I0544450

Cuba, 1952.

Twenty-year-old Ernesto Ruiz is determined to save his family's cigar business by exporting directly to the American market, but he'll need to learn about American customs and lifestyles first. That's why he takes a part-time job at an American guest house.

Hank Mannix, a beefcake magazine model, enjoys his carefree life in Havana, where new men come and go every week. But his immediate attraction to the new gardener is different. He's drawn to the young man in a way he's never experienced before.

A fateful encounter in the garden results in a misunderstanding that upends both their lives. As they begin to acknowledge the true depth of their feelings for each other, they must navigate through a city and country on the brink of revolution. Ernesto and Hank strive to secure their own happiness in a world where the future is uncertain, and their love is forbidden.

With vivid historical detail and memorable characters, Havana Bay is a captivating story of love and revolution in a time of change.

This story can be read on its own; however, characters from book one, Dublin Bay, and book two, Turtle Bay, play prominent roles as secondary characters, so it's recommended to read those first.

Havana Bay

Tides of Change, Book Three

John Patrick

A NineStar Press Publication

www.ninestarpress.com

Havana Bay

© 2023 John Patrick
Cover Art © 2023 Jaycee DeLorenzo

This is a work of fiction. Names, characters, places, and incidents are either the product of the author's imagination or are used fictitiously. Any resemblance to actual persons living or dead, business establishments, events, or locales is entirely coincidental.

All rights reserved. No part of this publication may be reproduced in any material form, whether by printing, photocopying, scanning or otherwise without the written permission of the publisher. To request permission and all other inquiries, contact NineStar Press at the physical or web addresses above or at Contact@ninestarpress.com.

First Edition, June 2023

ISBN: 978-1-64890-668-8

Also available in eBook, ISBN: 978-1-64890-667-1

CONTENT WARNING:
This book contains sexual content, which may only be suitable for mature readers. Depictions of war, revolution, violence, and attempted rape.

Chapter One

MARCH 1952

ERNESTO PAUSED IN his work to watch the spectacle unfolding on the beach.

He leaned his rake against a palm tree and raised a hand to shield his eyes against the sun's glare. Next to him, his cousin Ivan placed his pruning shears on top of a high stone wall and squatted to rest in its shade.

His father's admonition echoed in his mind. "Never slouch or squat, Ernesto. Always stand tall; otherwise, you'll look like a peasant." And Ivan *did* look like a peasant, with his sweat-stained T-shirt and worn cotton pants, cut short at the knees.

Ernesto wore denim pants, but they were clean—more or less—and fit properly. His lime-colored button-down shirt highlighted his amber eyes, and his black hair was oiled and slicked back from his forehead accentuating its silkiness.

Ivan was several shades darker than Ernesto and had features pointing to an African ancestry. Ernesto leaned more toward the Spanish side of the island's genetic mix. It wasn't supposed to matter—not in modern postwar Cuba. Not in 1952.

But it did matter, of course.

Both of them were darker than *los gamelos blancos*—the white twins—as the workers at Casa de Ada called them. They were wrestling on the beach, wearing tight bathing trunks, even whiter than the twins themselves. A film crew circled them, rolling their cameras and calling out directions in English.

Ernesto knew English, but Ivan had never tried to learn. There was no need to translate, however; the action was self-explanatory. The twins grappled in an easy way, more for show than dominance. Their oiled torsos gleamed in the sharp morning light, and their hands moved quickly, gripping a bicep, cupping the back of a head, sliding down a flank.

They weren't really twins. In the few months Ernesto had worked at Casa de Ada, he'd learned to distinguish between its two most famous residents. The one who sometimes *looked* at Ernesto—looked him right in the eye—was slimmer than the more muscled one and not as hairy. He was beautiful, and when he did catch Ernesto's eye and offered a knowing wink, it was terrifying.

He didn't see him every day. Ernesto only worked a few hours in the mornings, cleaning up the gardens before most of the guests were up and about. But the twins were sometimes out early—when the light was best for photographs and filming.

They sank to their knees, and a wave washed over them, soaking their trunks, rendering them nearly transparent. Ernesto steeled himself against reacting.

Below him, Ivan snorted. "*Locos*," he said and laughed as if he were watching a comic before a movie show.

Ivan was right; they were all such curious creatures, these *Americanos* who passed through Casa de Ada—the young, handsome ones as well as the older, rich ones. Who could say why they did what they did? Why they lay in the sun for hours even though their pale skin blistered and peeled. Why they drank so much, even in the mornings. Why they acted like girls sometimes and called each other "dear" and "darling."

On the beach, the director called out instructions. "Mannix, flip Cordero over and get on top."

Mannix. That was his name, the one who *saw* him.

The men switched places and Mannix pinned Cordero. He was looking up, away from his opponent and the cameras, across the beach and into the gardens. He caught Ernesto's eye, and they locked gazes. Mannix offered a cocky grin and raised an eyebrow.

"Good," said the director. "Good. Nice. Now push up into him, Cordero."

Ivan turned to Ernesto. "What is he saying?" he asked.

"Nothing. Just giving directions," Ernesto responded. "We should get back to work."

"Sure." His cousin stood and wiped his hands against

his pants. "This is our chance though. What I told you about. Look at them." With a nod of his head, Ivan indicated the mostly older white men—guests at Casa de Ada—who had gathered around to watch the show. They were transfixed by the white twins.

"That's a wrap," the director called. Mannix reached a hand down to help Cordero up. A soft smattering of applause rippled through the onlookers.

"Remember what I told you," Ivan instructed. "Don't make eye contact, but be certain they see you. Take one of the secluded paths into the deep parts of the garden. One will follow you."

Ernesto wasn't convinced he wanted to do that. Sure, it was easy for Ivan; he always talked of girls and all the sex he claimed to have had. He would view whatever happened at the end of a garden path, hidden behind a hedge, as purely transactional.

It was different for Ernesto. He couldn't quite picture what Ivan had described went on in the thickets, and when he tried, it was all too close to what he thought he might enjoy anyway if the right boy were to come along. He thought about Mannix's eyes, and his knowing smile.

"It doesn't mean anything, Ernesto," Ivan assured him, as if he were reading his mind. "It doesn't make you a *maricón*. It only makes you a Yankee dollar richer. And you just have to stand there; the Americans do all the work. You don't even have to look at them. You can close your eyes and think of a girl."

Ivan reached up to retrieve the shears from atop the wall, and Ernesto took a step back. Ivan smelled ripe—a stronger odor than a morning's work would account for.

It was as if he hadn't washed with soap and water in days. Ivan had come to stay with Ernesto's family in the city, and failing to wash properly wasn't the only bad habit he'd brought with him from his family's rural tobacco farm.

It was absurd to think someone, even a loco Americano, would pay money to...do things...to Ivan. Ernesto wanted no part of it.

Still, a dollar...and maybe many more dollars if he didn't find it too objectionable.

And he needed the money. That was without a doubt. If he did get into university—this time—there would be textbooks to buy, new shoes, supplies of all sorts, not to mention tuition. Ernesto's father insisted they'd find a way to pay, but it was difficult to see how.

The small group of guests on the beach began to disperse, and the film crew started packing up, carefully placing the cameras into their large padded cases. The Americans were shifting about, sharing grins and slapping one another on the back. A few started ambling toward the gardens.

Ernesto looked for Mannix, but the white twins had already disappeared.

"I'm going this way," Ivan said, pointing his shears toward the path that went alongside a row of palms and eventually turned to disappear behind the main house. "Don't follow me."

Ivan headed off, and Ernesto considered his options. He decided to put off any final decision regarding the Americans and their dollars until he had to make one. After all, he worked in the gardens, so he could hardly avoid them. He picked up his rake and headed in the opposite direction from Ivan.

One of the Americans who had been moving casually toward the path Ivan was on changed course when he saw Ernesto heading the other way. Ernesto told himself it was a coincidence, but he heeded Ivan's advice and avoided eye contact. Did he want to encourage the fellow? He wasn't sure.

He continued on his way, occasionally pausing to rake dead leaves and palm fronds into a pile, or to snip a spent flower from its stem. He passed the main house and followed the twisting path through the gardens leading to the fish pond at the far end of the property. There was a small bench there, and Ernesto hadn't attended to the area in a couple of days.

It was cooler in the shade of the closely bunched palms, and it took his eyes a moment to adjust to the dim light. It was quiet too. The sounds of the film crew on the beach faded away. An iguana scuttled through the dead leaves beside the path.

He reached the pond and was greeted by bright flashes of yellow and orange beneath the water as the fish—koi, he remembered they were called—approached him for food. "I'm sorry," he told them. "I have nothing for you."

There was a rustling sound from the bushes in front of him. "Maybe they're just happy to see your handsome face." It was Mannix.

He'd been shielded by a flowering shrub, but as he spoke, he stepped into view. He wore a loose robe, and Ernesto struggled between relief and disappointment that the damp swim trunks weren't on display. Mannix's gaze shifted to something over Ernesto's shoulder. "We're busy here," he said.

Startled, Ernesto turned to see the American had followed him, but the man quickly nodded and disappeared.

He turned back to Mannix and was surprised he'd continued to move closer. Ernesto could reach out and touch him if he wanted to. Or Mannix could touch Ernesto. He tightened his grip on the rake and swallowed. They stared silently at each other for a moment.

Mannix looked puzzled. He cocked his head. "*Habla Inglés?*"

"Oh. Yes. I speak English."

Mannix smiled. "Good. I thought you would. You look like a student."

Ernesto swelled with pride and stood straighter, scrambling for something to say, but his mind had inexplicably emptied. Mannix was even more strikingly handsome up close. A blue-black shadow of a beard covered his jaw, and he smelled like citrus-scented oil.

His heart raced, thumping deep inside his chest, tapping out a rhythm that echoed through his body. Did Mannix want to...do something? To him? He'd happily let him and forgo the dollar too. He wouldn't even close his eyes.

But Ivan hadn't been clear on *how* this was supposed to happen. He'd implied no words were needed, that both parties understood the nature of the transaction. Ernesto waited for Mannix to make the first move.

"I keep food for them," Mannix said, "in a tin over there." He nodded to the opposite side of the pond, where a narrow wooden bench with a slatted back was tucked into a dense copse of tall bushes. Ernesto was embarrassed to see how many fallen leaves littered the area.

The path narrowed as it circled the pond, and without waiting for a response, Mannix began making his way to the other side. Ernesto followed. Somehow, the fish knew to follow too, and they moved under the water in a flashing, golden swirl of tails and fins, their mouths opening and closing in anticipation.

The path was only wide enough for one man, and Ernesto slowed his pace to keep his distance. Mannix moved through the garden with a liquid grace, like a jungle cat stalking its prey. His hair was as black as Ernesto's, but it hung in loose curls, covering his ears and brushing the nape of his neck. The robe he wore was short, not even reaching his knees, and Ernesto admired the muscles of his thighs and calves as he moved.

Mannix's white skin glowed in the shade of the trees. When he'd first stepped out onto the path in front of Ernesto, his robe had been tied at the waist in a loose knot. Now it hung open, and the sides flapped with his strides.

Had it fallen open? Had Mannix untied it?

Ernesto envied the fish, so sure of their goal, certain of what was to come.

"Watch out here," Mannix called as he stepped over gnarled roots crossing the path. He glanced over his shoulder at Ernesto. "We wouldn't want you tripping into the pond. I'd have to jump in and pull you out." The image of Mannix hoisting him out of the pond, both of their bodies wet and slippery, nearly caused Ernesto to catch his foot on the roots despite Mannix's warning.

They reached the bench, and Mannix bent to retrieve a small tin tucked behind a rock at the base of a flowering shrub. He unscrewed the lid as he came back to Ernesto. He sat and loosely folded his robe across his lap.

The partial glimpse of the white trunks beneath the robe was distracting. Ernesto's heart raced alarmingly, urging him to do...something. Anything.

Mannix opened his palm and tilted the tin above it, tapping it with his index finger. A shower of small grey pellets dropped out.

"Here," he said holding his open palm, now filled with a small mound of pellets, to Ernesto. He slid to the side of the bench. "Sit."

There wasn't really enough room for two men, but Ernesto sat anyway. Mannix's naked thigh, warm and solid and dusted with dried sand, pressed against Ernesto's leg. Ernesto remained motionless. Mannix jiggled his leg and nudged Ernesto's arm. "Come on. Take it," he said. "They're starving."

Mannix leaned in, moving his open palm closer to Ernesto. The fold of robe covering his trunks fell open.

Am I actually going to feed the fish with one of the white twins?

He wished Ivan was there so his cousin could tell him what to do, could explain how to go about things, how to get from here to there. *No. I'm glad he's not here.*

He reached forward with his hand and offered his open palm. Mannix smiled and pulled his own hand back slightly—taking care not to spill the pellets—so that it hovered over his lap, forcing Ernesto to bring his own hand even closer, just inches above Mannix's crotch.

Warmth radiated from Mannix's body, along with an earthy smell below the citrus oil.

"Steady now," Mannix said. He reached out with his free hand to grasp Ernesto's wrist, pulling it lower still, until Ernesto was afraid his own trembling hand might accidentally bump against the man's privates. His fingers were warm against Ernesto's pulse.

"We don't want to spill anything." He tilted his open palm and tipped the pellets, one by one—a slow, sensual dropping—into Ernesto's palm.

Ernesto closed his eyes. He hadn't wanted to, but the tension was unbearable. Mannix's fingers slid along the back of his hand as he released his grip from Ernesto's wrist. "Do it," he whispered into Ernesto's ear.

Yes. But what?

He opened his eyes to find Mannix had pulled back, just a little. His smile hinted at a shared secret, and he dropped his gaze to Ernesto's lap, causing Ernesto to blush furiously at what must surely be discernable there, even though he tried to shield himself with his palm filled with koi pellets.

Ernesto leaned forward, stretching his arm as far as he could reach, then opened his fingers over the swirling mass of fish. The pellets dropped into the water all at once, and the fish thrashed about in a frenzy, spraying droplets of rank pond water.

Mannix sighed. He stood and turned to face Ernesto. "Now that wasn't so hard, was it?" he asked in a calm, almost bored tone, completely at odds with the circumstances. Mannix's tight swim trunks were at Ernesto's eye level, no more than two feet away. He didn't want to stare, but his brain betrayed him—intent on discerning what each curve and swell of fabric might be concealing.

The frenetic activity in the pond quickly died down. "They're hungry little beasts," Mannix observed. He slipped two fingers beneath the waistband of his swimsuit to reach a spot low on his belly, as if scratching an itch there. "Are you hungry too?"

Yes.

Ernesto slowly leaned forward, moving as if in a trance. Mannix's fingers inched lower.

A distant part of his mind clambered for attention. This wasn't how it was supposed to happen. If he did this, it would mean *he*, Ernesto, was the—

"Wait," he said. "Stop. This is...backward."

"What?" asked Mannix. He pulled his hand out from his trunks.

"I'm not—" Ernesto began. "You're supposed to—" He took a deep breath, trying to regain control of himself.

Mannix peered down at him. "What's wrong?"

"It's just that Ivan said, well, he said you'd..." Ernesto couldn't find a way to continue. What if this had all been a misunderstanding?

"What? For god's sake, spit it out." Mannix huffed. "Who's Ivan?"

"My cousin. We work together." At Mannix's blank look he added, "Here. Gardening?"

Mannix frowned. "Oh, the grubby one I see you with."

Ernesto didn't want to dishonor his cousin by saying yes, so he simply nodded.

"What did he tell you?" At some point in the last few

moments, the robe had been retied. "Wait, oh...*oh!*... You thought... You thought that *I* would, what? *Pay* you!"

Ernesto's face was flaming; the garden shimmered at the edges of his vision. Any thoughts of...whatever he'd been thinking, hoping for...shriveled away to nothing. "No, I...that is...well, Ivan said I could make a dollar—"

"Stop!" commanded Mannix. "Not another word. I have *never* and will never—" He huffed and tightened the knot on his robe. "Why am I explaining myself to you?"

Ernesto had no idea.

"Get back to work," he said with a sweep of his arm, taking in the state of the garden. He turned away from Ernesto and retreated down the path.

*

ERNESTO HAD A long walk home, which gave him plenty of time to think.

Or panic, more accurately.

Clearly, he'd angered Mannix and insulted him by suggesting he'd be willing to pay Ernesto to...do things...to him. And of course he'd been insulted! Imagine, one of the white twins paying a gardener for...sex. Even if it was sex of some loosely defined sort, difficult to precisely imagine. It was ridiculous.

He should never have believed Ivan. Sure, some of the older white men might seek out a young Cuban and even be willing to pay a dollar for a quick encounter to brag about later.

But obviously Mannix had no need to do that. He was a god. And he made movies where he and the other white twin—Cordero, that was his name—wrestled and...and... well, Ernesto didn't know what else they did when they were indoors in private. But he'd heard rumors there were pictures of them naked. Together.

Ernesto's imagination took over, and he was nearly struck by a taxi as he stepped onto the Miramar Bridge. Its horn blared, and Ernesto jumped. A group of boys on bicycles laughed as they swerved around him. Below him the fetid waters of the Rio Almendares moved sluggishly into the Gulf of Mexico.

Will they fire me?

That was his biggest worry—that he'd have to tell his father he'd lost his job working with the Americans. It wasn't the money; the gardening work didn't pay as much as his afternoon job at his father's factory. Rather, it was the opportunity to work with the Americans themselves his father valued above all else.

"Get in with the Americans, *mijo*," he'd tell Ernesto. "America is the future. Learn from them."

His father didn't know Ernesto's work at Casa de Ada consisted exclusively of gardening, or that he had never even been inside. His father also didn't know his own brother's son, Ivan, was letting white *maricóns* service him for money. Or that Ernesto himself had considered allowing that to happen. Had maybe even wanted that to happen.

Getting in with the Americans was proving to be complicated. Ernesto shut down the imaginary conversation with his father—one that would never happen anyway—and continued on his way.

Casa de Ada was on Havana's north coast, several

miles across the city from the railroad station near where Ernesto's family lived above their small factory. He had two hours before his shift started, so Ernesto took the longer route home, passing through the university's campus.

He could have taken a bus, but he enjoyed strolling through the campus, imagining himself as one of the students hurrying from building to building, carrying books and excitedly talking to his companions about things Ernesto could only hope to learn someday.

And he was grateful for the saved bus fare. Every bit would help—if he was admitted this time. His two prior rejections still stung. At twenty, he'd already be older than most of the first-year students. If he had to wait another year, his age would start to make things awkward.

"You'll get in," his mother insisted. "Keep trying."

"Read more," his father advised. "Practice your English. That will be important with the Americans."

"We're all counting on you, Ernesto," his older sister Marta told him. She was the most honest of all of them. His family was losing its precarious grip on the middle class, and the small factories like his father's were fading away quickly. Marta, who was twenty-one, would need stronger prospects to make a good match.

A young man—a student—came toward him on the path. He wore his oiled hair back like Ernesto's, and he offered an easy smile and a nod as they passed each other. His large gold wristwatch identified him as wealthy, as did his finely laced shoes and green silk vest.

What would it be like to know such a boy? To share a class with him? To discuss literature or politics?

The clocktower tolled noon, and Ernesto picked up his pace. His shift started at one, and he hoped to have a sandwich before that and maybe a limonada if his mother had made him one. She often did before he started work; she claimed it was good for his voice.

From the pristine elegance of the university, the city declined—geographically and economically—as it approached Ernesto's neighborhood and the train station. Well-maintained colonial villas gave way to mixed neighborhoods of factories, shops, open-air bars and small residences.

Ernesto made it home with fifteen minutes to spare. He entered the factory with its rows of worktables and its small, high windows, opaque from years of dust stirred relentlessly by the ceiling fans. The two dozen or so *torcederos*—cigar rollers—seated along the wooden benches were hard at work. A few looked up at the sound of the door and smiled when they saw Ernesto.

Behind the glass wall separating the office from the workers, his father poured over the ledger books. He shared a long table with Marta, who had an eye for color and design, and who prepared all the family's cigar boxes, carefully illustrating and decorating both the inside and the outside.

Their mother knew nothing of cigars and had no interest in learning. She occupied her own space in the back half of the office where she did seamstress work. American fashion magazines were piled on a corner of the desk. Dozens of pages depicting elegant white women in fancy dresses had been tacked to the wall. Ernesto's mother was renowned among the local women for her ability to modify an existing wardrobe to align with shifting styles—raising or lowering a hemline, reshaping a collar, strengthening or softening a shoulder line.

She always had work.

When she saw Ernesto, she smiled and waved him into the office. A *mixto* with pickles and a limonada waited for him.

"How was your morning?" she asked as Ernesto hurried to eat his lunch. She meant "Do you like that job with the Americans? Does it suit you? Is Ivan all right?" They all worried about Ivan. He'd always been...volatile, and now that he'd come to live with them, he seemed even more so.

"Good," he replied. Ernesto didn't like to lie to his mother, but what else could he do? He glanced through the glass window onto the factory floor and noticed Ivan's customary space at a worktable was empty.

He was reminded of a different time, many years ago, and a different empty space at a worktable. But it was a shameful memory for Ernesto, and as he always he did, he shut it down before it could fully form in his mind.

He chewed and then swallowed a bite of his sandwich. It was delicious; the pork was still warm and fat mixed with mustard drizzled down his chin. Inexplicably, the sensation made him think of Mannix. He didn't explore that thought.

"Did you speak English with the Americans?" his father asked. "Do they like you?"

Yes, I spoke English with one who wanted me to give him a blow job. But he didn't say that to his father. *And your brother's son, Ivan, actually gets paid for sex by these American maricóns.* But he didn't say that either.

"Yes. And one thought I was a student." At least that was true, as far as it went.

"Good." His father beamed. "That is good, mijo. You're going places; that's for sure."

Ernesto hoped so. But for now, the only place he was going was to his post on the factory floor. He finished his drink, cleaned his face with a damp cloth, kissed his mother on the cheek, and told Marta he liked the design of the box she was working on.

He took deep, calming breaths as he entered the factory. He walked to the open section in the middle, climbed the three steps to the small square platform holding his chair, and sat.

He cleared his throat, put all thoughts of the morning out of his mind, opened *The Count of Monte Cristo,* and began to read to the torcederos.

Chapter Two

"WHY SO GLUM?" Cordero asked before downing the last splash of whiskey remaining in his tumbler.

Mannix shrugged in response and twisted his empty glass in small circles on the bar top.

Nearby, a slot machine jangled, the sound of nickels pouring into the coin hopper announcing a winner. A woman in a white mink stole swept past them, her perfume competing with the cigarette smoke filling the air of the gambling floor. Ceiling fans with wide blades lazily moved the blue haze in soft swirls.

In front of them, a bartender wearing a dinner jacket poured a bright blue cocktail from his shaker into several glasses he'd lined up along the bar. When he finished, he looked at Mannix. "Another, sir?"

"Two more, please," Mannix responded, nodding to indicate Cordero's empty glass.

Across the room, an orchestra was setting up on the

stage.

"Come on," urged Cordero. "Spit it out. You know you're going to tell me eventually, and soon we won't be able to hear each other over the music."

Mannix let out a sigh. "You're a good friend, Tony." He nudged Cordero's knee with his own.

"I know. I always tell you that, don't I?" Their drinks arrived. "Come on, Hank. What's eating at you?"

Mannix twisted his stool to face Cordero directly and took a deep swallow from his glass. "Right. So, I think I may have put one of the gardeners in an awkward situation."

Cordero grinned. Mannix was always creating awkward situations. "What did you do this time?"

"Well, I was walking in the garden—"

"Wait," Cordero interrupted. "Were you walking in the garden or *lurking* in the garden?"

"Well..."

Cordero shook his head. "Hank. We've talked about this. You don't need to keep doing that sort of thing. You *shouldn't* keep doing it." He looked his friend in the eye. "For god's sake, you're thirty years old."

"I'm twenty-nine," Mannix objected. But that wasn't the point, and Mannix knew it.

"It's not like the old days in New York when you needed the money, and you sure don't need the validation." Cordero took a sip of his whiskey. "Heck, half these men choose to stay at Ada's just for a chance to see you. In the flesh, I mean, rather than just jerking off to pictures of you in *Pumped*."

"To see *us*," Mannix corrected. "You're famous too."

"Hardly. I'm just your foil. And besides, I...well, never mind that. Back to your gardener. What happened? Did he come upon you unexpectedly while you were giving some account manager from New Jersey the time of his life?"

Mannix looked away and took a sip of his drink.

"Which gardener saw you?" Cordero continued. "Not the grubby one, I hope. There's something off about him. I don't trust him; he might use something like that against you."

"No," Mannix replied.

"Oh god, not the old guy with the missing finger? You might have shocked him into an early grave."

"No," Mannix said again. "You see—"

"Wait, was it the cute one? The one who looks like he'd faint if you so much as talked to him?" Mannix was silent. "It was him, wasn't it? What did he say when he saw you?"

Mannix finished the rest of his drink in one swallow. "Yes, it was the cute one. Except he didn't come across me with someone else. He...that is...we..."

"Good lord, Hank! Please tell me you didn't seduce the gardener."

"Shh." Mannix glanced at the bartender. "Keep your voice down."

Cordero took a drink, then leaned closer to whisper, "Honestly, Hank, this is too far, even for you. He's likely to have a father or big brother who'll come punch your lights out. What were you thinking?"

"Well, obviously I *wasn't* thinking, Tony." Mannix let out a huff. "And it's worse than you're imagining."

Cordero finished his drink and signaled the bartender for two more. "I don't know how it could be."

"Well, it seems the cute one's cousin...the grubby one...told the cute one he could make a dollar if he let an American...perform oral sex on him...in the garden. At least, I *think* that's what he intended."

"Wait, the grubby one told the cute one or the other way around? Do these gardeners have names?" Cordero asked.

"Not that I'm aware of, no."

"So go on...you tried to seduce a member of the staff at Ada's—Hans will be furious, you know—and, no, wait." Cordero paused for a moment before continuing. "You said he thought he could earn a dollar. But who would he...?" Cordero trailed off as Mannix blushed.

"Oh. Oh, my God." Cordero clapped his hands. "You! He thought *you'd* pay *him*!" Cordero didn't try to disguise the delight he took in Mannix's discomfort. "He thought you, Hank Mannix, would get down on your knees and—"

"Enough, Tony!" Mannix hissed. He glanced again to make sure the bartender wasn't within earshot. "I'm humiliated enough already. There's no need to rub it in."

A girl in a short skirt selling cigarettes approached them, and Mannix waved her off.

"Well, did you?" Cordero asked.

Mannix rolled his eyes. "Of course not." He ran a hand through his hair, then adjusted his tie. "The thing is, I may have gotten rather angry at the boy and gone all American on him, making him feel small and telling him to get back to work."

"Ouch," said Cordero. "Poor guy. It's not his fault you're closing in on thirty and crossing the threshold from young and poor to rich and needy."

"If you don't stop grinning, I might punch *your* lights out," Mannix said.

Their third round of drinks arrived. Cordero lifted his in a toast. "To the cute one, for humbling the mighty Mannix!"

"You're not the least bit funny," Mannix complained, but he lifted his glass anyway. "To the cute one," he agreed. He downed half his glass. "And you know, up close, he really is handsome. In entirely different circumstances, it would be tempting."

Cordero raised an eyebrow. "He's just a boy, and you're—"

"We don't need to keep talking about my age, Tony. And he's not a boy. I think he's...well, old enough anyway." He picked up his glass and finished the other half of his drink. "And honestly, I think he *was* interested. In me, I mean. I think it would have worked if he hadn't gotten distracted by the advice he'd gotten from the grubby one."

"We need to give these boys names," Cordero said. "And I think you owe the cute one an apology. He's probably terrified."

Across the hall, the orchestra launched into a lively swing number and couples began making their way to the dance floor.

Cordero leaned in and raised his voice to be heard over the music. "Come on, old man. Let's get out of here before someone asks us to dance."

Chapter Three

IT HAD BEEN three days since the incident in the garden, and Ernesto was beginning to think he might be in the clear. Maybe he wouldn't get fired. Maybe he'd blown it out of proportion, and his memory of the morning was exaggerated.

That must be it, he thought, as he skimmed the long-handled net across the water of the pool, scooping up leaves, palm fronds, and dead or dying bugs of various sorts. There had been a rainstorm in the middle of the night, with strong winds, so there was more debris in the pool and throughout the gardens than there normally would have been. Ernesto had arrived early, anticipating the added work.

His mind kept returning to the potential consequences of the incident in the garden. If anything were going to come of it, surely it would have happened by now. If they were going to fire him, they would have done it already.

It was simple, really. He and Mannix had both been embarrassed; there'd been a mix up—a misunderstanding. It was easy to mistake body language from a different culture. And maybe Mannix hadn't been *angry* as much as he'd been shocked at Ernesto's foolish misunderstanding.

Yes. That was what must have happened. And if so, Mannix would be over it by now.

A piece of debris—some sort of cloth—floated in a small circle in the middle of the pool, just out of reach. If it was a leaf, or even a palm frond, he'd ignore it and see if it had moved closer to the edge where he could capture it before he left. But the longer he studied it, the more convinced he became it could be something soiled, a used napkin perhaps, or a cleaning rag.

He couldn't leave such a thing floating in the pool even for a short while.

Ernesto considered his options.

He could strip down and dive in to retrieve it. But he wasn't permitted in the pool at all, let alone naked, and if anyone were to see him...no.

He could tie his shirt to the net, maybe extend its reach by a few inches. That could be enough. But it was a nice shirt, made from fine cotton in a rich burnt-orange color, and he thought using it that way might ruin it.

In the end, he decided to go back to the pool shed and see if there wasn't a towel he could use for the task. If he tied it to the net, he might just gain enough reach to snag whatever was floating in the pool.

It was dark in the shed, and the air was thick and

musty. There were shelves and boxes, goggles and life rings. And there, hanging on a nail by the door, was an old pair of swimming trunks.

I could do it. Change in here, slip on the swimsuit, and be in and out of the pool in less than a minute.

It was the best plan he could think of. He removed his shirt, kicked off his shoes and began unfastening his trousers.

"There you are," Mannix said as he poked his head into the pool shed. "I've been looking for you. I need to—" He broke off abruptly as he took in Ernesto's state of partial undress.

Ernesto quickly refastened his pants. This was it; he'd be fired now, and it would be doubly humiliating to go through such a thing exposed as he was in the close quarters of the pool shed.

"Oh. Don't stop on my account." Mannix braced one hand against the door jamb, as if he was unsure if he should step all the way in or leave.

"*Lo siento, discúlpame,*" Ernesto said. "*Solomente—*"

Mannix held up a hand. "English, please."

Ernesto blinked. Had he just spoken in Spanish? Yes, he realized, playing it back in his head. What a disaster. He reached for his shirt, and braced himself for the bad news.

Mannix appeared to make up his mind and stepped fully into the shed. "Not that I'm complaining"—he pointed his finger toward Ernesto's bare chest—"but *why* are you getting naked in the pool shed?"

Ernesto's arm got stuck as he hurried to force it into his twisted shirt sleeve, and he had to wriggle it out to straighten the shirt so he could start the process again. Mannix reached over and untwisted the sleeve, freeing Ernesto's arm.

"The pool," Ernesto mumbled.

Mannix cocked an eyebrow. "You wanted to go swimming? Naked?"

"No, no, I—"

"Wait. Are you the only one getting naked? Should I be getting naked too?" Mannix placed a hand on the top button of his shirt.

"No, please." Ernesto waved his hand at Mannix—trying to stop him from taking his shirt off? Trying to make the entire situation disappear? Ernesto wasn't sure. "There's something in the pool. Something floating in the middle. I couldn't reach it."

"So, you were going to jump in naked to get it? And I missed the show?"

Ernesto finally managed to get his shirt back on. "No, there's a pair of swim trunks there." He nodded to the shorts hanging on the nail.

"I see. Well, don't do it. Those are disgusting; they've been there forever. They're probably moldy. You don't want them rubbing up against your privates."

Ernesto squirmed uncomfortably at the mention of his privates and finished buttoning his shirt.

"Well, no sense staying in here if you're putting your clothes back on. I'll go see what's in the pool while you finish getting dressed." Mannix left the shed, and Ernesto stooped to put his shoes on. If he was going to be fired, he wanted to be dressed for it.

After a few moments, he rejoined Mannix, who had

moved to one of the poolside tables. A glass of what looked like orange juice sat on the table—although you never knew with these Americans. He looked at the pool and saw the offending item had made its way closer to the edge, near enough to be retrieved with the net.

"Now's your chance," Mannix said. "But you'll regret it."

Before Ernesto could think through what that could mean, he picked up the net, reached out over the pool, and dragged the item closer. Then he scooped the net underneath and lifted the item out of the water. He brought the net closer and turned it over on top of the stove pavers.

A sopping pair of men's undershorts plopped to the ground.

"Things got a little wild last night," Mannix said. "I wouldn't touch them if I were you."

Ernesto poked at the shorts with the pole end of the net. "I can't just leave them there."

Mannix shrugged and took a sip of whatever was in the glass.

Ernesto hooked the shorts with the tip of the pole and carried them to the trash bin he'd already filled with garden debris. If no one claimed them and Mannix didn't say anything, perhaps Ivan would find them and at least something positive would come out of his being fired. Ivan definitely could use a decent pair of undershorts.

Mannix put his glass down and stood. "Well, now that all the excitement is over, time to get down to business. I need to talk to you. Follow me, please."

Ernesto was resigned to losing his job; he just hoped

this wasn't going to be drawn out. He followed behind Mannix and was surprised when they stopped at the greenhouse attached to the kitchen. Mannix opened the door. "After you," he said, waving his arm in front of him.

He'd been in the greenhouse once before when he'd been asked to carry out a heavy clay pot filled with a dead shrub. It wasn't the same as being in the house itself—where Ernesto had never been—but still, it was a place usually off-limits to him. And he was a mess from all his hard work. He was sure he had bits of leaves and grass stuck to his clothes.

And why would he be brought to the greenhouse to be fired?

No use worrying about it. I'll find out soon enough. He crossed the threshold into the humid room. The spicy scent of herbs filled the air.

A glass wall made up one side of the room, and there was a small round table with two padded chairs pulled next to it, facing out into the garden. Ernesto had occasionally seen Hans—the owner of Casa de Ada—reading there in the morning. A pitcher of orange juice sat on the table next to an empty glass.

"Have a seat," Mannix said as he stepped through the doorway behind Ernesto.

At the table? Ernesto hadn't washed his hands, and he quickly checked his shoes for mud.

"Sit," Mannix said again, pointing to one of the chairs.

Well, that was clear enough.

Ernesto lowered himself onto the edge of the seat, perching there and willing all the bits of leaves and dust to stay on him and not fall onto the floor. He nervously ran a hand through his hair and a dead beetle dropped out, landing with a soft *click* on the marble tabletop. It fell next to the empty glass, at least, and not inside.

But still...

Mannix had picked up the pitcher and had just begun to pour when the beetle intruded. He paused midmotion, staring at the dead bug. "Huh," he said. "If you'd only gone swimming naked as you'd planned, you would have left all these outside parts outside where they belong."

He filled the glass. "And I would have had a pleasant little show. Or maybe a big show," he added wistfully. "Who knows?" He slid the glass closer to Ernesto. "Have some orange juice."

Ernesto had no idea what was going on or why drinking orange juice would be part of getting fired, but all he could focus on was the beetle. Sadly, he'd been mistaken when he'd assumed it was dead. It lay on its back with its little legs twitching in the air.

"Can I *please* take this outside," he begged.

Mannix looked relieved by the suggestion. He pointed to the door. "I'll wait right here."

Ernesto picked up the bug and stepped outside. He thought about simply running, but decided against it. He placed the bug on a palm tree and went back inside to face his fate.

He stood by the table, but Mannix stared him down without speaking, then smiled when Ernesto gave up and took his seat.

"Good," said Mannix. "Now, I wanted to talk to you because I think I owe you an apology."

An apology? From one of the white twins?

Ernesto knew he was probably supposed to say something, but his mind had gone blank, which seemed to happen whenever he was around Mannix. "I'm not being fired?" he finally asked.

"What? No." Mannix shook his head and took a deep breath. "Look, we got off on the wrong foot. I...overreacted. Let's start again." He held his hand out across the table. "I'm Hank Mannix."

Ernesto stared at Mannix's fingers. They were slender, long and white with softly polished nails. And clean. His own hands were grimy, but he was clearly expected to shake. He was glad he hadn't handled the dirty shorts.

"This is the part where you say, 'Hello, I'm the cute one; pleased to meet you.'"

What was happening? "Uh..." *Think, Ernesto! You know how to introduce yourself.*

Mannix grinned. It was the unnerving smile that seemed to imply so much. "Take your time," he said. "We can just keep doing this until we get it right." He withdrew his hand and then slowly held it out again. "Hello, I'm Hank Mannix..." He paused, then added, "And you are...?"

"Ernesto. Ernesto Ruiz." He let out a trembling breath he hadn't known he'd been holding.

Mannix's hand still hovered over the table between them. "And now the hand part, Ernesto." He wriggled his fingers.

What the hell is wrong with me? Just shake the white twin's hand, and get it over with.

He rubbed his palm vigorously against his thigh,

then raised it from his lap and inspected it. "My hand is dirty," he said.

"Good clean dirt though," Mannix said. "Come on, my arm is getting tired." He wriggled his fingers again.

Ernesto reached forward and placed just the tips of his fingers against Mannix's palm. Mannix closed his grip and gave two quick squeezes before letting go. "Well, it'll do for now, but if you expect me to pay you a dollar, you're going to need to show a lot more enthusiasm."

Ernesto's face flamed with embarrassment. "I'm sorry. That was— I mean, I've never done anything—"

"Oh stop," Mannix interrupted, waving a hand to dismiss the apology. "And of course you haven't; that much was obvious." Mannix took a sip of orange juice. "I have though."

Ernesto wasn't sure what Mannix was telling him. He couldn't mean...

"Earned a few dollars that way," Mannix clarified. He leaned forward and winked. "I've had a very sordid past."

So, he *did* mean what Ernesto thought he'd meant. But before Ernesto could formulate a reply, or ask a question, Mannix changed the subject.

"But tell me about you. You're a student, right? Why are you working here as a gardener?"

The orange juice was cold and acidic. He forced himself to swallow a sip, giving him time to think. He wasn't being fired. But beyond that, he wasn't sure what was happening. It would be best to be brief and truthful.

"I hope to attend university next term. In the afternoons, I work in my father's factory."

"Oh." Mannix frowned, and Ernesto was concerned

he'd offended him somehow. Or perhaps disappointed him was more accurate. "But if you work in a factory...in your *father's* factory, why spend time gardening here in the mornings? Surely it doesn't pay as well as the factory work?"

A sour ball of anxiety filled Ernesto's stomach. He did *not* want to talk about this, but he was asked a direct question, and politeness required a response. "My father thinks it will be good for me to work with Americans."

"But...why?" Mannix seemed honestly bewildered, glancing outside at the gardens. "How can being a gardener here help you?"

It was too late to come up with a different story, so Ernesto told the truth. "He doesn't know I'm just a gardener. He thinks...well, I'm not sure what he thinks..." He trailed off, unclear even in his own mind how to finish the thought, let alone express it to Mannix.

"Oh, gosh. That's—"

"Hank?" a man called from the house. The door from the kitchen opened and Ernesto recognized Hans, the owner of Casa de Ada, as he stepped into the room. "Is it done? Have you fired—" Hans stopped when he saw Ernesto. "Oh."

"I haven't even started," Mannix replied. "He's not in yet."

"Oh," Hans looked at Ernesto again. He turned to Mannix. "So, he's not the—"

"For god's sake, Hans. What's the point of having eyeglasses if you aren't going to wear them?"

"They make me look old," Hans grumbled as he dug into the pocket of his long floral dressing robe.

Hans was an odd one; none of the workers at Casa de Ada knew what to make of him. Whenever Ernesto caught a glimpse of him, he thought he looked like an American starlet fresh off a movie set. He had shoulder-length blond hair and wore soft and flowing clothing—not ladies' clothes exactly, but certainly not what men normally wore either.

He was slight of frame, and his bright blue eyes dominated his face. He found his glasses in the second pocket he searched and fumbled with them before putting them on. He came forward and peered at Ernesto.

"I see," he said, after studying Ernesto's features for an uncomfortably long moment. He turned to Mannix. "You were right about this one, Hank. He's delightful."

It was the first time in his life anyone had called him delightful, and Ernesto struggled to identity what quality of his could have prompted it. Hans turned back to Ernesto. "I'm Hans Schmidt," he said. He held out his hand but kept his palm facing down and allowed his fingers to dangle.

Ernesto wasn't sure how to respond, but he knew he should be standing if he was meeting the boss. He pushed back his chair with an abrupt motion, causing it to scrape across the tiled floor. Everyone winced at the sound. "Sorry," he mumbled. He reached forward and touched his fingers to Hans's.

The man's frown confirmed Ernesto had done the wrong thing. Again.

He was puzzling out what he might have done differently when Mannix spoke up. "He's very bad at remembering his name. Hans, this is Ernesto Ruiz. Ernesto, this is the queen."

Hans pulled his hand away and smiled. "Never mind him; he's just teasing you, dear. I'm not really the queen. Well, I suppose I am—of my own little kingdom here."

Once again, Ernesto flushed in embarrassment. Hans's eyes sparkled behind his wide-framed glasses. "Oh, that's a lovely shade you're turning. Please, don't let me interrupt. Sit."

Sitting was the very last thing Ernesto wanted to do. He spied Ivan outside poking through the bin containing the abandoned undershorts. Good. "I really need to get back to work."

Hans had followed Ernesto's gaze outside. "Hank, the grubby one is here. Come find me when it's over." He tilted his head at Ernesto. "It's a shame about your friend, but I can't have speculation and rumor around my business. I run a quiet, respectable house."

Ernesto thought about the undershorts floating in the pool, and the strange encounter with Mannix in the garden, and the nearly naked wrestling on the beach. But who knows what Americans meant by quiet and respectable? He nodded his understanding.

"It's so nice to finally have a real name for you, dear, although I'm afraid 'the cute one' is probably going to stick for a while. It fits." Hans left and Ernesto remained standing.

Mannix stood too. "I guess you've figured out I need to fire your cousin. What was his name again? I'd hate to have to ask him."

"Ivan." *The grubby one.*

"Right. See, the thing is, there's talk about sex for

money here. Hans can't afford that, you understand, not with Arthur's job."

Ernesto had no idea who Arthur was but knew better than to ask. "Of course," he said. Although, hadn't Mannix just implied…

He let the thought drift away. It was too much for him to figure out. There were rules for the white Americans and rules for everybody else.

What on earth was Ivan going to do now?

*

MOONLIGHT FILTERED THROUGH the hazy Havana sky, bringing a soft glow to Ernesto's small bedroom window. He was far too worried to sleep. His concerns and anxieties tumbled in circles in his head. He should have heard from the university by now. Why had he bungled the early morning conversation with Mr. Mannix and Mr. Schmidt? Why had Ivan arrived late for work again this afternoon?

His father's sense of family obligation toward Ivan wouldn't extend to out-and-out charity.

He rolled onto his side and peered over the edge of his bed. Below him, Ivan rested on his mattress, which Ernesto folded and stored under his own bed every morning. His cousin stared back at him. It seemed no one was having an easy time sleeping tonight.

"Do you miss the farm?" Ernesto asked.

His uncle's family was on the raw materials side of the business—growing the tobacco, drying and curing it, then baling it for delivery to his father's factory in the city.

They lived deep in the countryside and didn't have the middle-class luxuries Ernesto's family did, like electricity or indoor plumbing.

Ivan snorted. "Miss it? The constant stink of fermentation? The work in the blazing sun? Dust everywhere. No."

"Did you tell my father you were fired?"

"Of course not. And don't you tell him either. He'd send me home. I'll find something else." He sat up on his mattress and twisted to rest his elbows on Ernesto's bed. The soft moonlight reflected off his scruffy hair. It was clear it hadn't been washed recently. "I don't get why it's a big deal to work with Americans anyway. I can just go full-time at the factory."

He was probably right. He didn't need to learn the ways of the Americans; Ivan wasn't destined for a career in business.

But Ernesto was. It was his dream to take the family business to the next level. To become a direct exporter of cigars to the American market, rather than just selling to a wholesaler. But to do that, he'd have to learn about international trade, corporations, financing, and any number of other things he couldn't even think to ask about.

And to do *that*, he'd need to go to university.

"If you're going to work at the factory full time, you'll need to show up when you're supposed to."

Ivan nodded, but Ernesto couldn't see his face clearly enough to know if it was sincere.

"Okay," Ivan said. "I want to show you something." He stood and went to the dresser, stooping to open the bottom drawer—the one Ernesto had cleared out when

Ivan came to live with them. He removed an envelope and something else and came to sit on Ernesto's bed.

He put the envelope on the mattress but held the other thing out to Ernesto. "Look."

Ernesto sat up against the headboard, then took what Ivan was holding. It was a crumpled wad of bills. He flattened them out and counted—four American dollars.

"What's this?" Ernesto asked, despite his growing fear he already knew the answer.

"This morning, after the white twin fired me, I went to the *malecón*, down to the very far end where one of the Americans said I should go. All you have to do is stand there, by the spot hidden behind the seawall where men go to take a piss." Ernesto nodded; he knew the place. "Rich Americans go there, looking for young Cuban guys. They say it's busy at night, but I had the whole place to myself this morning."

Ernesto considered his words carefully. This would kill his father, and Ivan's too.

"You should go back to the farm, Ivan. Learn the fermentation process. It's a real art; you could make a name for yourself."

Ivan took the four dollars from him. "I don't think so."

Ernesto reached out and touched Ivan's arm. "No, seriously. It would be a good living. And when I have the export business up and running—"

"You're a fool, Ernesto." He waved the four dollars in front of his cousin's face. "This is *real* money, here and now. They'll never let you own an export business. How many times will you be refused entrance to the university before you give up?"

Ernesto's failure to get in weighed heavily on him, and his face flamed with shame.

"And look at these." Ivan opened the envelope and took out a photograph. It was too dark to see clearly, but Ernesto saw a naked male backside, and he looked away quickly. "Put that back," he hissed. "Where did you get it?"

Ivan stuffed the photograph back into the envelope. It looked like there were several more inside.

"I stole it from one of the maricóns before I was fired."

"You went into the house—into a *room*? You could have gotten caught."

"I'm always careful," Ivan said. He tapped the envelope. "I saw him showing these to another guy in the garden. I figured I could sell them."

"Ivan, you'll never get a good job if you steal."

"A good job," Ivan scoffed. "Like cleaning up after your American friends?" Ivan moved his arms from the bed and sank back onto his own mattress. "Forget your fantasies, Ernesto. You should come with me to the malecón. We could both be rich."

Chapter Four

MANNIX LOOKED ACROSS the breakfast table at the pained young man whose name he'd forgotten. Mark? Mack? Alan had only recently arrived with the boy, after sailing to Havana on that ridiculous boat of his. "It's a yacht," Alan would reply to anyone who called the *Greek Prince* a boat.

Alan came to Casa de Ada a few times each year, and always with a different young man. They were all the same: shorter than Alan, which ruled out many possible candidates, and muscled in an obvious way, as if the purpose of biceps was simply to display them. They tended to have short blond hair cut in a military style.

This one was no exception.

And he clearly was not feeling well; clutching his coffee mug and squinting his eyes against the morning light filtering into the dining room. Alan was nowhere to be seen. "Did you sleep well, dear?" Hans asked him.

The boy grunted.

Cordero, an annoyingly chipper morning person, came bouncing into the room. "Hey, Matt," he said, giving the boy a manly slap on the back.

Matt, that's it.

"Where's your daddy?" he asked.

Mannix and Hans looked at each other, and Hans shrugged. It wasn't always clear when Cordero knew what he was saying and when he was just being...Cordero.

Matt rubbed the bridge of his nose. "He's at the yacht club."

The annual Saint Petersburg to Havana yacht race had ended earlier in the week. After nearly two days at sea, Alan had swept triumphantly into Casa de Ada. Or he'd tried to anyway, but it was difficult, given the state of his young companion. Alan's disgust with Matt was evident from the moment they stepped into the reception hall.

"How was I supposed to know I get seasick?" Matt had complained. He'd slumped into the chair by the counter as soon as they'd dropped their bags. He'd been sweating and trembling, and Hans had used his foot to nudge the garbage pail closer to him.

"I don't know," Alan had snapped. "But you should have been able to lean over the rail instead of vomiting all over my deck."

Mannix shuddered to think of it—forty hours of vomit, anger, and resentment. Matt had gone directly to their room after they'd checked in, and Alan had gone to the casino for drinks with the other yachtsmen. He imagined the two wouldn't be seeing much of each other once they arrived safely back in Florida.

Mannix felt sorry for the young man sitting across from him. He looked lost.

Two older men from Allentown sat at the end of the long table, whispering to each other. They'd checked in three days earlier and hadn't stopped eyeing Mannix and Cordero in a frankly obvious way ever since. This morning, they'd turned their gaze on poor Matt, perhaps sensing an opportunity there.

Cordero stood at the sideboard, pouring himself a cup of coffee. "Where is everyone?" he asked. "There's no one working the grounds. The garden hasn't been raked since yesterday."

Mannix was wondering the very same thing. He hoped he hadn't overwhelmed the cute one yesterday. He was concerned the boy had become angry about his cousin being fired, or maybe the teasing about him swimming naked had just been too much. Or perhaps having to fish underwear out of the pool had been the last straw for him. Mannix eyed the men from Allentown and wondered if one of them had been to blame for that.

"You didn't accidentally fire everybody yesterday, did you?" Cordero asked him. "It would be a shame to lose the cute one."

The men from Allentown nodded their agreement.

"He certainly is handsome," Hans offered.

"I saw him shirtless in the pool house," Mannix said.

One of the men from Allentown dropped his fork.

Cordero grinned. "Knowing you, I'm surprised you didn't talk him out of the rest of his clothes."

"Well, I *did* try to—" Mannix began.

But Matt interrupted with a groan. He looked up from his coffee, bleary-eyed. "Is every young man's worth defined *solely* by his looks?"

A stunned silence descended around the table. Outside, a truck rumbled by, blaring something from a loudspeaker.

"Unless he's rich, yes," replied Mannix. Everyone laughed. Well, everyone except Matt, who groaned again and rubbed his temples.

"It *is* odd none of the Cubans showed up today," said Hans. His eyeglasses dangled from a pink, beaded chain around his neck. He lifted them and slipped them on, peering out into the garden as if the workers might be there after all.

Cordero went to the sideboard and lifted the cover off the dish holding the scrambled eggs. He dragged the serving spoon through the bowl, but evidently changed his mind. After replacing the lid, he took a banana muffin from the tray. "The eggs don't look very hot," he observed.

"It's a lot of work making breakfast every morning," Hans said. "Maybe if you helped out now and then…"

"Do I look like a houseboy?" Cordero asked through a mouthful of muffin.

The men from Allentown must have thought it a serious question.

"Well, you're very nice to look at," one offered.

"But probably too old for a houseboy," suggested the other.

"You could be a fitness instructor though," the first one said. Cordero had posed as an athletic coach in a photo spread for *Pumped* magazine. Mannix had been his "student," but no one at the publisher bothered to explain why the scenario called for Mannix to lay on his back, wearing nothing but a posing strap, while Cordero bent over him, pushing Mannix's knees up over his shoulders.

"Yes, or maybe a maintenance worker or a plumber," said the second. That had been one of the more popular *Pumped* photo shoots. Both of them in posing straps, but with thick leather tool belts added to the mix. They worked *very* close together under a wide-open sink. Mannix still had nightmares about claw hammers.

"Or an FBI agent," Mannix offered enthusiastically.

Hans spluttered.

Cordero *had* been an FBI agent back in New York, before they'd all come to Havana, but it wasn't something they talked about with the guests. Arthur had been one too, although he was with the other group now, the new one that was all spies and secrets. Mannix struggled to remember the name. The CIA—that was it.

Arthur had left on one of his frequent trips to DC the week before. He was probably in some bigwig meeting right now, saving the world from Communism and eating warm eggs, while the residents at Casa de Ada drank luke-warm coffee and discussed the need for a houseboy.

"*You* could be a houseboy," one of the Allentown men told Matt.

"He could be *our* houseboy," the other said. "We've talked about getting one."

Matt groaned. It sounded to Mannix like they were discussing getting a golden retriever. He decided to get some of the cold eggs.

"So, who won the boat race?" Cordero asked Matt.

Cordero was good that way; he could soldier through even the most awkward social interactions.

"How the hell should I know?" replied Matt, which was pretty effective as a conversation stopper.

"Well," continued Cordero, as if Matt had asked a reasonable question. "You were on one of the racing yachts. And obviously you didn't win, because I'm sure Alan went slow to minimize your discomfort."

Everyone at the table knew that for the lie it was.

"But didn't Alan tell you who the winner was yesterday after the final results came in?" Cordero continued, "I heard they were hoping for a record. Thirty hours, isn't it? Something like that?"

Matt paled even further at the idea of another two days on the yacht. He shook his head as he pushed his chair away from the table. "He didn't come back last night. Said he'd stay at the club." He walked over to the sideboard. "More coffee," he mumbled.

Mannix turned to Hans. "If you had a houseboy, guests wouldn't have to pour their own coffee."

"And the eggs would be warm and fresh too," Cordero added, before popping the rest of the muffin into his mouth. Before Hans could respond, the door banged open, and Alan rushed in.

"Pack your bags," he said to Matt. Mannix thought Alan may have already forgotten the boy's name. "We're leaving."

"We're changing inns?" Matt asked. Mannix couldn't tell if the idea disappointed the young man or not.

"No, we're going home. Today. Now."

It seemed impossible Matt could have gone even

whiter, but he did. "I can't. I can't get back on that boat so soon. You said we'd have a week here."

Alan's eyes narrowed. "It is a *yacht*. And I have half a mind to leave you here."

"Fine. I'll stay."

Mannix didn't know any five-year-olds, but he imagined that is what one would sound like if he didn't get his way.

"Suit yourself," Alan said coldly.

Hans removed his glasses and let them dangle against his chest. "Well, there is the slight matter of the bill..."

"Why the rush?" asked Cordero.

Alan stopped glaring at Matt and turned to face the table. "There's been a coup."

"Oh no," exclaimed Cordero.

Hans clutched his eyeglasses to his chest.

Mannix exchanged glances with Matt. He figured the young man might be as clueless about the news as he was. "Uh, is that bad?" he asked on their behalf.

"Only if you don't like tanks in the streets and dead bodies at the presidential palace," Alan said, and Mannix was reminded just how much he didn't like the fellow.

"But what happened?" asked Cordero. "Who did it?"

"Batista is back in power," Alan told him. "He took over last night. They say there's at least one guard dead at the palace."

"Well, that explains why the Cubans aren't here," Hans said. He peered into the garden again. "How did they hear about this before us?"

Mannix looked at his friend and decided to go easy

on him. "Uh, maybe it's because they speak Spanish. Might have something to do with those trucks that drove by a few times already with the loudspeakers."

Alan poured himself a cup of coffee and moved right past Matt as if he wasn't there.

"There was a message from the State Department tacked to the Yacht Club's bulletin board. It advised us all to leave for home immediately." He turned to Matt. "You should come with me. But you have to promise to lean over the rail when you're throwing up."

Mannix smiled at Alan. "Is this a first date you two are on, or did you know each other before?"

Alan glared. "You better watch yourself, Mannix. You don't want to get on my bad side." He turned to Matt. "I'm packing, and then I'm leaving." Alan left the room and his footsteps pounded angrily down the hallway.

Matt's coffee mug trembled slightly in his hands.

"He did put a deposit down for the whole week," Hans told Matt. "I'm happy not to refund it if you decide to stay."

Matt avoided looking at the men from Allentown. "But how would I get back?" he asked.

"Take a real boat," Mannix said. "Big steamships go between here and Miami all the time. Huge steady boats with bathrooms for throwing up in."

The men from Allentown whispered to each other again. "We're heading back on a steamship next week," one said. "You could come with us."

Matt looked down the hallway toward where Alan had disappeared, his indecision reflected in his face. Mannix could tell he didn't want to leave with Alan, but he didn't want to become indebted to the men from Allentown either.

"Or you could fly," Mannix offered. The men from Allentown frowned. "But that's expensive."

Matt looked into his coffee cup. "I don't have any money," he mumbled.

"We'll come up with something," Mannix said, even though Hans was frantically shaking his head at him behind Matt's back. "Tell Alan to take a long walk off a short pier."

Alan was slamming things about in the distance. "I just can't get back on that boat," Matt said. "Not so soon."

"It's a yacht, dear," Hans offered, and everyone laughed.

The front door opened and a tall, heavyset Cuban stepped through. He wore thick-rimmed black glasses, a white shirt, and a boldly patterned green and orange tie. "Oh good," he said. "I managed to catch you in time."

"Eduardo, dear." Hans rose to greet the newcomer. "What brings you out so early?"

"I rushed here as soon as I could to warn you. There's been a coup." He was breathing heavily, and Mannix suspected he really had run, or, well—knowing Eduardo—walked very quickly, all the way from the university.

"Golly," exclaimed Mannix. "Another one?"

All eyes turned to Mannix with a mixture of disbelief and pity. Mannix finished pouring a cup of coffee for Eduardo, then turned to face the room. "Honestly, I'm disappointed no one would see that as the joke it was."

Cordero grinned and slapped Mannix on the back. "It's so hard to tell with you sometimes, pal."

The men from Allentown bent their heads together and whispered.

Eduardo accepted the coffee from Mannix with a nod of thanks. "I'm never entirely sure what's happening when I'm here," he said.

"And yet you keep coming back," Mannix observed. "We're irresistible; aren't we?"

The Cuban's eyes landed on Matt. Eduardo was well into his thirties, but his tastes ran to younger men. "Well, some of you are." He walked over to the young man. "I'm absolutely certain we haven't met. I'm Eduardo Martinez." He held out his hand.

"Matt Lansing." They shook, and when Eduardo added a second hand, Matt smiled. "Is it dangerous out there right now, Mr. Martinez?"

"It may be, yes. They're telling everyone to stay off the streets." He dropped Matt's hand and turned to face the others. "It's why I came over here; I wasn't sure if you'd heard the news." He turned back to Matt. "But please, call me Eduardo."

"Or Eddie," Mannix added.

"You know, I really prefer Eduardo—"

"Oh, stop." Mannix waved the objection aside. "We're all friends here."

"It's not so much about being *friends*, exactly—" Eduardo began. But he was interrupted by the reappearance of Alan, dragging two packed bags behind him.

"I threw your stuff into your bag," he said to Matt. "Come on. We need to leave now."

Matt cringed at the tone, and Eduardo put his hand on the young man's shoulder, giving it a squeeze. "We should all be staying inside today."

Alan squinted at Eduardo's hand on Matt's shoulder. "Who the hell are you?" he asked.

"We've met before," Eduardo said. "When you've visited in the past. But, of course, you'd have no reason to remember me." He left unsaid all the reasons why someone like Alan wouldn't remember someone like Eduardo. "But I remember you. You are the American with the big boat and the small—"

"Anyway," Mannix jumped in. "Alan, this is Eddie Martinez. He works at the university, and he stopped by to warn us about the coup and to let us know the new government has started confiscating Americans' boats."

"What!" Alan strode forward and grabbed Matt's arm. "Come on. Now."

Eduardo tightened his grip on Matt's shoulder. "No one should be out on the streets right now. And the young man looks as if he's not up for traveling on your boat."

"It's a...oh, to hell with it. I'm leaving. Are you coming, Matt, or not?" He picked up his own bag and left Matt's sitting on the floor.

The men from Allentown leaned forward in their seats.

Matt looked at Mannix, who gave him an encouraging nod.

"I think I'll stay."

The men from Allentown grinned and began whispering to each other again.

"Well, there you have it," Mannix declared. "Safe travels," he said to Alan. "Oh, and better luck in next year's race."

*

ONCE ALAN LEFT, and the dust settled, Matt collapsed into his chair at the breakfast table. "What have I done?"

"The right thing," Mannix responded. "That man is a cad."

Matt's stomach grumbled. "Do you feel ready to eat yet, dear?" Hans asked.

Matt eyed the serving table with the bowl of cold eggs. "Uh…"

"Oh no. Do you not feel well?" Eduardo asked.

"No. It's just a headache. I was seasick yesterday." He took another sip of his coffee. "I do feel a little better now."

"And that evil man was going to drag you back onto his boat," Eduardo said with all the indignation he could muster. Which was a lot, Mannix thought. "Come with me to the kitchen. I will make you proper Cuban food." He took Matt's elbow to help him out of his chair.

"Let's all go," announced Mannix. "Maybe Hans can learn a thing or two."

Hans cocked an eyebrow at Mannix.

"Not me," said Cordero. "If it's not hamburgers or spaghetti, I'm not interested." He finished the coffee in his mug and grabbed another muffin. "If we're going to be stuck here all day, I'm going to clean the area around the pool so the guests have somewhere to relax." He glared at the men from Allentown. "Even if I'm too old to be a houseboy."

"Oh, but you're still glorious to look at," one of them said.

"Just in a more mature way," the other added. "Come on," he said to his companion. "Let's go claim the good lounges so we can watch him work and grab our spots before the others start getting up and learn what's happening."

"Don't forget we have a photo shoot this morning," Mannix called to Cordero as he headed toward the patio doors and the pool beyond.

"Wouldn't miss it," he called back. "Maybe I'll have to do some shirtless pushups on the pool deck to get primed." He winked at the men from Allentown, who both blushed and whispered to each other.

*

EDUARDO KNEW HIS away around Casa de Ada's kitchen. "I hope you still have my red sauce," he said to Hans as he opened a cabinet next to the stove.

"You're the only one who uses it." Hans said. "So, I'm sure it's right where you left it."

Mannix made a face. "I can't even smell that stuff without my eyes watering."

At Matt's panicked look, Eduardo said, "Don't worry. It's not that bad. You'll like it; it'll put hair on your chest." He looked at Mannix. "Is that the right English phrase?"

"Yes," Mannix said, "It's meant to...wait." Mannix looked at Matt. "*Do* you have hair on your chest? I mean, now that Eddie has brought it up, I need to have the visual."

"Hank, please," Hans said, as he opened a drawer and pulled out a cutting board. "The poor boy will be with us for the rest of the week. I suspect you'll have plenty of time to...learn more about him."

Matt was turning a pinkish color, which only deepened when Eduardo chimed in. "I must confess I'm curious about the hair and the chest too." Still, pink was better than the sickly white he'd been earlier.

"Enough, you two," Hans snapped. When he took control, it usually worked. Mannix went back to cracking eggs, and Eduardo began chopping peppers and onions, as if it was perfectly normal to include those vegetables in breakfast food.

They worked together in silence for a few moments. "Thank you for coming to warn us, Eduardo. Will it be bad, do you think?" Hans asked.

"It's too soon to say," he replied. "But if Batista settles into power quickly, and the city remains calm, there might not be much of a disruption." He picked up the cutting board and slid the chopped vegetables into a brightly colored bowl. "It's Cuba. We've done this before."

"Not since before the war," Matt said. "The last two presidents were democratically elected."

Everyone stopped and looked at Matt. He'd been slicing a loaf of bread, and when he noticed the drawn-out silence, he put the knife down and looked up. "What?" he asked. "I study political science at NYU."

Eduardo's eyes glimmered. "Oh, my dear boy," he said. "An American who knows more about Cuba than rum, cigars, and sugar."

Mannix simply stood, blinking, as he reassessed the situation.

Eduardo approached Matt. "I want to hug you," he

said, opening his arms wide.

"For a start," Mannix mumbled.

"That's okay." Matt waved the Cuban off. "Thanks anyway."

Eduardo didn't seem offended. "But how did such a smart boy like you come to be involved with that horrible man?" he asked.

Matt didn't seem offended by the question either. "Well, it's not so uncommon, is it? He has wads of money and promised me a vacation in Cuba in exchange for my...company. We took the train from New York to St. Petersburg, which was fun. I'd never been on a sleeper train before. But then we had to get over here and I didn't know about how it would be. On the boat, I mean."

"Yacht," said Mannix.

Hans shushed him.

No one ever offered to take me on a vacation, Mannix thought. *It was always just a quick encounter in a semi-public space in exchange for cash.*

"I suppose things are different now that the war is behind us." Mannix said, as if he'd shared his thoughts out loud. "So much more money sloshing around."

"Um, different than what?" asked Eduardo.

Mannix refocused on the discussion in the room. "Different than when I was...well, just different is all."

He was spared the need to explain further by one of the men from Allentown rushing into the kitchen. "Ice! Ice!" he exclaimed.

"Good lord, what's happening?" Hans asked, wiping

his hands on his apron. It was yellow, with cartoon chickens dancing around the hem.

"Cordero's hurt!"

Matt pushed past Mannix and headed for the patio doors. "I know first aid," he said, as he rushed out of the kitchen, Eduardo close on his heels.

Of course he does.

Hans busied himself gathering ice from the freezer and placing the cubes into his apron pockets. "Grab some towels," he told the man from Allentown. "How badly hurt is he?"

"I don't know. He fell onto the diving board. There was a terrific *whack*."

"How do you fall *onto* a diving board?" Mannix asked as he grabbed a handful of tea towels from the drawer by the fridge.

"Well, *first* he fell onto the diving board, then he slipped from that and landed on the stone pavers. It was our fault. We were encouraging him to do one-armed push-ups. And on a slippery diving board! What were we thinking?"

By the time they arrived with the ice and towels, Matt had already gotten Cordero propped into a sitting position. He sat against Cordero's side, letting him lean against his shoulder for support. "Keep it tightly pinched. Lean your head forward." Blood was running from Cordero's nose. He looked up at Hans. "Good. Hand me a towel."

While Cordero squeezed his nose shut, Matt delicately tilted the man's chin so he could dab at the blood from the split lip. After a moment's inspection he said,

"Good." He reached out a finger and touched Cordero's cheekbone.

"Ouch!"

"Sorry." Matt tilted Cordero's head again. "I don't think it's fractured. Just badly bruised." When Matt pulled back, Mannix leaned in for a closer look, then let out a slow whistle. "You're going to have quite a shiner."

They debated a trip to the hospital, but when Eduardo pointed out there could be bodies piling up around the city, it was decided the best course of action was to wait it out. Thankfully, after fifteen minutes, Cordero's nosebleed diminished to a trickle, and they were able to lead him cautiously back into the kitchen.

"Coffee," Cordero said as he slumped back into his chair at the table.

"No," Matt replied. "No caffeine. You need to rest. Eduardo, would you take him to his room please?"

The men from Allentown seemed disappointed they hadn't been tapped for the task.

"Of course, Matt." Eduardo helped Cordero up. "You're a very impressive young man," he said before steering Cordero down the hallway.

Other guests had begun arriving for breakfast and were seated at the table, pushing cold eggs around their plates or eating muffins. Hans set about making a fresh pot of coffee, while Mannix refilled the orange juice pitcher. They'd both returned to the dining room just as the two photographers from *Pumped* entered.

"Good morning," one of the cameramen said to the assembled guests. "How is everyone doing today?"

*

IT WAS A lot to take in.

The coup, Alan's departure, Cordero's injury. No wonder the photographers seemed a bit shell-shocked. And then there was Matt.

"But who *are* you? When did you get here?" one of them asked. Hans had gone through it once already, but Eduardo told the story again. Mannix thought he embellished Matt's role to the point of embarrassment, but Matt only smiled.

"And Cordero?" the other photographer asked. "He's not available for the photo shoot at all?"

"I don't know," Mannix said. "Are you doing a special spread for Halloween?"

"Uh, no," said the first one. He took a bite of his eggs and made a face. "Ugh. These are awful." He looked at Hans accusingly.

"I know," said Mannix. "We're getting a houseboy."

"Actually, we haven't decided about that yet." Hans corrected.

The photographers whispered together and Mannix decided there'd been too much whispering in the break-fast room for one day. "What?" he asked, a touch too loudly.

One of them nodded at Matt. "The new guy," he said. "He has great features."

"Very defined," the other added.

Mannix grasped the end game immediately. "You want me to wrestle with Matt?" It was an exciting idea and one he could enthusiastically support. He'd gotten used to Cordero—how he moved, how he felt—and they worked well together. But he wouldn't mind grappling with Matt; he was fit, attractive, perhaps a little cocky—but Mannix liked that.

Too bad it wasn't Ernesto though.

Where the hell did that *come from*?

"Not wrestle, no," one of the *Pumped* men said. "We're planning a poolside shoot today."

"We can do that," Mannix said. He'd just pulled a chair up to the table, but he pushed away the plate he'd brought with him. "I guess one muffin will be enough for me this morning."

"We'll have to verify he checks out first though. Get him into a pair of trunks, make sure he still looks good." One of the photographers was writing in a small note-book.

As Matt watched the exchange, his eyebrows inched higher and higher up his forehead. "Hello?" he said, finally. "Don't I get a say in any of this?"

The *Pumped* man put his pencil down and closed the notebook. "You get twenty dollars—cash—for just a few hours work."

"Where do I sign?" asked Matt.

*

IT TURNED OUT Matt did have hair on his chest—a downy feathering of the palest gold that stretched between his pecs then narrowed down to a thin line ending just above his navel. He wore turquoise swim trunks and stood awkwardly next to the diving board waiting for the crew to finish staging the pool area for the shoot.

The blood had been mopped up, and all of the inn's guests—a dozen or so men who had nowhere else to go due to the coup—had been corralled into an area of the garden outside of the camera's view.

Matt looked nervous, but Mannix was sure he'd loosen up once they started working together, following the director's instructions and moving in sync with one another. A large inflated beach ball and a life preserver had been brought onto the set.

"All right, you two," one of the photographers said, "just start tossing the ball back and forth. We'll get a sense of how you look together, how the rhythm flows."

Mannix and Matt got to work, and sure enough, Matt seemed to blossom in front of the cameras. He laughed and grinned, and Mannix admired the way his muscled body moved. He thought they made a good pair—Mannix, sleek and smooth, in black trunks that matched his black curling hair, and golden Matt, powerful and compact. He was looking forward to the grappling part of the photoshoot.

But the photographers were frowning, studying the scene before them then checking their notes. "Stop a moment," one called. They bent their heads together. More whispers.

One of them nodded then looked up. "Mannix, head back a little bit into the edge of the garden. We want to try you in the shade with Matt in the sun." he wrote something in his notebook. "For the contrast," he added.

Mannix moved back, and the guests of Casa de Ada shuffled farther back too, getting out of the camera's viewfinder. Matt and Mannix began tossing the ball between them.

The photographers shook their heads.

"Stop," called one. "Matt, come over here and sit on the diving board."

Matt walked to the pool, his body glistening from the exertion in the sun. He hopped onto the diving board and sat, dangling his legs over the side. The turquoise trunks hugged his body, and Mannix noticed he filled the suit out nicely.

"Where do you want me?" Mannix called to the cameramen.

"Take a break for a few minutes," one called back without looking away from his camera.

For the next half hour, the photographers took photos of Matt—lying on the diving board, lounging in the deck chair, sitting poolside with his legs in the water. Then more photos of Matt in the pool—floating, swimming, diving.

When at last they were finished, the photographers were smiling and writing notes furiously in their pads. "Perfect," one said. "That's it for this morning. Thanks, men." They began packing up their equipment.

Mannix strode forward out of the shadows. "Guys? What about me?"

"Oh, right," one said. It was almost as if he'd forgotten Mannix was there. He looked at his colleague, and Mannix sensed the unspoken communication passing between them. Finally, the other spoke up. "Sorry, Hank. We can't use you and Matt together."

"But there's such great contrast," Mannix objected.

"Dark and light, short and tall, stocky and slim." Mannix sucked in his stomach when he said slim. It was starting to be a stretch to refer to himself that way. He decided he'd start using the word lithe going forward.

"Young and old," one of the *Pumped* men said.

A murmur rippled through the gathered crowd.

The other photographer put his hand on Mannix's arm. "He's just kidding."

No, he isn't.

"You're not *old*. It just that...well, our readers don't want to think of *themselves* as old, and seeing you two together..."

The other photographer spoke up. "What he means is there's an obvious age gap, and when our readers see the pictures, we don't want to remind them they're...admiring...the form of someone so much younger."

"Like, less than half their age," the other added unnecessarily.

Mannix flushed. "But I'm not twice as old as Matt, I'm not even—"

"Not *you*, Hank. You're great. You and Cordero still work well together. For now." Both photographers smiled at him as if they hadn't just killed him. "It's just, when you're together with Matt, it's looks a little..."

Mannix waited for the insult. The *Pumped* men equivocated, evidently searching for a word that would get the point across without offending. "Lecherous," one concluded, missing the mark entirely.

Chapter Five

ERNESTO'S FAMILY GATHERED in the office. Just because the factory was closed didn't mean they couldn't work.

A truck rumbled by for the third time that morning. "General Batista is in control of the government. Order is being restored. Remain inside." The truck moved off into the distance. Its message repeating as it faded into the eerie silence of Havana.

"He wasn't so bad when he was president before," Ernesto's father said. "It would be good for business if the corruption was brought under control."

"But the elections," his mother said. "Will they still be held?"

Ernesto thought that a naïve question. The elections wouldn't be held. They were less than three months away, and Batista himself was a candidate. Would a man stage a coup if he thought he might win an upcoming election?

"We'll see," his father said, but Ernesto knew from his tone he saw the truth too. "That's beautiful, mija," he said to Marta, who was completing the interior decorations on one of the boxes that would hold their best cigars—the ones destined for the most expensive international markets.

If only we could export them ourselves. And why haven't I heard from the university yet?

"No, Ivan. The band is upside down," his father said. "And it needs to go on the cap end, not the foot." He took the cigar from Ivan, removed the band, and replaced it with a new one. "See?" He handed it back to Ivan, who barely glanced at it before passing it on to Marta.

Ernesto's mother didn't think Ivan would ever make anything of himself. She would never have told Ernesto that directly, but it was hard not to overhear when his parents argued, even privately. She also thought his cousin was a bad influence on Ernesto, and given what had almost happened in the gardens, she was probably right.

"And he's so dark," she said once, at the end of one of their fights about Ivan. "What must the neighbors think when they see him as part of our family?"

"Isabel," his father had responded, "that's beneath you." His tone carried a warning.

She sniffed. "I'm not saying it's right, but people notice these things." His father clenched his fists but turned away and left the room. "You can't pretend they don't, Raúl," his mother called after him. "It's the way people are."

Ernesto suspected Ivan had overheard at least part

of that argument; he'd been cold and distant for days afterward. How difficult it must be to constantly disappoint people, although Ivan brought most of the disapproval upon himself. Not all of it though. He may exercise poor judgment and lack any semblance of a work ethic, but it wasn't his fault he was dark.

And what did it matter anyway? The Orthodox Party stressed there was only one Cuba, and everyone was a part of it.

Ernesto believed that.

But he couldn't help noticing all the light-skinned students at the university, and the darker faces that worked in the factory. And the still darker faces working in the fields.

The Cuban people were like the cigars they made—a wide spectrum of colors, from *double claro* to *oscuro*. But in the end, they were all just shades of brown.

Ernesto thought of Mannix, with his slender white hands and teasing manner. Had he mistaken the signs of interest there? Was the white man simply toying with him? It didn't matter. He needed to put all his focus on getting into the university.

The salsa music playing on the radio stopped, and the family paused in their work to hear what would come next. An announcer came on—a deep, masculine voice, calm and reassuring.

The new government was installed, and the city would reopen tomorrow. There had been no violence. The elections would be rescheduled. The university would remain closed for the week.

"Why the university?" Ernesto asked.

"Young people," his father answered. "They have their heads in the clouds, always thinking the world should be different than it is." He picked up the cigar on which Ivan had just placed a band and peered at it, tilting it one way and then another. "Better," he said.

Ernesto thought about what Ivan had done that morning on the malecón. The details were vague, thankfully, but as much as Ivan put on a show of bravado, Ernesto didn't believe his cousin would have chosen this path if he'd had better choices.

"I think the world *should* be different," Ernesto said. "We could make it better."

His mother put down her sewing and smiled at him across the worktable. "Then you'll fit right in at university, mijo."

"But our son will be a sensible student," his father said. "He's no radical. He'll follow the rules and make the world a better place for all hardworking Cubans." Everyone glanced at Ivan. Ernesto wasn't the only one in the family who wondered if his cousin fell into the category of hardworking.

His father selected a cigar from the stack in front of Marta. After she finished preparing the box, Marta would select the premium cigars for color consistency then carefully pack them. He placed the cigar in front of Ivan. "What color is this?" he asked.

It was an easy question. The cigar was wrapped in a reddish-brown leaf, a rich, earthy color. It would be characterized as maduro, the closest to oscuro on the dark end of the scale.

"Um…colorado claro?" Even in this, Ivan was deficient. He was at least three colors off.

"No, Ivan," his father said with a frown. "See the deep color, like damp soil? This is maduro."

Ernesto admired his father's perseverance and commitment to his nephew. But there was no point. Ivan was never going to grasp the details of cigar manufacturing, much less the nuanced aspects of packaging and marketing. It had been a mistake to send him to the city to learn a trade.

Ivan shrugged and shot Ernesto a challenging glance. "Four dollars," he whispered.

"What was that?" his mother asked.

But before he could respond, there was a knock on the front door of the factory.

The family froze and looked at each other. Who could possibly be at the door with the city under curfew? Ernesto went to the window to peer out, and his heart jumped. Why would the police be showing up now? Did someone report Ivan? "It's the *caballito*," he whispered.

His father stood. "Is it the usual one?" he asked.

Ernesto leaned farther to the side and looked again. "Yes," he replied just as the knock came again.

"Let him in. Quickly."

Isabel looked as if she'd object, but she remained silent. Her gaze settled on Ivan. It was clear to Ernesto she wished his cousin wasn't there.

"Señor," Ernesto said as he opened the door and stepped aside to allow the officer to enter.

The caballito had been to the factory many times, but

never so early in the month. Raúl strode forward, stretching a hand out in greeting. "Señor, welcome. Is everything all right?" The men shook hands, and the officer was led into the office. He nodded to the women, and they smiled back at him. He frowned at Ivan, and Ivan looked away.

"Everything is fine, Raúl," he said, surveying the worktable. "It seemed a good day to stop by and make sure you had no worries about the new government, to ensure no one was harassing you or bothering you in any way."

Ernesto turned that over in his mind. He concluded the caballito was worried someone might take advantage of the situation and move in on his turf. Ernesto hadn't considered that possibility, and he added it to the growing list of things to keep him awake at night.

"No, Señor," his father replied. "You have been our only visitor."

"Good," he said. He picked up the cigar Ivan had just banded and ran it under his nose, breathing deeply. "Beautiful. A criollo wrapper leaf, no?"

"Yes, our finest," Raúl said. The men looked at each other.

It was only the second week of March. This shouldn't be happening yet.

Ernesto's father seemed to consider his options and concluded he had none. "Please take it, as our thanks for your checking in on us on such an uncertain day."

The caballito held the cigar and smiled at Ernesto's father. The silence lasted for what felt like an hour, but must have only been seconds. Raúl swallowed. "Take a couple for your fellow officers too. It must be a difficult day for all of you.”

Isabel's smile twitched at the corners of her lips. Ivan stared at the floor.

“Thank you, Señor Ruiz. You are a good man.” He reached forward and picked up four more cigars. “Stay safe, and call on me if you need my help.”

He turned and walked to the door. Ernesto hurried to escort him out.

*

THE FOLLOWING MORNING, the city gradually returned to life. There was no gunfire, no protests, no dead bodies in the streets. Rumor had it a guard had died at the palace, maybe two, but beyond that there had been no violence. The torcederos began trickling back into the factory, and Ernesto read the morning news to them as they worked.

The university—a hotbed of political radicalism—was to remain closed for the remainder of the week. The whereabouts of President Prío were unknown. The coup was necessary to eliminate government corruption and to prevent the former president from seizing control himself. Elections would be scheduled at the earliest possible opportunity.

The people of Havana should make every effort to return to normalcy as quickly as possible.

The torcederos nodded and silently rolled their cigars, betraying nothing of their feelings about the sudden change in the government. Ernesto decided he should return to work at Casa de Ada the following morning.

By the afternoon, one could imagine nothing out of the ordinary had happened at all. Shops and cafes reopened. Buses rumbled by outside the factory, spewing black exhaust across the city.

Mail delivery resumed.

Ernesto received his third rejection from the university.

Chapter Six

THE DAY AFTER the coup, Mannix half-heartedly raked up the garden area by the pool.

It gave him something to do rather than fret about the humiliating photo shoot the day before. Cordero was still too banged up to work, let alone be seen in public with his gruesomely swollen face.

Breakfast had been a vast improvement. Eduardo had stayed the night, as he sometimes did, and he and Matt had managed to put together a fine spread. Mannix had given a stern warning beforehand. "Just normal food, Eddie. None of your mysterious vegetables. And nothing spicy."

He raked the palm fronds and leaf litter into a pile to be picked up later by the Cubans—assuming they ever returned, waved to Hans who was sitting in his reading chair by the window in the greenhouse, and then headed deeper into the garden to feed the koi.

He removed the tin from beneath the bush and threw a handful of food into the pond. The water churned as the fish flashed white, gold, and orange, their gaping mouths opening and closing on the surface. The men from Allentown appeared, but he scowled at them, and they retreated.

He remembered Ernesto sitting on the bench, nervous and aroused.

Mannix had thought back to that moment frequently, envisioning all the ways it could have gone better. He could have tried to befriend the young man rather than seduce him, although Cordero was right—sex was like an obsession with him. It colored everything and everyone.

And he *was* too old for it.

Not for sex, of course, but for this...pursuit of conquests, for this lifestyle of turning tricks and seeing every encounter as a homage to himself. As a validation of his desirability.

And what had he thought would happen when he'd come on so strong, practically shoving his cock in the young man's face? It would have been degrading for Ernesto to have followed through on that.

I should have known better. I should have been *better.*

And yet.

There had been interest there—he was sure of it—on both their parts, and Mannix was probably more confused about that than Ernesto was. Mannix had actually been tempted. For a moment, he'd considered switching roles, *giving* pleasure rather than simply being worshipped.

And that had been such a shocking, unexpected thought.

Then everything went to hell in a handbasket when Ernesto mentioned his ridiculous idea about payment, and Mannix...blew up. He lost control. He could admit that now, but it was a hard pill to swallow; he was a man who prided himself on always being in control.

There was just something about Ernesto that had him in a twist.

He'd kept his eyes open for the young man the last two days, hoping to find him in the garden. But none of the Cubans had come back to work yet. He hoped Ernesto was safe, and regretted how little he knew about any of the workers at Casa de Ada. Where did Ernesto live? What was his family like? What kind of factory did his father own?

It was difficult imagining him on an assembly line, welding parts onto cars or whatever it was factory workers did in Cuba.

He brought his attention back to the fish and tried to think of something other than Ernesto.

*

"STOP DOING THAT," Cordero said. He had his feet propped up on an ottoman and an ice pack pressed against his forehead, just above his swollen eye. They were in Casa de Ada's parlor, and Mannix was reading a newspaper while he sat in a brightly upholstered armchair across from Cordero.

"Stop doing what?" Mannix asked as he lowered the paper, looked at Cordero, and shuddered.

"That! Looking so repulsed every time you see me." Cordero lowered the icepack and pointed an accusing finger at Mannix. "My bruises can't keep coming as a surprise. You're just doing it to needle me."

Mannix suppressed a smile. "Maybe a little," he acknowledged.

"I'm not missing the show tonight," Cordero insisted.

Mannix put the paper aside. "You *can't* go out in public like that. We have a reputation to maintain."

Cordero sighed and moved the ice pack from his forehead to his swollen lip. "I know; I know. The white twins, blah, blah, blah...but, I don't know, maybe it's time to—"

"No. It's *not* time to...whatever it is you're thinking." Mannix snapped the paper back into place in front of him.

Cordero wasn't giving up. "We have to go tonight though. You know they'll only let Eduardo in if he's with us. And he's looking forward to showing the new Mannix—"

Mannix cast the paper aside and stood, pointing a finger at Cordero. "Do *not* call that upstart 'the new Mannix,' or I swear I'll—"

"Did I hear my name?" Eduardo asked as he came into the room.

Mannix and Cordero exchanged a guilty look. Of course Eduardo understood the situation, and it wasn't Mannix's fault Cuban men faced discrimination in their own country, but still. It was awkward and uncomfortable to discuss it in front of him.

Cordero lowered his icepack, and Eduardo flinched. "Ouch," he said. Mannix snickered.

Cordero frowned and winced in evident discomfort. "We were wondering if you wanted to head out to the casino tonight?" he asked.

"You'd go out looking like that?" Eduardo asked.

"See?" asked Mannix.

Cordero leaned his head back and covered his entire face with the icepack. He waved his hand at the other men. "I'm done with both of you."

Eduardo shrugged. "Well, thank you for the offer, but I have to get back to the university. I don't want them thinking I've been rounded up with all the radicals." He walked to the sideboard and poured himself a cup of coffee. He took a sip and scrunched his nose. "Cold," he said.

"We really do need a houseboy," Mannix replied.

Cordero moved the icepack away from his mouth. "Well, maybe now that you'll have more free time..."

Mannix turned to Eduardo. "Is it unseemly to punch a man who's already injured?"

Eduardo considered the question. "You know, I could write a book about what it's like—behind the scenes—with the white twins."

"Better write fast," Cordero mumbled from behind the icepack. "Their star is fading."

"Whose star is fading?" asked Matt as he walked into the room, all shiny and glowing and muscled.

Mannix muttered under his breath. "Coffee?" he asked Matt, pointing to Eduardo's abandoned cup.

"Uh, no thanks." Matt went to Cordero's side and stooped. "Move the icepack; I need to check on my patient."

Cordero exposed his face for inspection. Matt tilted the man's chin toward the light and leaned in for a closer look. "Good," Matt said. "The swelling is going down. Does this hurt?" He placed his finger on Cordero's chin below the split lip.

"No."

"Good. This?" He touched his fingertip to Cordero's brow, just above his bruised eye.

"Ouch."

"Sorry." He traced his finger down the side of Cordero's face until he reached his chin. It was a strangely seductive motion, and Eduardo frowned. "You'll be fine. We maybe should have gotten a stitch or two in your eyebrow. You'll likely have a small scar there." Matt leaned back and smiled at Cordero. "It'll look sexy."

Eduardo stepped forward. "Stop touching his face; you don't know where it's been."

Mannix laughed.

"Besides, we've got to go," Eduardo told Matt.

"We?" Mannix cocked his head.

"Yes," Eduardo replied. "I need to get back to the university, and Matt wants to see the campus. Do you think Hans would let you drive us in the house car? Matt will need a way to get back."

The last thing Mannix wanted to do was play chauffeur for Eddie and Golden Boy. Still, it would get him out of the house, and he was curious about how things were after the coup. "It's only to be used for guests," he said.

"Matt's a guest," Eduardo pointed out.

Mannix considered arguing the point. Alan was the guest; the young upstart was just Alan's...whatever. But Cordero had already jumped on the idea. "Road trip!" he exclaimed, lowering the ice pack and swinging his feet off the ottoman.

"No!" Mannix and Eduardo said at the same time.

"Honestly, Tony. You can't go out looking like that," Mannix pleaded.

"He's right," Eduardo agreed. "Not today. You'll start a rumor the new government is roughing up Americans."

Cordero sighed, leaned his head back against the chair, and replaced the ice pack.

"One of you is riding up front with me," Mannix said. "I don't want to have to think about what might be going on in the back seat."

*

THE HOUSE CAR was a 1937 Packard Super Eight that Arthur had picked up on the cheap when the owner of a local nightclub failed to pay his protection money. It was painted a dusky, elegant blue and had a gorgeous cream interior. Even though it was over ten years old, it was still elegant, and Mannix found it more attractive than the bulkier new models beginning to make their way onto the island.

Eduardo sat up front, and it soon became evident he was directing Mannix on the most circuitous route possible to the university. He kept up a running monologue for Matt, pointing out historic landmarks and cultural sights.

Mannix was enjoying being out in the city, so he tried not to take offense at being treated like a servant: "Turn here. I want to show Matt the parrot market;" or "Go back. We passed the cathedral;" and "Oh, take this right. We can drive along the malecón."

It was as vibrant as ever along the seaside. Street vendors were out in full force. Guitar buskers competed with each other. It was as if the coup had never happened. At one point, Mannix locked eyes with a dark young man in dirty jeans, leaning against a stone wall and projecting an attitude and a message Mannix could have read a mile away.

Good lord! It's the grubby one.

Mannix looked away, then looked back. Yes, it was him. He'd just fired the man two days ago, and he wouldn't soon forget his face.

He'd have to tell Ernesto. Turning tricks in the garden was one thing. Publicly prostituting himself on the malecón was another. That was dangerous, both physically and legally. Perhaps Ernesto could talk some sense into him. Grubby or not, there must be something the young man could do to earn a legitimate living.

But will I ever see Ernesto again? His heart sank at the idea he might not.

*

MANNIX PARKED BY the main gate of the university.

Eduardo had been checking his watch obsessively during the last few minutes of the ride. "I'm sorry, Matt. We took so long on the city tour that I don't have time now to show you the campus." He'd twisted all the way around in his seat and was leaning precariously into the back.

"That's all right," Matt replied. "I enjoyed learning so much about Havana."

They both just sat there, staring at each other, and Mannix was convinced if he'd let them both ride in the back seat there'd be a kiss goodbye at this point, like some sappy first date in the movies. Instead, Eduardo stretched his arm toward Matt then grasped his hand. "Let's do the campus tour this week while you're still here." That was followed by even more arm stretching and hand clasping and silence.

"Eddie, there's a little handle thingy there on the side of your door. If you twist it, then push, you can get out."

Mannix glanced in the rearview mirror in time to catch Golden Boy rolling his eyes.

Eduardo reluctantly released Matt's hand. "I'll try to stop by tomorrow if I can get away."

Please, no.

"Okay," Matt said with a smile.

Eduardo finally opened his door and climbed out of the car. Before he walked off, he tapped on the glass in the back window and gave a little wave. Mannix laid on the horn, causing Eduardo to nearly topple over.

"Jesus," grumbled Matt.

Eduardo collected himself, gave one last jaunty salute, and headed off into the campus. After a few moments of silence, Mannix said, "Well?"

"He seems nice," Matt answered. "And he's a good cook."

"I meant, are you getting up front or are we sitting here all day?"

"I know what you meant. I was just teasing you, Pops." Matt slid across the seat and stepped out of the car. Mannix considered driving off, but he suspected he'd never hear the end of it, and, much as he'd like to, he knew it wouldn't be right to abandon the boy in the middle of the city.

Once they were both settled, Mannix put the car in drive—he hadn't bothered turning off the engine—and pulled onto the roadway. Matt stared out the open passenger window as they drove. Mannix slowed once they reached the malecón, and he scanned the crowd as they passed. The tang of the ocean air competed with the smell of roasting meat and exhaust fumes.

"What are you looking for?" Matt asked. It was the first time either man had spoken during the drive.

"Mind your own beeswax," Mannix shot back. He continued searching the crowd and thought he might have spotted the grubby one—*Ivan, that was his name*—but his view was soon blocked by several parked cars and an ice cream vendor. "Hang on," he said as he made a sudden sharp left into an alley.

The alley turned out to be a dead end, but at least it widened somewhat at the end, and Mannix managed a tight K-turn, avoiding a couple of chickens and an inconveniently positioned basket of laundry while he did so. They stopped when they reached the mouth of the alley and waited.

After a few moments and several gaps in the cross traffic, during which Mannix could have pulled back onto the main road but didn't, Matt said, "What are we waiting for?"

Mannix considered the question. He was uncertain how much he should share about what happened with Ivan.

"You don't like me much," Matt observed.

Mannix kept his focus on the men passing by on the malecón. "Nonsense. I don't even know you.

"Which makes it that much more rude," Matt pointed out. When no further information was offered, he sighed, leaned his head back against the seat, crossed his impressive arms over his chest, and closed his eyes. "Fine. Wake me up if you need me."

Mannix glanced at the young man. It wasn't his fault he was beautiful. Even his eyelashes were an arresting shade of burnished bronze. His biceps threatened to break through the tight short sleeve cuffs of his shirt. He was so young.

But none of that justified Mannix's resentment of the fellow. If he was honest with himself, he was simply jealous. Jealous of how easy it was for Matt—rich men whisking him away on international trips, university administrators fawning over him like besotted teenagers, magazine photographers treating him like…like…

Don't say the new Mannix. Don't even think *it.*

Still. Mannix was disappointed with himself. He'd had his own lucky breaks, after all, as well as his fair share of setbacks. And you can't judge a book by its cover, can you?

He drummed his fingertips on the steering wheel. "I'm sorry," he said. "I have no reason to be cross with you. I'm looking for someone."

A young boy selling cigarettes pushed a packet through Mannix's window. "Mister, mister. American cigarettes?" Mannix waved him off.

Matt opened his eyes and turned to Mannix. "Who are you looking for?"

An older American man walked by Matt's side of the car, twice, slowly passing each time and staring at Matt intently. Matt rolled his window closed.

"A young Cuban fellow," Mannix responded. "Dark, scrawny, rough around the edges, looking to make some cash."

Matt squeezed himself closer to his door, and gave Mannix a disgusted look. "Jesus, man. I'm not one to judge, but do you have to do that *now*? With me in the car? Can't you drop me back at the inn first?"

Mannix whipped his head around to look at Matt. "What? No. Not to *hire* him! What the hell is happening? Why does everyone suddenly think I have to pay for sex?"

Matt didn't look entirely convinced, but he held his hands up in surrender. "So why are you looking for him, then?"

"I had to fire him a couple days ago." Mannix turned his gaze back to the crowd. "I want to tell his cousin where to find him, talk some sense into him."

"Oh, right. The guy you call the grubby one, because all young men are valued solely on the basis of their looks."

Mannix turned back to Matt. "Are you being serious right now, Golden Boy? Do you think you'd be vacationing in Cuba if you didn't look like you do?"

Matt sat up straight in the seat. "I know why I'm here. I know why you're here too. And I know you fired that poor boy for doing the same thing in the gardens that you've done all along."

"It wasn't the same thing at all. And what the hell do you know about it? You just got here." The chickens had made their way to the front of the alley, and one flew up to land on the hood of the car. Hans would kill him if he scratched the Packard. Mannix honked the horn, the chicken flew off, and everyone within earshot turned their way.

"Eduardo likes to gossip," Matt said. "I learned a lot yesterday. Plus, I've seen the magazine pictures, and Alan said he'd show me even better ones—like that's something I'd want to see. As if he was doing me a favor by offering to look at photos of naked men together. I'm so glad he's gone."

Mannix wasn't exactly naked in the magazine pictures. The iconic *Pumped* cover photo—the one that started it all—featured Mannix in a posing strap, crouched in a boxer's stance. It had made him famous within the small circle of the men's magazine crowd. It was taken eight years ago, but there were still several copies of the magazine floating around Casa de Ada.

The ensuing modeling career had paid the bills, mostly. Mannix didn't like to dwell on the other things he'd had to do to make ends meet when he came up short.

Hans had been a lifesaver at the time, offering him a place to stay at his New York City boarding house. Hans collected misfits back then, all men of a certain persuasion seeking new lives in the city. Mannix had even come to grudgingly like Hans's G-man boyfriend, Arthur.

And once Mannix met Cordero, the two of them became a sought-after modeling duo, and the rest was history, as they say.

Only, yes, he still turned tricks in the gardens, but it was all in fun, and it gave him a thrill to know these men sought him out. They chose to stay at Casa de Ada because of him. He was appreciated. He was a celebrity!

It wasn't the same as what Ivan had been doing. Not at all.

"I get it though," Matt said. "White men, white rules."

This was absurd. "Can you hear yourself?" Mannix asked. "One look at you and men give you whatever you want. You even—"

"How long ago was that picture taken?" Matt interrupted. "The boxer one, I mean, not the more sordid ones Alan hinted at."

More sordid ones? He couldn't possibly know about that one time— No. He must mean the films he was doing with Tony. And they weren't exactly sordid.

"You looked like you were in your prime back then. My age maybe? At least a decade ago or so?"

Mannix was getting annoyed. "Why, you little—"

Suddenly the car filled with the unpleasant stink of sweat. "Hey, maricón." Mannix whipped his head to the window to find Ivan, leaning well into his personal space, his arms resting on the roof of the car. He'd ducked his head into the window opening. "You fire me, now maybe you want to hire me?" He laughed and took a step back then ran a hand down his stained and torn T-shirt and grabbed his crotch.

"Jesus," Matt whispered, pressing himself once again into the passenger door.

"Look, Ivan. You shouldn't be doing this. It's dangerous," Mannix said.

He laughed again. It sounded unstable.

"Talk to Ernesto. Maybe he could get you a job with him at his factory."

Ivan stepped up to the window again, and the car filled once more with his smell. Matt lowered his window.

"Two dollars, American man. You want?"

Mannix began rolling his window up. "Talk to Ernesto," he said again and drove off.

Chapter Seven

ERNESTO READ THE note three times.

Beyond the shock of the message itself—"I'm leaving. I won't be back. Thank Uncle Raúl and Aunt Isabel for feeding me"—Ernesto had never seen his cousin's handwriting before. It was a series of ill-formed, blocky letters, little better than an untrained child could manage.

One more brick of bad news on the rapidly growing wall.

After yesterday's devastating letter from the university, even his mother had stopped pretending he'd get in. "It'll all work out, mijo," she'd said at dinner. But her eyes were puffy and red.

"You don't *need* a degree to be successful in business," his father had said. "We'll focus on the factory and improving our product. You have good marketing ideas. We'll get there."

Marta had asked to be excused from the table early,

claiming she didn't feel well.

So, it was with a heavy heart at breakfast the next morning that Ernesto handed over the note he'd found tucked into his underwear drawer. His father looked worried, but his mother only nodded. "I feel bad for your brother, Raúl, but that boy was nothing but trouble from the beginning."

Marta looked relieved. Ivan's presence had caused tension within the family.

"You'll need to go to the farm, Ernesto," his father said. "Tell your uncle what has happened. They might want to look for him."

His mother huffed out her doubt about the likelihood of that outcome.

"I planned on going back to work with the Americans this morning," Ernesto said. His parents hadn't raised it yesterday, and he was afraid his father might prefer he join the family business full time now.

"Well, plan on going to the farm tomorrow then," his father said. "But we'll need to think about where you spend your time. You'll need to start learning more of the business than just reading to the torcederos."

"Being a lector is honorable work," Ernesto insisted.

"It is," his father agreed, "but it won't help grow the business or increase exports."

Ernesto nodded his understanding. It was true, after all. He'd probably have to leave his job at Casa de Ada. He'd miss it, odd as all the men there were. He'd miss Mannix. He'd like to feed the fish with him again, and not screw it up so badly next time.

"I'll get some of those little cakes from the bakery for

you to bring," his mother told him. "And a few items from the pharmacy your Aunt Clara can't get down there." She shook her head. "I don't know how they live like they do, so far from everything, with no electricity or running water."

"We grew up on that farm, Isabel," his father admonished. "Don't make it sound worse than it is."

She sniffed, then smiled. "I guess I married the right Ruiz brother then."

"Like you had a choice," his father said. Then he kissed his wife on the forehead.

*

ERNESTO SAT ON the bench by the koi pond. The tin of food was missing.

He'd cleaned up the area twice, and there was no justification for lingering. He'd hoped to talk to Mannix to explain that he wouldn't be here for a couple of days, and that maybe he couldn't come back at all. It was absurd to think they'd hold his job for him, but he'd rather speak to Mannix than Hans about it. Hans made him nervous.

So did Mannix, but for different reasons.

Ernesto stood and gave one final look at the pond. The fish had abandoned their hopes for breakfast, but he could still see them in the shady waters, muted rusts and golds undulating in the depths. He imagined them saying goodbye and wishing him well.

It was silly, really; he'd only fed them once and hadn't even known about the pond a few months ago. But he'd come to think of this secluded spot in the garden as a magical place. A place where all of his half-formed dreams of the future could be made real. A place where the yearnings he didn't understand—and couldn't even name—would blossom.

A place where he could become himself, whoever he was to be.

But those doors had all closed. The university, his job here with these mysterious men, his dreams of a cigar export business. He took a deep breath, gathered his rake and bag, and stepped back onto the path leading to the house.

"Don't you dare leave now," Mannix called as he rounded the narrow path and stepped into view. "I just got here, and I brought the food." He shook the metal tin to prove his point.

Ernesto's heart skipped a beat, as it always seemed to when he was in the man's presence. Mannix wore perfectly tailored cotton slacks and a gaudy short-sleeved shirt with pictures of brightly colored seashells scattered across it. His hair was mussed, sticking out at angles, as if he'd just woken up.

For a moment, that thought triggered a vivid picture in Ernesto's imagination: Mannix stretched out on a white bed, one arm hanging languidly over the side, a silk sheet partially draped across his naked form, his lips softly open in sleep, his eyelids fluttering with a dream only he knew.

Dumbstruck, Ernesto stood motionless. He was so caught up in the vision it took him a moment to realize Mannix had reached him, and based on the expectant look on his face, had asked him a question.

Ernesto came back to himself and blinked in confusion.

Mannix frowned. "Oh dear. We're back to this again." He shifted the tin of food to his left hand. "Well, I did say we'd practice until we got it right." He held out his right hand. "Hello, I'm Hank Mannix, and you are…?"

Ernesto smiled and grasped Mannix's hand. "Ernesto Ruiz. It's a pleasure to meet you, Mr. Mannix."

"Oh, look at that. You even did the hand thing without prompting this time. That's progress." Mannix released his grip, and Ernesto felt the man's fingertips trail across his palm as he did so. He wondered if that was an American thing.

No, the yearning, dreaming part of him answered. *It's a Mannix thing. And you* like *it.*

"Now, you did forget the part where you call me Hank, not Mr. Mannix."

"Hank," Ernesto said.

Mannix laughed, an appealing, musical sound Ernesto wanted to hear again.

"Oh no. You make me sound like a goose, or a taxi cab. Try again."

Ernesto blushed. It was a difficult sound for him to make.

"Hank," he said again, making a special effort to get the harsh, raspy sound of the vowel correct.

"Better," said Mannix. "And I didn't mean to embarrass you. I like your accent. It makes me think of warm summer nights and sultry music."

Mannix's accent made Ernesto think of televisions and subway cars and elevators. He didn't say any of that.

"You didn't embarrass me. I know I need to work on pronunciation."

"No. No. You're fine. You can call me Honk if you'd like to. I like it." Mannix smiled and held out the tin. "Shall we feed our little friends?"

Ernesto nodded, and Mannix pointed toward the bench. They sat, and this time Mannix left some space, although it was still a tight fit for two men. The fish had figured it out, and they splashed noisily at the pond's edge in front of the bench. Mannix offered the open tin to Ernesto, who pinched out a few pellets and sprinkled them into the maelstrom.

"I was afraid you wouldn't come back," Mannix said. "After the coup, I mean."

I might not come back. This could be the last time I feed the fish. Or see you. Ernesto was suddenly overcome by the emotion of it all—the university rejection, Ivan, the unnerving episode with the police at the factory, his entire future slipping away—and he choked back an unexpected sob.

Mannix put the tin on the ground. "Sorry." He turned to face Ernesto directly. "I seem to be saying all the wrong things today. I just meant, you know, I've never seen a picture of this Batista fellow, so I worried maybe he was you, and you'd taken over the government, and I'd never see you again."

That startled a laugh from Ernesto, which unfortunately prompted a case of the hiccups.

"Oh dear," Mannix said.

And because the tears hadn't been far behind to begin with, the hiccups turned into a sob, and before he could stop, Ernesto was out and out crying—a humiliating, teary thing alternating between hiccups and gasps for breath.

Mannix reached his arm around Ernesto's shoulder and pulled him into a hug. "It's all right. It'll be fine." He guided Ernesto's head to his chest. "Take your time. Just breathe."

Ernesto tried to concentrate on getting his breathing under control, but he became increasingly distracted by Mannix's hand combing through his hair. His left eye was scrunched closed against Mannix's chest, but through his right eye he could see the watery outline of a pink conch shell, and he worried he was getting tears—or worse—on the beautiful shirt.

"There, there," Mannix whispered as Ernesto's breathing calmed.

He raised a hand to his face and wiped at his nose. He was about to lift his head, but Mannix was stroking his hair and making soft noises, and he could hear the man's heartbeat, right against his ear, and it was all so...perfect. He let his hand settle flat against Mannix's chest, enjoying the slick feel of silk above the hard muscle.

He was tempted to let his fingers explore further.

As if echoing Ernesto's own thoughts, Mannix said, "I could just sit here like this all day."

Yes. Let's.

"But then, I wouldn't trust myself not to do something you might find objectionable."

Ernesto couldn't imagine objecting to anything Mannix might want to do.

"Besides," Mannix continued. "Tony's right. I

shouldn't be so...singularly focused...all the time." He shifted his weight, and Ernesto's head slid down his chest a few inches. He was horrified to feel the cold dampness he'd left on Mannix's shirt where his cheek came to rest. "And you're emotionally distraught, so I should be focused on comforting you, not...the other thing."

Ernesto didn't know who Tony was, but if "the other thing" meant they could stay here, just as they were, with Mannix stroking his hair and Ernesto's hand—which had slid to Mannix's belly—rising and falling with the man's calm, reassuring breaths, he was all for it.

The fish were becoming impatient. One leapt out of the water and fell back with a great splash, sending droplets of water everywhere. Mannix trailed his fingers from Ernesto's hair to his nose, where he wiped away a drop of pond water. He allowed his finger to trace the edge of Ernesto's lip before he pulled away.

"So," Mannix said, as he gently lifted Ernesto's head from his chest and helped the young man upright. They both pretended not to notice the mess Ernesto had made of the shirt. "Tell Honk all about it."

*

HE DIDN'T TELL Mannix everything, but he did explain he'd be going away for a couple of days, maybe even three, in order to tell Ivan's family his cousin had disappeared. He told Mannix he knew it was unreasonable to expect his job would still be there when he returned.

"Oh, I think two or three days might be manageable," Mannix said. But he looked upset. "I wouldn't want to go without you longer than that though." And for just an instant, Ernesto allowed himself to think Mannix might be speaking of more than the gardening work. "But why do you need to be gone for so long? Couldn't you make a day trip out of it?"

"No. The farm is outside of San Cristóbal, almost fifty miles away. And the bus makes many stops along the coast. It takes most of the day just to get there."

"Hmm," Mannix said, drumming his fingers against his thigh.

As much as Ernesto didn't want to risk his prospects at Casa de Ada, he decided he owed the man the truth, or at least more of the truth. "Listen," he said, "there's something else. I...I might not be able to keep working here."

"What! Why?" The fish were in a frenzy, having not received any food since Ernesto began explaining his situation. The churning waters sprayed a continuing rain of droplets onto the bench. "Oh, for God's sake," Mannix exclaimed. He stood, put his hand out toward Ernesto, and said, "Stay," as if he were commanding a pet dog. He walked to the edge of the pond and dumped the contents of the tin into it.

The fish rioted in a maelstrom of water.

Mannix returned to the bench, sat—closer this time, pressed against Ernesto—and grasped his hand. "That's better. Now, tell me why you could possibly want to leave us."

Chapter Eight

"NO," SAID HANS. "Absolutely not."

They were sitting in Casa de Ada's parlor. It had been a long day and had been raining steadily since late afternoon. Rumbles of thunder echoed through the evening, and the air was thick and damp inside the house. Most of the guests had gone off to the casinos or nightclubs, but the sitting room was crowded nonetheless.

Cordero had finally given in to the obvious and was staying out of public view until the swelling and bruises diminished. He was sitting in the corner chair, watching the back and forth between Mannix and Hans as one would a tennis match.

Matt was at the small card table, reviewing plans for the next day's shoot with the *Pumped* photographers, and that didn't help Mannix's mood one bit. And because Matt was there, the men from Allentown were there too, sharing the love seat and offering whispered commentary to each other.

"It's out of the question," Hans repeated. "I really must put my foot down." He uncrossed his legs and stomped his foot on the floor to drive the point home, but the effect was muted by the fact he was drinking tea from a delicate china cup while sitting in a Queen Anne armchair.

Plus, he was wearing a pair of pink lady's bedroom slippers with faux fur trim around the ankles, so his foot didn't stomp so much as it only softly slid atop the rug.

Mannix was beginning to fear he wouldn't be able to talk Hans around, which was a problem because he'd already told Ernesto he could do it. "It's less than fifty miles," he said again. "We'd be there and back while it's still daylight."

"No, Hank, and that's final." Hans was reaching his limit; Mannix had a good sense of such things. Cordero knew it too, and he shot Mannix a warning look. "The house car is for transporting guests only." Hans smoothed the front of his shirt and picked up a magazine, signaling an end to the discussion.

Mannix was still trying to determine if there was any possibility of a way forward when one of the *Pumped* men said, "Oh, yes, that's a good idea. Let's try it." He motioned to Matt, who stood and removed his shirt.

The room was transfixed.

"Like this?" Matt asked as he raised his arms high above his head and assumed the pose he would take as if he were about to dive into a pool.

The men from Allentown clasped each other's hands.

Even Mannix had to admit it was a spectacular sight,

and he reminded himself not to hold Golden Boy's beauty against him.

"Yes, that's amazing," one of the photographers said. He turned to his colleague. "I see now what you mean by how his pecs look lifted up like that."

"And the V shape of the torso. It's perfect," said the other. "Twist to your right, Matt."

He did, and the men from Allentown whispered excitedly to each other.

"Try it with Hans's slippers," suggested Cordero. Honestly the man was getting more jaded by the day. Mannix made a mental note to follow up with him about what he'd meant earlier when he said it might be time. Time to what?

The *Pumped* men talked Matt through a few additional poses, then he put his shirt back on while the photographers finished writing their notes. Mannix was gratified to see Matt missed a button, so that his shirttail hung lower on one side. It humanized him somehow.

"Driving into the countryside," Cordero said, pulling the conversation back to life. He shook his head and pointed at Mannix. "What I want to know is why? Why do you want to go out of your way to help this boy? I mean, sure, he's nice to look at..."

Evidently everyone else wanted to know the answer to that question too. The room quieted, and all eyes turned to Mannix.

"Is every young's man value determined exclusively by his beauty, Tony?" Mannix didn't look at Golden Boy when he asked the question. One of Hans's carefully plucked eyebrows rose. The men from Allentown tilted their heads in confusion.

"Well, it's what allowed you to get your start," Cordero responded.

"True," Mannix acknowledged. "And please don't talk about my beauty in the past tense. I'm still quite spectacular. You've seen me naked, so you know."

One of the men from Allentown spoke up. "Actually, we haven't *all* seen you naked. Not yet; perhaps if you—"

"I'm not finished," Mannix interrupted. "My point is, beyond physical appeal, every young man has other attributes—like drive and intelligence and a desire to improve his position in life."

"And the cute one has these 'attributes'?" Cordero asked. "That's what makes you want to help him?" He pointed to his own head. "You can't see it because of the bruising, but this is my skeptical face."

"Yes, he does," Mannix insisted. "I admit, it helps that he's very attractive." Across the room, Matt frowned. "But I spoke with him for a long time this morning, and he's very...intense. He wants more from life than to work in his father's factory."

"Oh," Hans said. "I didn't realize he was a factory worker. What kind of factory does his father own?"

"I don't know," Mannix admitted. "We didn't talk about that. A steel factory maybe?"

The men from Allentown giggled.

"What's so funny?" Mannix asked.

"Nothing, dear," Hans said. "It's refreshing to see you being so...altruistic."

Cordero was slowly nodding his head. "I think I get it," he said. "Here I've been thinking our young Mr.

Lansing was the new Mannix—" The "old" Mannix began to offer an objection but Cordero held up his hand. "But really," he continued, "it's the cute one who's the new Mannix—young and scrappy, handsome, too, sure, but off to a tough start in life and trying to pull himself up by his bootstraps."

Mannix was taken aback. *Was* that what this was about? Did he see his younger self in Ernesto and want to help guide him along? Maybe.

But he couldn't just shut the old Mannix off, no matter how much he might decide to turn over a new leaf—to be less obsessive about sex. There was simply no denying Ernesto triggered a lot more in him than simple respect. He *wanted* the young man.

"His name is Ernesto," Mannix told Cordero. "And there *is* no new Mannix."

"Hoo boy," exclaimed Cordero. "You've got it bad. I've never seen you fall for a fellow before."

Everyone waited for Mannix to reject the assertion, but he found he couldn't. As uncomfortable as it was, as *new* as it was, he had a thing for Ernesto, and it was consuming him.

Hans softened. "Hank, I'm glad to see you...interested...in someone other than yourself—"

"For a change," muttered Cordero.

"But there are rules for the house car, and, technically, it's Arthur's, and I promised him I wouldn't allow it to be abused."

Mannix sensed an opening and was formulating his best plan of attack when Matt spoke up.

"Oh, would you look at this," he said while fingering

the buttons down the front of his shirt. "I've got it all wrong." He began undoing the buttons as he moved across the room toward Hans. He removed the shirt and made a show of inspecting one of the collars. "Oh no." He held the shirt to Hans. "Do you think this stain will come out?"

He'd moved very close to Hans, and Mannix saw Hans try not to stare at the naked torso in front of him. His hands trembled slightly as he reached to grasp the collar. "I don't see a stain," he said after a moment.

"No?" asked Matt. "It's right here." Their fingers brushed as Matt tried to find the stain. Mannix noticed Hans suppress a shiver.

My God, the kid is good. But what is he up to?

"Huh," Matt said. "It must have been the light. He withdrew the shirt from Hans's hands, very slowly, almost as if he was reluctant to move away from the man. He didn't put it back on but remained standing next to Hans, half naked.

"You know," he said, resting a hand on the arm of Hans's chair and leaning in slightly to look Hans in the eye. "Eduardo told me about a cathedral in San Cristóbal. He said I should see it before I go home. Perhaps Mannix could take me?"

Hans's mouth moved but no sound came out.

"I'm sure Ernesto would be welcome to come along too," Matt said to Mannix as if it had been decided.

And, of course, it had been.

*

VERY EARLY THE following morning, Ernesto arrived at Casa de Ada, prepared for a road trip. Mannix had wanted to pick him up at his home, just to get to know him better—to fill in the missing contours of what he understood of the young man's life.

Ernesto had refused. He said he didn't want his parents to know a white American was driving him to his uncle's farm; there would be too many questions. It would be better, he'd insisted, for him to simply arrive home late in the day and explain what happened, after it was all over.

Since Mannix didn't know how he'd answer the questions Ernesto's parents were sure to pose, he reluctantly agreed they should meet at Casa de Ada.

But then there was the question of Matt.

He didn't want Golden Boy elbowing his way into his day with Ernesto, even though he owed him one for moving Hans off his position against the trip. And Mannix had been turning the question over all night—*why* had Matt gotten involved? Why do such a good turn for him when Mannix had been nothing but irritating since they'd met?

Ernesto and Mannix were in the kitchen finishing a breakfast of coffee and yesterday's bread with cheese and sliced meat. Ernesto had brought an overnight pack, which he'd no longer need, and two bags filled with items he said were gifts for his aunt from his mother.

There was an awkwardness between them. Their planned expedition seemed so unlikely now that a day had passed since Mannix first wildly conceived of the idea.

"If you'd rather not—" Ernesto began for the second time.

"Stop. We're doing this. Relax." Mannix swallowed the rest of his coffee. "It'll be fun."

He looked at the wall clock. Golden Boy had two minutes to show, or they were leaving without him.

At precisely 6:30 a.m., Matt strolled in, not exactly dressed for a day in the country. He wore cotton slacks and good shoes and a deliciously tight teal-colored shirt that accentuated his eyes.

Mannix was once again grudgingly impressed by the young man's ability to present himself in the best light. Matt smiled when he saw Ernesto—the kind of smile that would disarm the harshest critics and light a room like summer sunshine. He held out his hand and walked to Ernesto. The corded muscles of his forearm flexed.

"You must be Ernesto," he said. "I'm Matt Lansing."

"Oh," Ernesto said. He turned to Mannix. "I didn't know... You didn't say..."

Mannix sighed and looked between the men. The two very young men. They were striking together. Each was beautiful in his own way, but next to each other, they were astounding, a study in sexual contrast. Mannix didn't like the way Ernesto was staring.

He turned to Matt. "He's still learning this part," he stage-whispered. Then he turned to Ernesto. "You know, you don't *always* need to do the hand thing. Sometimes you can just wave. I suggest you do that now."

But Ernesto closed the gap and grasped Matt's hand. "Hello, Matt. I'm Ernesto Ruiz. It's a pleasure to meet you." Matt kept hold of Ernesto's hand and gave him a slow inspection. The wattage of his smile increased.

"I see what all the fuss is about," Matt said.

Before Mannix could step in and pull the boys' hands apart, one of the *Pumped* men came stumbling into the kitchen, scratching his belly and yawning. He came to an abrupt stop and stared at Matt and Ernesto. He blinked, then rubbed his eyes.

"Oh my God," he spluttered. "This is incredible. The two of you. Holy smokes!" He looked at Mannix as if to confirm the reality of the vision in front of him. Mannix was beginning to regret the day's arrangement. He wanted to get Ernesto away from Matt as soon as possible.

"Stay right there," commanded the photographer before turning and hurrying out of the room.

Matt tugged Ernesto's hand. "Come on, let's skedaddle before the other one gets here and they try to photograph us naked together. Pops here wouldn't like that one bit."

He's right about that.

Ernesto managed to swallow, and Mannix managed not to kill anyone. As they walked through the garden toward the garage tucked away in the rear of the property, Matt turned to Mannix and said, "I hope you brought a lot of cash."

"I've got gas money and enough for Ernesto and I...and you, I suppose now...to have lunch." Mannix worried that perhaps he'd forgotten something. "Do I need more?"

"Yes," Matt replied. "Did you really think I was going to waste my day touring the countryside with you two?"

He punched Mannix in the bicep. "You're going to drop me at the university. I'm hoping I can find Eduardo, and he can show me around. But just in case he's not available, I'll need taxi money to get back here."

Mannix grinned. The day was looking up.

"And," Matt continued, "if you want to throw a few extra dollars my way for making this work with Hans, I wouldn't say no."

"Gladly," said Mannix. "I'll be right back." He turned and hurried toward the house to collect more cash, smiling. Golden Boy was clever as well as handsome. And manipulative too.

Maybe he's the new me after all.

Chapter Nine

ERNESTO HAD NEVER been in a car before.

He'd ridden in tractors on his uncle's farm and had taken the bus on a number of occasions but had never sat in a private automobile—the kind rich people used to get around all by themselves. The Packard was sleek and far more attractive than the squat, blocky American cars beginning to appear along the malecón.

He was fascinated by all the switches and buttons, the long gear shift knob rising up from the floor, and the thin steering wheel with its delicate spokes stretching out from the center. He wanted to know what each of the round gauges arrayed in a line along the dash were for, but Mannix was already arguing with Matt, and he didn't want to interrupt.

"You can't just wave down a taxi like you do in New York. Look at you; you'll stick out like a sore thumb. You could be kidnapped and murdered, and then Hans will never let me borrow the car again."

"Thanks for your concern. That's very compassion-ate." Matt leaned impatiently over the seat back and pointed to the dashboard. "Can we get going now before those photographers come and drag us out of the car?"

"First you have to promise me if you don't find Eduardo, you'll have someone from the university get a taxi for you."

"Okay, Pops. Whatever you say."

Ernesto didn't believe Matt, but the back and forth between the two men was layered with context he didn't understand, so he couldn't be sure. He didn't know what to make of the young man from New York. He'd never met anyone like him; Matt was impossibly sculpted, as if he'd been intentionally designed by a marketing company for use in magazines or movies. Ernesto couldn't quite put his finger on it. He knew lots of muscled guys who worked hard in the fields, or labored in Havana's facto-ries, but none of them looked like Matt.

And even the white twin—Hank, he reminded him-self, call him Hank—wasn't quite so, well, *white*. Maybe it was the straw-colored hair, or the icy blue eyes, or the milkiness of his skin, but Matt looked unfinished some-how, like a well-shaped loaf of bread that hadn't yet been baked.

Mannix started the car and pulled onto the street, turning left toward the Rio Almendares. He glanced over at Ernesto. "I drove to the university a couple of days ago, but we took a very roundabout route. What's the best way to get there?"

Ernesto had no idea. He knew how to walk to the

university from Casa de Ada, and he knew the bus route to his neighborhood near the train station, but he'd never taken a bus that went past the university. He quickly ran through his walking route in his head and didn't immediately identify any reasons why they couldn't do the same in a car.

"Turn right after the bridge," he said.

They made their way along the northern edge of the city and had only gone a few blocks when Ernesto realized how little he paid attention to traffic patterns when he walked. The right-hand turn they needed to take turned out to be a one-way street—the wrong way—and when they took the next right to circle back, that street curved away to the left in the opposite direction from their destination.

"Try that one," Ernesto suggested, pointing off to the left.

"Uh, the sharp left or the angled one?" asked Mannix.

"The angled one?" replied Ernesto. But it was more of a question than guidance, and once they made the turn and navigated around the bicycles and box trucks, they had once again gotten turned about.

"Um," said Ernesto as he scanned the street ahead for any clues as to what they should do next.

"Manhattan is mostly a neat grid," Matt offered unhelpfully. Then he reached forward and put his hand on Ernesto's shoulder. "You don't drive, do you?"

"No," replied Ernesto, struck by how little any of them knew about each other.

"Neither do I," said Matt. "There's no need in New York."

"Well, I do," Mannix said. "And I need to know which way to turn here." He was stopped—mostly blocking the intersection—and a horn blared behind him.

"Look!" said Matt, leaning forward and pointing to a road sign on the corner. "Does that word mean university?" he asked.

"Sí," Ernesto replied, his anxiety pushing him into Spanish.

Mannix took the sharp left the sign indicated. After just a few blocks, Ernesto recognized the buildings of the campus. "There," he said, pointing ahead to the entrance gate. He recalled too late that the other men had been to the university already; they'd recognize the campus as easily as Ernesto did.

"Uh...thanks," offered Matt from the back seat.

They found a spot by the gate to pull over to the curb. Mannix turned to Matt and said, "Don't forget what I told you about getting a taxi. I'm serious."

"You got it, Pops." Matt opened his door and stepped out.

"Matt," Mannix called to him, and the young man stuck his head back into the car. "Thank you," Mannix said.

Matt smiled, nodded at Ernesto, and closed the door behind him.

*

MANNIX DIDN'T PULL back into traffic. "So...I guess I shouldn't have assumed, but, well, do you know how to get to your uncle's farm?"

Ernesto's face heated and dampness bloomed under his arms. He *did* know how to get to his uncle's farm. At least, he knew the route the bus took, and could probably manage to avoid getting lost if they took the more direct inland road rather than following the bus's winding path along the coast.

That was his plan, anyway. But he'd have to start from the bus terminal, and he didn't know where that was. He'd never driven before and had no idea how to get anywhere from the university.

He turned to Mannix. "Yes." He looked away. "But..."

Mannix reached across the seat and tapped Ernesto lightly on the shoulder. "Hey, look at me. Don't be embarrassed. What's the 'but'?"

"I don't know how to get out of the city," Ernesto admitted. "We need to be on the north road, heading out of Havana to the west along the coast. But I don't know how to get us there." Ernesto waited for Mannix's disappointment. Maybe he'd even change his mind about the trip.

"Oh, that part's easy." Mannix grinned. "It's the secret to driving. You just go along in what you hope is the right direction until you figure out where you are."

Ernesto thought that was probably true of many things. Maybe it was true of everything.

"So, north it is, then," Mannix declared, starting the car and putting it in gear. "We'll just head back toward Casa de Ada, and as soon as we see water we'll turn left, and then we'll keep going until all the crowds are behind us."

Could it really be that easy?

Mannix pulled into traffic and started driving along

the tall stone wall in front of the university. When they reached an intersection, Mannix stretched his neck over the wheel and peered around the corner. "North is that way, right?"

"I guess so," Ernesto responded, looking down the street in the opposite direction, as if a large compass might reveal itself. "Sure."

*

IT TOOK OVER an hour to get out of the city proper. Eventually, they found themselves on a rural stretch of road, but there were still plenty of trucks, pedestrians, and occasionally livestock to slow them down. The graveled road soon turned to dirt, and Ernesto was surprised he hadn't noted what bad shape it was in the last time he took the bus.

But that had been months ago, when he'd gone to the farm to collect Ivan and bring him back to Havana. And the bus always bounced and jolted. Even the ones in the city did that.

Ernesto stared at Mannix's hands, gripping the steering wheel so tightly his knuckles had turned white. He regretted being the cause of all this...distress. He wondered once again *why* Mannix was doing this.

His curiosity about Mannix's motivations warred with his desire not to tempt fate. He was enjoying being with the man, and couldn't have imagined, even a week ago, that the American he knew only as a white twin would show an interest in him. That he'd actually be alone with him, in a car, for hours.

He wondered again about their first encounter in the garden, and how things might have gone differently if he hadn't stupidly asked for money.

"I'm sorry if I offended you," Ernesto said.

Mannix cocked his head but didn't respond immediately. He drove carefully around a wide, shallow depression in the dirt, then paused while two tethered goats led by a very old woman crossed in front of them.

Once he'd straightened out the car and was moving forward again, he glanced at Ernesto. "Is this going to be a thing with us? You'll have complicated little dialogues in your head, and then include me in the middle, when I don't know what's going on?"

Ernesto looked down at his lap. "Sorry."

Mannix smiled. "And then you'll apologize, even though you didn't do anything wrong." He reached over and tapped his fingers against Ernesto's thigh, then let his hand come to rest there just for a brief moment, before withdrawing, leaving a ghost of a presence, tingling and empty. "This will be fun."

Ernesto tried to puzzle through what 'a thing with us' could mean, but he failed to make sense of the comment.

"Why are you doing this?" he asked instead.

Mannix sighed. "Haven't we been over this already?"

No, they hadn't.

He gave Ernesto a few moments to reply, but when he remained silent, Mannix added, "Because I like you. I want to help."

Ernesto tried to wrap his head around that. Hank was everything Ernesto wasn't: bold, self-confident, sexual... modern. *Free.*

"But you don't even know me," Ernesto objected.

Mannix shook his head. "That's not true. I know a lot about you. I know you're a hard worker who's always on the job early. I know you're always neat and clean even though you do gardening work. I know you care about your cousin."

"That's hardly a lot."

Mannix glanced at Ernesto and both men jolted when the car ran over a bump Mannix hadn't seen.

"Okay, how about this then? I know my eyes are always drawn to you when I see you in the gardens. I know I like how relaxed you look when you don't think anyone is watching you. I know you like to look at me too. Don't you?"

He did. He always had an eye out for Hank, and when the man was posing for the cameras, Ernesto could barely breathe.

"Don't you?" Mannix prompted.

Ernesto nodded, not trusting himself to speak.

"Listen, Ernie—can I call you Ernie?"

No! "Um..."

"The thing is," Mannix continued, without waiting for an answer, "ever since that time in the garden—the first time, not the time when you ruined my shirt..." Ernesto flinched at the reminder.

"Well," Mannix continued, "I keep thinking about you. About what might have happened if we hadn't messed that up so badly. If we'd come at things properly."

Me too.

"But that was real, wasn't it? I mean, we both felt a connection, right? An attraction, at least?"

Ernesto nodded again.

"Good." Mannix reached over and squeezed his knee. Ernesto wished they were back at the fish pond, where Mannix didn't need to use both his hands to drive a car. "So, let's get to know each other. Like we're starting from scratch. Um...what do you like to do? Do you have any hobbies?"

Hobbies? Ernesto couldn't think of any. He worked two jobs, and when he wasn't working, he was studying to get into university—though that wasn't going to happen now—and when he wasn't working or studying, he was helping out around the house or the factory or looking out for Ivan or trying to convince Marta everything would be fine.

No, he didn't have any hobbies. He thought again about his job. He was a lector. It wasn't a *hobby*, exactly, but...

"I like to read," he offered.

"Oh, there's a start. What do you like to read?"

Ernesto read a little bit of everything, but mostly it was up to the torcederos. That was the tradition. He'd read the news to them first thing each day, but then they got to decide what he'd read for entertainment. It was surprisingly varied. He was currently working his way through *The Count of Monte Christo*, but when he wasn't reading fiction, the workers would usually ask for political essays, which often leaned toward Marxist theory and sometimes made him uncomfortable.

Most recently, they couldn't seem to get enough of the writings from a young lawyer running for congress, or, he *was* running before Batista took over and postponed the elections. He was one of those politicians always railing against corruption and capitalism. The torcederos loved him. Ernesto had a number of his essays, but he tried not to read more than one a week to the workers, and never when his father could hear.

"Right now, I'm making my way through some political essays by a lawyer named Fidel Castro. He's running for office—if they still have the elections, that is. He's a bit of a radical."

Mannix blinked. "Oh. I thought maybe you'd say '*the Hardy Boys*' or something. Do they have them here?"

"Who?"

"*The Hardy Boys*? Young sleuths, finding dead bodies, solving crimes, that sort of thing?"

"I don't know what you're talking about," Ernesto said.

Mannix sighed. "I think that's going to be a thing with us too."

*

FOR THE NEXT hour, they tried to learn more about each other as much to pass the time, Ernesto thought, as to build something between them. It was more challenging than it should have been.

"Do you like to read?" Ernesto asked after the strange exchange involving the boy detectives and Castro. Hank had a puzzled look on his face, as if he wasn't sure about the answer, which made no sense. He either liked to read or he didn't.

"Actually, now that you mention it, no. I can't remember the last time I read anything for pleasure."

That was a surprise. Ernesto thought all Americans must read. They seemed so...worldly. "Well then, what are *your* hobbies?" Ernesto asked. Mannix drummed his fingers against the steering wheel. Twice it appeared as if he'd answer, but then he changed his mind.

"I suppose starting with hobbies wasn't a very good idea," he finally replied. "I know. Tell me about your family. You have a sister, right?"

He normally liked talking about his family, but his failure to get into university had been weighing on him. He knew he'd become a disappointment to them. "Yes, Marta. She's a little older than me, and she's still not married. It was going to be my responsibility to make sure she met the right people—after I got into college."

Mannix's grip tightened on the wheel. "Oh, well, that's..."

"I know. I let her down. I let the whole family down. I couldn't even protect Ivan." Ernesto sighed and looked out the window.

"That's not what I was going to say. I just think that's...a lot...to put on you, all that responsibility."

"I'm the only son," Ernesto replied. No one was putting anything on him. Ernesto shook his head. Everyone had responsibilities. That's how it worked. And when you failed to meet them, or ignored them, you ended up like Ivan. Did Hank not see that?

"And you're so young," Mannix added. "How old are you, anyway?" He asked the question in a casual way, almost as if it was an afterthought, but Ernesto was beginning to get a better sense of Hank, and the way he kept his face expressionless while he waited for the response told Ernesto the answer was important.

"I'm twenty," he replied.

Mannix's features softened, and he smiled. "That's a relief!"

"Why? How old are you?"

"I'm twenty...five," Mannix replied, not taking his eyes off the road ahead of him.

Ernesto had no reason to doubt it; who could know how old these white Americans were? But for some reason, he thought Mannix had just picked that number. And that it wasn't true. It was a mystery he put to one side.

"Tell me about your family," Ernesto said instead.

Mannix frowned. "I don't really have one," he replied.

That was an incomprehensible statement. Everyone had a family. Ernesto turned back to the window, and both men let the landscape pass by in silence for a few minutes. Soon, they came to a church with a statue of Our Lady of El Cobre towering in front of it. It was painted in various shades of gold, red, and blue. Ernesto had never seen anything like it.

Oh no.

"I think we missed our turn."

Chapter Ten

THEY WERE ALMOST out of gas.

Mannix had been keeping his eyes open, but they hadn't passed a service station since they'd left the city. And now they'd missed a turn and needed to backtrack. He pulled into the dusty parking lot of what he guessed was a church, given the larger-than-life statue out front. It was of an imposing woman in voluminous robes holding a scepter. He imagined she was a saint of some sort.

"We need to find a gas station before we go too much farther." He said it calmly—if anything downplaying the immediacy of the situation, but as he suspected would happen, Ernesto looked panicked. The fellow was wound tighter than a clock.

"I don't know where any stations are," he said.

"It's all right, Ernie. We'll just ask someone." Mannix waited to see if Ernesto would object. He didn't. "How about him?" he asked, pointing to the priest making his way from the church to the car.

"All right," Ernesto responded. He opened his door and stepped out. Mannix began to open his door, but Ernesto said, "You stay here."

Bossy. He liked that. Mannix settled back into his seat and rolled down the window so he could hear the conversation.

Ernesto and the priest spoke for a few minutes—longer than it would take for the man to simply direct them to the nearest service station. Mannix couldn't understand a word of it, and his mind drifted to all the mistakes he'd made already on this drive.

His ill-conceived "getting to know you" questions only served to highlight what different worlds they lived in. And *hobbies*? What had he been thinking? And what was wrong with him, anyway? Why couldn't he think of a single hobby?

He'd almost said posing for beefcake magazines or drinking with Tony, but those weren't really hobbies. The nearest he could come to an actual hobby was turning tricks in the gardens, but that would have been a poor choice to share on a first date—and wasn't this trip a date? Maybe? Mannix didn't know—he'd never been on a date before.

So instead, he'd remained silent, looking dull and uninteresting.

He was a mess.

Ernesto and the priest walked over to the driver's door. "He wants to sit in the car," Ernesto said. "And he asked me a lot of questions about you. I think he wanted to make sure you weren't kidnapping me."

Mannix swallowed his pride. They *were* an odd sight, the two of them driving through the country in a city car. "Okay, tell him to hop in."

"Um...he wants to sit behind the wheel."

Hans would never forgive him. "Does he know where we can get gas?"

"Yes. He says we can find fuel at the bus station in Cayajabos. And we're not on the wrong road. This is the inland drive to San Cristóbal, which is what we wanted. I've just never been here before and didn't recognize the church."

That was good news, so Mannix stepped out of the car and waved a hand to allow the priest to take a seat. The fellow gripped the wheel and touched all the knobs and toggles. He ran his hands up and down the gear shift while he made *vroom-vroom* sounds and leaned side to side through imaginary turns.

He looked like an older version of Ivan, which was disturbing. Mannix hoped he'd be able to wipe down the steering wheel with a cleaning cloth at the service station. The priest looked at Mannix, who was standing just outside the open driver's door. "Movie star," he said carefully in English.

"Sure, Pops," Mannix responded, borrowing a phrase from Matt and knowing the priest couldn't understand him. "Maybe with the right agent, and better clothes, you could make a go of it."

"Not him," Ernesto said from the other side of the car. "You. I told him you were a movie star shooting a film in Cuba. He's a priest; I couldn't lie to him."

Mannix grinned. A movie star! *I can work with that.*

*

THEY WERE SPLUTTERING along on fumes by the time they made it to the bus station, which turned out only to have diesel, which did them no good at all. A worker at the station directed them to a farm supply store a mile or two farther down the road, but they only made it about a half mile before the Packard went silent, and Mannix glided it to a stop along the edge of a field.

"Well," Mannix said, "this is a pickle."

Next to him, Ernesto twisted his hands in his lap. "I'll go," he said. "I'll get a can of gasoline and bring it back."

"Nonsense," replied Mannix. "We're not splitting up. What if someone comes by and I need to communicate with them? We'll both go; it'll be nice to stretch our legs." Mannix glanced at his watch, and tried to hide the worried look that came over his face. They'd been in the car for hours, and they still hadn't made it to the farm. If they didn't get there soon, it would be getting dark by the time they made it back to Havana.

Hans would be furious, especially if Matt returned first and spilled the beans.

"I'm sorry," Ernesto said.

Mannix groaned. "Listen, Ernie. None of this is your fault."

Ernesto grimaced.

"Well, the part that makes me want to kiss you all the time is probably your fault somehow, but you have to stop apologizing. Understood?"

"You...you want..." An open-air truck with a dozen farm workers in the back chugged by dangerously close to the Packard, stirring up a cloud of dust as it went.

"But we can't sit here making out in the car, or we'll never get back." Mannix carefully observed Ernesto's response to his reference to kissing. He couldn't be sure, because Ernesto always looked worried and anxious, but he thought the interest in kissing just might be a mutual one. At Ernesto's nod, Mannix said, "Good. Let's get going. The sooner we're back, the sooner we'll be on our way."

It felt more like three miles rather than one, but neither of them wanted to hop into the back of the handful of trucks that offered them a lift. The situation was uncomfortable enough as it was without having to squeeze between sacks of fertilizer, crops and, in one instance, loose chickens.

Their luck improved at the farm store, where they were able to get a gallon of gas in a metal canister—sufficient fuel for the car to make it back to the gas pump where they could fuel up properly and buy extra gasoline to take with them for the ride back.

When they reached the car, a small crowd had gathered around it, and several young men were leaning against the hood or running their hands down the glass windows. They seemed particularly fascinated by the hood ornament.

A distant part of Mannix's brain noted how the car's blue paint highlighted fingerprints and smudges. Maybe if he avoided Hans for the next month or two it would all blow over. He dispersed the crowd and filled the gas tank.

Shortly after they were back on the road, Mannix's stomach let out a loud rumble. "It's way past lunch time," he said.

"I know. I'm hungry too," Ernesto agreed. "Do you want to stop along the way? I could find us something you'd like. Probably."

Mannix shook his head. "No offense, Ernie, but I'm not sure my system could handle local roadside fare."

Ernesto let out a sigh. "So, um, I wasn't going to say anything, but about the nick—"

The car juddered violently over a large rut hidden by a pool of water. There was a loud popping sound and a grinding noise. Once again, Mannix brought the car to the side of the road.

"What was that?" Ernesto asked.

"Nothing good. Let's find out." Mannix opened the door and swung out of the car, Ernesto close behind him. At the back of the car, on the passenger side, they found a flattened tire.

"I'm sorry," said Ernesto.

Mannix walked behind the car and opened the trunk. "You said 'I'm sorry' again."

"Oh. Sor—" He stopped himself.

There was a spare tire in the trunk standing up in its cubby leaning against the side of the wheel well. "So, here's the thing, Ernie. I'm about to change a tire—something I've never done before in my entire life. And you're going to help me. I assume you've never changed a tire either?"

Ernesto nodded.

"Right. And I will *not* have you saying 'I'm sorry' each time I drop a doohickey or hit my thumb." Mannix began rocking the tire out of its slot.

"Okay. S—I'll try."

Mannix freed the tire and rolled it to the edge of the trunk, then lifted it with a groan and let it drop to the ground, where it bounced once but remained upright. "Damn, that's heavy." He poked around in the trunk until he found the jack. "So, here's what we're going to do—to get me through this ordeal."

"Hold this, please." He handed the jack to Ernesto and went around to the passenger door to—hopefully—find the Packard's user manual in the glove box. He let out a relieved breath when he saw it. "Every time you say 'I'm sorry,' I'm going to count it as a kiss you owe me."

"Um, what?" Ernesto blinked and tightened his grip on the jack.

"You heard me. I know we haven't kissed yet, but I hope to at some point, and I'm hoping you wouldn't mind if we did." Mannix was pleased by how furiously Ernesto was blushing. "So, if we ever do become the kind of fellows who find themselves kissing each other, I'm going to build up a little bank of kisses I can claim whenever I want. Does that sound fair?"

He handed the user manual to Ernesto. He waited a long time while he traced the emotions racing across Ernesto's face. Just as he was beginning to think he'd overstepped, Ernesto nodded and said, "Yes."

"Good," Mannix said. "This is all your fault, you know."

"I know; I'm sorry, I—"

He was interrupted by Mannix's laughter. "Oh, this is going to be so easy."

Ernesto smiled. "Not fair," he said.

"Sure it is. Listen, Ernie, I'm going to be busy working on the tire, so you're going to have to keep count of the kisses. Go ahead, say it: 'One.'"

Ernesto frowned. "One," he said.

"Good man! Now, find the page describing how to change a tire and start reading it to me.

Ernesto flipped through the paper booklet. "Here it is. Page seventeen. *If a rear wheel is to be changed, and the car is fitted with wheel shields, the shield is removed by reaching up under the shield at the rear, grasping the handle of the tightening lever, and pushing the handle inward to clear the flange and then down and forward. The shield will then drop outward at the top and can be lifted clear of the fender brackets at each end.*"

Ernesto finished reading and looked at Mannix.

"Are you reading in Spanish? None of that makes any sense at all," Mannix complained.

"Sorry."

"Ha! Count."

"Two."

"Very good. Now we're getting somewhere. Let's skip the parts that don't make sense. What's next?"

Ernesto turned back to the booklet. "Um, here we are. Is the hand brake set?"

"Yes, I did that before I got out of the car."

"Okay, um, next it says, *Remove the hubcap using the flattened end of the combination wheel wrench and jack handle as a pry.*"

"Where's the hubcap?" Mannix asked. "Do you think it's behind the big flat disc covering the wheel? Do you think that's the wheel shield?"

"I don't know," Ernesto said.

"Come on, Ernie, you're supposed to be helping here."

"I'm sorry. I—oh, I see what you're doing."

"Clever, aren't I? Count."

"Three."

"Good. Now read the first part again about taking this thing off."

Ernesto read the first part again, and after fifteen minutes of trial and error, the wheel shield popped free. Mannix groaned in relief when the hubcap was exposed. "Tony should be here; he's good at these sorts of things."

"Who's Tony?" Ernesto asked.

"He's the other white twin. That's what you call us, right?"

"Oh. You know about that?"

"Sure do. Tony and I both think it's offensive too."

"Oh no, sorry. We don't mean—" He stopped himself that time. "Four."

Mannix laughed again. "I never knew how much fun changing a tire could be. Now hand me the flattened combination thingy so I can pry this off." Removing the hubcap took even more time than the wheel shield had, but eventually they managed.

"It's getting late, Hank."

"I know. Don't worry. We'll figure it out. What's next?"

Ernesto turned his attention back to the booklet. *"Loosen the wheel mounting nuts not more than a turn or two."*

"Which is it, Ernie, one turn or two?"

"I don't know. It doesn't say. Sorry. Dammit! Five."

Mannix whistled happily as loosened the mounting nuts. "The fun part's next, right? We raise the car using the jack?"

Ernesto read further and nodded his agreement. A half hour later they had the car lifted high enough to remove the wheel, and no one had gotten seriously hurt though Mannix had pinched his finger. "All right," Mannix said. "You take that side and I'll take this side and we'll slowly wiggle it off. Ready?"

"Yes," Ernesto replied.

Both men bent to the task at the same time, and their heads collided. "Ouch," exclaimed Mannix.

"Sorry," said Ernesto; then he rolled his eyes. "Six."

They'd both dropped to their butts and were sitting shoulder to shoulder in front of the raised tire. Mannix rubbed his forehead. "Those kisses are piling up," he observed. "Would it be terribly wrong to collect one now? Just in case the actual tire changing part ends up killing me?"

They were grimy and sweaty and hungry. But after a moment—a long enough moment that Mannix began to worry he'd gone too far, pushed too hard too fast—Ernesto turned to face him, leaned in, and brought their lips together. And, oh, how Mannix wanted to deepen the kiss, to pull Ernesto into his arms, right there on the side of the highway in the dust and gravel. But he allowed the kiss to remain sweet and gentle; then he sat back.

"Oh," said Ernesto. He put two fingers against his lower lip.

"Thank God, there's still five left," whispered

Mannix.

*

THEY MANAGED TO get the tire changed, but not before Ernesto dropped the wheel mounting nuts and had to scramble into the brush to find the last one. That episode alone brought the count up to eight.

It was nearing dusk when they passed the road to the farm.

"Oh," Ernesto said, turning behind him. "That was it. That was our turn. Sorry, I usually come here on the bus from the other direction. I didn't recognize it in time."

Mannix grinned.

"What? Oh. Nine." He sighed, but Mannix noted the smile he tried to hide.

"It's just about a mile down this road." Ernesto sounded nervous. Mannix considered the time and imagined how difficult it would be to navigate these roads in the dark. They'd need to figure out a plan, but first things first.

"I don't want to seem rude to your family, but the very first thing I'll need to do is use their bathroom and then use their phone."

Ernesto looked at him. "It's a farm in the country, Hank. There is no phone."

Hans was absolutely going to kill him.

"And there's no bathroom either, at least not inside. If you need to take a piss just step behind one of the barns. Otherwise, there's a small outhouse, but you'll want to be quick about it."

Mannix wasn't a man given to self-doubt, but for the first time that day he wondered if he'd made the wrong decision. Not about helping Ernesto or trying to develop a relationship with him—the kiss had validated that, and Mannix was excited to imagine where they could go from there—but about this mad idea to drive the Packard to the farm and back in one day.

Even without getting lost and running out of gas and getting a flat tire, he wasn't sure they could have done it.

But the idea of using an *outhouse*! Mannix shuddered.

As they made their way down the road, vast fields of tall, broad-leafed plants spread out on either side. They were about shoulder height, and the leaves were the size of dinner plates.

"That doesn't look like corn," Mannix observed.

Ernesto tilted his head. "Why would it look like corn?"

"I don't know. When I think of a farm, I think of corn. What is it, wheat? No, that's not right either. What's the other one they grow on farms? Oats of some sort?" Mannix slowed as he passed one field where the plant's leaves had been cut off the stalks and grouped into small bundles then draped over long horizontal poles.

He'd never seen anything like it.

"It's tobacco," Ernesto said.

Mannix looked more closely, but he couldn't imagine how any of these broad leaves became cigarettes.

"Your uncle grows cigarettes?" he asked.

Ernesto laughed. It was a beautiful sound, and Mannix wondered why he'd never heard it before. He vowed to hear it again. Often.

"No one *grows* cigarettes, Hank," Ernesto laughed again and tapped Mannix's bicep playfully, as if Mannix had made a joke. He'd be happy to play the fool forever if it meant Ernesto would keep laughing, keep touching him.

"It's tobacco for cigars. And it's very high quality too." There was a note of pride in Ernesto's voice, and Mannix tried to put all the pieces together.

"So, your uncle makes cigars...?" They were approaching a...what? House would be too strong a word. Cabin maybe?

"No. They just grow the tobacco here. This is where it's cured and fermented too. Then it's delivered to our factory in the city. That's where the actual cigars are made."

Mannix had let the car slow to a crawl as he focused on understanding what he was hearing. "Do you mean the factory you work at makes cigars? Not steel or cars or something?" They were almost at the cabin, and people had begun to emerge at the sound of the car.

Ernesto laughed again, but there was a nervous edge to it, like maybe he thought Mannix wasn't entirely joking. Mannix swallowed.

"Well, people make the cigars. They're called torcederos. But come on, there's my aunt and uncle. Come meet them." Two people were walking toward the car. Several children slipped out behind them, and a handful of other adults began appearing from the various barns and sheds nearby.

"*Tía* Clara," Ernesto called as he walked to the

woman, embracing her in a tight hug. When they pulled apart, he shook the man's hand. "*Tío,*" he said.

They began speaking rapidly to each other, with all three of them glancing at Mannix and pointing to the car. It was as if a switch had been flipped in Ernesto. He was animated and fluid; he spoke quickly and at a volume Mannix had never heard before.

In fact, Mannix was certain he'd never heard Ernesto use as many words in the entire time he'd known him than he had since he'd gotten out of the car. For the first time, Mannix realized how difficult it must be for Ernesto to always plan what he would say and be careful about how he pronounced his words.

He stood there simply listening to Ernesto, enjoying the rapid flow of the language and the sensual sounds of the words.

"Hank, come here," Ernesto called. "I'd like you to meet my uncle and aunt, Jorge and Clara Ruiz." Mannix approached, and Ernesto turned to him. "Say *mucho gusto,*" he whispered.

Mannix did, more or less. "Ernie, I'm sorry, but I really have to go use the back of a barn."

Ernesto exchanged a few words with one of the workers who'd wandered out of the nearest barn to see what was happening. The man nodded. "He'll show you," Ernesto told Mannix.

As Mannix followed the man, he thought about the many times he'd wandered off into the gardens with a fellow to find some privacy and marveled at how quickly his life seemed to be changing. He should be worried about that, but Ernesto's melodious voice was soothing, and he dismissed the thought.

Ernesto seemed to be arguing with his aunt and uncle, their voices getting louder as he moved away.

Once Mannix and the other man were behind the barn, the fellow pointed to a large bush with pale pink flowers. He'd been keeping up his own Spanish monologue, and it didn't seem to bother him that Mannix couldn't understand a word of it. In case Mannix hadn't gotten the message, the man stepped up to the bush, unbuttoned his trousers, and began urinating into the foliage.

Mannix had never been one to avoid providing a show, so he did the same, pleased to note the not-so-subtle stare of his companion. In entirely different circumstances, this could have been interesting. But the thought of Ernesto and the kisses he was owed put him off the idea of pursuing anything with this fellow, now or later. And wasn't that a kicker.

There's a first time for everything.

The argument back at the cabin—if that's what it was—intensified, and both men hurried to finish. Coming around the barn he saw several children of various ages had gathered around the Packard. Two had clambered onto the hood and were sliding down the windshield. All were filthy.

He rushed forward to shoo them off. They laughed and scattered, leaving smears of dirt and grime all over the car.

I should kill myself now—deprive Hans of the satisfaction of doing it once he sees the car.

Ernesto was hurrying towards him. "Uh, Hank?"

Ernesto looked nervous and worried, which, admittedly, was his default state, but he seemed even more so as he approached. "We...um...have to spend the night here." Ernesto looked down at his shoes.

"What! Why?" Although, once he thought about it, Mannix knew why. Even if they dropped off the care package, gave them the bad news about Ivan, and left right away, they couldn't possibly make it back to Havana in daylight. There were no lights on the road, and relying solely on the Packard's headlamps to avoid animals, potholes, and wrong turns was beyond foolish.

"I'd never hear the end of it if we refused to stay for dinner," Ernesto explained.

As hungry as Mannix was, the thought of eating food prepared in that cabin made his stomach churn. Maybe there'd be a lot of bread or pretzels or something he could fill up on. He sighed theatrically. "I can't believe this is happening. This is all your fault, you know."

Ernesto cringed. "I know. I'm sorry, I—"

Mannix laughed and slapped Ernesto on the back.

Ernesto groaned. "Twelve," he said.

Mannix squinted his eyes. "I think you're only up to nine."

"I know," Ernesto replied. "I'm throwing in a few extras for your troubles."

*

ONCE THEY WERE inside the cabin, Mannix realized it was even more rustic than he'd expected it would be. An acrid blue smoke hung in the air, and his eyes watered.

He tried not to cough. Why would they have a fire going inside when the weather was so warm?

Things made sense when Ernesto's aunt swung a heavy pot over the open fireplace. The pot sat on the end of a solid metal bracket, so that it could be moved nearer to the flames or farther away. She was cooking. On an open fire. Inside.

Mannix quickly searched the walls and ceiling for signs of light fixtures, and concluded there was no electricity. It was like going back in time.

A number of children swarmed about, and Mannix saw there were additional rooms in the back, beyond the long wooden table. All three adults kept up a rapid-fire conversation Mannix wasn't sure he could have followed even if they'd been speaking English. He heard the word Ivan a few times, and could tell by the tone, and the looks on their faces, that they were at the serious part of the discussion.

The smoke and close quarters were making him lightheaded, and he caught Ernesto's eye then pointed to himself and then the door. Ernesto rolled his eyes. "You can say, 'I'm going outside.' I haven't lost the ability to speak English."

Right. Of course not. He wasn't thinking.

The air was clearer outside, but as he got closer to the barn, there was a background smell of something that made his eyes tear up, like an old lady's apartment with too many cats. He went back to the car—the now filthy car with its mismatched tires—and sat in the passenger seat. He left the door open to catch the late day breeze; it was warmer here than it had been in Havana.

Was that only this morning?

Everything was happening too quickly. Only two weeks earlier, he'd been Hank Mannix, pinup boy to a small but devoted community of a certain type of man, with a best friend who wasn't complicated and didn't make mysterious statements about it 'being time,' and a ready supply of men at his beck and call who would—and this was the best part—go home when their vacations in tropical paradise were over.

His life had been perfect. He'd given absolutely no thought—none, zero, *nada*—to kissing a handsome young Cuban man or wanting to make him laugh or gazing into his eyes or holding him while he cried. Or *caring* about him.

What the hell was going on?

Ernie. That's what was going on.

Mannix leaned his head back and closed his eyes. He remembered the first time he'd spotted Ernesto in the garden. Mannix had been having coffee with Hans in the greenhouse, and outside, a handsome young Cuban was clipping dead fronds from the tops of the palm trees lining one of the walkways. His brown skin glowed a burnished gold in the sunlight, and a sheen of perspiration sparkled on his forehead.

He was reaching far above his head with the pruning shears—too far, really, and his arms wobbled with the awkward angle and the weight of the clippers. His neatly tucked shirt kept pulling up and out of his trousers, revealing a smooth, toned torso that had Mannix transfixed. Each time it happened, the young man would stop his work, put the shears down, and tuck his shirt back in securely, which would hold only for a few minutes before he'd have to repeat the process.

It was endearing and ridiculous. He was a gardener after all.

But the more he watched the fellow the more he found the young man's quirks appealing. Unlike the others, he wore work gloves when carrying debris and always fixed his hair after he removed his hat. And something about how he carried himself, his posture, perhaps, or his graceful movements, conveyed a sense of dignity Mannix was drawn to.

And what a contrast he was to the young man he worked beside—a stringy, dirty fellow who slouched and took no care as to his appearance. And from that first moment, even as Mannix sat admiring the gardener and ignoring Hans's ramblings about something or another, he'd mentally dubbed them the cute one and the grubby one.

He'd kept his eyes open for the cute one after that. He made it a point to wake up in time to sit in the greenhouse when the cute one would arrive for work, always before the others showed up.

"You've been getting up early," Hans noted one morning.

"Oh, you know, turning over a new leaf and all that," Mannix replied.

Hans's gaze had drifted into the garden where the cute one was sweeping the path. "I see," he said.

Still, as much as he enjoyed watching the cute one, it came as a revelation when he caught the cute one watching *him.* He'd been posing for photos by the pool with Tony at the time. Both of them wore bathing trunks, and Mannix was flexing his bicep while Tony squeezed his fingers around the muscle.

"Try to look amazed at how big it is," one of the photographers had called out.

"But he has his bathing suit on," Tony had responded.

The photographer sighed. "Har-har, Cordero. Maybe just do your job without the commentary, okay?"

Mannix had thought the joke was funny, and he turned his head away from the camera to hide his grin, only to meet the cute one's gaze locked onto his. He was a distance away, at the edge of the garden, half hidden by the hibiscus bushes. But it felt as if they were mere inches apart.

The cute one looked away quickly as color bloomed on his face. But Mannix knew the look he had seen. Desire. Longing.

Something had stirred deep inside him then, and he'd grinned in anticipation of the game ahead.

"Good, Mannix," one of the photographers had said as the cameras clicked. "That's perfect."

*

MANNIX'S RUMINATIONS WERE interrupted by the opening of the driver's door. Ernesto slipped into the car and tapped Mannix on the leg. "Were you sleeping?" he asked.

"No," Mannix replied. "Just daydreaming."

Ernesto rested his hands on the wheel.

"It's sort of scary seeing you in the driver's seat, even without the car running."

Ernesto gripped the wheel and made *vroom vroom* sounds, just like the priest had done. Mannix grinned at seeing Ernesto more relaxed and open and considered again how difficult it must be for him to operate in Mannix's American world. Although this farm wasn't Ernesto's world either. He was a city boy, and he belonged at university.

"I *am* sorry about all of this, Hank."

"Thirteen is an unlucky number," Mannix replied.

"Oh. I didn't know that. Then let me say I'm also sorry that my aunt and uncle insist you sleep in their bed tonight." He gripped the wheel tightly, probably in anticipation of Mannix's objection. "Fourteen," he added quickly.

"No. Absolutely not." An echo of Hans's refusal to permit this trip drifted through his mind. What goes around comes around. "Wait. You don't mean *with* them, do you?"

Ernesto cocked his head. "You know, I used to think it was just a language issue, but sometimes I don't know when you're serious."

"I get that a lot," Mannix admitted. "And I don't know. About the bed I mean. Why would they want me to sleep there or with them or whatever?"

Ernesto ran his hand up and down the gear shift. It was distracting.

"Because you're a guest. And I told them I work for you, and that—"

"You work for Hans, not for me."

"But you could fire me. It's the same thing."

Mannix didn't know what to say to that.

"And I told them Ivan had worked for you. And you'd tried to provide him with...guidance, I guess." Ernesto shrugged, seemingly unsure how to talk about the activities Ivan was involved in. "And I told them you were a movie star!"

Mannix groaned.

"They asked if you'd been in any movies they might have heard of." Mannix laughed, and even Ernesto chuckled at the idea. "And anyway, it's the only real bed in the house. And, just in case you *weren't* kidding—no, they don't want to share it with you. They want you to have it tonight."

Images of what the bed must be like floated through Mannix's mind. And the sheets! Did they even have sheets? And would they be able to wash them before bedtime?

"No. I, um, couldn't impose like that."

"But they *want* you to. They want to be good hosts."

Mannix frowned and twisted in his seat to look Ernesto in the eye. "Listen, Ernie. Here's what you're going to do. I know you're related to these fine people, but you're going to go in there and you're going to lie to them."

Ernesto began to object, and Mannix held up a hand.

"No. I don't care what you tell them. Tell them I...wait. They're not priests, are they?"

"What? No, how could they possibly be—"

"Fine then. So, lie. Tell them I can't tolerate the smoke, or the smell, or the dirt, or whatever. I'm not sleeping in their bed—with or without them." He stared hard at Ernesto, waiting for an indication he understood. "I'll sleep right here in the car."

Ernesto sat in silence, staring forward out the windshield. Mannix was beginning to understand this was what Ernesto looked like when he was deep in thought, that he wasn't just shutting down. He waited.

Finally, Ernesto nodded. "I'll be back." He left the car and closed the door behind him.

Mannix watched him walk off and disappear into the cabin. Farm workers went in and out, some bringing tables and chairs outside, others carrying bundles towards the barn, then bringing more tables from the barn out into the yard. Children ran about but wisely stayed away from the car, perhaps because Mannix scowled at them any time they came near.

Finally, Ernesto reappeared then slipped back into the car.

He leaned back against the seat and let out a long sigh, like a warrior exhausted from battle. Mannix looked at him expectantly and raised a questioning eyebrow.

"Okay," Ernesto said. "But you can't sleep in the car."

"I'm not sleeping in their bed, Ernie, I just—"

Ernesto held up a hand. "I know. It's all right. You don't have to. But, um...you're sleeping in the barn instead."

"What?" Mannix looked over at the imposing building, open to the elements on the ground level, with its wide gaps in the siding under the roof. "Why? No, I think I'll just stay here." He settled himself into the seat, trying to convince Ernesto he'd be comfortable.

"You *can't* sleep in the car, Hank. They'd be offended."

"But they don't mind putting me up in the *barn*?"

Ernesto blushed. "Well, I told them you were filming a movie about tobacco growing, and you wanted to spend the night in one of the barns to really experience it, so you could make sure the movie producers got it right."

"Who would want to watch a movie about tobacco farming?"

Ernesto turned to face Mannix directly. "That's not really the important point here, is it?"

"No. No, it's not. That was a good lie though, Ernie. I'm proud of you."

Ernesto frowned. "I'm not sure lying well is something you should be proud of me for. And, well, about the nick—"

"Wait," Mannix interrupted as he began to envision the night ahead. "Are there *animals* in the barn? Will there be...I don't know...bugs, or worse, *snakes*?"

"I don't think so. I mean, sure, bugs and stuff, but I don't think there are any dangerous animals. Not here anyway. But there is equipment you could hurt yourself on and places where you could trip or fall." Ernesto's blush deepened. "That's why they asked me to sleep in the barn with you."

A sizzling energy shot through Mannix. "We're going to sleep together?" He couldn't keep the excitement out of his voice. "I mean, you know, in the barn, not, you know, the other thing. I think."

"It was all I could come up with. Sorry. I'm not very good at making things up."

"I'm not sorry at all," Mannix said. "And that's fifteen, by the way."

Ernesto just shook his head and ran his hands along the steering wheel. "First, we have to get through dinner." He nodded his head toward the tables being set up in the yard. "A lot of people will come by. It's a small community. Word would have spread about us arriving, and everyone wants to know what's happening in the city since the coup. And they'll all want to meet the movie star too."

Mannix didn't care about dinner, or whether everyone thought he was a movie star. "But after all that—the dinner and stuff—we'll get to sleep together? In the barn? Alone?"

Ernesto's grip on the wheel tightened. "*Sí, es verdad.*"

Chapter Eleven

ERNESTO THOUGHT THE dinner would never end.

Switching back and forth between English and Spanish always gave him a headache, and he was forced to do so throughout the evening, translating for his aunt and uncle or for Hank or for all of the workers who'd brought their families—who'd brought, in particular, their daughters—to be presented to Hank and even to Ernesto as if either man might decide a trip to the countryside was also the perfect time to pick up a wife.

It was exhausting. And hanging over it all was the other thing, the thing that made it nearly impossible to focus on anything else.

I kissed Hank!

But what did it mean? What did it make him? What did it imply for his future that his first kiss was with another man? That he'd loved it and wanted more?

He looked at the pretty girl sitting across from him

with her perfectly braided hair and her embroidered blouse—the one she probably wore to church. She smiled shyly at him. Her mother reached across the table and handed Ernesto a neatly arranged plate of churros. "Elena made these, Ernesto. Try one. And take some home to your mother."

My mother—who would have to approve of the cooking skills of any girl I'd marry.

And he'd have to marry someday, surely. He'd want a family and children and grandchildren eventually; wouldn't he? How could he marry such a sweet girl when it took every ounce of his self-control to stop him from inching his hand along the bench to his left and letting it rest against Hank's thigh?

"Those look fantastic," Mannix said as he reached out for one of the churros. And, as if bidden by Ernesto's will alone, Mannix's right hand slid along the bench and came to rest against Ernesto's thigh.

Ernesto fought back a smile, or maybe a grimace. He was ridiculously pleased to feel Hank touching him. And embarrassed. And a little bit frightened. It was all too much to think about—the big picture questions about what the kiss meant, or who he was and what his future might hold.

But the kiss itself was nice to think about, as were the fifteen others taking up all the space in his head when he tried to imagine the future. He was lost in the memory of his first kiss when his aunt interrupted his musings.

"Ernesto," she repeated. "I said ask him who he thinks is going to win the presidential election when it's rescheduled."

This was pointless. He knew Hank well enough to know he'd have absolutely no opinion about the Cuban elections.

Mannix's index finger traced a delicate line along the side of Ernesto's thigh. "What did she say?" he asked.

Ernesto turned to face Mannix, resigned to his role as interpreter. But then he had a better idea.

"She wants to know how many young men you've kissed." Ernesto *did* want to know this. It had been troubling him since they'd changed the tire. Is this something Mannix did all the time? Is it normal for Americans to do such things? Does it mean anything, or is it just a game of some sort for him?

"What! How did she—oh, I get it. Clever." Mannix leaned across Ernesto—ostensibly to grab the pitcher of water—but he brought his hand up on top of Ernesto's thigh as he did so. "Tell her just one recently. There's something about the way he blushes and the way his bright eyes sparkle like copper in the sunlight. I just can't help myself."

Mannix poured himself a glass of water from the pitcher, and Ernesto had a moment's thought that maybe he should have warned Mannix to stick to beer, given how white people sometimes responded poorly to local food and water. But all thought flew from his head when Mannix's fingers softly crept up his thigh. "And the fifteen more I'm looking forward to collecting," he added. "Tonight."

Mannix withdrew his hand and took a long drink of water. He smiled at the girl across the table.

There was a throbbing sense of absence where

Hank's fingers had been. Ernesto turned to his aunt. "He thinks Socarrás is going to win."

"Oh, that's good," she responded. "Ask him what he thinks about this fellow Castro who's running for Congress. The one all the field-workers seem to like."

He turned to Mannix. "She wants to know what you meant by 'only one recently.' She thinks that's not a particularly helpful answer."

Mannix licked his lips. "Well, ask her if she believes in redemption. Ask her if she thinks it's possible for a fellow to turn over a new leaf."

Ernesto didn't know what Hank meant by turning new leaves over, but he knew his aunt, and he knew for sure she believed in redemption; she was a Catholic. He turned to her. "He doesn't know anything about Fidel Castro. But the torcederos like Castro too. They're always asking me to read his essays."

"You're such a smart boy," she said. She patted his cheek. "You'll do well in university." He hadn't told them about his third rejection. "I wish Ivan was more like you."

No, you don't. Not really. If Ivan pulled himself together, he might end up with a pretty young wife like Elena. Ernesto only saw doors closing ahead of him.

He was spared from having to respond by the cheer that went up when his uncle appeared with a thick clay jug. Ernesto knew what was in there. It was potent stuff, brewed by his uncle in the small shed behind the curing barn. It was going to be a long night.

The women began clearing the tables; they'd be gone soon, and the men would drink until the early morning hours.

Mannix waved at a few flies that had gathered on his plate and took another deep drink of water. "Oh, this looks interesting,' he said, eyeing the jug. Someone put a wooden bucket filled with small glasses on the table, and the men began gathering around, choosing a glass and filling it with the clear liquid from the jug.

Mannix did the same.

"Be careful, Hank. It's strong."

Mannix waved away the warning just as he'd waved away the flies. "Oh, please. I was drinking booze when you were still just a boy." He took a sip, grimaced, then downed the rest of the glass.

"But you're only twenty-five." Ernesto said.

"What?" Someone refilled his glass. "Oh, that's right. I am, aren't I?" He lifted his glass. "Bottoms up," he called out before swallowing the contents. The men cheered, although Ernesto knew no one understood what Hank had said.

Ernesto himself rarely understood what Hank was saying.

He worried Hank was drinking too quickly. "Let's go get a space set up for us in the barn," he said as he took Mannix's elbow and steered him away from the table. As he'd hoped, Mannix perked up at the mention of the barn. They'd only gone a few feet when Ernesto's uncle called to them.

"Where are you going?" he asked. "We're just getting started."

"He wants to see the barn while we still have enough light," Ernesto replied. And although it had only been an excuse he'd made up in the moment, now that he thought about it, they *did* need to get themselves situated before darkness fell. Any open flame—even a well-secured oil lamp—was a bad idea in the tobacco barn.

"Oh, right," his uncle said. "Here. Take this with you." He picked up Mannix's empty water glass—his very tall water glass—and filled it with the clear liquid from the jug. Mannix reached for it, but Ernesto managed to get it first.

"Thanks," Ernesto said, silently vowing to spill most of it on the way to the barn.

There were three large barns in the immediate area around the house. The nearest was a low building with wide doors and small vented openings high on the walls below the roof line. It was just beyond the Packard, and Mannix cast a nervous look at the car as they passed it. "Hans is going to kill me."

Ernesto would have liked to disagree, to assure Hank everything would be fine, but the car was a mess. And as much as he was able to deceive his aunt and uncle about Hank's job and his interest in making a movie about to-bacco, failing to tell the truth didn't come easily to him.

"Killing you probably wouldn't be worth it for him. He could get in a lot of trouble." Ernesto thought that was a good compromise—comforting, perhaps even reassur-ing, but still true.

But Mannix only laughed, and then he reached for the glass. "Careful," Ernesto said. "Don't spill any." But what he meant was, "Don't drink too much."

Maybe Mannix got the message, because he only took a small sip and handed the glass back. As they ap-proached the closest barn, he scrunched his nose. "What is that smell?" he asked. "It smells like cats."

"It's ammonia," Ernesto replied. "It's stronger inside. But you get used to it."

Mannix hung back. "We're not sleeping in there, are we?" Beads of sweat had begun to appear on his forehead.

"No, this is the fermentation barn; that's why it smells that way. We're sleeping in the curing barn. But I thought you'd want to see the entire operation. For your movie, right?" In truth, he just wanted to get Hank moving and away from the never-ending flow from his uncle's jug.

He thought Hank wasn't looking too good.

"Right. Okay," Mannix said as they stepped into the dark barn. In addition to the ammonia smell, it was warm and humid inside. Knee-high mounds of tobacco leaves ran in straight rows down the length of the barn.

Ernesto led the way, guiding Mannix along a path between the piles. "The fermentation step is actually the last stage in the process, so we're sort of starting at the end." Midway down the row, he lifted a large turning fork from a post and carefully levered into a pile of leaves.

A wave of heat and an even stronger smell of ammonia emerged from the opening.

Mannix wiped his brow. "It's *really* hot in here."

"I know. Fermentation gives off a lot of heat. These piles are kept at around eighty-five degrees. They need to be turned now and then to keep them from overheating."

"No," Mannix said. "I mean it's way too hot in here." Sweat ran down his cheek. "I need to get out." He turned and hurried toward the open doors.

Ernesto thought he looked unsteady on his feet. He

followed him out into the waning sunlight.

"Phew," Mannix exclaimed, bending at the waist and taking a couple of deep breaths. "Do people actually work in there?"

Before Ernesto could answer, there was a loud rumbling sound, like distant thunder over the hills. "Oops," Mannix said. "That was me. My stomach's been acting up." He glanced at Ernesto's hands, probably looking for the alcohol, but Ernesto had dumped it on his way into the barn and left the empty glass inside on a shelf by the door.

"Just as well," Mannix mumbled to himself. "Shall we continue the tour?"

"Are you sure you're up for it?" Ernesto asked. Although it was noticeably cooler outside of the barn, Hank still looked off. He was surprisingly pale given how hot he'd said he was.

"What choice do I have? You said I couldn't sleep in the car. Might as well go see where I'm bedding down." His stomach emitted another rumbling growl. "This is all so overwhelming."

Did he mean the farming operation? The food and alcohol? His stomach acting up? How the day was turning out generally?

Ernesto couldn't be sure, but he agreed with the sentiment. He thought about the kiss, but wouldn't allow himself to dwell on what might happen that night in the barn. He was overwhelmed too.

As they neared the curing barn, Mannix continually wiped perspiration from his forehead. "How did they take the news about Ivan?" he asked.

"All right. He's gone off on his own for a day or two before, so they're not too worried."

Mannix offered a noncommittal grunt. "Did you tell them about...what he's doing?" He paused for a moment and took a deep breath, rubbing at his belly, then he offered a weak smile to Ernesto.

"No. How could I? Even I don't know what he's doing," Ernesto said. Mannix grunted again. "At least, not exactly," Ernesto finished.

"Ernie, I saw him walking the malecón. *I* know what he's doing. And it's a lot worse than just letting some fat cat American suck him off in the garden for a dollar."

Ernesto winced. That was awfully blunt. He was embarrassed for Ivan and for himself, too, given he'd considered allowing the same thing. *Was that only four days ago?*

"Maybe he'll stop and come back to work." Even as he suggested it, Ernesto knew it was unlikely. He'd seen the look in Ivan's eyes when his cousin talked about the money he could make on the malecón.

"Maybe," Mannix replied but offered nothing more.

They approached the curing barn, which was the same shape and size as the fermentation barn. Mannix twisted around to look behind them. "Did we just go in a circle?" He turned back to Ernesto and swayed slightly after the sudden movement.

Ernesto grabbed Mannix's arm to steady him. "No, Hank. This is where we're sleeping." It was obvious Mannix had had too much alcohol too quickly. "You don't look so good. Maybe we should go in and lie down." The grumble from Mannix's stomach seemed to second that idea.

"Yes," Mannix said. "Let's go get laid." He laughed. "Down. Get it? Laid down?" He hiccupped, then hiccupped again.

No, Ernesto didn't get it, but he knew better than to ask.

"Come on, Hank." He led the man by the elbow into the barn.

Once inside, they stood for a moment letting their eyes adjust to the dimness. Mannix hiccupped, then took a deep breath. "Oh, much better," he said. "The smell I mean."

And it was better. Ernesto had always loved the smell of the curing barn, where the freshly cut tobacco leaves were hung to dry. It was a sweet, earthy smell, much more pleasant now that all the ammonia had leeched out.

The broad leaves were tied together in bundles of a dozen or so, and they hung from poles in long rows running the length of the barn. Ernesto began explaining the process—how the leaves were grouped by color, shape and purpose, and how they'd hang in this barn for weeks.

He untied one of the bundled *manos* from its pole and turned to hand it to Mannix. These were wrapper leaves, unblemished and still pliable, like a very soft leather. "Feel this," he said.

Mannix reached out his hand unsteadily, but a loud rumble from his stomach interrupted his movement.

He turned away and vomited on the barn's floor.

*

ERNESTO KNEW HE was a worrier.

His parents had told him that all his life. "You always expect the worst, mijo," his mother would say. "It's never as bad as you think it will be."

But for all his propensity to visualize disaster, to anticipate the many things that can go wrong, that *would* go wrong—even he hadn't imagined what a catastrophe the night would be.

It hadn't been just the alcohol. Maybe it was something he ate, or even the water, but Mannix was sick—shivering, sweating, looking-like-he-wanted-to-die sick.

The entire farm was thrown into chaos.

Workers ran between the barns and the house carrying buckets and rags. "The movie star has the shits," they yelled.

Twice, Ernesto managed to get Mannix to the outhouse in time, but usually he didn't.

The curing barn didn't smell as sweet as it had earlier in the day.

They tried to keep up with shovels and pails of water, and mostly managed, but the first few hours were rough.

Eventually, well after midnight, Mannix settled into an exhausted stupor, curled into a fetal position on the third blanket the farm hands had managed to scrounge up, alternately sweating and shaking. Surely, whatever poison had been coursing through his intestines had been purged. There couldn't possibly be more to come out.

"Ernie. Ernie," Mannix whispered. He waved his arm about as if he were a blind man. In his defense, it *was* very dark in the barn. Only one small candle set securely in the middle of a metal box dimly illuminated the space around them in shifting shadows. And even it looked like it wouldn't burn much longer.

Ernesto decided there would be better times to have the discussion about his nickname.

"I am, so, so sorry," Mannix said. It was the most recent in an endless string of apologies he'd offered over the last few hours. If Ernesto had been the one banking the kisses, he'd have amorous riches beyond imagining.

He sat crossed-legged on his own blanket next to Mannix. "It's all right, Hank. None of this is your fault. You were kind to bring me here. We just didn't...think it through."

Mannix groaned. Whether from pain, frustration, or something else entirely, Ernesto couldn't be sure. He took a small sip of the boiled tea Ernesto's mother had made for him, then swished the tea in his mouth before swallowing it and licking his lips. "Listen. Just for the record, if we make it through this, you should know that thinking things through isn't my strong suit. You're going to have to be the one who thinks things through for us."

Ernesto smiled. Those were the most words Mannix had spoken since he'd gotten sick—a good sign. But then the import of what the words meant sunk in. Mannix was suggesting they had some sort of future together—with assigned roles—and, okay, that last bit was odd.

But was it just Hank being Hank, or was he delusional from his illness, spouting nonsense?

He reached his hand out and held it against Mannix's forehead. It was still clammy, but he was no longer drenched in sweat. The candle sputtered and then went out.

In the sudden darkness, his hand still resting on Mannix's brow, Ernesto decided to go with the fantasy. "All right. I'll think things through. But what's your job going to be?" He moved his hand to Mannix's hair and gently stroked it back from his face.

"Me? I'm all about the possibilities." Mannix groaned again, stretched, then rolled onto his other side, his back toward Ernesto. "Stick with me, Ernie. The sky's the limit."

*

THE MORNING WASN'T much better.

Twice during the night, Mannix had woken up, rolled off his blanket, and vomited into the dirt. It was too dark to clean effectively, so Ernesto was glad there couldn't have been much left inside of Mannix to come out.

As soon as daylight began filtering into the barn, Ivan's mother came with more boiled tea. Ernesto rose and took the jug from her, thanking her again for her efforts.

"Do you think he could eat anything," she asked. "I could bring an egg."

He looked down at Mannix, who was sound asleep. He seemed...peaceful. Ernesto recalled the vision of Hank he'd had in the garden, languidly stretched across a white bed with only a thin sheet covering his waist. That image had been arresting—sexual and projecting power, even while the man slept.

Now he looked...innocent. Like a vulnerable man

who needed looking after. "No, I don't think so," he re-plied. "I'll let him sleep. Let's see how he feels when he wakes up."

It was another three hours before Mannix finally opened his eyes and levered himself into a sitting posi-tion. He rubbed his head and blinked at his surroundings, taking in the puddles of thin vomit, the soiled clothes, the *smell*.

"Oh God, Ernie. I am so sorry."

"Yes, you've mentioned that." Ernesto smiled, re-lieved Mannix was able to sit on his own and speak coher-ently.

"This isn't how I thought sleeping with you the first time would go," Mannix said.

Well, mostly coherently, Ernesto thought.

"I hate to ask, but could you help me up? I need to go find a bush." Ernesto grasped one of Mannix's arms and helped lift him, but he'd only made it halfway to a stand-ing position before he collapsed back onto the blanket. "Ouch."

"Oh, sorry," said Ernesto.

Mannix grimaced as he pushed himself into a kneel-ing position to try again. He reached his hand out for Ern-esto's support. The unvoiced "sixteen" hung between them. "Please tell me I didn't try to collect on any of those last night."

"No. I think you were preoccupied with not dying." Ernesto grinned as the two of them managed to get Mannix up on his feet.

"Christ," Mannix said. He didn't relinquish his grip

on Ernesto's arm, but instead tried to steady his wobbling. "I might have been better off if I had. Hans is going to kill me anyway once we get home and he sees the car."

When he was stable enough to shuffle outside, Ernesto led him through the barn doors and around the back of the building. The fresh air was a glorious revelation, but he was alarmed how much it took out of Mannix just to make it that far.

He brought Mannix to an appropriate bush and paused, unsure how to proceed. "Um, do you need... help?"

"No." Mannix steadied himself, then slowly turned his back to Ernesto and faced the bush. "I'm not normally shy about these things. But I want it to be a special moment." He unzipped his trousers. "You know, when you're first blinded by the glory that is me. You're not ready for that yet."

As he listened to Mannix relieving himself, Ernesto thought he wouldn't mind at all being blinded by the glory that was Hank. But he agreed this probably wasn't the best time.

It seemed to take forever, but after Mannix finished, they made their slow way back to the front of the barn. Even several feet away from the open doors, the smell from inside was overwhelming. "I can't go back in there," Mannix said. "I'll get sick again if I do. But I need to sit."

He wasn't the only one who didn't want to go back into the barn, so Ernesto led him back to the tables and benches still sitting in the yard after last night's party. Mannix barely made it and was shaking with the effort by the time he slumped onto a bench and rested his arms on the table.

The sun was beginning to warm the morning air, and tendrils of mist rose from the fields. It would be beautiful if everything wasn't so...horrible.

Mannix had lowered his head to the table. His cheek pressed against the wooden surface. "I want to go home," he mumbled.

"I know. Are you able to drive?"

Mannix lifted his head and gave Ernesto an incredulous look. "Of course I can't drive. I can't even hold myself upright." As if to prove the point, his head plopped back onto the table. "You're going to need to drive, Ernie."

"But I don't know how," Ernesto exclaimed. He hated the note of panic in his voice.

Several workers who must have slept on the farm overnight crossed the yard with cleaning supplies, heading towards the curing barn. They didn't make eye contact with Mannix or Ernesto.

"Maybe one of these fellows can teach you."

They couldn't stay here forever, and it wasn't fair to Hank to keep him here while he recovered. It could be days before he was well enough to drive. But Ernesto was terrified by the idea of driving. Once, when he visited the farm as a boy, he drove one of the tractors on a dare from Ivan and nearly ended up killing them both.

He could ask his uncle to take them back, but he knew what an imposition that would be, especially since it was clear after his visit to the fermentation barn that a large batch of tobacco was ready to be baled and shipped to the factory. For Hank's sake, he could try to learn how to drive.

"You're thinking," Mannix said into the tabletop. "That's good. I'm glad I know what that look is now."

Ernesto stood and touched Mannix on the shoulder. "I'll be back." He headed toward the barn to talk to the workmen. When he returned a few minutes later, he had to gently nudge Mannix to get his attention.

He lifted his head an inch from the table. There were pieces of dirt, or maybe food, stuck to his cheek. "Huh. Wha—?"

"Oscar is going to teach me. I need your keys."

"Right pocket." Mannix leaned to the side with a groan. "Please don't ask me to stand."

Ernesto squatted and braced his left hand on Mannix's shoulder while he began to squeeze his right hand into the pocket. He didn't immediately feel any keys, so he dug deeper, trying not to think too much about what his fingers were rubbing against behind the thin fabric.

"They're not here." Ernesto's pulse quickened. What would happen if they'd lost the keys in the barn, or worse, during one of the stumbling rushes to the outhouse?

Mannix managed a grin. "Oh, did I say right? I meant left." He leaned in the other direction pressing into Ernesto's side.

"What? How could you—?" Ernesto closed his mouth when he realized he'd been played, but he was too relieved Hank was up to the joke to be angry about it.

"Felt nice though," Mannix mumbled before suddenly trying to push Ernesto aside and twisting away to vomit onto the ground behind the bench. Ernesto's relief evaporated.

Not much came out. Mannix raised his head and wiped spittle from his mouth with his arm. "I thought that part was over," he said.

Ernesto found the car keys, then rubbed the back of Hank's shoulders. "It's going to be okay," he said. But he didn't really believe it.

*

OSCAR PROVED TO be a not-very-good driver. "This isn't how the tractor works at all," he kept telling Ernesto as they maneuvered through the farmyard. And Ernesto proved to be even more inept at the task of driving than he feared he'd be.

It didn't help that whenever he was behind the wheel, he kept looking for Hank, trying to see if he was getting sick again. And it also didn't help that whenever he did manage to catch Mannix's eye, Ernesto would grind the gears, or stall the car, or accidentally shift into reverse. Mannix would simply shake his head sadly, then go back to resting it on the table.

It wasn't at all like locking gazes in Casa de Ada's gardens.

At least Hank had moved—or someone had moved him—farther down the bench away from the puddle of vomit.

His uncle came out of the house and brought another jug of boiled tea, then waved to Ernesto, calling him over to the bench.

Ernesto managed to bring the car around but didn't quite manage to stop in time before nudging an empty bench, tipping it on its side, and pushing it under the table. He tried not to think about the metallic crunching sound that accompanied the tap.

Even Oscar looked at him like maybe he couldn't tie his own shoes.

He got out of the car and walked behind it, avoiding the front fender entirely. Mannix's head still rested on the table, so he hoped the bump with the bench had gone unnoticed. And it had been such a light tap, it couldn't possibly have left a mark.

"There's a dent up here," called Oscar, who'd gone around to the front of the car to inspect the damage.

Ernesto shot a guilty look at Mannix.

"Good thing the movie star doesn't understand Spanish," his uncle said.

Mannix groaned against the tabletop.

"Listen," Ernesto's uncle said. "You obviously can't drive, and we need to get this American out of here before he ruins the whole farm."

Ernesto bristled at the choice of words, but upon reflection, he agreed leaving puddles of various objectionable bodily fluids in the barns, the fields, and the farmhouse yard was a pretty bad outcome.

"So, here's what we're going to do," his uncle continued. "I have a new maduro wrapper leaf that's ready. It's from a *corojo* plant your father hasn't seen yet. The leaves finished nicely; they're beautiful and perfectly shaped. I don't want them damaged in shipping with the filler leaves."

That made sense. The wrapper leaves were the most

important part of the cigar's appearance, and a new maduro leaf could be used in their high-end products, if they ever managed to get into the export business directly.

If only I'd managed to get into university.

"I'm going to send several manos of leaves back with you. See what your father thinks about them and write to us to let us know. Oscar will drive and return on the bus." Hank wasn't going to like that, but what choice did they have?

"Your aunt is also sending some things back for Ivan for when he shows up again. Tell him Elena is always asking for him." His uncle winked at him. "Or don't tell him, and come back yourself to let Elana know how much you enjoyed her churros."

Ernesto nodded, but he didn't think either of those two things was likely to happen.

Chapter Twelve

MANNIX RODE IN the back of the Packard, sometimes sitting up but mostly stretched out on his side across the wide bench seat. He thought he might be feeling a little bit better. At least the smell from the sacks of tobacco in the trunk wasn't making him feel nauseous any longer.

But every time Oscar hit a bump, or bungled shifting gears, Mannix's stomach lurched.

Oscar. He was the one who showed Mannix the pissing bush the day before and who'd shown more than a little bit of interest in Mannix himself when they both stood, exposed, before each other in front of the bush.

And now there he was, driving the Packard and letting his hand rest on the gear shift knob, just inches from Ernesto's thigh.

Mannix didn't like that. Not one bit. And he didn't like that he couldn't understand a word they were saying to each other. Oscar would laugh occasionally at something Ernesto said, and he didn't like that either.

The car swayed into a turn—far too fast, Mannix thought—and his bile rose in his throat. He closed his eyes and concentrated on his breathing, trying to steady himself. When he opened them again, he saw Oscar's fingers lightly brush against Ernesto's thigh, as if by accident—a light touch, then back to the gear shift, then a light touch again, longer that time.

Mannix knew every trick in the book, and he was having none of it.

"Hey, Ernie."

Ernesto turned in his seat and smiled at Mannix. "Are you feeling any better, Hank?"

"Tell the driver if he wants to keep his fingers attached, he needs to keep them to himself." The implied threat was diminished when Mannix clutched at his stomach and let out a soft moan. "And tell him to slow down."

When Mannix thought about that, he realized it would only prolong their time together with Oscar. "Never mind. Tell him to get us there as soon as possible."

Ernesto looked confused, and Mannix didn't blame him. He didn't translate any of that for Oscar, but he did shift farther in his seat toward the door, taking him away from Oscar's easy reach. Mannix decided to count that as a win.

But if he didn't understand the words, Oscar must have sensed the tone, because he swung aggressively into the next turn, causing Ernesto to press against the door and Mannix to slide across the seat.

Mannix felt what was about to happen. "Stop the car! Stop the car!" he called.

"*Qué*?" Oscar asked with a grin.

Ernesto braced himself against the dash and said, "He's asking you to pull over. I think it's an emergency."

But it was too late. Mannix scrambled for the window handle and cranked it down, but had only managed to hang his head halfway out when he vomited. It ran down the upholstery, across the window crank, and onto the floor. Most of it did, anyway. Mannix had never given much thought to what was *inside* of a car door, down in the space where the window descends, but he thought about it now and decided he didn't want to see what the window might look like when it was rolled back up.

The stench from the pooling liquid in the footwell competed for dominance with the earthy scent of the tobacco in the trunk. The vomit won.

The front seat passengers rolled down their windows. Oscar was frowning. If he'd thought the prank was funny before he certainly didn't any longer. They stopped at a farmhouse to borrow a bucket of water and a rag, offering some of Elena's churros in return.

They cleaned up as best they could, but it didn't help when the rooster hopped through the open window and pooped on the dash.

All in all, thought Mannix, the trip to the country was an excursion best forgotten.

Except for the kiss—that made everything else worth it.

*

GOLDEN BOY AND Eddie were waiting for them on the street by Casa de Ada's driveway. They'd brought out folding chairs and books and looked as if they'd been prepared for a long vigil. They stood when the Packard pulled up, and Matt said, "Jesus," as he began to take in the state of the car.

Oscar put the parking brake on, and Ernesto opened the passenger door and jumped out.

"You can't let Hans see this," Matt began. "He's angry enough as it—oh, who are you?" he asked when he realized Mannix wasn't driving.

"That's Oscar," Ernesto said. "Hank is sick." He nodded to the back seat.

Eduardo and Matt went to the rear door and Matt opened it. They leaned away when the smell assaulted them. "Jesus," Matt said again.

Eduardo leaned into the passenger compartment. "Hank, good lord. What happened?"

"Ernie will fill you in," Mannix managed through gritted teeth.

Matt raised an eyebrow at the nickname, and Ernesto gave a shy little wave to Eduardo by way of introduction. Mannix tried to slide out of the car but collapsed back onto the seat. "I can't walk all the way to the house."

Eduardo slid into the backseat next to Mannix. "Go warn Hans," he told Matt. Ernesto jumped back into the passenger seat, and the ruined Packard made its way slowly up to the house. Oscar stalled the engine once, but even Mannix didn't think he'd done it on purpose. It took a few attempts to restart.

Mannix risked a peek out the window ahead of them

and wished he hadn't. They were all there—Golden Boy with the men from Allentown right behind him, the *Pumped* photographers, Tony with a beer in his hand, and front and center, with his arms crossed in front of his chest and his pink-slippered foot tapping impatiently, was Hans.

The Packard came to an abrupt stop right in front of him. Oscar turned off the engine and something metallic dropped from the undercarriage with a *clang*.

Hans's mouth opened and closed as he looked over the car, taking in the spare tire, the dent in the front, the grime on the doors and windows. The smell from inside reached him, and he scrunched his nose.

"What...?" he began. "How...?"

Tony handed his beer to one of the men from Allentown and came to help Eduardo get Mannix out of the car. They half carried/half pulled him out, and when Hans saw him in his stained clothing, unsteady on his feet, exhausted, Hans's eyes welled up, and he rushed to his friend, embracing him in a tight hug.

"Oh, Hank, darling."

A camera clicked behind them.

Hans whipped his head around. "I swear to *God*, I'll rip the film right out of that camera." The *Pumped* man looked chagrinned.

"Sorry," he murmured.

"Tony, help Hank inside. Get him cleaned up; then get him to bed." Hans turned to Ernesto. "You, young man, are coming with me. You're going to explain everything."

Mannix was relieved to be home, to have Hans's

compassion and Tony's support.

Still, he couldn't help but feel sorry for Ernesto as he watched the young man trail after Hans, head hanging low, braced for what was to come.

*

"A MOVIE STAR!" Cordero said again, chuckling. "Oh, if they only knew."

"Stop," said Mannix, pressing his hand against his side. "It hurts to laugh."

They were in their small shared bedroom at Casa de Ada, an arrangement meant to be temporary when they first arrived in Havana five years earlier, but one which both men had allowed to settle into something more permanent.

Mannix was in his bed, still recovering from the events of the prior two days. Cordero sat in the room's one chair, his feet propped on the side of Mannix's mattress.

"Hans was trying to be very stern," Cordero said, "but he almost cracked a smile when Ernesto shared that." Cordero reached to the bureau top and grabbed his beer. "He's a very serious fellow, isn't he? Your Cuban boy?"

Mannix sighed. "I hope he made it home okay."

"I'm sure he did. Eduardo promised he'd make sure he got there in one piece."

"I hope he comes back. I hope I haven't driven him off."

"Why would you have? Just because you got sick in their barn?"

"Both barns!" Mannix said. "And the fields and their front yard. They'll be cleaning up after me for years." Mannix looked away. "And it wasn't just vomit either."

"I did *not* need to know that." Cordero smiled and reached over to touch Mannix's arm. "Hank, he'll be back. He's surprisingly devoted to you."

"*Surprisingly*, Tony?"

Cordero leaned back and took a swig of beer. "Well, you can be a hard man to like, sometimes."

Mannix carefully sat up and swung his legs over the side of his bed, pushing Cordero's feet out of the way. "Nonsense," he said. "You like me and you're devoted to me."

Cordero harrumphed, but didn't offer a denial.

"Listen, Tony. I want to ask you something, and I'm being serious." He waited for Cordero to nod his agreement. "Have you ever kissed anyone?"

"Do you mean...have I ever kissed a man?"

"No," Mannix said. "I mean anyone, ever."

Cordero looked perplexed. "Hank, I'm over thirty years old; of course I've kissed people! More girls than I can count." He tilted his beer bottle toward Mannix. "Who hasn't? Why, you must have kissed hundreds of people by now, men *and* women, I'd imagine."

Mannix wrung his hands in his lap and looked at the floor.

"What an odd question," Cordero continued. "Why would you...?" He stopped when Mannix looked up.

"Good God, Hank. You're not saying that you...that you've never..."

"It's true. I really haven't," Mannix said. "Not in any

way that mattered. Not where I felt something."

"You mean, in all those encounters, there's never been *kissing*?" Cordero sounded incredulous.

"Well, sometimes a particularly boorish fellow might have tried to smash his lips into mine. But no, I never let them get that far." Mannix warmed as color rose in his face. "But I have now," he whispered.

"*Ernesto*?" Cordero seemed shocked. Mannix couldn't tell if it was because he'd kissed Ernesto or had never kissed anyone before.

"But you..." Cordero waved a hand at Mannix. "You're always..."

"I know what people think, Tony. But I'm not really how people see me."

"But even we've..." Cordero waved his hand between the two of them. "I mean, there've been plenty of times you and I have—"

"Kissing is different, Tony. Despite all the times we may have...lent each other a helping hand...we've never *kissed*. Kissing is...intimate."

"But, back in New York and even here in the gardens, you're always—"

"That's *different*, Tony. In New York it was...transactional. And here, well, it's just a...hobby." He smiled when he recalled the disastrous get-to-know-you conversation he and Ernesto had had on the drive.

Cordero put down his beer, leaned back in the chair, and let out a breath. "Hoo boy."

"Exactly. Hoo boy." Mannix planted his hands on his knees. "I'm going to stand," he warned Cordero. He carefully rose, swayed briefly, then made his way to the room's single window. It looked out into the gardens, but Mannix only saw his reflection in the glass, with Cordero frowning in the chair behind him.

He touched his cheek. "Good lord." He turned to face Cordero. "Please tell me it's the light in the reflection and I'm not really this pale."

"Sorry, Pops—you know Matt calls you Pops, right?" Mannix winced, then nodded.

"But, yeah, you really are that pale." Cordero stood and walked to the window. He wrapped an arm around Mannix's chest and pulled him back to rest against him. "Our little boy is growing up," he whispered.

"Ass," Mannix said and elbowed Cordero in the gut. He studied their joint reflection in the window. The White Twins. Having spent two days with Ernesto and the others it began to make sense.

"I think..." he began, searching for Tony's eyes in their dim reflection. "I think, maybe, we should stop...you know...being the way we are, sometimes, with each other."

"Shh," Cordero whispered into his ear. "I know." He brushed Mannix's hair back from his forehead. "I'm glad for you, Hank. Ernesto's a good kid. Even Hans warmed to him as he told us the story. He did everything he could to make none of it seem like your fault."

Mannix smiled and lifted his hand to rest it on Cordero's hand, which was still pressed against his chest.

"But he didn't fool us," Cordero continued. "Hans and I both know it was all your fault." He released his grip and walked across the room to pick up his beer. "He didn't mention anything about kissing though. When did that happen?"

Mannix turned away from the window and steadied himself with a hand against the sill when he swayed. "During the tire changing, if you can believe that."

Cordero shook his head. "I still can't believe you actually changed a tire! How are your nails?"

"Funny," Mannix said. "But the kiss, Tony. It was...glorious. I had no idea."

Cordero kept shaking his head. "You've got it bad, pal. I hope for your sake he feels the same way."

"Me too," Mannix replied as he lowered himself back onto the edge of his bed. "Because if he does, I've still got, like, sixteen more."

Cordero tilted his head. "Did you get a concussion too? You're not making any sense."

Mannix smiled. "Ernie tells me that all the time."

Before Cordero could respond, there was a knock on the door.

"Hans," the men said to each other, and Mannix nodded his permission for Cordero to open the door. But it wasn't Hans; it was Eduardo.

"Eddie!" Mannix said. "How's Ernie?"

"Can you not hear how wrong that is?" Eduardo asked as he stepped into the room.

"He really can't," Cordero said. "It's not in his nature."

Eduardo let the door swing open and come to rest against the doorstop. "It's so hot in here. Can't you open a window?"

"No, too many bugs," Mannix replied.

Eduardo sighed. "Ernesto is fine. Safely home." He

walked to the metal fan sitting on top of the bureau and toggled the switch. The blades began turning lazily with a loud metallic clacking sound. "Wow. That's even worse than the heat." He turned off the fan and moved to stand next to Mannix's bed. "How are *you*? Ernesto told me you were very sick."

"I've been better." He looked up at Eduardo's concerned face. "I feel like I've left half of myself behind at the farm."

"Serves you right," Eduardo said. "That was a stupid thing to do. What made you think you could drive there and back in a day?"

Cordero put down his beer and turned to Mannix. He seemed curious about the answer too. "It wasn't that *far*," Mannix complained. "And Ernie didn't seem to think it would—"

"Ernie doesn't drive," Eduardo interrupted. "And Ernie is in no—" He rolled his eyes. "Arg. You've got me doing it now. *Ernesto* is in no position to advise you on how long it would take to drive a private car to San Cristóbal." He shook his head. "And to make no planning effort at all. Not even for gas!"

"But Ernie's the one who's supposed to think things through, not me."

Cordero grinned. "That makes sense. To assign someone the job of being your brains."

"And that must be why he thinks this is all his fault," continued Eduardo. "Even though none of it is. He made me promise to tell you he's sorry."

A warmth blossomed in Mannix's chest. *Seventeen.*

"You were lucky Matt found me at the university yesterday. I knew right away you wouldn't be able to make it there and back. At least we were able to stop Hans from creating an international incident."

"He was still plenty angry though," Cordero observed. "But you were also lucky he learned Arthur is coming home in two days. So even though he's still trying to be furious with you, I think he's mostly in good spirits."

That was a relief. He waited to see if either man was going to continue blaming him, but they both seemed to be finished. Cordero drank the last of his beer. "Would you like a beer?" he asked.

"God, yes," said Mannix.

"I didn't mean you. You're still recovering."

"Yes, please," said Eduardo. Cordero left, and Eduardo sat on the bed next to Mannix. "He's a nice kid. Be sure not to hurt him."

Mannix huffed. "He's twenty years old; he's not a kid." He didn't bother denying he could hurt him. Badly. Mannix worried about that too.

"Still, he's very...innocent. And you're...not." Mannix concluded Eduardo had decided to sit next to him so he could avoid looking him in the eye. "Look, I know you Americans get up to all sorts of—What's the word? Hijinks?—here at the house, and I admit I enjoy being on the edge of things, looking in. But Ernesto isn't like that. And he's one of us, so I feel protective."

One of us. There were so many ways to mean that. So many circles of people.

"I don't want to hurt him," Mannix offered.

"I know you don't, Hank. I'm just saying it would be

easy to do. Accidentally." He did turn then to look at Mannix. "Do you understand what I'm saying?"

Mannix shook his head.

And it came with an unexpected jolt of clarity that the opposite was true too. Ernesto could easily end up hurting Mannix. He couldn't say that though. Not out loud.

Cordero returned with two beers and handed one to Eduardo.

"Oh," Mannix said. "I forgot to tell Cordero. Tony, did you know Ernie works in a factory where they make cigars? Can you imagine such a thing? Not cars or steel. Cigars!"

"Yes, Hank. I've been caught up."

"Which doesn't make sense to me," Mannix continued. "He's smart. He reads all the time. I hate to think of him working on an assembly line, even if it is just cigars rolling along on a conveyor belt."

Eduardo's grip tightened on his bottle. "*Diós Mio*. He doesn't work on an assembly line. He's a lector."

"Oh," said Mannix. "Well, that's good. I guess. Or not, maybe. I don't know. What is that?" He looked at Cordero, who simply shrugged.

"A lector is an educated worker who sits up on a platform in the middle of the factory floor and reads to the workers as they hand roll the cigars."

"Well, that's different," Mannix said. "So, no assembly line at all?"

"No. It's a nice shop, actually. I saw it this evening. His family lives above the factory. Nice people too." He took a sip of beer. "They weren't too upset about everything once Ernesto explained, and once they saw the new wrapper leaves you brought back."

"Hmm. That part of the trip is all sort of fuzzy for me." Mannix reached for Cordero's beer and was allowed to take a swallow. "When he told me he likes to read I thought maybe he meant *the Hardy Boys* or something—"

"Oh, those are good," Cordero offered.

"I know. But he never heard of them. Can you imagine never having heard of *the Hardy Boys*? Anyway, he said he'd been reading some politician. Casper? Caesar? I can't remember."

Eduardo put down his beer and rubbed his temples. "Sometimes, I don't know if you're being serious or not."

Mannix looked at Cordero and opened his palms. "See?"

"It's Castro," Eduardo said. "And he's dangerous. At least he is for folks like you, and even more so for people who own factories, like Ernesto's family."

"Well, we can take care of ourselves," Mannix said. "If he comes around here, we'll set him straight." Cordero nodded his agreement.

Matt appeared in the doorway. "Who are you beating up?" he asked.

Eduardo's face lit with a broad smile. "Matt, come in." Mannix rolled his eyes, and Matt came through, already holding a beer.

"Fidel Castro," Eduardo answered with a smirk. "They said they'd take care of him if he comes around here."

Matt tilted his head. "They don't know who he is, do they?"

Cordero took a deep swallow of beer. "All right, smarty-pants," he said, "why don't you tell us."

"He's a politician who's going to free the Cuban workers from the yoke of capitalism."

Eduardo spluttered. "Well, Matt, I-I'm not sure—That's not exactly how—"

"Oh look, Tony," Mannix interrupted. "They're going to have their first argument, right here in our overly crowded bedroom."

"We're not arguing," Matt objected. "I just have strong opinions about right and wrong. And since I'm sticking around for a while, you'll need to—"

"Sticking around?" Mannix asked with a growing sense of dread.

"That's right," Cordero exclaimed. "You wouldn't have heard the news yet."

"News? What news?" Mannix felt like he might vomit again.

"The *New Mannix* is going to be attending university here in Havana." Cordero made no attempt to keep the glee out of his voice.

"Just for this semester," Eduardo rushed to add. "I spoke with his school back in New York, and they were thrilled to have him study abroad, especially with all the...political interest right now in Cuba."

There was no point further alienating Golden Boy unnecessarily, and he had done Mannix a good turn by concocting the plan to borrow the car. Plus, it was clear now he didn't have his sights on Ernesto anyway.

"Congratulations," he offered, much to Eduardo's relief and Cordero's disappointment, who evidently had been looking forward to a bit of a scrap. "I don't get it though. If it's that easy to get into university, why did Ernie tell me he was rejected? He's smart and resourceful. He reads all the time and is a hard worker."

"It's not that easy, Hank," Eduardo said. "Not for Cubans who aren't from the right families. I mean, yes, admission is supposed to be based on merit alone, but the upper classes like to keep things separated."

Mannix huffed. Poor Ernesto; he never had a chance. "That doesn't seem very fair. To say everyone has an equal chance but then game the system so only the rich can get in. It doesn't seem very American to me."

"Ha!" Matt scoffed. "It's the most American thing about this island. That's why people like Castro are—"

Hans stepped into the room and everyone fell silent.

"This room is way too small for five fully clothed men," Mannix complained.

"Out," Hans said. "Everyone out." Mannix began to push himself up. "Not you, Hank."

The others shuffled out. Mannix took Eduardo's beer. "Good luck, my friend," Cordero whispered as he left.

Hans closed the door behind them and toggled on the fan. "It's stifling in here." He quickly turned the fan back off when he realized what a racket it began to make. "I can't believe I get away with charging money for these rooms."

"Not every guest house has my star power as a draw," Mannix proclaimed.

"Hmph," Hans said as he sat next to Mannix on the bed.

"Hans, please. Can we just jump to the part where you forgive me? I know what I did was stupid and indefensible and reckless. And I'll pay for repairs to the car...eventually. I just can't bear you being angry at me, especially when I already feel like I want to throw up."

"Oh, Hank." Hans pulled Mannix into a tight embrace. "I've already forgiven you. You know I can't stay angry at you for long." Mannix relaxed into his friend's embrace. "Do you ever miss our time in New York?"

Mannix sniffed. He was unexpectedly teary. "What, with your G-man boyfriend breathing down our necks because he thought we were communists?"

"Oh, come now. In the end, Arthur did the right thing. I don't know. New York was more...uptight, less hedonistic, I suppose."

"And you miss that?" Mannix mumbled against Hans's shoulder.

"A little bit. Maybe it's just that the rules were clearer."

Mannix didn't understand what Hans meant. Getting around the rules had always been the guiding principle of his life, so he couldn't grasp wanting more of them.

"Anyway, this new young man of yours. He's quite impressive. I believe he's smitten with you." Hans squeezed Mannix's hand, then gently moved him away. "But tell me how you feel about him."

Hans was his oldest and dearest friend; he deserved the truth. "I wish I knew. He's turned my life upside down. I've never cared for anyone before." He thought about it and realized that didn't sound right. He cared for Hans and Cordero and even Arthur in his own way. "I mean, cared for someone where I feel so exposed—at risk of being hurt.”

“That’s good, Hank. You need someone in your life.”

Did he? He’d always assumed the opposite—that committing to someone was a fool’s game, leading only to frustration and resentment.

“I don’t know anything about him. I thought he worked in a steel factory, for God’s sake.”

Hans barely managed to hide his smile. “The men from Allentown found that very amusing.”

“Oh sure. I used to be a celebrity; now I’m just a laughing stock.”

Hans tsk-tsked. “Nonsense. You’re not a laughing stock. But you are at a crossroads. You need to decide who you want to be. Next, I mean. Especially now that we have a new Mannix.”

“Not you too,” Mannix groaned.

“Sorry. It was a joke. Mostly. But he is staying on, you know?”

Mannix sighed. “Yes, and good for him, I guess. It just doesn’t seem fair for Ernie, who desperately wants to go to college, that Golden Boy just flits in here and grabs a spot.”

“Yes, Ernesto told me about how he wants to improve the family business, get into exports directly. He’s very smart.”

“That’s what I told Eddie. Hey, I wonder if he could pull a few strings like he did for Golden Boy?”

“Maybe. Let’s talk more when Arthur’s here. He’ll be home the day after tomorrow, and he always has something reasonable to add.”

Mannix cocked his head. "Like the time he called you broken?"

"We all get a chance to grow and learn from our mistakes, Hank. Even you."

There was a shriek out in the garden, followed by peels of girlish laughter. "What is *that*?" Mannix asked.

"That shady-looking fellow who drove you home is out by the pool with the men from Allentown." Hans looked toward the window, but only low glints of the distant garden lights could be seen through the dark foliage.

"Why is he still here?" Mannix asked. "He's a sneaky one."

"Well, it was either allow him to stay here or send him home with Ernesto. And from Ernesto's story, I suspect you wouldn't have liked that very much."

"True," Mannix said, imagining the man bunking with Ernesto all night long.

Another shriek, followed by a splash and more laughter.

"They seem to get along famously," Hans said, "even though they don't speak the same language."

"Oh, I suspect they do," grumbled Mannix.

It was going to be a long night.

Chapter Thirteen

"BUT, MIJO, I still don't understand. Why did the American drive you to the farm in the first place?" Ernesto's mother poured him more juice, and he cast a covert look at his father sitting across the breakfast table, newspaper open in front him, pretending not to listen.

"I told you. He wanted to see the operation for a movie he's making."

"But how did he even know—"

"That's enough, Isabel." His father folded the paper and placed it on the table. "It all worked out in the end with the new wrapper leaves. I think they're going to be superior to the ones we've been using. Ernesto and I have work to do, figuring out how best to use them." His mother didn't look convinced, but she dropped the topic.

"Actually, I was planning on going back to work at the guesthouse this morning. I want to make sure Mr. Mannix is all right and maybe even talk to Dr. Martinez again." Ernesto knew Eduardo wasn't actually a professor at the university, but instead had some sort of administration job. But when he'd told his parents the story last night, they'd assumed he taught there, and Ernesto chose to let them continue to believe that.

"Not today, mijo," his father said. "It's time we both started giving thought to how you'll fit in here, and how to improve operations."

Marta looked at him, then quickly looked away. She also must have heard the finality in their father's tone.

"Of course, Father, but—"

"No buts, Ernesto." His father stood, then drank the rest of his coffee. "Come on. Finish up. We'll go see what we can do with the new corojo leaves my brother sent us."

Ernesto had no choice but to follow his father into the factory. The first few torcederos had arrived and were taking their places at the rolling tables. His father greeted each by name. Ernesto glanced longingly at the lector's platform and his empty chair. The two men continued across the factory floor and into the tabaco storage room.

Bales of tobacco were piled in the middle of the floor. Metal ceiling fans kept the air gently moving and open transom windows high on the wall provided ventilation. A sweet, musty smell permeated the room, and Ernesto was reminded of the time he spent here as a boy, hiding from his sister or reading one of his books or just daydreaming about an entirely different world than the one he lived in.

The new corojo wrapper leaves were neatly stored by the doorway, and both he and his father got to work lifting bundles and carrying them into the inspection room, with its clean tables and bright lights.

His father placed a pile of leaves onto the white workbench and spread the manos apart. "Let's see what we have here."

Ernesto did the same with his bundle and both men began spreading the leaves out. His father would pick one up and hold it to the light, carefully studying the veins and structure of the leaf and searching for even the smallest blemish.

"These are beautiful," he said. He rolled a leaf along his thumb, testing its pliability. "And strong without any brittleness." He brought it to his nose and took a deep sniff, then handed it to Ernesto. "What do you think?"

Ernesto thought this was what the rest of his life would be. Making cigars, perhaps finding some small success in marketing the family's brand. Maybe marrying Elena and having children. At least he'd enjoy the churros.

He was resigned to it. There were worse lives to be led. And he did know a thing or two about tobacco. "These are better than any wrappers we've worked with before," he said, impressed despite the melancholy track his thoughts had taken. Then he had an idea.

"Maybe the Americans could help me understand the market there better. We could specifically develop a cigar to appeal to them." He continued to examine the leaves before him, as if the suggestion was of little consequence.

"I don't know, mijo." His father responded.

"Well, it's just an idea," Ernesto said. "We should do what we can to maximize the value of these leaves, leverage their strengths into a premium product." He wasn't sure he had used the right words, but he counted on knowing the language of marketing better than his father did.

Apparently, he was successful. His father nodded his agreement. "You're right about that," he said. "But is it proving useful to spend all this time with them? What is it you actually *do* there?"

And that was the rub of it, wasn't it? He could hardly say "gardening" without significantly weakening his argument. But he didn't want to lie to his father.

"Whatever needs doing, mostly." Which was sort of true. He'd moved that heavy pot out of the greenhouse once, and retrieving dirty shorts from the pool wasn't exactly gardening. "And just yesterday I spent over an hour talking to the owner, answering his questions about tobacco farming."

Hans hadn't actually been asking about farming so much as demanding to know why his car was filled with "stinking rotted vegetables."

Ernesto shuddered as he recalled the hour he'd spent with Hans. It had been an intense grilling—no, more than that—an interrogation. Why had Hank offered to take him to the farm? What did they talk about in the car? When did he get sick? Where did they sleep?

The list went on and on, and although Ernesto thought Hans may have been trying to restrain himself, he considered the questions overall to be far too personal and intrusive. Still, as the hour wore on, Ernesto began to suspect Hans was mostly just worried for his friend, and Ernesto could respect that.

He'd been as truthful as he could be, without revealing anything about the kiss.

And then, at the end, there'd been the...what? Job offer?

"You should leave the gardening to others," Hans had said. "Come work inside as a houseboy. Lord knows I could use the help. And you seem personable enough." Ernesto had simply nodded, trying to make sense of the offer, if that's what it was. "Talk to Hank about it; see what he thinks."

He wasn't ready to explain any of that to his father yet. He didn't understand it himself. And the very term—houseboy—seemed like a job for a servant. He could be proud of his gardening work; it was honest labor, physical, a man's work.

But houseboy? He didn't know what to think.

"He asked you about farming?" his father said.

Ernesto nodded.

His father held a leaf up to the light. "Look at this color, Ernesto. I can't decide if I'd call it maduro or oscuro." He handed the leaf to his son. "Is it dark enough for oscuro, do you think?"

Ernesto studied the leaf. It was unblemished and thickly veined, with the texture of soft, paper-thin leather. "I think we'll need to see what it looks like as a wrapper before making a final assessment."

His father nodded his agreement. "Perhaps keeping in contact with the Americans could be useful." Ernesto remained silent, not wanting to risk an interruption. "But maybe less time there, and more time here at the business, yes?"

*

THEY SPENT SEVERAL hours carefully sorting the new leaves by size and color, and making special notations about their scents. Then they rebundled them for storage in the coolest part of the warehouse, where they kept the crates of finished cigars for shipping.

Late in the morning, Ernesto took his familiar spot in the chair on the lector's platform and read the morning papers to the torcederos.

It was reported that Batista claimed he would remain in power only until order could be restored and fair elections were held. This announcement triggered a fair bit of grumbling among the torcederos, many of whom could remember the first time Batista took power by a coup twenty years earlier. He'd ended up staying in office then for a decade.

It was announced the police had seized the headquarters of the Federation of Cuban Workers, and that some members of its leadership were unaccounted for. The Federation was described as a front for the more radical elements of the Partido Ortodoxo, and this prompted even more grumbling. Many of the workers were supporters of the Orthodox Party and had intended on voting for its members—including the popular Fidel Castro—in the now postponed elections.

Finally, the paper admonished students at the university for promoting false beliefs about Marxism and Communism. The campus was described as a political hotbed of radicalism, and a veiled warning was issued about the government's willingness to take actions as necessary to curtail subversive behaviors.

Ernesto wondered about that. Why would young people of means and privilege seek to overturn a system that puts them at such an advantage? It didn't make sense, and he suspected something else was going on, something the paper wasn't reporting.

He put the paper down, and the torcederos began talking softly among themselves while they formed their cigars. He heard the name Castro several times, and he looked forward to reading for pleasure in the afternoon. They'd picked Don Quixote as the next book to read, and Ernesto was eager to start in on it.

He rejoined his family for lunch where his father extolled the virtues of the new leaves and asked Marta to design a cigar band to accentuate their rich color. "Maybe we could name them something special too," Ernesto offered.

"Yes," his father agreed. "Come up with some ideas, and ask the Americans which would work best."

His mother raised her eyebrows. "So, you're going back there?" She looked to her husband for confirmation.

"Yes," his father confirmed. "The owner of the inn seems to be interested in the tobacco industry, so that changes things." He looked at Ernesto and seemed to recall their earlier conversation. "Not so often though, yes?"

His mother cleared the lunch dishes, then brought a plate with the remaining churros on it. "She's a good cook, this Elena," she said. "A solid country girl who knows the household arts. She'd be useful. A man could do worse."

Marta pushed back her chair and quietly left the table.

*

"TURN OUT THE light, mijo," his father called through the closed bedroom door. "It's eleven o'clock; you need to get to sleep."

"Yes, Father," Ernesto replied. "Good night."

He took the flattened cigar band he used as a bookmark from his narrow bedside table, tucked it into his copy of *Don Quixote*, placed the book on the floor where Ivan used to sleep, and turned out the lamp.

He'd been enthralled by the story as soon as he'd started reading it. He could identify with Alonso, a hidalgo clinging to the very bottom of the respectable social order, searching restlessly for something, *anything*, to prove himself, to give his life meaning.

Perhaps feigning madness wasn't a bad strategy. He could choose his own title—Don QuiErnie!—and embark on eccentric adventures. He could hold himself above accountability and respectability, go wherever the winds blew him.

He glanced over the side of his bed at the book and the empty floor. But isn't that what Ivan had done? And where had that gotten him?

And isn't that—possibly—what the men at Casa de Ada were doing? It was a confusing and disturbing thought, and Ernesto drifted into a troubled sleep.

Chapter Fourteen

"IT'S AWFULLY EARLY to be doing this," Matt complained as he climbed into the passenger seat of the Packard. The car had been cleaned, but not exactly fixed. New rattling sounds came from underneath, and it still sported the mismatched tire.

Mannix pulled into traffic and adjusted his grip on the wheel to accommodate the new pull to the right the car was exhibiting.

"So, you'll be early. It'll give you a chance to enjoy a cup of coffee, maybe learn some Spanish so you're not sitting there in class like a brick."

"I know a little Spanish," Matt huffed. "And the professors all speak English so mostly I'm just auditing the courses and talking to the professors afterward."

"Nice work if you can get it," quipped Mannix. He was still struggling with how unfair it was that Ernesto couldn't get in, but Golden Boy got to uselessly take up a spot.

"Besides, Eduardo is helping me with the language."

"Oh, is that what you kids call it these days?" Mannix hit the brakes hard when he realized he was about to miss his turn. A flatbed truck loaded with barrels almost rear-ended them.

"Jesus," Matt said, bracing his hands against the dash.

"Sorry," Mannix replied. "But I need to get to Eduardo before the day gets away from us." He turned to Matt and waggled his eyebrows. "I have a plan."

"I'm sure literally everyone who knows you shudders when they hear that."

"Probably." Mannix looked at Matt again, taking in his pressed chinos and button-down oxford shirt. "You know, you clean up really well when you're not presenting as a gigolo."

"I know!" Matt grinned. "You should see the looks I get from some of the guys in class."

"I can imagine," said Mannix. "I've gotten plenty of those looks myself." And for the first time, Mannix wasn't panicked by the thought his pinup boy days might be behind him. He pulled to the curb near the gate to the university. "Let's go find your boyfriend and then get you to class. We don't want to disappoint your fans."

They got out of the car and began walking through campus. "You know, Pops, I think we could almost become friends."

Huh. "Well, let's settle for a truce for now."

*

"ARE YOU SURE this is the right way?" Mannix asked, peering out the driver's side window at the increasingly dilapidated neighborhood.

"Yes," Eduardo replied. "I brought him home two days ago. I know where he lives. It's not much farther now." He pointed out the front windshield to three dogs trotting across the street. "Watch out."

Mannix steered around the pack. "I almost forgot. I need a pack of cigars—cheap ones."

"I didn't know you smoked. And can we maybe wait until we're back at the house for that?" Eduardo craned his neck to read a street sign as they passed an intersection. "Turn right up ahead."

"They're not for me. They're a prop." Before they reached the intersection Mannix noticed an elderly man selling fruit, gum, and cigars from a push cart. "Oh, there," he said.

"I don't know, Hank. They won't be very good."

"Perfect," Mannix said as he brought the car to a stop by the cart. "Grab me a pack, would you?"

Eduardo shook his head but did as he was asked.

Before long, they reached their destination, a wooden two-story building hemmed in on both sides by similar looking structures. A row of opaque windows ran along both sides of the doorway.

"This is it?" Mannix asked. It looked decrepit, and he couldn't imagine someone as dignified as Ernesto coming from here. "And the family lives here?"

"Yes, Hank. On the second floor. It's a common arrangement in Cuba."

Mannix glanced back at the car as they walked to the

factory door. "Will it be safe parked there?" The only other vehicles on the street were work trucks and motorcycles.

"Safer than it was with you in the countryside," Eduardo replied. "And don't be so parochial. The whole world isn't like New York City." They reached the door and Eduardo stepped through, holding it open behind him for Mannix. "No sense frightening them by sending in the white man first."

Mannix wasn't sure if he was joking.

The door opened directly into the factory with its rows of long tables and benches filled with men rolling cigars from the piles of tobacco leaves in front of them.

Oh, now I understand.

"Hello guys," Mannix said. The torcederos all stopped their work and silently looked up. One of them stood and walked into a back room.

Behind a glass wall on the far side of the factory floor, Mannix saw a woman stop her own work at a sewing machine, and a pretty girl about Ernesto's age put down a tiny paintbrush and turn to the door. *That must be Marta,* he thought. *She looks like Ernesto.*

The woman rose and came out of the office. "*Profesor* Martinez," she said, reaching her hand out to Eduardo. Then she said something else Mannix couldn't understand.

Mannix raised an eyebrow at the term "professor," and Eduardo subtly elbowed him to keep him quiet.

"She asks if anything is wrong," Eduardo told Mannix. "I'll tell her no, then introduce you." That was as far as they'd planned. Mannix hadn't known who to expect and decided he'd go with the flow in the moment.

After he made the introductions, Eduardo indicated with a nod that it was his turn. Ernesto's mother offered a tentative smile. She was clearly confused as to why this white man was standing in her home. Nonetheless, she ushered them off the factory floor and into the office. Marta kept her gaze on the table before her.

"Good morning, Mrs. Ruiz. It's a pleasure to meet you. I see where Ernesto gets his good looks."

Eduardo rolled his eyes. "Sure, Hank. That won't be alarming at all." Ernesto's mother looked back and forth between the two men, waiting for Eduardo to translate. "I'm just going to tell her you'd like to speak with Ernesto if he's here, okay?"

But then Ernesto came into the factory from the back room, followed by a man who must be his father. Mannix tried to interpret the look on Ernesto's face but couldn't come up with anything more encouraging than panic.

As Ernesto's father crossed the factory floor, the torcederos immediately took up their work. The two men came into the office, and Eduardo made the introductions once again. Ernesto's mother said something, and her son replied before turning to Mannix and saying, "I told her, yes, you were the movie star who got sick all over the farm."

"Oh," Mannix said. "So that story got around?"

"What are you doing here, Hank?" Ernesto asked.

Good question. His plan had seemed solid when he first came up with it, but now, with everyone looking at him expectantly—or suspiciously, he thought, keenly aware of Ernesto's father's puzzled frown—he wasn't sure how to proceed. "See, this is why *you're* supposed to be the one who thinks things through."

Ernesto blinked in confusion. Eduardo cleared his throat. "Um, I don't know what your plan is, but maybe it had something to do with the cigars?"

"Oh, right! Thank you, 'Professor' Martinez." He opened the bag he'd carried in from the car and pulled out the package of cigars Eduardo had bought from the street vendor. He turned his attention to Ernesto's father. "We were expecting your son to show up at work this morning. We were hoping to get his opinion about these cigars." Mannix handed the package to Ernesto's father.

As Eduardo translated, Ernesto blushed, and his father opened the package and sniffed the cigars. He frowned and handed them off to Ernesto.

"You see," Mannix continued, "we offer these to our guests, but one of the American businessmen staying with us this week said they were inferior, and we should think about providing a better cigar."

Eduardo sniffed. "So now you want me to start lying for you?"

Before Mannix could respond, Ernesto began explaining to his father what Mannix had asked. The two men had a lengthy exchange. "What on earth are they talking about?" Mannix whispered to Eduardo.

"Ernesto is telling his father all about the movies you shoot with Tony, and what the pictures of you in *Pumped* Magazine look like."

"You're a funny man, professor."

The Ruizes kept talking, and everyone but Mannix

was focused on the discussion. At one point, Marta was brought into the conversation, and she quickly disappeared into the back room.

"Unbelievable," Eduardo muttered.

"What are they *saying*?" Mannix demanded in as quiet a whisper as he could manage.

The two men stopped talking, and Mr. Ruiz held his hand out to Mannix. "Thank you for—" he began in halting English before turning to Ernesto for guidance.

"Taking care of…" Ernesto prompted his father.

"Taking care of my son," Mr. Ruiz concluded. Ernesto said something to his father and then repeated it. "My son says to tell you—" He turned to Ernesto again, having already forgotten what Ernesto had told him to say.

"He's sorry for the trouble he caused," Ernesto told his father slowly, so he'd be able to repeat it back to Mannix. There was an impish gleam in his eye.

"He's sorry for trouble," said his father.

Sorry. "Nineteen!" Mannix exclaimed.

Marta handed the box to Ernesto, who then turned to Mannix and said, "Okay. Let's go."

Mannix grinned. He couldn't believe it had been that easy. "Really? Just like that?"

"What is it you Americans say?" asked Eduardo. "'We better get going while the getting is good,' I think."

*

"WHAT JUST HAPPENED?" Mannix asked as he maneuvered the car through the streets of Havana heading toward the university.

"To start with, you flirted with Ernesto's mother," Eduardo said from the back seat.

"I missed that part," complained Ernesto. He was sitting next to Mannix clutching the box Marta had handed to him before leaving the factory.

"Yes. And here's the best part." Eduardo reached forward and put his hand on Ernesto's shoulder. "He told her it was clear where you got your good looks from."

Ernesto sucked in a breath and turned to Mannix. "You told my mother you thought I was good-looking?"

"Well, indirectly, I suppose. I wasn't thinking about it that way. It's just a thing that's said to compliment a woman."

"I'll have to ask Matt about this," Eduardo said. "Whether it's normal in America for women to be complimented by the fact that their sons are considered attractive by older homosexuals."

Ernesto shrank into his seat and gripped the box more tightly.

"Don't worry," Eduardo patted him on the shoulder. "I didn't translate it."

"Was Marta listening?" Ernesto asked. "She speaks some English."

"She was there," Eduardo said, "but she didn't react in any way."

"Oh, come on," objected Mannix. "It wasn't that bad. I was just being polite."

"And *then*," continued Eduardo, "after you told Ernesto's mother that you found her son sexually attractive, you—"

"I *didn't* say—"

"You lied to his father about the cigars." Eduardo plopped back against his seat with the finality of a lawyer closing his case in a jury trial.

"Oh, so that's how that happened," mumbled Ernesto.

"It was just a white lie," Mannix insisted. "We do have American guests who like to smoke cigars sometimes."

"And *then*," Eduardo continued, "you asked *me* to lie to Ernesto's father."

"I was there for that part," Ernesto said. He turned to the back seat to face Eduardo. "Sorry."

"Twenty!" Mannix exclaimed. "Or, does that not count since it wasn't directed to me?"

Ernesto sighed.

Eduardo looked puzzled. He leaned forward and said, "You know, Hank, sometimes I don't have any idea—"

"What I'm talking about," Mannix finished for him "Yes, I know. It's a thing with me." He drummed his fingers on the steering wheel. "But I made up the rules, so I'm going to say it counts."

"Fine with me," said Ernesto.

"*What* are you two—?"

"Oh look, we're here." Mannix pulled to the curb, and Eduardo climbed out of the car. "Tell Golden Boy we said hi," Mannix called to him. "And, Eddie, don't forget what we talked about yesterday. It's important."

"I'll do my best," Eduardo said as he shut the door

behind him.

*

"SO," MANNIX SAID. "You and me again, driving through Havana on a bright sunny morning. Why, it's almost like the last three days didn't even happen."

The Packard made a loud grinding noise and shuddered. "I'm pretty sure they happened," Ernesto replied.

"I don't know. It's all so hazy. I thought I remembered kissing an incredibly handsome young Cuban fellow, but…that couldn't have happened. Could it?" Mannix smiled and reached over to trail a finger up Ernesto's thigh. "Maybe if it happened again, I'd remember for sure."

Ernesto pushed his hand away. "Hank, we can't do that here. Anyone could see."

"There you go, thinking things through again." He put both hands back on the wheel.

"Can we drive along the malecón? Just in case he's there."

Mannix wasn't sure he wanted to seek out Ivan. The boy would probably be so far gone into the lifestyle of the streets that it would only be painful for Ernesto and not at all helpful for Ivan for his cousin to see him like that. Still, he understood the desire.

"Sure, but just one pass. We do need to get back. You start your new job today."

"Then Mr. Schmidt was serious about that?" Ernesto asked. "I don't… I don't even know what a houseboy is. Or what I'm supposed to do."

"You can work all that out with Hans. What he needs most is just help with making sure guests have everything they need. Breakfast, of course, keeping the coffee fresh and the eggs hot—that sort of thing. But also getting extra towels if they're needed, helping with pool chairs. Whatever needs doing, really."

Mannix waited while Ernesto thought about that. He turned onto the main road heading to the malecón.

"It sounds like a maid," Ernesto finally said.

"Not at all." Mannix slowed to let a pushcart cross in front of him. "He has a maid. You'll be more like...a butler...and a local expert."

Ernesto was quiet again. "What else?" he asked. "You're fidgety, Hank. You're not telling me something."

Mannix realized he'd been tapping his hand against the wheel and jiggling his knee. Ernesto was already able to read him easily. "Fine. You're right." He let out a breath. "Traditionally, a houseboy is also a young, attractive man who the guests would enjoy interacting with. Maybe flirting a little, you know?"

"But, not like Ivan? I wouldn't be expected—"

"No!" Mannix exclaimed. "God, no. I wouldn't permit that. I couldn't bear to think of it."

Even as he said it, Mannix realized that was probably revealing too much. Who was he to stake such a claim on Ernesto? They'd shared one kiss; that was all. And sure, it was his first kiss, and probably Ernesto's first kiss too, at least with a man. And just because *his* life had been turned upside down by his unexpected feelings for Ernesto, it didn't mean Ernesto felt the same.

A sudden memory from the barn intruded on his

thoughts. He was "washed up," he'd told Ernesto. Or thought he had, while gripped by delirium. He remembered thinking he should warn Ernesto off, confess to being old and useless and aimless. He wanted to tell Ernesto to find someone else, someone with a future ahead of him. But then Ernesto would wipe his brow, or rest his hand on his shoulder, or make soft comforting noises in his musical language, and Mannix would want Ernesto to stay with him forever.

Is this what this was all about? Was he *clinging* to Ernesto? Like a drowning man to a life buoy?

"There!" Ernesto said, pointing to the corner, where a shirtless young Cuban fellow lounged against the wall of a pharmacy. It must have been his fondness for his cousin that allowed Ernesto to think—even for a moment—the handsome young man could have been Ivan.

Even from halfway down the block, in a line of traffic on a busy street filled with shoppers and vendors, the fellow made eye contact with Mannix. And why not? A white man driving a fancy car, cruising along the malecón. Chances were good he was looking for just such an opportunity.

The youth pushed himself off the wall and grinned, then noticed Ernesto in the passenger seat and looked away. Either he thought Mannix had already found a companion, or he wasn't into a group thing. By the time the car pulled to the corner, he'd turned away and Ernesto had realized it wasn't Ivan.

"This is hopeless, isn't it?" Ernesto asked as he scanned the crowd.

"No, not hopeless. He's out there *somewhere*,"

Mannix observed. Or he might be dead, he thought—there were a thousand things that could go desperately wrong on the streets—but he didn't say that out loud.

"We need to head back. Arthur's coming home today, so Hans will be very busy."

"I've heard others mention Arthur. Are they...?" Ernesto left the question open.

"A couple? Yes, much as I tried to stop them from getting together back in New York." Mannix continued driving along the malecón, keeping one eye out for Ivan, although he thought it highly unlikely they'd see him.

He smiled, recalling the incident at the Easter Parade, when he'd first met Arthur. Hans had...oh. Hans. Ernesto didn't know about Hans.

"There's something you should know about Hans," Mannix began. "He's more...feminine than a lot of the other guys."

"I know. The gardeners all think he's mysterious. He's who I was thinking of when I came up with the idea to tell people you were a movie star. He looks like that to me."

Mannix chuckled. "You know Tony and I aren't really movie stars, right? I mean, sure, we're in movies, sort of, but they're not...well..."

"I know what they are, Hank. Mostly." Ernesto seemed suddenly nervous. "I think... I think I'd like to watch one sometime. But then I think, maybe I don't want to see you and Mr. Cordero like that." He looked down at his lap, and Mannix knew he must be blushing.

Mannix reached over and put his hand on Ernesto's knee. "I'm embarrassingly pleased that would bother you.

And, you know, it's just acting. Tony and I aren't like that. Like you and I are, I mean. We don't..." But then he stopped because, well, they *did*. Or they used to.

Mannix was grateful he'd had the talk with Tony two nights ago, and that they'd agreed they'd stop doing...whatever it was they used to do. "Helping a friend out," as Tony put it. And then with a sickening jolt he thought of the private photos that had been taken a few years back—when they'd been so desperate.

Those photos *were* quite explicit and went far beyond the simple drunken fumbling he and Tony occasionally engaged in on their own.

He'd tried hard to forget the pictures had even been taken.

They'd both been uncomfortable going so far with each other—they were friends, not lovers, and they were awkward around each other for weeks afterward. But a very, *very* wealthy man from New York had paid an extravagant sum to have the photographs taken, and the proceeds had carried them for quite a while.

He shook his head to clear the memory and turned back to Ernesto. "You don't need to see the movies; you've seen the filming. In the flesh." He winked.

"True," said Ernesto. He looked very uncomfortable. "So, there aren't more? No movies where you and Mr. Cordero are...naked?"

Where on earth had he gotten that idea?

"No!" Mannix replied, not actually lying because the naked ones were those damned photographs, not movies. Still, it was deceptive. "Why on earth—?"

"It was Ivan. He said he heard there might be—"

"Ivan," Mannix spat the name out. "I would think after what happened in the garden between us the first time, you'd have learned not to listen to your cousin." Ernesto blushed, and Mannix felt bad for dragging the poor fellow back to that moment. But he'd had to do something to redirect the conversation and to get Ernesto to stop thinking about what had gone on between him and Tony.

That was all in the past.

"Sorry," said Ernesto. And they both laughed when they realized they'd lost count.

Chapter Fifteen

HANS WAS IN a state.

"Oh good, you're here," he said when Mannix and Ernesto arrived. He pointed to Ernesto and began snapping his fingers.

"Ernie," Mannix supplied.

"Right," said Hans.

"Actually, my name is Ernesto." The remark went unacknowledged.

"Well, whatever you're called, I'm glad you're back." Hans ran a hand through his hair. "I couldn't take another day of Hank's drama, wondering if he'd ever see you again." He stepped to Ernesto and leaned in, appearing to conduct an inspection of some sort. Ernesto stood silently. "I don't know what you've done to Hank, young man, but do be careful. He's more fragile than he looks."

"I'm not—" Mannix began.

Hans snapped his attention back to Mannix. "This

won't do at all, Hank. Take him to Luigi's as soon as possible. He needs an appropriate uniform."

Uniform? There was nothing wrong with Ernesto's clothes.

Hans handed Mannix a few bills. "Don't go overboard."

Ernesto must have made a panicked sound because Hans turned to him and said, "Don't worry, dear. You're quite presentable as is. We just want to make sure you look like you belong; you understand?"

No, Ernesto did not understand. He conducted a quick survey of what the other men in the room were wearing. Hank looked more like a businessman than he normally did, but Ernesto thought he'd probably dressed that way to be more persuasive with his father. Mr. Cordero was slouched in a corner chair, looking fairly rumpled.

There were also two men Ernesto didn't recognize. They were sitting by themselves in a far corner of the parlor, heads bent together, whispering. They looked...Ernesto wasn't sure how to describe it. He thought they looked as if they'd gone to a menswear shop and bought outfits from posters of exotic vacations like they were wearing some type of costume.

Hans looked unusual and alluring in a green chiffon smock and white trousers that only came halfway down his calves, but Ernesto was coming to understand Hans wasn't expected to "fit in" anyway. And besides, he was the boss.

Ernesto couldn't see anything wrong with his own clean, serviceable outfit. He didn't feel out of place, or that he didn't belong.

Hank must have been reading his mind. "He means something tighter," he whispered.

Ernesto swallowed. Mannix had placed the box of cigars on the end table when they'd entered, and there they sat, forgotten.

"Look at this place," exclaimed Hans, sweeping out his arm to encompass the entire room. "Arthur will be here in only four hours, and it's a total mess." He squinted suspiciously at the cigar box.

Ernesto had never seen such a clean and neatly tidied room before.

"Hans," Mannix said. "Relax. The place is spotless, and Arthur doesn't care about those things. He'll just be happy to be home."

"Oh, but that's just it"—Hans twisted his hands together in front of him—"I've received a telegram this morning. He's not coming alone. He's bringing his awful boss with him."

"That Denton fellow he complains about all the time?" Mannix asked. "But why?"

"I don't know, Hank. It was only a telegram." He paced the room, then turned to Ernesto. "You're not a communist, are you?"

"No, sir."

"Well, that's something, at least. They *hate* communists where Arthur works."

Mannix put a hand on his friend's arm. "Hans, it'll be fine. You've got hours to prepare. Arthur mentioned the CIA wants to set up something permanent here. Denton is probably coming to do that. He might not even come in. Maybe he'll just drop Arthur off."

"No," Hans said. He reached into his pocket, pulled out the telegram, and handed it to Mannix.

Mannix read it and frowned. "I see. He wants to meet you."

From across the room Cordero snorted. "Arthur has talked you up too much. It's not *you* he wants to meet, Hans."

The two men at the other side of the room whispered excitedly to each other.

Ernesto was confused. They were speaking so quickly, and Mr. Schmidt was clearly distressed. But he felt he must have missed something. Did Arthur's boss want to meet Hans or not?

And he couldn't call all these white Americans by their first names. If he was going to work here, he'd need to know how to address people. "What is Mr. Arthur's name?" he asked.

Hans turned to him. "Why don't you start, dear, by cleaning up the remains of breakfast in the dining room and getting it in shipshape? They might want a snack or coffee or something when they get here. Then Hank will take you to see Luigi."

It wasn't a question; it was a dismissal. That was fine with Ernesto. He was here to do a job, after all. And although the job was ill-defined, it was beginning to look like it would involve a lot of cleaning.

Still, it kept him close to Hank, and after his daring rescue from the factory this morning, keeping close to Hank was becoming increasingly important to Ernesto.

On his way to the dining room, he heard Hans say,

"And Tony, take our guests to the casino this afternoon. We can't have all these men underfoot."

*

LUIGI TURNED OUT to be an elderly Italian who owned a tiny men's clothing shop tucked into an alley off a narrow side street. A sign in the window advertised same-day tailoring. A metal bell above the door jingled when Mannix and Ernesto entered the store.

"Mr. Mannix!" Luigi exclaimed, taking off his close-work glasses and rising from the counter where he'd been operating a pedal-driven sewing machine. "What a pleasure to see you. Do you need to have the waist let out again so soon?"

Mannix blushed, and it was the first time Ernesto had seen him do so. He liked it.

"Golly, Luigi. Can't a girl have any secrets at all?"

"I'm sorry, Mr. Mannix. I didn't mean to be indiscreet." He turned his attention to Ernesto. "And you've brought me such a treasure."

"Luigi, this is Ernie. He's Hans's new houseboy."

He hurried across the small shop and took Ernesto by the arm, steering him to a raised platform surrounded by a three-paneled mirror. "Of course you are," he said.

"My name is Ernesto. It's nice to meet you."

"Step up here, my boy." He steadied Ernesto in front of one of the mirrors, slipped two fingers into his waistband, and tugged hard, nearly causing Ernesto to tumble off the platform. "Please tell me we're replacing these?" he asked Mannix.

"Or taking them in at least. We'll see what kind of deal you can offer on a full package."

Ernesto didn't think that was a good idea. His mother would know right away if his clothes had been altered. There would be questions he didn't want to answer.

Luigi hummed to himself as he turned Ernesto this way and that. "Now turn around, my boy." Ernesto did and the tailor grabbed a fistful of his pants leg at the top of his thigh, cinching it together and pulling the fabric tight across his buttocks. "Oh my," Luigi said.

"I know," agreed Mannix.

Luigi let go of his pants and asked him to take off his shirt. "We'll need to see how much we need to cover and how much we can show," he told Mannix.

Ernesto wasn't comfortable with any of this. He'd never been so...assessed. But he couldn't give up on the Americans now, so he took off his shirt.

"Oh my goodness," said Luigi.

"I know," agreed Mannix.

"Well then, houseboy, you said?" Luigi asked.

"That's right," Mannix replied, "so it can't be too...obvious."

"Pity."

Once again, Ernesto had no idea what they were talking about. No one had suggested otherwise, so he shrugged back into his shirt.

"All right, hand me your trousers, and I'll pin them up." He turned to Mannix. "He can try them on, and we'll make sure they're the fit you're looking for."

Ernesto was getting tired of being talked about as if he wasn't there. "You can't alter my trousers. My mother would be upset."

Luigi and Mannix exchanged glances. "So new ones then, but you can't charge me an arm and a leg. Hans has limited funds here."

"Understood," Luigi headed to the shelves along one wall and began fingering his way through piles of folded slacks. "I think a soft cream with a front pleat?"

Ernesto assumed the question was for Mannix. "Yes, but not too much of a pleat; it's not a jazz club. And definitely light-colored. We'll want to reveal as much of his...form...as possible."

"These, I think," Luigi said, holding up a pair of soft milk-colored trousers. "With a tight, high-waisted jacket in dark orange—to bring out his eyes."

"Perfect," said Mannix.

"All right, my boy," he handed the pants to Ernesto. "Put these on and we'll get you pinned up."

"Here?" Ernesto asked. "Out in the open?"

"No one can see back here from outside. It's just us. Hop to it."

Ernesto handed the pants to Mannix to free up both his hands, and then he quickly undid his own trousers and kicked them off. He reached for the new ones but was stopped by Luigi. "Wait. That won't do at all."

"No," agreed Mannix. "No wonder you couldn't fully appreciate his form underneath the pants."

Ernesto was frozen in a half crouch. He didn't have any generalized objection to nudity, but it felt odd to be standing in front of Mannix in just his drawers when they'd only kissed once and would probably do more. Maybe.

"What's wrong?" he asked the tailor.

"It's the underwear," Mannix said. "It's hardly...stylish."

He thought of the white briefs he'd fished out of the pool. They were stylish, he supposed, but, well, skimpy. Too skimpy for his taste.

He looked down at his shorts. They were the same shapeless boxers he'd worn since he'd turned thirteen, and the kind his father wore too. True, they were gray and faded, but they were clean, and no one would see them, so what did it matter?

"They're fine," Ernesto protested. "I like them."

"Ernie," Mannix said. "They're as big as a circus tent. They'll get all bunched up under your new trousers and will look silly."

Ernesto wasn't convinced, and Mannix must have seen that. "They'll make you look sloppy. Like you're not a very neat person." That did it.

Ernesto sighed. "What would I have to wear instead?"

Luigi had already been busy making his selection, and he returned with a pair of white briefs in hand. "These," he said.

Ernesto took them and held them in front of him. Mannix grinned. "Ooh, perfect."

Ernesto hated them. They were ridiculous. They looked like Marta's panties. Thin and smooth and...small. Very small. "I'm not sure there'd be room in those for...you know...me."

"They'll stretch," Luigi assured him. "They're even able to hold Hank, here, and that's saying something."

"Barely," Mannix said.

Ernesto's brain might have overloaded then. There was just too much happening. The idea that he'd be getting new clothes he could never in a million years have afforded on his own. The thought that he'd actually have to wear those tiny briefs. The idea that Hank wore them, and the shock of how much he wanted to see that. And the further shock of what Luigi had implied about Hank, and that he'd seen Hank in the revealing briefs.

"Put them on," Luigi ordered. Hank locked eyes with him and nodded. Something passed between them. Sexual interest, yes—lust, actually—but something else too. Trust, perhaps? A promise of some sort?

"You can get changed behind that curtain," Mannix said. Ernesto realized it must have cost him a great deal to make the suggestion, and he was grateful not to have to insist on privacy.

It took Ernesto a couple of attempts before he figured out how to arrange everything to fit securely in the briefs, but in the end, Luigi had been right. They'd stretched enough to provide a sense of—if not modesty, exactly—at least coverage. Nothing was poking out, and although they were quite revealing, they weren't obscenely so, like the wet swim trunks Hank had worn.

The briefs were definitely not sufficient to hide what would happen if he kept thinking about Hank in his wet swimsuit, so Ernesto took a deep breath, steeled himself, and stepped out from behind the curtain.

"Oh my," said Luigi.

"I know," agreed Mannix.

Ernesto was embarrassed, but Hank's dumbstruck

look of appreciation also emboldened him. He felt exposed, yes, but also empowered in some way he didn't fully understand and had never experienced before.

"My God, Ernie," Hank whispered.

"Ernesto," he replied. He strode to the platform and stepped up, admiring himself in the mirror as he did so. "Let's do this," he said.

He put the trousers on, and they were tucked and pulled and pinned until Ernesto was sure they'd rip across his behind. But Mannix was providing feedback and guidance, so Ernesto let the experts do their job.

Hank and the tailor reached an agreeable price, and Luigi even included a pair of soft leather loafers that were clearly only designed for inside wear. Ernesto had never worn an outfit so fine, and he was already dreading the day he'd have to leave Casa de Ada and leave the clothes behind.

Luigi agreed to complete the alterations while they waited. "It's been an honor to work on such an amazing specimen," he'd said. Ernesto refused to wait around in his skimpy briefs, much to Hank's disappointment, so he dressed in his old clothes, and they went for a walk in the city while waiting for Luigi to finish.

"I need to make a stop," he told Ernesto after pausing outside of the local *caballito*.

"Is anything wrong?" Ernesto asked.

"No. Just making a little shakedown payment. Is that a word you recognize?"

Ernesto thought he did. But he was surprised the white Americans had to do it too. "I thought it was just us," he said.

"Oh no, we've been paying ever since we landed in Havana. It's not actually due yet, but I don't want our friendly officer showing up when Arthur and his boss are here. Hans has enough to worry about."

Ernesto thought about the visit they'd received at the factory just a few days ago, and how it had been a surprise to have the money demanded so early. "This is smart," he said to Hank. "They showed up early at my family's house."

Mannix frowned. "Wait here," he told Ernesto.

When he returned fifteen minutes later, his frown had only deepened. "Let's go," he said. Something about his tone warned Ernesto against asking questions.

Back at the tailor's, Ernesto tried on his new outfit and attempted to hide his excitement. Vanity was unattractive, but as he studied himself in the mirror, he couldn't help but admire how incredible he looked. Yes, the pants were too tight, but they weren't uncomfortable. He only perceived them as too tight because they highlighted the shape of his privates, but again, not obscenely so, just more than Ernesto was accustomed to seeing on men.

"Beautiful, yes?" asked Luigi.

"So much more than that," replied Mannix.

And the square, short jacket covering a finely woven shirt *did* end up making Ernesto's amber eyes seem larger, although he couldn't understand how that happened. He smiled to himself in the mirror.

"Um, listen," Mannix began. "I know we agreed to a final price, but I just visited the *caballito*, and—"

Luigi held up a hand. "Say no more." He tore his gaze

away from Ernesto. "They demanded more than they should have, didn't they?"

Mannix nodded.

"It's this damned coup. Everyone is trying to grab what they can before things settle." He looked back at Ernesto and smiled in a sad way. "Hopefully, they *will* settle." Luigi handed Mannix a bag containing Ernesto's street clothes.

"I'll bring the rest tomorrow," Mannix said as he handed over a folded stack of bills. "If that's okay?"

Luigi put his hand on Mannix's back. "Only if you promise to describe the look on Hans's face when he sees our boy here."

*

CASA DE ADA was quiet when Mannix and Ernesto walked into the parlor. Mannix placed the bag of clothes on the floor near the end table where Ernesto's box of ci-gars sat.

"I guess Mr. Cordero managed to get everyone out."

"Listen, Ernie, if you're going to work with us, you have to stop using last names all the time. It's Tony, not Mr. Cordero, and Hans, not Mr. Schmidt. Well, most of the time."

"All right," said Ernesto, "but about the names we use for each other, I really—"

"There you are." The most elegant woman Ernesto had ever seen walked into the parlor. "I thought I'd been abandoned."

Hank smiled broadly, then wolf-whistled, which

stunned Ernesto. How could he make such a rude sound to such a...such a...

"Ada." Hank smiled and held his hand out to her.

She offered her own hand to Hank, and Ernesto could barely breathe. The owner! Where had she come from? Where had she been?

Mannix kissed her outstretched hand.

She held herself with such grace and refinement, Ernesto was immediately reminded of a movie he'd seen last year. What was it? A rich young woman, just like this. *The Philadelphia Story*! That was it. Ada was exactly like Katharine Hepburn.

She turned her gaze toward him, and Ernesto could only stand and stare in awe.

"Sweet Jesus, Hank," she said. "That's...he's...*my God.*"

"I know," agreed Mannix.

Wait, Ernesto knew that voice. It was a different tone, lighter and more refined, but he knew it. But from where? He'd remember meeting such a glamorous woman.

"Those trousers! Turn around, dear," she said, twirling her finger in a circle to illustrate her command.

As if under a spell, Ernesto did.

"Extraordinary. Well done, Hank. I hope you gave Luigi a bonus."

"I think he got his money's worth," Mannix said.

The mysterious woman and Hank stood quietly for a moment, admiring Ernesto. He still couldn't quite believe his own transformation and the effect he seemed to now have on people. He was embarrassed by the attention, but a little bit invigorated too.

The woman smiled at Mannix and tilted her head toward Ernesto. "Well?" she asked.

"Of course," said Mannix. "Where are my manners?" Ernesto knew Hank well enough to see that he was hiding something. A secret perhaps, but a...good one. Maybe? He could barely contain his smile. "Miss Ada Werner, may I introduce your stunningly handsome new house-boy, Ernesto Ruiz."

So, Hank does know my name!

She held her hand out to Ernesto, and he took it, holding it for just a few seconds as he'd seen Mannix do moments ago.

She cocked her head and said, "Goodness, the penny still hasn't dropped, has it?"

Wait, that sounded exactly like... But how could...?

"And after all the time we spent together in this very room as I grilled you about your intentions toward our Hank, here."

Mr. Schmidt! *Dios mio*, Schmidt was Ada, or Ada was Schmidt, or...or...

"Mr. Schmidt, I—" he stammered.

"No, Ernie," Mannix said. "It's only Ada, or Miss Werner when she's like this. Never anything else. Do you understand?"

No. Not even a little bit. But he could follow instructions. "Yes, sir," he said to Mannix. "Yes, Miss Werner," he added with a nod to Hans.

"Good," said Ada. "Now, when Arthur and Mr. Denton arrive, bring them anything they ask for, but otherwise, just stand quietly in the corner and look handsome."

"Yes, Miss Werner." And for the first time in his life, Ernesto realized he really could simply stand and look handsome, just like the white twins.

"Can I squeeze into the corner with him?" Mannix asked.

"Hank, I'll have none of your monkey business. Hopefully, they'll be in and out in minutes and I can relax." Ada patted her hair to make sure it was in place. Unlike Katharine Hepburn, Ada's hair—well, wig, Ernesto realized, although it was impossible to tell—was blonde, and fell in soft, loose curls to her shoulders. "You are staying, aren't you, Hank? I need your support."

"Of course I'll stay, Ada. But let's not call too much attention to me. I know Arthur is CIA now, and the FBI is different, but I didn't leave the Bureau on the best of terms."

FBI! That hadn't come up during the disastrous getting-to-know-each-other conversation in the car.

"FBI? When—" Ernesto began.

"No time for questions right now, Ernie," Mannix said.

"That was a long time ago, Hank. And I hate to say it, but with Ernesto in the room, I don't think there will be too much attention called to you at all."

"Ouch. If you weren't a dame, I'd sock you."

Ada pretended to be shocked, but before they could continue their banter, the door in the front hallway opened.

"How do I look?" Ada whispered to Mannix.

"Ravishing," he said and kissed her cheek.

Ernesto felt a confusing mix of jealousy and fondness. He had no time to process any of it before two men stepped into the room.

"Arthur, darling," Ada said by way of greeting as she approached with both hands held out. The man who must be Arthur took the offered hands and even dared to press a kiss to Ada's cheek.

"Ada," he said. "You look gorgeous. This is the man from work I've told you about, Peter Denton. Peter, this is Miss Ada Werner, the extraordinary woman I go on and on about whenever I have the chance."

"Yes," Ada said. "You must be the one who keeps Arthur away from Cuba for far too long." She offered a hand to Denton, who took it and actually *kissed* it, as if Ada were royalty. Ernesto wondered what the man would do if he knew the truth.

"It's a great pleasure to meet you, Miss Werner. And now I see why Mason always wants to return to Havana."

Behind Denton, Mannix rolled his eyes, and Ernesto fought a smile.

"Please, you must call me Ada." She held her arm out toward Mannix. "This is Hank Mannix, my house manager." Ernesto saw Arthur roll *his* eyes. But then Mason's gaze shifted to Ernesto, and they widened slightly. He quickly looked away and turned toward Hank, but not before Ernesto registered the appreciation in his glance.

"Mannix," Mason said with a nod.

"Mason," acknowledged Mannix.

Mason. That must be Arthur's last name. "Please, gentlemen, have a seat," Ada said. "Can I get you anything? Coffee?"

Ada glanced at Ernesto to indicate he should be pre-pared to bring coffee in if they asked for it.

"Whiskey, if you have it," Denton said.

"Certainly," Ada said. Ernesto was relieved to see Hank give him a slight shake of his head. Ada would han-dle the drinks. She walked to the sideboard and poured whiskey into two tumblers, which she then placed on the round table between the wing chairs occupied by Arthur and Mr. Denton.

"Thank you, dear," Arthur said.

"To the beautiful Miss Werner," Denton said, lifting his glass and tilting it toward Ada. "Thank you for looking out for our Arthur here. He won't have much free time soon, though. We're opening a permanent location in Ha-vana, and Arthur will be in charge there with more agents to oversee."

Ada schooled her expression. Obviously, this was news to her.

"And," Denton continued, "now that I'm in Cuba, how about we enjoy a nice Cuban cigar?"

Ada, Hank, and Arthur all glanced at the empty glass cigar jar on the sideboard. Ernesto had noted it with dis-approval when he'd first entered the room. It wasn't a proper humidor, and it was no place to store a fine cigar.

"Um, I may have left a cigar or two in my desk drawer..." Arthur said.

Ernesto and Denton cringed. A cigar left in a drawer? For days—maybe even weeks? It would be ruined.

Without pausing to think about what he was doing, Ernesto walked to the cigar box his father had given him and brought it to Denton. He held the box in front of him, allowing Denton to admire the fine artwork Marta had put into its design, then he lifted the hinged lid and offered the neatly arrayed cigars for Denton's inspection. "Sir," he said.

"Oh, that's beautiful." He studied the intricately detailed illustration on the inside of the box. "Ruiz, is it?" he asked, reading Ernesto's family name emblazoned on the crest.

"Yes, sir." He continued to hold the box open for Denton, allowing the man time to make his selection. He ran a finger lightly across the row of cigars. "Oh, I see. It's like a sampler arranged by color. Very clever."

He selected the darkest cigar on the end, lifted it from the box, and ran it under his nose, sniffing deeply. "Beautiful," he said again. "I love a good maduro." He studied the band. "I've never heard of the brand before."

"It's brand new," Mannix said. "A small-scale, boutique-type thing. I've been to the operations personally to ensure the cigars are of the highest quality. We've just started offering them to our guests."

Ernesto marveled at Hank's ability to lie without actually lying.

Ada and Arthur were perfectly still, as if any false move could expose the layers of sham that were happening in the room.

"Does anyone have a cutter?" Denton asked.

"Um, I think maybe in my room—" began Arthur.

"Tucked into the side wall of the box, sir." Ernesto tilted the case to reveal the tightly stitched pocket on the outer wall. "There is a *cortapuros*..." He struggled to remember the English word. "A guillotine, yes, in the pocket."

Denton fingered the small metallic cutter out of its slot. "Now that *is* clever!"

Ernesto noted with approval that Denton first dampened the cap end of the cigar in his mouth before removing just a sliver of the tip with the guillotine. While Denton was preparing his cigar, Ada managed to find a box of matches in the sideboard drawer, but she seemed not to know how to proceed from there.

Before she could hand the matches to Denton, Ernesto took them, lit one, and held the flame about two inches below the foot of the cigar. Denton smiled and slowly turned the cigar above the flame. After a moment, Ernesto blew out the match and struck another, repeating the process as Denton continued to rotate the cigar.

"This boy knows what he's doing," Denton said to Ada. Ernesto swelled with pride, and Hank looked at him like he was considering collecting all the kisses due immediately—and then some. "I should bring him back to Washington."

Hank's look shifted into something else, something far more protective and *claiming*. It shot a thrill through Ernesto.

With the third match, Denton finally assessed the tip of the cigar, concluded it was evenly glowing, and drew in a small amount of smoke, which he allowed to settle in his mouth before drifting out. "Glorious," he said.

Ernesto offered the box to Arthur, who selected a cigar at random and tried, with limited success, to parrot the motions his boss had gone through. Hank waved him off when he offered the box, then cleared his throat meaningfully when Ernesto turned to do the same for Ada. Of course, a woman wouldn't be offered a cigar.

"Can we get these in the States, Mason?" Denton asked.

"Um…"

"Not yet, sir," Mannix cut in. "The family is just now exploring options for the export market. They're still researching distribution channels, exclusive markets, that sort of thing."

He took three soft puffs from the cigar, then leisurely let the smoke escape. "Well, I'd like to see these in Washington. The tobacco is excellent, and the box is a work of art. And it's so clever to include a small guillotine with the package." He studied the wrapper leaf and band. "What does a box like this sell for?"

Hank and Ernesto exchanged glances.

"The family is still researching the market pricing, sir. They want to make sure to get it right."

"A family-run operation, is it? That can be good for quality control." He motioned to Ernesto to bring the box back to him.

"Oh yes," Mannix said, clearly warming to his new role of promoting the Ruiz's family business. "It's totally integrated, too, from tobacco field to cigar box—all the same family. In fact, I spent some time on the farm just this week, assessing the operations."

Echoes of "*The movie star has the shits*" ran through Ernesto's mind, and he stifled a laugh.

Denton rested his glowing cigar in the heavy glass ashtray Ada had scrambled to find and place on the table.

He examined the lid and the latch keeping it tightly closed; then he studied the interior artwork more closely. "This is marvelous. There seems to be some sort of foil inlay in the letters of the family name."

That is very observant, Ernesto thought. Marta collected bits of scrap foil and used them very sparingly to provide a hint of *el brillo*—a shine—to bring the colors to life. And it was all drawn by hand. Ernesto smiled, anticipating how much Marta would enjoy learning about this conversation.

"Cigars of this quality, once there's some brand recognition, would get at least fifty cents per cigar, maybe even seventy-five. But the whole box, with this stunning artwork... I think you could sell it for eighteen, maybe even twenty dollars." He handed the box back to Ernesto and picked up his cigar, taking two more slow puffs. "The fellow who designed this has a real talent."

"It's a girl," Mannix said.

"Really?" Denton seemed surprised. "Well, it's good for a woman to have a skill, I suppose."

Ernesto was quickly running through calculations in his head. They only received five cents per cigar from the wholesaler they sold to. Imagine ten times that! Of course they'd have to create a lot more boxes; nearly all of their product was currently sold in bulk. The few boxes the wholesaler took only brought them a few dollars each.

And they didn't have a ready supply of them. His father had thrown together this selection at the last minute.

It would take time, and Marta couldn't do all the boxes by herself, but was it possible? And what about branding? Once again, Ernesto yearned for a university education so he would know about these things.

Denton let the ash grow to about an inch before he placed the cigar in the ashtray and gave it one tap with his finger. The ash column fell apart as it dropped. He picked up his whiskey and swirled the glass. "You seem quite informed about the cigar industry, Mannix. Do you have many contacts with local business people?"

Ernesto thought that was unlikely. He suspected he and Eduardo were the only two Cubans Hank knew.

Hank must have reached the same conclusion. "At the university, perhaps."

The cigar smoldered in the ashtray, its sweet scent filling the room in a blue haze. Denton finished his whiskey and pointed at Mannix with his glass. "Contacts at the university could be useful too. Lots of radical agitators there."

Batista had said something similar. What did these Americans think was going to happen?

"All right, Mason, finish up." Denton took three heavy puffs on his cigar. "We need to get your little lady out on the town." Ada smiled brightly, but Ernesto was becoming familiar with these strange men at Casa de Ada, and he could see how fake it was.

Mason ground the burning tip of his cigar against the bottom of the ashtray, demonstrating he had no idea what he was doing. Denton frowned at him. "Maybe we'll need to start up some courses on cigar etiquette back in DC."

Ada's smile grew more brittle.

Denton finished his cigar with one last deep inhalation, then left the stub on the ashtray to burn itself out.

"Let's go explore these casinos I've heard so much about."

*

AFTER THE OTHERS left, Ernesto realized he was alone with Hank. No one was throwing up, or offering them churros, or wrecking the car. It was just the two of them.

"Follow me," said Mannix. He stood, picked up the bag he'd placed by the door earlier, and walked out of the parlor, leaving Ernesto no choice but to trail behind along the hallway. They stopped next to a door which he suspected was where Hank and Mr. Cordero slept. He knew they slept in the same room. Hans had told him that much during his interrogation.

But he trusted Hank, and Hank had told him he didn't have that kind of relationship with Mr. Cordero.

Still, when they entered the room, it was uncomfortable to see the small beds so close together, the single chair and shared bureau. A pile of clean and folded undershorts on one of the beds could have been either man's, and that was somehow disconcerting too.

Mannix placed the bag on the bed by the window. "Your clothes." Hank's bed looked nothing like the fantasy he'd had of the white silk sheets draped around Hank's naked form. It was small and sagged in the middle, and even though the sheets were pulled across the top, they were rumpled and sloppy.

Ernesto eyed his bag of clothes. He knew he couldn't bring his uniform home. There would be far too many questions. But he hadn't thought about the mechanics of where to change or how to store his new clothes when he wasn't here working.

And now here he was in Hank's bedroom—just the two of them.

"Ernie," Hank said. He moved closer and took Ernesto's hands in his. "I *need* to kiss you. Right now. Please, let me have that."

"Yes, Hank. I'd like that."

Mannix pulled him into a tight embrace. Ernesto thought it would be sweet and sensual like the promise of the nearly chaste kiss when they'd changed the tire. But it wasn't. Not at all. It was as if Hank needed to draw Ernesto's very breath into his own body—as if he needed to consume him.

It was dizzying, and after a moment, Ernesto braced his hand against Mannix's chest and pushed for space to breathe.

"God," Mannix said, panting, "that asshole is *not* taking you back to Washington."

"No, he's not," agreed Ernesto. He tilted his head forward to continue the kiss, but Mannix held him away, just inches from his lips.

"You're *mine*, Ernesto. No one else's. Do you understand that?"

It was aggressive and assertive, and Ernesto liked it. He couldn't imagine being anyone else's. Mannix's arms trembled with the effort to hold Ernesto at a distance.

"Yes, Hank. Only yours."

It must have been what Mannix needed to hear because after that Ernesto was consumed by Hank—his mouth, his hands, his entire body wrapping around Ernesto, pushing him up against the wall, enveloping him.

After what could have been minutes, or maybe hours, they broke apart, dazed. Mannix held Ernesto's shoulders as they both took deep, heaving breaths. "Do you remember the day we met in the garden?" Mannix asked.

The shame of that moment came flooding back to Ernesto. How foolish he had been to think what Ivan allowed men to do to him for money could have possibly interested Hank. "Yes, I remember. And, Hank, I'm so—"

"Shh." Mannix pulled him into a kiss and then released him. "I'm going to do what I was too stupid to do then." He sank to his knees and reached up to finger the button on Ernesto's far-too-tight trousers. "I'll stop if you want me to, but, Ernie, I'm dying here. I'm about to explode. I *need* to have you."

Could this really be happening? What he'd longed for? What he'd dreaded?

Mannix popped the button and tugged the pants down his thighs. Ernesto thought of the desperate young men he'd seen along the malecón, the shorts he'd fished from the pool, the sordid nature of what Ivan did in the gardens. He let out an anguished sound and looked down into Mannix's eyes.

Hank must have seen the anxiety on his face. "It's just us, Ernie. None of the rest of it matters. This is you and me." He stroked his thumb across the front of Ernesto's briefs, which clearly could no longer contain him. "I know you want this. Let me give it to you."

Yes, just us. Ernesto nodded.

Mannix pulled the briefs forward to release Ernesto. Then carefully rolled them down. "Jesus, Ernie. Look at you! We're lucky these didn't rip. Hans would kill me."

"Enough about Hans, Hank."

"Right." Mannix looked up at Ernesto, and if a man could come undone just by the intense longing in another man's eyes, Ernesto would have finished right there. But he didn't have the chance because suddenly his world shrank to nothing more than warmth and moisture, Hank's tongue and fingers. Time stopped and rushed forward simultaneously.

Had he tried to warn Hank as the end neared? He couldn't remember. He'd been in some transcendent space he'd never visited before but vowed to return to. Already, mere moments after it was over, with deep, echoing pulses still thrumming through his body, the intensity of the experience was slipping from his memory. Could it really have been that glorious?

He realized he was moaning, loudly, and that Hank was making his own strangled sounds of pleasure, even with his mouth clamped tightly around Ernesto. Hank's hair was wrapped between his fingers, and Ernesto was *pulling* it, hard.

"*Dios mio!*" He released his grip. "*Lo siento tanto.*"

Mannix pulled off Ernesto with a wet *plop*. "Yes, to whatever you just said." He wiped the side of his hand across his mouth and chin.

His legs were trembling, and even though it was warm in the room, the air felt cold against his exposed, damp privates. Mannix rose unsteadily to his feet and pulled Ernesto into a tight embrace. "Thank you, Ernesto, for allowing me to give you that," he whispered into his ear.

So that's *what it takes to get him to use my name.*

He was returning to his senses and aware that his pants were at his knees and his briefs were still coiled around his thighs, at risk of being dripped on. But Mannix was still fully clothed, and shouldn't he…reciprocate?

"Hank, I don't know what to do…"

"Nothing, Ernie." *So, they were back to that.* "You don't need to do anything. That train has left the station, I'm afraid."

Ernesto didn't know the phrase, but he saw the wet stain spreading on Mannix's crotch and understood. "The things you do to me, Ernie." Mannix shook his head. "I'd love nothing more than to climb into that bed with you and do it all over again."

Ernesto thought he *could* do it all over again—even this soon afterward—and what a surprise that was.

"But we need to get you cleaned up and safely home."

Home to his parents. Would they be able to tell just by looking at him? Would the torcederos see it in him tomorrow and snicker? Did he do something shameful? It hadn't felt shameful. It had felt…honest…and true.

"I see you in your head there, Ernie, fretting and worrying." Mannix took a cloth from a drawer and handed it to Ernesto. He stripped off his own trousers and bent to pull on a clean pair. He had an extraordinary backside, and Ernesto decided that, yes, he could very much do it all over again, right now.

But Hank was right. There was no time. He hurried to pull his old clothes on.

"Stop overthinking it." Mannix folded Ernesto's new clothes into a pile and placed them on top of the bureau. "If you want to be the fellow who thinks things through, figure out when we're going to find the time to do this again."

Ernesto smiled. He could do that.

Chapter Sixteen

"ARE YOU SURE you won't come with us?" The men from Allentown were standing in the foyer, packed bags at their feet, waiting for the taxi that would take them to the steamship dock. Matt shook his head, and Mannix fought back a laugh.

It was Saturday, and Matt was waiting for Eduardo to come pick him up for another day of sightseeing. Or so he said. Mannix had his doubts about what the pair actually got up to, but he didn't think they did much sightseeing.

"It's a nice big ship, very stable. We'll rub your back if you feel sick."

Mannix would be glad to see the backs of these fellows. It had been a long two weeks. Still, they were regulars, and they'd be back again next year, so Mannix managed a polite smile. "Maybe you can write to him?" he suggested.

"Oh yes, dear." One of the men removed a sheet of paper from the stack on the reception desk and took a pencil from the tray. "Write down your address." He held the sheet out to Matt. Before Matt could ruin the moment by saying he'd rather curl up into a vomiting ball on Alan's yacht than give these two his home address, Mannix interceded and took the paper.

"He'll be staying here while he's at university. We'll make sure he gets any letters."

The men from Allentown frowned but must have realized they'd come to the end of the line with Matt. "Very well. And Mr. Mannix, are you certain an unclaimed pair of white briefs haven't shown up anywhere? They were quite expensive, and I bought them especially for this trip."

"Sorry. No, haven't seen them." That was a lie of course. Ernesto had told him what had happened after they'd been lifted from the pool. *Ivan will get a lot more action out of them than you ever would have.* But that was an uncharitable thought; poor Ivan had sunk to the lowest depths a human could reach, assuming he was still alive. He offered a silent apology to Ernesto for thinking such a thing about his cousin. "If they show up, we'll keep them safe for next year."

A honk announced the arrival of their taxi. *Honk.* Mannix smiled, thinking of how Ernesto pronounced his name. He helped the men out with their bags and breathed a sigh of relief when the car drove off. They were the last of the guests departing this Saturday. A new crop would be arriving late in the afternoon.

The housekeeping service was busy inside with towels and linens, and Ernesto and Hans were hard at work too, ensuring the rooms had their ashtrays and matches, books and pamphlets with local recommendations, discount coupons to the casinos and maps of the city.

Ernesto had brought ten boxes of his best cigars to display and sell in the parlor. Denton had assured them he'd take three more when he left in a few days.

Matt, meanwhile, was doing nothing of use. To be fair, Alan had prepaid for the room through that morning, so technically, Matt was still a guest. But it rankled nonetheless. For some reason—and not the obvious one—Hans seemed unusually fond of the boy and had worked out some sort of arrangement for Matt to pay his way from what the *Pumped* photographers were paying him to model for them.

Mannix suspected it didn't cover the cost of a room, but Hans said the entire arrangement was good for business. "And after all, something has to keep the customers coming now that you're...maturing."

Mannix was too excited about the afternoon ahead to let his annoyance ruin his mood. Ernesto had told his father about the American's interest in the Ruiz cigars, and despite his misgivings, Mr. Ruiz had permitted Ernesto to return to his morning schedule working at Casa de Ada and had agreed he could spend all day working at the guesthouse on Saturdays.

Mannix and Ernesto hadn't managed to find any time alone since their first encounter in the bedroom, but Mannix had high hopes for later in the day. If Ernesto was going to be here all day, he'd surely have a break at some point—maybe even be able to stay for a while after his work was done.

The front door opened and Eduardo strode in.

Matt's face lit up, and Mannix wondered if he looked as sappy whenever he spotted Ernesto. Probably. "Mannix," Eduardo said by way of greeting. He smiled at Matt. "New Mannix." He never got tired of that.

"Doctor Doolittle," Mannix replied. It made no sense as a nickname; it was merely silly and childish, but it annoyed Eduardo to no end, and ever since Ernesto's parents mistook Eduardo for a real professor, Mannix had decided to use it.

The Cuban sighed. "I almost miss 'Eddie.'"

"Never mind him," Matt told Eduardo. "Let's get out of here. Can we go to the protest on campus?"

"Matt, no," Eduardo said, even though it clearly pained him to deny Matt anything. "We talked about this. Those demonstrations are dangerous, and I can't be seen mixing with radicals."

"They're not radicals," Matt complained. At Eduardo's raised eyebrows, he added, "Well, maybe some of them are. But mostly we just want to protest the canceled elections."

"We?" Mannix asked.

"Yes, Pops, *we*." Golden Boy seemed to be itching for a fight. "All the workers of the world need to unite."

"I thought you said it was about the elections," Mannix pointed out.

Eduardo wrung his hands. He was itching *not* to have a fight.

"It's all the same. The workers don't have any power

to change things," Matt said.

"So, the students are workers now?" Mannix asked.

"*Caballeros, por favor—*" Eduardo tried to cut in.

Mannix ignored him. "*You're* a worker, Golden Boy? Posing half-naked for the camera? Flitting around the world while your parents pay for your education?"

"Gentlemen," Eduardo said again, waving his hands. "We all work; that's not the point."

"So, what is the point, Professor?"

"Well, the Marxists think it's all about who owns the means of production. You see..." But Mannix let the man's voice fade away. He simply couldn't be expected to pay attention to anyone who used the words "means of production."

Besides, Ernesto had just passed by in the hallway, heading in the direction of his and Cordero's bedroom.

"Gotta go, gents." Mannix walked out of the room, leaving behind a tedious argument about systems of power and revolution. He headed to his room, pushed open his door, and found Ernesto sitting on the edge of his bed.

"What a pleasant surprise," he said, closing the door behind him. Ernesto smiled, but he looked nervous. Of course he always looked nervous. "I haven't stopped thinking about the last time we were here," Mannix whispered. "I can't get you out of my mind—even for an instant."

"Yes," Ernesto said. "I keep wondering if it was real."

Mannix moved to the bed and sat next to Ernesto. "Let's find out," he said and gripped Ernesto's thigh.

"I only have a fifteen-minute break."

"What? Hans works you too hard. You should revolt and take over his means...of something." He ran his hand up Ernesto's leg.

"I don't know what you're talking about." Ernesto shook his head. "Although here you are mentioning Hans again, and we're down to twelve minutes."

"Right, stand up."

Ernesto did, and Mannix flicked open the button at his waistband, then tugged the trousers down to reveal the white briefs.

"My God, I missed this," Mannix said.

"It's been less than a week, Hank." Ernesto said. Mannix was running his fingers along the waistband of the increasingly tight shorts. "But I missed it too."

The door opened, and Cordero stepped in. "Hey, Ernesto. Nice briefs."

"Cripes! Can't you knock?" Mannix exclaimed as Ernesto struggled to pull up his trousers. Clearly, he'd have to wait a bit before trying to fasten them.

"It's my room too." Cordero took a deep breath. "It smells like sex in here."

Ernesto blushed a charming deep red. "It does *not* smell like sex in here," Mannix countered. "And that's entirely you're fault."

"Can't be helped," Cordero responded, as if he hadn't just ruined Mannix's entire week. "I need to get changed." He was wearing tropical-patterned shorts and a loose T-shirt. Mannix had seen him earlier in the morning preparing the pool for the new guests. "Arthur and his asshole boss are coming over. Hans wants me to help keep them occupied."

Ernesto started to inch his way toward the door, holding his pants closed with a fist.

"Don't leave on my account," Cordero said. He stripped off his shirt and dropped his shorts, then walked to the room's tiny closet and opened the door. "I'll only be a few minutes; then you can get back to...whatever." He found the shirt he'd been looking for and removed it from its hanger.

"We only have ten more minutes," Mannix complained.

He placed the shirt on his bed and pulled a pair of slacks from the bureau drawer. "Huh. I've seen you clock in under that, Hank."

Mannix looked at Ernesto, who seemed to be puzzling through the expression. Mannix hadn't *lied*, exactly, when he'd told Ernesto that he and Cordero didn't have that kind of a relationship. But they did have a...complicated history.

Still, if Tony were to leave in, say, the next two minutes...

But it was too late. Hans came into the room.

"There you all are." He paused to take in the scene. "Well, I never thought I'd walk into a room with three men in it and find *Hank* the only one fully dressed."

Ernesto frowned.

"Oh, that's very funny," Mannix said.

"Tony, there's been a change of plans."

Ernesto finally managed to fasten his trousers. Hans shook his head. "Honestly," he muttered. "Hank, put on nicer clothes. You're coming out with us."

"What? Why?" Mannix looked at Ernesto, all his

hopes for the day slipping away.

"Because Arthur called, and now we have to go to *dinner*, and then *dancing*." He said dinner and dancing like he was anticipating a root canal. "And I need you to come with us so I don't have to listen to talk of communists all evening. Plus, you need to dance with me anytime it looks like Denton might ask. You know how Arthur hates to dance. Tony needs to stay here to check in any late arrivals."

"But...but I can stay and do that," Mannix insisted, a small flicker of hope rekindling in his breast. "And Tony's a good dancer."

"No." Hans snuffed the flame. "Leave you here alone with Ernesto? There'd be a throng of men abandoned in the parlor, looking for someone to check them in."

Ernesto's face fell. "Mr. Schmidt, please, I'd never—"

"Oh, it's not your fault, dear. Hank is a bad influence on everyone."

"Hey, now wait a—"

"And how many times do I have to tell you to call me Hans when we're not with guests?"

Ernesto nodded and looked at the floor. "Yes, sir...Hans."

Cordero buttoned his shirt, then pulled on his pants. As he moved to sit on the edge of his bed to manage his socks and shoes, he nearly collided with Matt, who pushed into the room with an overly dramatic flair.

"Eduardo just stormed out. He called me a revolutionary." He looked around expectantly for...what? Validation? Consolation? Empathy?

Mannix was annoyed the fellow was so damn attractive. The sparkling blue eyes, the muscles that just begged to burst through his shirt sleeves. And Doctor Doolittle was absolutely smitten. Mannix didn't know what other charms Golden Boy might be hiding, but the obvious ones were enough.

"It's the eyes, I think," Mannix said. Everyone looked at him.

"My *eyes* make me look like a revolutionary?"

"Um...you're doing it again, Hank," Ernesto said. "Not making sense?"

"Get used to it," Cordero said after he'd managed to squeeze through the crowd and find an open space to sit and pull on his socks.

"What I meant," Mannix said, "is that he'll be back."

"Of course he will," Matt confirmed brightly. "But listen, Hans. Now that Alan's week is up, and I've vacated the room, where should I bed down tonight?"

Hans looked about the small bedroom, and Mannix was struck once again how ridiculously crowded five grown men made it feel. But Hans's gaze was assessing, and Mannix's stomach sank to the floor.

"I suppose we could squeeze another cot in here."

*

THE PIANIST WAS working through a collection of Cole Porter classics in a soft jazz style as the orchestra was setting up.

Their little dinner party had moved from the dining room to the ballroom, and the sounds of the casino—

spinning roulette wheels, coins tumbling into slot machine hoppers, the occasional gasp of delight or groans of disappointment—competed with the piano and the conversations around them.

"Am I underdressed?" Ada asked. They were able to speak freely; Denton was off somewhere meeting with the club's owner.

"You look beautiful, darling," Mason said.

"You're the prettiest gal in the casino," Mannix confirmed, lifting his cocktail in a toast. It was a bright orange concoction Denton had ordered for them, overly sweet and complicated. He looked around at the women in the room, studying them.

Everyone seemed to be a blonde these days, except for a few bright copper-colored redheads. The jewels were large and colorful—costume, Mannix assumed, otherwise they'd be looking at millions of dollars around necks and wrists alone—and there were more than a handful of mink stoles, absurd in the Cuban heat.

"But they do all seem to be a little more...extravagant than they used to," Mannix said.

Ada nodded. "That's what I thought too."

Mason searched the room as if he was missing something. Which he was. He simply didn't notice these things. "It's all right, G-man," Mannix said. "Miss Werner assures me you have other skills."

Ada was dressed in a shimmering silver cocktail dress. It was formfitting and displayed to great advantage the padded hips Mannix had helped construct earlier in the day. It was cut in a high-collared oriental style, and Ada's platinum hair was brushed away from her face in tight waves. A small satin hat with ivory pearls completed her outfit.

The entire effect was one of understated elegance. But Ada was right—the other women here seemed to be going for gaudy display.

"It's this island. It changes people," Mannix said.

"I don't know about the whole island," Mason replied. "But the Americans who come here sure do let loose. It's nothing like this back at home."

"How are things back home?" Mannix asked. "Is it getting better? For people like us, I mean?"

"Just the opposite I'm afraid." Mason reached over and placed his hand on top of Ada's. "That lunatic in the senate, McCarthy, keeps ramping up his accusations against alleged communists and homosexuals. They've forced hundreds of workers out of government jobs by accusing them of homosexuality."

Mannix grimaced. "This obsession with sex—it's like a sickness."

"It is," Mason agreed. "And since you and I left the FBI, they've hired thousands more agents to investigate people."

In the casino, a cascade of coins on metal was followed by applause and whoops of joy as bells rang and lights flashed.

"But why are people putting up with it?" Ada asked. "Surely Americans don't want to live under that kind of constant scrutiny and fear, not by their own government."

Mason turned Ada's hand and squeezed their fingers together. "That's the worst part. People seem to have just gotten used to it somehow. When it all started back in '47, remember how it seemed so shocking to us? Now, McCarthy is pushing for public Senate hearings and people just...look away."

They sat silently for a few moments, contemplating the grim picture Mason had painted.

The piano trailed off and the orchestra's musicians began taking their seats. There was still no sign of Denton. His half-smoked cigar had gone out, and now sat propped in the ashtray, the Ruiz logo on the band reminding Mannix just how much he didn't want to be there.

Ada followed his gaze and changed the subject. "So, Hank, tell me how this boy managed to capture your heart."

"Not something I ever thought I'd see," Mason said. "That's for sure."

It was a question Mannix had been asking himself, and he still hadn't landed on a solid answer. Yes, Ernesto was sexy and smart, and yes, he reminded Hank a little of himself at that age—restless and ready for his life to really *start*.

But there was so much more, and it was hard to put his finger on.

"He...he changes me. He makes me a better person. Somehow. I don't know. Does that make sense?"

Mason shrugged, but Ada said, "Yes, Hank, it does. It's important for us to have someone we care about. It's just..." She took a sip from her drink, as another crowd from the casino pushed past their table to find spaces by the dance floor.

"Go ahead," Mannix said. "I'm a big boy. Say it."

"I don't want to see either of you get hurt. He idolizes you, and that makes sense because you're so...glamorous."

Mason covered a laugh with his fist.

"But you're also...worldly," Ada continued. "And Ernesto is innocent to the ways of men like us. Not that you'd try to hurt him, but what's going to happen when he finds out how much experience—" Mannix opened his mouth to object. "—history, then, if you prefer. He can't possibly know about your past."

"He knows enough. There's his cousin, after all, and I hinted I'd lived like that for a while."

"Still." Mason cut in. "It's awfully unbalanced, don't you think? Between the two of you?"

Mannix spun his empty glass in a circle on the tabletop. "We both kissed a man for the first time this week."

That prompted a stunned silence, and before either man could respond, Denton came back. He slid into his chair and relit his cigar. "Sorry that took so long."

"Quite all right," said Hans. "We were just catching up on local gossip."

"Speaking of the locals," Denton said. "These cigars." He studied the band. "Ruiz. Mannix, did you mention they're a local family business? Not one of the big internationals?"

"That's right." Mannix thought of the small factory with its rows of tables and the elevated chair from which Ernesto read to the workers. How much he'd like to see him do that!

"And they're looking to make a name for themselves?

Break into exports?"

Mannix stopped daydreaming about Ernesto and pulled himself back into the conversation. Something important was happening here. He could sense it.

"Yes, something like that," he confirmed.

"Well, I want to explore that further. Might be we could help each other out."

Ernesto would be nervous about that.

"What do mean, boss?" Mason asked.

"We need eyes and ears on the ground here. Someone who can keep us informed on what the workers are thinking, how much traction the revolutionaries are getting. A small factory, with an interest aligned with ours. That could be helpful. Very helpful."

"Aligned with ours?" Mason asked.

But Mannix already saw it. Who better to help the Ruiz family launch an international export business than the CIA? And in exchange, Denton would have informants in the country, close to the labor movement. Mannix suspected Ernesto wouldn't like the idea. It would make him seem too much like he was spying on his own workers.

"Yes, Mason, mutual interests," Deton said. "Did you know this casino doesn't have an arrangement with any manufacturers to sell high-end cigars? What a wasted opportunity."

Mannix watched Mason put it all together. "I see," he said. And Mannix thought he did. Given how pale Ada had become, Mannix thought she got it too.

"We could start here," Denton said. "Have the Ruiz's sell their cigars to the high rollers, let them spread the word about them back home" He looked around the table at the other men. Mannix nodded. "And if the arrangement proved useful—for us, I mean—then we could see about expanding with the cigars internationally." He waited a moment to let the others absorb the plan. "What do you think?"

"I can see how it *might* work..." Mason began noncommittally.

"Well, I...I..." said Ada. Denton didn't let her finish.

"Good. Because I just finished arranging the exclusive sales deal for the Ruiz's with casino management."

The orchestra struck up a dance number that precluded any further conversation at the table. Couples began filling the dance floor, and Denton cocked an eye at Mason. He pushed his chair from the table and stood. "And since Mason here doesn't seem to be interested in taking his little lady for a spin on the dance floor—"

Mannix jumped in before Denton could finish. "Then it looks like I'll have to do the honors." He stood and extended his hand to Ada, who accepted gracefully and allowed herself to be led onto the floor.

"Watch out for that one, Arthur," Denton said after Mannix and Ada disappeared into the crowd. "He might just try to steal Ada away from under your nose."

Chapter Seventeen

"TO THE *LEFT*," Matt said, his annoyance clear.

Ernesto spent a brief moment confirming to himself he understood left and right in English. "This *is* left," he insisted. The mattress wobbled between them as they tried to negotiate the turn into the bedroom.

"*My* left," Matt grunted.

They'd already moved Matt's meager possessions into Mannix's and Cordero's—and now Matt's—cramped bedroom. The mattress had come out of the storage closet. It was small but unwieldy enough to be difficult to maneuver through the twists and turns of the narrow hallways across the length of the inn.

Matt was convinced Eduardo would return soon, so he'd taken off his clean, pressed shirt and carefully placed it on the back of the room's only chair. Cordero was in the reception hall, ready to check in the new guests who'd be arriving soon. Ernesto was still in his houseboy uniform.

He'd have work to do after this, helping the newcomers with luggage and anything else they might require.

Ernesto was in front, and therefore walking backward, and he nearly stumbled as Matt made a final push into the tight curve through the doorway. The room's ceiling light reflected off Matt's damp, white chest. "Jesus," he said, as he dropped his hold on the mattress, leaving Ernesto leaning into his end.

Matt wiped sweat from his brow and surveyed the room. "This is grim."

Ernesto thought about how much he'd love to sleep in such close quarters with Hank. "I'm losing my grip," he said. "Where does this go?"

"There's no space," Matt complained.

Ernesto let the mattress drop. "It's going to have to block the closet door. You'll need to move it anytime someone wants to get dressed." He thought of Ivan's mattress—smaller and thinner than this one—and how he'd roll it under his bed each morning. He wanted to talk to Hank about trying to find his cousin again.

They pushed the mattress across the floor until it sat squarely in front of the closet.

"Do you think they snore?" Matt asked. Ernesto didn't know; it wouldn't be fair to judge Hank based on the noises he made all night when he was sick, so he said nothing. "Or worse," Matt continued. "You don't think they would, you know...*do anything* together, do you? Not while I'm in the room, right?"

It took a moment for Ernesto to understand what Matt was implying. At first, he was angry, but then he realized Matt might not know how much he and Hank had come to mean to each other. It was still so new and surprising even to Ernesto.

"No, of course not," he said. "Hank told me he and Mr. Cordero aren't like that. They don't do anything together. It's just for the magazine people." How had Hank put it? "They're just acting."

"Oh," Matt said, but he didn't seem convinced. "Are you sure? Because Alan seemed to think they might, and the guests here at the inn all spread the same rumors."

"Well, that's the nature of rumors, isn't it?" Ernesto felt bad for Hank, with people talking so freely about him behind his back. "And who's Alan?"

"He's the guy who brought me here. He lives in New York, and he's in the yacht race every year. He tried to convince me to go back with him when the coup happened, but he was such an asshole. And then Eduardo stepped in to save the day."

Ernesto still didn't know how to feel about that. He was happy for Matt—maybe—but resentful that the American could get a spot at the university, even if it wasn't an official slot. It just seemed unfair, and he was suddenly reminded of one of Castro's essays he'd read to the torcederos, about power and privilege.

"Anyway," Matt continued. "Alan had a friend in New York who said he saw them—Hank and Tony—doing more than they do for the cameras here. He said there were—"

"Enough," Ernesto interrupted. "They don't do anything like that, and why people in New York might think they know better is crazy. You should get sheets from the linen closet." He turned to walk away but almost ran into

Cordero heading into the room.

"Well, shit," he said, staring at the new mattress. Then he turned to Matt. "Your boyfriend's on the phone."

"See," Matt said to me. "I told you he'd—"

"No," interrupted Cordero. "Not the nice Cuban one. The asshole from New York."

"Alan? He's actually calling me? From New York?"

"I know. Crazy," Cordero responded. He was still staring at the new mattress like he hoped it would just disappear. "It must be costing him a fortune. More than most people make in a week. The bastard."

Matt hurried down the hallway.

Ernesto wrestled with asking Mr. Cordero about the rumors but decided against it. He didn't know the man well enough to ask something so personal, and besides, Hank had already said they didn't have that kind of relationship, and that was good enough for Ernesto.

"Come on," Cordero said, "Let's see what's going on."

Matt stood behind the reception desk with the telephone's handset pressed against his ear. He pulled open the narrow top drawer that held pencils, city maps, a few brochures, and casino advertisements. It also served as the lost and found drawer.

"No, we didn't find any white envelopes... Photographs? But why...? Oh, *those*... Yes, we'll check again... Mannix? Why would he care?" Matt rolled his eyes at Ernesto, then shuffled through the contents of the drawer once again.

Ivan's envelope! The one he stole.

"Well, they're not here... I understand... Yes, Alan, I'm *sure* I didn't take them." He covered the mouthpiece with his hand and whispered, "What an asshole."

"Yes, I'll ask Hans to hold them for you when we find them... Right, not Mannix... Got it. Okay, so long." He hung up the phone.

"What was that about?" Cordero asked.

"Alan can't find an envelope with photos in it. He thinks he left them here."

"Photos?" Cordero asked. Ernesto thought he looked more upset than Alan leaving an envelope behind warranted.

"Yes, pornographic photos," Matt responded. "He's such an asshole; he carries these photos around in New York and shows them off in bars, hoping to entice young men. He tried to show them to me once, but I didn't want anything to do with them."

Cordero looked suddenly pale. "You didn't see them?"

"No, why would I want to? They're illegal, you know—if what he says they show is true."

Ernesto tried not to react to what he was hearing. He didn't want to get Ivan into more trouble, but his cousin shouldn't have those pictures in his possession. If he could get the envelope back from Ivan, Ernesto decided he'd slip it into the drawer without telling anyone his cousin had stolen it.

"Why did he mention Hank?" Ernesto asked.

"He doesn't trust Mannix to hold on to them for him. I think there's some history between them," Matt replied.

"There's sure is," Cordero said. "Mannix rebuffed him, publicly, last year when Alan offered to pay him for sex."

"See," Matt said. "He's an asshole. Anyway, he's convinced the envelope is here, and when we find it, he wants Hans to hold on to it until he comes back." Matt slid the desk drawer closed. "I can't believe I ever agreed to come here with him."

Ernesto needed to get to Ivan, and soon.

*

THREE DAYS WENT by before Ernesto managed to find himself alone with Hank.

He'd just finished his morning shift and was hoping to track down Hank before having to head back for his afternoon work at the factory. He'd fruitlessly searched the house, and had just stepped into the front garden, ready to acknowledge defeat, when Hank pushed his way out the greenhouse door. He held up the tin of koi pellets, gave Ernesto a wave, then disappeared down the path into the rear gardens toward the pond.

Ernesto followed.

The farther he moved from the house, the more neglected the garden appeared. By the time he reached the koi pond, the path was nearly covered in dead leaves and fallen palm fronds. He made a mental note to speak to someone about it, but then realized he didn't know who he would talk to. Both Hank and Mr. Cordero seemed to unofficially have some responsibilities around the inn—it was Hank who had fired Ivan, after all—but it wasn't clear who was actually in charge of anything.

And besides, he didn't intend to waste any private moments with Hank discussing the state of the garden.

And there he was in a crisp blue shirt and pale linen trousers, sitting on the bench waiting for Ernesto. He was beautiful. But he was always beautiful, even when he'd been sick and vulnerable, his beauty shone through. Well, maybe not when he'd been vomiting in the car.

He made his way through the clutter to the bench. "The garden is a mess," he told Mannix. He hadn't meant to; he just couldn't help himself.

"We lost our best worker. He's moved to indoor work."

Ernesto sat next to Hank and was immediately pulled into an embrace. Mannix kissed him lightly on the lips, then said, "I can't believe how long I've had to wait to do this." He kissed him again, harder that time, then slid his hand to the top of Ernesto's thigh. "Or this," he added.

"Hank, we can't. Not here." But he didn't pull away. "It's too public."

"Public? Look at the place. Obviously, no one ever comes here." Mannix went in for another kiss, and he ran his hand low across Ernesto's stomach.

"And Mr. Schmidt would be furious if anyone found out."

Mannix groaned and sat back against the bench. "How come every time we're about to make out, someone ends up talking about Hans?"

They were interrupted by footsteps crunching through the dead leaves, and two men appeared from the garden path. Ernesto didn't know their names; they were new arrivals from a city he had a hard time pronouncing.

"Oh, we're sorry," one said. "We didn't think anyone

would be here." But they made no move to leave, and their sly grins made Ernesto think they were lying. They looked like they were waiting for…something.

"Great," said Mannix. "The men from Schenectady have arrived. Sorry, boys, nothing to see here. You should head on back."

"But we'll be very quiet," one said.

"You won't even know we're here," the other added.

"Scram," commanded Mannix, a bit harshly, Ernesto thought, but it had the desired effect. After the men from Schenectady were gone, Mannix took Ernesto's hand. "You're right though. Sex in the garden is demeaning, even for me. And certainly for you."

Still. Ernesto had been thinking about what Hank had done to him in his room for days, and he thought he'd very much like to try returning the favor. After all, he had yet to be "blinded by the full glory" of Hank, as Hank himself had put it at the farm, and if he had to be just a little bit demeaned to experience it, well…

"We could go to my room…" Hank suggested, but then quickly abandoned the idea. "But Tony or Golden Boy could be there, or worse, either of them could come in at any moment. And you don't have much time, do you?"

He didn't. He'd be expected to start reading to the torcederos right after lunch. And they were at a very exciting moment in the adventures of Don Quixote. He should be on his way back already.

"It's so unfair," Mannix complained. "How are we supposed to…do this, if we can't find time alone together?"

By "do this" did he mean…? What *did* he mean? "Hank, what *are* we doing? I mean, beyond the kissing, and…the other thing you did?" *The thing Ivan gets paid for.* But he pushed that thought aside. It was different with him and Hank.

"Well, dating…I guess. I don't know. I've never done it before."

Dating? Like what would be expected of him and Elena? But how could that be? Ernesto was quiet for a few moments while he considered what that could mean. He and Hank couldn't have Sunday dinners with family, or go to a *fiesta* together, or sit with each other at Mass.

"Are you even Catholic?" Ernesto asked.

"Seriously, Ernie?" Mannix cocked his head. "Oh, you're doing it again, aren't you? Having some internal conversation with yourself, then inviting me in at the end."

"Uh, yes. I guess." Ernesto ran his hand nervously through his hair. "It's just the word dating makes me think of going to Mass together."

"Oh, how romantic." Mannix squeezed Ernesto's hand. "Still, I'd have thought the whole 'two penises' thing would have been more of a hurdle to overcome than religion."

"See!" Ernesto exclaimed. "It's not even possible to *think* about—two men dating."

"Maybe not how you're thinking about it. Going to Mass and such. But it's perfectly possible for two men to have a relationship, to build a life together. Hans and Arthur have done it, and we have good friends back in New York who are practically mar—"

"But you're Americans, and white." Ernesto wrang his hands. "You make your own rules."

"All men can make their own rules, Ernesto."

What an odd thing to say. What an odd thing to think.

"Even in Cuba," Mannix continued. "Do you think Eddie is going start dating some girl, change who he is just so he can sit with her in a pew?"

It took a moment for Ernesto to remember Hank's nickname for Mr. Martinez. And then he remembered how he and Matt behaved together. Was that possible for him and Hank?

"No," Ernesto admitted. "I guess he isn't."

But Eduardo Martinez was an academic. Things were different for them. Probably. Although the more he thought about it, the more he realized just how little he knew of people whose lives were different from Ernesto's—academics, artists, actors, and writers, even politicians. There were *lots* of people who operated outside the rules Ernesto thought were supposed to apply to everyone.

"So...so we..." Ernesto wasn't sure how to complete his thought.

"Look, Ernie." Mannix put his arm around Ernesto's shoulder. "Let's not try to figure it all out right now. We don't need to. You want to spend more time with me, right?"

Ernesto nodded. That was very true.

"And I want to spend more time with you. You're all I think about."

Ernesto felt the same way. He nodded again.

"So, we're dating, then," Mannix concluded. "Not sitting-in-church-together dating. But we'll do it our way." He shook Ernesto's shoulder. "All right?"

Ernesto wanted to be convinced. He wanted to say yes. But he just didn't see a path forward. "But what will we *do*? How will we find time together?"

"Don't worry," Mannix said. "I have a plan." There was almost nothing Hank could have said that would have caused Ernesto to worry more.

He groaned. "Is this like your plan to visit the farm?"

"Unfair, Ernie." Mannix knocked his knee against Ernesto's. "That was as much your fault as it was mine."

"I know. I'm sorry." They both grinned at the apology.

And in the few minutes they had remaining, Mannix sketched out his plan.

*

ERNESTO HURRIED DIRECTLY home, forgoing his walk through the campus. His mind was spinning with all the implications of Hank's plan. He knew he was missing something. It didn't make sense.

Hank and Mr. Schmidt had already told him about Mr. Mason's boss asking the casino to feature his family's cigars. That was extraordinarily good news, and his family was excited to get started in the new venture. Marta had spent all her time the last few days creating new cigar boxes and redesigning the Ruiz logo for the bands.

But why would the United States Government—the

CIA, Hank said—spend money to set up a sales and storage space for Ruiz cigars at the casino? Hank had said not to worry about that part yet. Then he learned a new phrase: Don't look a gift horse in the mouth.

He liked that one.

He picked up his pace as he hurried through the city, but he tried to pay attention to the tobacco shops as he passed by. How did they display their wares? How were cigars marketed? Things were looking up for his family, and for the first time, the sting of the university's three rejections felt a little less sharp.

They were finding a way to increase business, maybe even getting a toehold in the export business—all without the expense of an advanced education.

And then there was Hank. They were dating!

A bus blared its horn as Ernesto nearly stepped in front of it, lost in thought about what it could mean that he was dating another man. An American man. It still seemed impossible, but exciting too. And the more he was around the Americans the more he understood just how men could craft lives for themselves that were very different from anything Ernesto had come to expect.

"A room at the casino, Ernie," Mannix had said, waggling his eyebrows. "Where we can be alone."

*

HE MADE IT home with only fifteen minutes to spare, just enough time to grab something to eat and drink before he took up his post in the lector's chair. The family was gathered in the office, and his mother waved excitedly to him through the glass as soon as he stepped into the factory. What looked like a cake box from *la panadería* sat on the table.

"Mijo!" His mother wrapped him in a hug when he entered the office. His first thought was that they'd received bad news about Ivan, but she was smiling and there was the cake box.

"Ernesto," his father said, "Read this." He handed him an envelope from the university addressed to Ernesto. He wasn't surprised they'd opened it. He pulled out the letter and scanned the contents. Stunned, his hands shook, and he had to drop the letter onto the table, next to the cake with *Felicidades* written across the top.

"I was accepted?" He couldn't quite believe it, not after everything that had happened.

"Oh, mijo." His mother wiped away tears. "I'm so proud of you."

He glanced down at the letter and read it again to make sure he didn't misunderstand. A clerical error. An administrative mistake.

But it was clear. He'd been approved for admission and would start at the end of the summer.

Chapter Eighteen

MANNIX THOUGHT THE situation would be humorous if it wasn't actually happening to him.

First, Cordero would let out a rumbling snore, quickly cut off by a gasping snort. That would prompt Matt, lying only four feet away on his pathetic floor mattress, to sigh in a loud, aggrieved way, mainly, Mannix supposed, to prove he was being kept awake.

Mannix would begin a silent count to ten, and somewhere around seven or eight, the process would repeat itself. It was as if the Three Stooges had picked up stakes and moved to Havana. He couldn't continue living like this.

Mannix began his count again, and at three, rolled onto his side. And then suddenly it was upon him; he thought the fart was going to be a silent one. But, no.

"Jesus Christ!" Matt exclaimed, throwing off his thin blanket.

"Huh? Wha...?" Cordero had been startled awake.

"Jesus!" Matt said again as the stench began creeping through the small room. He waved his blanket up and down. Cordero groaned.

"It was the dog," Mannix said.

Matt glowered at him, and Cordero swung his legs over the side of the bed and stood. "I'm going to hit the head while the room airs out," he said, scratching at his hairy belly.

It was remarkable, Mannix thought. Three extraordinarily attractive men in one small room, each wearing only his skivvies, and there was absolutely *nothing* sexual about it. Just the opposite in fact. Matt's hostility and resentment filled the room in a pungent cloud more toxic than Mannix's flatulence.

"You'd think three fellas on the winning side of capitalism would be able to manage better accommodations," Mannix said. And sure, he did it just to needle Matt, who'd been going on and on about the unjust plight of workers and the glory of the upcoming revolution. Golden Boy was becoming downright dull. He hoped Eddie would come groveling back soon. Matt needed a good, hard—

"Did you tell him yet?" Matt asked, interrupting Mannix's thoughts.

"Tell who what?" he asked, although he knew. They'd been over it already a few times.

"Did you tell your boyfriend he and his family are going to be used as spies for the United States Government?" Matt settled into a cross-legged position, still fanning the air with lazy flaps of his blanket.

"You're exaggerating." Mannix propped himself up on an elbow and looked down at Matt. "They stand to make a lot of money selling cigars through the casino. Can't you just be happy for them?"

"Sure." Matt plopped down onto his back. "Maybe they can force the factory workers into a third shift to keep up with demand."

"Or," Mannix said brightly, "maybe they could hire more workers and pay them more, so someday the workers will have enough money to send their children to college in foreign lands where they'll scoff at their parent's values and end up working as escorts—"

"I do *not* work as an—"

"Boys, *please*," said Cordero returning from his trip to the toilet. "Do you have to do this"—he looked at the glowing hands on the wind-up alarm clock—"at one o'clock in the morning?" He climbed back into his bed. "And why are the men from Schenectady out at the pool so late?"

Mannix knew it was a rhetorical question. He rolled onto his back and folded his arms across his chest. "I bet if you went out and joined them, Golden Boy, you could make enough money to afford your own room."

"Go to hell," Matt grumbled as he turned onto his side to face the closet door.

*

MANNIX LIFTED THE last of the cigar boxes and placed it on the ornately carved wooden table that filled the back half of the tiny office. The room was too small to have served as guest quarters. Maybe it had been a large storage closet or a small meeting room where high rollers could make private phone calls to their bankers back home.

Whatever it had been, it was perfectly positioned to be the sales office for Ruiz cigars—just off the casino floor, and on the opposite side of the facility from the dining room and club lounge. The only thing lacking was a bed, but no sense getting ahead of himself, Mannix thought. It would do for now.

"Don't you think you've been a bit hard on the boy?" Cordero asked. He was on his knees maneuvering a file cabinet into a corner next to the door. Two chairs with an end table between filled the rest of the space.

"Ernie? No."

"Not Ernesto," Cordero responded, standing up and twisting his back until it made popping sounds. "Matt. What have you got against him anyway?"

He was about to deny it, but Tony had known him too long and would see right through the lie. He surveyed the table and its neatly stacked boxes. "We'll need to leave space for humidors and ashtrays too."

"So you're just going to ignore my question."

"No," Mannix sighed. "I'm thinking."

"I thought I smelled something."

"Har-har. You're a card, Tony." It was the type of comment his best friend found hilarious, and it was— usually, mostly—endearing. Mannix plopped into a chair and looked at the empty table next to it. "And whiskey. We need whiskey in here too."

Cordero took the other seat. "Tell you what, why

don't you get whatever's bothering you off your chest, and then we'll go have a drink in the lounge. Hell, I might even drop a couple nickels into the slots on the way, and if win, I'll buy the drinks."

"You're a good man, Tony."

"And so are you, Hank. So why are you being so rough on the new Mannix?"

He grimaced. How could his life be changing so quickly? And why *was* he dumping all over Golden Boy? "I think I just…resent…how easy everything is for him." God, that made him sound so small.

"Easy compared to who?"

Right. And that was just it. He could say "Ivan," but everyone had it easier than that poor boy. Or Eddie, whom Mannix genuinely liked, and who faced challenges Golden Boy never would, like needing an escort from white Americans to come into the casino. And Matt certainly had it easier than Ernesto, who had to work so hard for everything, and wouldn't have even gotten into university if Mannix hadn't pressured Eddie into pulling some strings.

"Compared to me," Mannix admitted, which was actually—shamefully—the true answer.

"I don't understand, Hank."

"When I was his age," Mannix began, but then he realized that made him sound like one of those old men who told tales of how they walked miles to school each day. He started over. "A decade ago, when we were at war and I was a twenty-year-old desperately praying to be spared from the draft— Sorry, I know you served, and I didn't. That's awkward, isn't it?"

"Not at all. We all did what we had to do. Go on."

"Well, you'll find this hard to believe, but I was a little cocky as a young man."

Cordero spluttered. "*Was?*"

"Fine. But I didn't know my limits then and lacked any semblance of good sense." Mannix glanced at Tony to see if he'd offer any further commentary on his continued use of the past tense, but he graciously remained silent and Mannix continued.

"Anyway, I'd become estranged from my family. That's what they call getting kicked out of the house as a teenager, right?"

"I'm sorry, Hank."

"Well, water under the bridge and all that. But my point is I was living on the streets, trying to get by on my good looks and charm." He scowled at Cordero. "Don't you dare say anything to that."

Cordero smiled. "No one would deny how incredibly charming you can be, Hank. Or how good-looking you are. Still."

Mannix relaxed. "I knew I liked you for a reason." He turned in his seat to face Cordero more directly. "And, well, I did things...a lot of things...that I wish I hadn't had to do." Cordero opened his mouth to speak, but Mannix waved him off. "I'm not ashamed of my choices. I had to survive. It's just that it was *hard*—some of the things I resorted to doing."

"We've all done things we wish we hadn't had to do," Cordero said.

Mannix was sure they were both thinking of the regrettable photo shoot they'd done for the rich New

Yorker. They *never* should have had sex with each other—especially not for money; it would have been better to go hungry. Still, he was grateful their friendship had survived it.

"And here's Golden Boy, ten years later, also getting by on his looks and his charm, but *he* gets international vacations and slots at university. I *never* had those kinds of chances." Mannix could hear how petty he sounded, and he hated it. But Cordero was right; he needed to work this through with his friend.

"Well, Matt wasn't exactly living on the streets. But you're right, there does seem to be more opportunity in the world today. But that's a good thing, isn't it?"

Of course it is. What is wrong with me?

"And you know," Cordero continued. "When Hans was just a few years older than Matt is now, he was being held in a Nazi prison camp."

And what a gut punch that was. Hans had been an academic in Berlin, and a gay man. He'd been one of the last to be rounded up.

"I know. Thank you. That helps provide perspective. I'm not the center of the universe after all."

"You're the center of *your* universe," Cordero said. "But why does it bother you that Matt's here and going to university?"

Good question. Mannix knew life wasn't fair. We end up where we do through a variety of choices and luck and fate. Look at Ivan and Ernesto. He should no more be resentful of Golden Boy's good fortune than he was of Ivan's miserable circumstances.

"But Golden Boy *tries* so hard. It annoys me. He's always rubbing our faces in it. The university education, the political smarts, falling into photo shoots the way he did, manipulating Eddie into falling for him—"

"I think that's mostly on Eduardo," Cordero interjected.

"Maybe," Mannix conceded. "But he's just so...driven. So achievement oriented." Mannix said that like it was a bad thing, but he was beginning to lose the thread of his own complaint, and he wasn't making sense even to himself.

"Just like Ernesto," Cordero observed.

"Yes!" No one was more driven than Ernesto. "I mean, no."

Cordero simply waited.

Mannix tried to think it through. Even Ivan was driven in his own way. He was wrong, and a lost soul, but he still was *striving*. Trying to make something of himself. And Ernesto's uncle, with his new strains of tobacco leaves. And his parents and sister, always finding ways to improve their product, to make their lives better. Even the factory workers, eager to learn new things from Ernesto's readings while they worked.

Whereas Mannix was just...coasting along, not working hard at anything. No goals, no obligations, just...oh.

A very, *very* ugly truth dropped into place.

"My God, Tony. We're wasting our lives!"

Cordero smiled. "Yeah, that's what I've been trying to show you for a while now. We've got to get the hell out of here."

That must be what he'd meant by "it's time." Mannix

looked around the small room. "Maybe, but not yet. I *do* have a purpose now, Tony. I need to help Ernie with this. He can't do it himself."

"Don't underestimate him, Hank. Ernesto is a smart man." Cordero cocked an eyebrow. "Except for his obviously poor judgment in men."

"I *don't* underestimate him. But he's not even allowed in the casino without one of us accompanying him. And he couldn't be expected to work directly with the G-men. Even I'm not sure I'm able to figure those guys out. Why, you're the only one I know who... Hey, I have an idea."

Cordero laughed. "I figured all this out already, Hank." He punched Mannix in the arm. "Of course I'll stay long enough to help you with the G-men. It'll be like old times, like it was back in New York."

"And then I'll do something utterly unforgivable and have to flee to another country, and you'll come with me." Mannix said it in a humorous way, but there was a serious question behind it.

"Well, hopefully it won't be *that* much like our time in New York."

That wasn't an answer, Mannix realized, but he knew it wasn't time to press the point. "Let's go get that drink."

Chapter Nineteen

THE BOXES WERE works of art. Marta had outdone herself.

Ernesto ran his fingers along the exterior border of the lid, feeling the smooth edge and the snug fit. They'd been experimenting with small boxes of just a dozen cigars. "Samplers," as Mannix referred to them. It had been Ernesto's idea—to create something Americans could easily carry home with them in a bag or slipped into their luggage.

He handed the box to the American who'd come into the "cigar room"—as the casino management called the little space. The man's wife lingered in the open doorway, seemingly uncertain about entering.

Ernesto offered her a bright smile, then looked away. Mannix had tried to explain it to him once: "The women are going to be very attracted to you, Ernie. Especially in that getup." His cigar-selling costume was similar to his houseboy uniform, except instead of a short jacket he wore a snug white vest, under an open-collared white shirt that revealed a fair amount of his smooth chest and accentuated his biceps.

The trousers were much the same, excessively form-fitting perhaps, but comfortable. The entire outfit was set off by a panel of multicolored cloth wrapped around his waist. The ends tucked around each other and were left to hang from his hips.

The outfit had nothing to do with cigars—growing or manufacturing—but Hank assured him that didn't matter.

"The women won't want to appear interested," Mannix had continued, "so you need to be unthreatening. Just smile politely—nothing that will make the husbands uncomfortable. Their wives will be drawn to you like moths to a flame."

Hank had been right. And a few of the men responded the same way too.

Ernesto was still trying to settle into this new reality, where he had power over people simply because of how he presented himself. He recalled his early days at Casa de Ada and how transfixed he was when he watched Hank and Mr. Cordero grapple on the beach wearing nothing but their swimming trunks. It was as if an enormous secret had been revealed to him.

"Honey," the man called out to his wife, "come see this artwork." He opened the lid and turned the box so his wife could see the interior. She offered a tentative smile to Ernesto—they always did—and stepped closer, then drew in a breath as she delicately traced the Ruiz logo on the inside of the lid with her finger.

"Oh, that's gorgeous." She brushed her blonde hair over her shoulder and took the box from her husband. "Even the cigars look like works of art." She gave her husband a sly grin. "The Harrisons would be very envious."

"You're right," he said. "How much is it?" he addressed the question to Mannix, who so far had simply stood silently as Ernesto offered the cigars for the American's inspection. It was the arrangement they'd settled on that seemed to work best. Mannix would wander through the casino with a display box, looking for Americans who'd just won big at the roulette table or the slot machines. He'd offer a free cigar and invite them into the cigar room to learn more.

Once a potential customer was in the room, Ernesto would display the wares and describe the cigar-making process, but Mannix would handle the business end of the discussion.

Americans became uncomfortable when they were dealing directly with Ernesto in matters of finance.

"Fifteen dollars," Mannix responded. "You won't find higher quality on the island."

"Hmm," the man said. "That's awfully steep." His wife frowned.

"Nonsense," Mannix proclaimed. "Each cigar is hand rolled by a...a...what do you call them again?" he asked Ernesto.

"Torcedero," Ernesto replied.

"Right," Mannix confirmed. "Torcedero." He tapped a framed photograph on the wall. It was a picture of the workers in the family's factory. Ernesto was in it too, up in his chair, reading from a newspaper.

The Americans came closer and peered at the photo. "Why is there a fellow in a lifeguard's chair?" the man asked, as Ernesto knew he would.

"Oh, that's our young Mr. Ruiz, here." Mannix nodded at Ernesto. "He's the owner's son. He sits up there so he can read to the workers. Everyone is always trying to improve themselves here. Everyone wants to be like the Americans."

The couple looked at Ernesto and then back at the photo. "Well," said the woman.

"And this is his sister," Mannix tapped the photo next to the one of the torcederos. "She does all the boxes by hand." Ernesto marveled at how Hank managed to make that sound special, as if other cigar boxes were mass-produced in a factory somehow.

"Oh," the woman said, leaning in for a closer look at Marta among her brushes and paints.

"It's delicate work," Mannix continued. "And steeped in tradition." He picked up an empty box and held it open. "Look at the stitching on the inside lining. Why, the box itself is practically a collector's item, like those pots the Indians make on their reservations, only not nearly so expensive."

Ernesto hated that line. It made him feel like he and his family should be in a museum or something.

"Still," said the man, "fifteen dollars..." He looked at his wife, and Mannix switched tactics.

He opened the drawer in the table and withdrew two photographs. "Look," he said, lowering his voice and glancing at the open door. "If you promise not to tell anyone else, I can give you these two photos." They were similar to the pictures on the wall, only these had been taken with a Kodak Brownie camera—the kind all the well-heeled American tourists carried.

Ernesto tamped down his smile. Unsurprisingly, the photos had been Mannix's idea. They'd taken dozens of shots with Arthur's camera.

"Wouldn't it be fun to tell the Harrisons you met the young man in person?" Mannix winked at the American woman to show he was in on the game too. It wasn't really deceptive; there was a photograph, and they *had* met the young man. The fact that the American couple hadn't been to the factory and hadn't been the ones to take the photographs didn't need to be revealed.

Ernesto watched as the woman played out the scene with the Harrisons in her mind. She took her husband's arm. "Let's do it, darling. It would be such a lovely souvenir."

Hank was amazing. *Fifteen dollars*!

After the transaction was completed, Mannix escorted the couple out of the room and then turned to Ernesto. "You have no idea how much I want to close that door and ravish you on the desk."

Ernesto didn't know that word, but he agreed with the general sentiment. "I know, Hank. But we can't. We need to be here for two more hours."

"Just ten minutes..." Mannix pleaded.

"Hank...this is too important..."

"I know." He licked his lips. "But later..."

Ernesto shivered. He loved Hank this way, all insistent and needy. "Yes...soon."

They looked at each other; then Ernesto burst into a grin. "Fifteen dollars!"

They'd been open for business in the casino less than a week, and they'd made at least a dozen sales in that time, but never for more than ten dollars. Most of the time the price was nearer to six. But even at fifty cents per cigar, they were earning ten times as much as the wholesaler paid them.

If they could keep this up, Ernesto's family would be able to end the arrangement with the wholesale company altogether and be that much richer. And it could happen too. Already a few Americans had sought them out after learning about their cigars from friends.

Mannix picked up the display box. "Off to find our next victim...er, customer." He left the cigar room and disappeared onto the casino floor.

Ernesto busied himself filling a new sampler box, selecting cigars from the satchel below the table by size and color and arranging them carefully in one of Marta's boxes. He admired the stylized *R* of the Ruiz seal and had a moment of intense pride that his family's circumstances seemed to have changed dramatically and for the better.

He had his back to the door when he heard someone enter. He assumed it was Hank, perhaps with a new customer, but even as he turned, smile at the ready, the stink of gin filled the room, and he knew he was mistaken.

"Whatchya got there, boy?" the American asked as he stumbled into the room. Ernesto's gaze darted past the man to the doorway, but there was no sign of Hank.

Many of the English language's subtleties were lost on Ernesto. Hank had referred to Mr. Cordero and others at the guest house as "the boys" on a number of occasions, always, as far as Ernesto could tell, with a sense of fondness. This man's use of "boy" felt different, hostile maybe.

He recalled Ivan telling him how older Americans would search the malecón for "Cuban boys," but he meant young men, and he'd spat the term out with obvious disgust.

The American came closer. His hair was disheveled, and he took the cigarette he was smoking from his mouth, dropped it on the floor and ground it underfoot. Ernesto had known his share of drunks, and he quickly tried to assess what type of drunk this one was. He suspected he was capable of violence but hoped he could still be talked to in a reasonable tone.

"Good afternoon, sir," Ernesto said. "How can I help you?"

"I asked you a question, boy."

Ernesto swallowed. "This is where the casino sells cigars." He decided it was best to keep the focus off himself and to make this more about the casino. This was not someone he was going to explain the family business to or point to pictures on the walls of how the cigars were made.

"Nice," the drunk mumbled. He may have been referring to the cigar boxes, but he was staring directly at Ernesto when he said it. When he grabbed at his crotch and leered, Ernesto understood there'd be no talking his way out of this one. He braced for a confrontation.

"You'll have to leave now, sir," he managed. But everything started happening so quickly. The man was big—much bigger than Ernesto—and even though he was drunk, it took no coordination at all to stumble into Ernesto and push him up against the table. The drunk's face was plastered next to his own, stinking of booze and cigarettes.

Ernesto tried to shove against the man, but he was heavy, and Ernesto was leaning backward over the table with all of the man's terrible weight bearing down on him.

This can't be happening. "Sir," he said again. *Why am I calling him sir? The man is attacking me.*

The man was rutting up against him and Ernesto felt a wet tongue against his neck. In just seconds, he'd managed to unravel the cloth around Ernesto's waist. With the sickening realization that he couldn't push him away, Ernesto felt the drunk groping his crotch and yanking at the clasp holding his trousers closed. He was preparing to yell when his attacker leaned back—just far enough to reach his hand between them to undo his own trousers.

Ernesto brought his knee up, hard, and the man roared in outrage. The distraction gave Ernesto enough of an opening for a solid punch to the man's torso, just above his stomach, and the drunk collapsed, bringing several cigar boxes off the table with him.

A woman by the doorway screamed.

A casino guard rushed in and tackled Ernesto to the ground. A second guard followed and pinned Ernesto's arms behind his back, holding him firmly against the wooden floor. A cigar rolled from one of the upended boxes—a lovely amber-toned Colorado—and Ernesto watched as a guard trampled it underfoot.

His attacker sat with his back propped against the wall, ignored, catching his breath.

Mannix rushed into the room. "What the hell—?" He stopped when he saw Ernesto on the floor.

"This Cuban attacked one of our customers, Mr. Mannix," proclaimed one of the guards.

"He attacked *me*!" Ernesto exclaimed. It was hard to speak with his face pressed against the floor.

"Sure," said one of the guards.

"The fucking little *bitch*," the drunk slurred. Everyone looked at him. Ernesto felt the pressure from the guards begin to loosen as they took in the man's wild state and his unfastened trousers. The guards looked away, seemingly unsure how to proceed.

"Jesus. Cover yourself," one of them said to the drunk.

The woman in the doorway had disappeared.

"Ernie!" Mannix rushed to his side and shouldered a guard out of the way. "Did he hurt you? Are you all right?"

Mannix helped him off the floor, but Ernesto almost tripped in the tangled cloth of his uniform's sash. The drunk hadn't managed to get Ernesto's trousers opened, so he focused on retying the band, but his hands trembled too much, and he let it drop back to the floor.

"I'm fine," Ernesto managed, his voice unsteady.

The guards had the drunk's arms and were trying to lift him up, but he kept wobbling and mumbling, "Fucking little bitch."

"I'd advise you to stop talking," one of the guards said.

The casino's floor manager came into the cigar room. He took in the situation and raised his eyebrows at the American's open fly. The guards looked away. "Mr.

Mannix," he said. "Do I need to remind you that Cuban guests in the casino are only permitted if they are accompanied by an American? That you are responsible for this young man's behavior?"

Ernesto couldn't believe what the man was suggesting, and in his shock, he wondered if the claim was even true. He suspected he didn't need an American chaperone, just a white one. An Englishman might do just as well, for instance, or a Canadian.

"Really?" Mannix asked. "So, who's responsible for the molester over there?" The guards flinched, and the floor manager frowned, then looked away.

The drunk slid back to the floor, leaned over, and vomited.

Mannix put a hand on Ernesto's elbow. "We're leaving." He turned to the guards. "Don't forget to lock up after you've cleaned up the mess."

*

"DID HE HURT you?" Mannix asked again once they were outside. It was a warm evening, and Ernesto sucked in deep breaths of the thick humid air. A mosquito buzzed nearby, and Mannix slapped at his cheek.

"No. My arm hurts a little, from the guard."

"I'm so sorry this happened. I shouldn't have left you alone."

That was absurd. Why should Ernesto not be able to be left alone? What was wrong with these people?

"Come on, let's get you back to the inn." Mannix took Ernesto's elbow again and began to point him toward the street. "I'll fix you a drink."

"No," said Ernesto. "I want to head home. I feel like a walk."

"But, Ernie—"

"My name is Ernesto." He shook off Mannix's hand and walked away.

*

THE FAMILIAR SIGHTS and sounds of Havana soothed Ernesto as he made his way home. Music, everywhere and always. The spicy aroma of roasting meats, the laughter of young people, the blare of horns, the choking exhaust of the buses. It all relaxed him, reminding him he wasn't one of them—the violent and frenetic Americans who made no sense.

Mannix had said all the Cubans wanted to be like them. Ernesto thought he was wrong about that. Sure, it would be nice to have the money, and all the things he read about in the newspapers: the cars and cameras, the dishwashers and televisions. But what was the point of such good fortune when they didn't even see it was theirs?

What do they want? Why are they here?

He could still feel the drunk's body rubbing against his, still smell the foul breath.

He wasn't in a hurry, so he took the long way home, making his way along the malecón, keeping an eye out for Ivan. He'd left his colorful waistband behind, and he must have seemed like an apparition, all in white, totally at odds with the vibrancy around him. A few young men cast appraising looks his way. Was he a performer? Competition?

The Americans drove by in their big cars. More than one slowed and stared.

What did the drunk see when he looked at me? Why did he think he could do that to me? Did he think I would welcome it?

Suddenly, everything about Casa de Ada felt... tainted. The films and the photographs, the late-night pool parties. The drinking. The men.

Did they all see me that way, as an object to be used on a whim?

He became uncomfortable with how he was dressed—the revealing trousers and tight vest—and he picked up his pace. It wasn't normal, this life he'd fallen into.

*

WHEN HE WENT to bed, he left his window open so the sounds of the city would fill the room, grounding him. It was hours before he fell into a troubled sleep. His mind replayed the events of the day, serving up a confusing mix of images: Hank kissing him, the drunk groping him, Ivan, Hans.

"*Primo*," a voice whispered. A hand shook his shoulder, and the stench of an unwashed body filled the room. Ivan. He was squatting on the floor next to Ernesto, his face only half visible in the dim light.

"Ivan?" he glanced at the open window, piecing together how Ivan had entered. "You climbed through the window?"

Ivan didn't bother answering. "I saw you today," he said. "Are you working the malecón now?"

His breath smelled nearly as bad as the rest of him. Ernesto fumbled for the lamp on the bedside table and worked the switch. They both squinted against the sudden brightness.

Ivan looked awful. He'd always been wiry, but now he looked as if he might be starving. His eyes were hidden deep in their protruding sockets. Even his nose seemed bony.

"Ivan." Ernesto could barely breathe. "My God."

"Are you?" Ivan pressed.

"What?" Ernesto played back the question Ivan had asked. "No!"

"You were dressed like a whore," Ivan accused.

"Ivan, no. I was looking for you." Ernesto reached out a hand, but Ivan leaned back.

"There're rules, you know, about where you can work, who you have to pay. If you want, I can help you." Ivan leaned forward again, and Ernesto saw how bloodshot his eyes were. "Be careful. They *lie*, primo. The Americans. Even when they don't have to."

Ernesto leaned away. He didn't want to, but Ivan's breath drove him back.

"They'll tell you that you don't have to do something, but then they make you do it anyway. Or they'll tell you they'll pay you, and then they don't."

Oh, Ivan. Ernesto braced himself and reached out to clasp his cousin's shoulder.

"No. I can help *you*, Ivan. For real now. Business is

good. We're selling to the Americans." Ernesto needed to rush forward, get it all out before Ivan disappeared again. "But I need that envelope with the pictures you showed me. It can get you in trouble, Ivan."

"It's hidden, I'm going to sell them."

"No, Ivan, it's too risky. Listen, I visited your parents. They're worried about you. Elana was asking about you too. I have work at the casino now. I could get you—"

Ivan spat onto the floor. It was shocking and disgusting.

"Listen to you, *primo*. The casino. The lying Americans. They're devils. They're killing us."

Once again, Ernesto felt the drunk's hands groping him, the wet lick of his tongue across his neck. He couldn't let that happen again. He couldn't become like Ivan.

Ivan climbed onto the chair under the window. He was leaving. "A storm is coming, primo. The devils will be swept away. And so will the Cubans who help them." He pulled himself onto the windowsill and swung halfway through. He looked like a skeleton climbing back into its coffin. "Find me when you're ready."

Then he disappeared into the night.

Chapter Twenty

"OH, COME ON, Tony. You have to help; there's no one else." Mannix handed Cordero a beer and took the seat next to him.

They were all in the parlor—Mannix and Cordero, Hans and Mason, even Matt—and Mannix had just finished filling everyone in on what had happened earlier in the evening at the casino. "Are you sure the boy's all right?" Hans asked again.

"No, I'm not. He said he was fine, but he didn't want to talk to me, and he seemed awfully out of sorts." Mannix took a swig of his beer.

"Well, who wouldn't be after being attacked?" Mason asked. He was squeezed into the corner of the love seat and Hans was tucked up against his side. Mason was massaging Hans's shoulder. Hans looked so much better now that Arthur was home. More relaxed, more himself.

He thought he might be beginning to understand

what it is to have someone else complete you like that.

"But you didn't actually see the attack, right?" asked Matt. He was sitting by himself at the small card table, flipping through his Spanish language workbook. "Maybe Ernesto was too friendly or didn't reject the guy's advance at first."

Mannix was about to bite Matt's head off, but Hans beat him to the punch. He rose from the love seat, pulled his silk shawl tight about his shoulders, then thrust a finger at Matt. "Mr. Lansing, I know Eduardo is fond of you, and I trust his judgment, but let me tell you this quite clearly. If you *ever* engage in victim-blaming again in my house, you will *not* be welcomed here." Matt blinked, and Hans held his gaze firmly.

"Do I make myself clear?"

"Yes, Hans." Matt swallowed. "I'm sorry. I wasn't thinking."

"No, you weren't." Hans returned to Mason's side. "It's bad enough men like us are met with suspicion and mistrust by the rest of the world, I will *not* have that attitude brought into my home."

"Yes, Hans," Matt said again. "I'm sorry."

"And you," Hans continued, next pointing to Cordero. "Of course you're going to help them."

"But, Hans—" Cordero began before Mason interrupted him.

"There's no point, Tony. You know how my man gets," Mason said. He pulled Hans back into his side and kissed him on the forehead. "Besides, you *should* help. Denton has been throwing money around Cuba like it's water. You and Hank will both be paid handsomely for the job."

"And then we can move out and get our own place," Mannix said.

Matt couldn't hide his enthusiasm. "That sounds like a great idea."

Cordero still looked like he wasn't sure. "Tony, please," Mannix said. "Much as I might like to, I can't be with Ernie constantly while we're at the casino. You need to help out. You wouldn't need to sell anything. Just be the American chaperone when I'm not there."

"That is so stupid," Matt said. "It's Ernesto's country, so why is he the one treated like an intruder?"

Mannix groaned. Golden Boy could be so...dense.

"And no one needs to move out," Hans said. "Hank, I was going to tell you this before you dropped your own bombshell, but you and Tony can each have your own room going forward."

Cordero—always the sensible one—raised the obvious question. "I don't know, Hans," he said. "Even if we do get paid well by Arthur's boss, your prices here are still steeper than we could afford."

"Not anymore," Hans said. "We've gotten three more cancellations for next week. It's the coup. The American press is making things seem very unsafe." Hans let out a sigh and settled in against Arthur's side. "And now that the elections have been postponed indefinitely...why, even those four men who come as a group each year from...where is it again, dear?" He pushed his glasses up his nose and twisted to look at Arthur. "I know it's a fruit of some sort, but I always forget..."

"It's one of the Oranges," Mason said. "The west one,

I think, or maybe the south one. Something like that."

"It's the east one," Mannix said. The four men from East Orange were inseparable. He fondly recalled one night several years ago when the five of them went for a midnight swim and they'd ended up—

"So, I get my own room?" Matt interrupted Mannix's musings.

Mason tilted his head. "I know I've been away, but as I understand it, the young Mr. Lansing is the only one of you three who's been paying anything at all to stay in that room."

"But Tony and I are stars," Mannix objected. "We're almost like a...a marketing expense, maybe."

"When was the last time the *Pumped* photographers wanted to take pictures of you rather than me?" Matt asked.

"Enough," Hans said. "You're all charity cases, and you know it."

Mason stroked the hair from Hans's brow. "And besides..." he prompted, leaving space for Hans to complete the thought.

Hans sighed and sat up straight on the love seat, but took hold of Mason's hand. "And besides—" He began, seeming reluctant to say whatever was coming next. "—I'm thinking of...ratcheting back."

"What?" Cordero asked. "Why?"

"Oh..." he waved his arm in a wide arc to take in...everything. "All this. It's just so different now. It's like a holiday house, not a refuge. I mean, all of these men traipsing through, just to party. Whether they're from Allentown or Schenectady or the—what are they again? West Lemons—?"

"East Orange," Mannix corrected.

"Exactly," said Hans. "They're just here to play. Which is fine. Really it is."

Mannix wasn't sure who Hans was trying to convince.

"But when we were in New York," Hans continued, "I made a real difference in the lives of so many young men." He turned to Matt. "You wouldn't believe it now, and it's only been five years, but so many young homosexuals were flooding into the city right after the war—all looking to start new lives where they didn't have to hide, or at least didn't have to hide as much. And certainly, they didn't have to hide at my boarding house."

Mason nodded. "Now everyone is hiding back home—from Congress, from the FBI, from the CIA. From each other," he said.

That was a horrible thought.

"Except they come here to Havana and act like all the constraints have been lifted," Mason continued. "They let loose what they've been bottling up back home." He squeezed Hans's hand. "And now the government wants to start keeping tabs on everyone here too."

The entire discussion reminded Mannix too much of the months leading up to their departure from New York. "But if you didn't run Casa de Ada, what would you do?"

"Oh, I'm not closing up shop anytime soon. I just want to cut back some, wait and see what develops with Arthur and his work. I think it would be good if we were in a more nimble position."

Nimble. So Mannix was right to be concerned. And

suddenly, with Ernesto in his life, being nimble had become a lot more difficult.

"So, we each get our own rooms, right?" Matt was having a hard time getting past his most immediate concern.

Cordero sighed and took a long drink of his beer. "I guess that means we're going to be seeing a lot more of Eduardo."

*

THE FOLLOWING WEEKS were frustrating.

It's not that Ernesto *disappeared* exactly—he still showed up at work each day, and he and Mannix, and Cordero now too, continued to work together selling cigars at the casino. But there was no *alone* time, and Ernesto seemed to be avoiding him. There were no longing glances exchanged over the breakfast table, no stolen kisses in the hallway.

No feeding the koi.

It was as if everything that had happened between them in the last month had been...erased. Something would have to be done.

Mason knocked on the door to Mannix's room after breakfast. As usual, he was wearing a narrow black tie, which he even wore around the house. Mannix thought it made him look like a spy. Which he was, in a way. "I need to talk to your young Cuban friend," Mason said. "The fellows back home need to see some results soon."

Results. Like Ernesto was an experiment or something.

At Mannix's nod, Mason stepped into the room and sat in the empty chair. Mannix was sitting on the side of his bed, and he realized he'd simply been holding the shoes he'd been about to put on, staring blankly at them as he thought about what could be done with Ernesto.

"Have you explained the situation to him yet?" Mason asked.

"No," Mannix admitted. "We haven't exactly been talking lately." At Mason's lifted eyebrow, Mannix hurried on. "It's not like we're *not* talking. We are. It's just that he's pretending there's nothing between us."

"You'll need to talk to him."

"I know. But he won't be caught alone with me now. At the casino he's all business, and here he won't even walk down the hallway where my new room is." Mannix scrunched his brow. "It's like he's expecting a trap."

"I can't help with your relationship, but we do need to talk to him about the information the CIA needs."

"What *does* the CIA need?" Mannix asked. He was fuzzy on all the anticommunist stuff. "Why is Ernie's factory so important?"

Mason sighed. "It's not the factory, particularly. It's the workers. The CIA is afraid the Soviets are trying to get a foothold in the Americas to set up communist regimes right on our doorstep."

Mannix still didn't understand why that would be so horrible, but he concluded that wasn't a good question for Mason. So, he focused instead on what was most important. "But why does Ernie need to be involved?"

"My bosses believe he can keep his finger on the pulse of what's going on with the workers. Identify the ones who might be rabble-rousers, so we can track them—the ones who might support that Castro fellow running for Congress."

"What business is it of ours who people want to vote for?" He bent forward and pulled on a shoe.

Mason leaned back in the chair. "If the revolutionaries get their way, there won't be any voting this time around."

"Another coup, then?" Mannix asked, pulling on the other shoe.

"Something like that," Mason responded cryptically.

Mannix looked up at his tone. "So, it's up to Ernie to save Cuba?" Mannix looked back down and began tying his shoes. "Seems like quite a lift."

"Hank." Mason paused until Mannix met his eyes. "This is serious business. Ernesto is far from the only one. The CIA has people all over Havana."

Mannix pulled the knot and the laces snapped. "Damn." He took the shoe off and began to unlace it. "Let's cut Ernie loose, then. You don't need him. I think this was all a mistake."

"It's too late, Hank. The CIA has already sunk money into this casino cigar scheme. They'll want to see something for it."

He pulled the lace out and assessed it. Maybe he could skip threading it through the lower holes. "And if they don't?"

Mason shook his head. "I'm sorry, Hank. You don't want to screw around with these guys."

Mannix tossed the torn lace onto the bed. It was too short to be useful. "Let me talk to Ernie first," he said.

"I'm the one who got him into this mess."

*

IN THE END, he did have to trap Ernesto into meeting with him privately.

He sat quietly on the bench, the tin of koi pellets at his feet. He fidgeted with the collar of his shirt—the one with the brightly colored seashells Ernesto had slobbered all over before. His impatience was mirrored below the water as the flashing mob circled hungrily.

When Ernesto appeared on the path and saw Mannix, he froze. He was holding a small tray with cookies and two glasses of orange juice.

Mannix watched as the indecision played across his face. "Oh," he said. "Mr. Mason told me two guests wanted to enjoy a snack at the pond."

Mannix smiled brightly and gave a jaunty little wave. "That's us!" He patted the bench next to him. "Come. Sit." Ernesto remained frozen in place, and for a moment Mannix feared he would turn and head back. But, as Mannix had hoped, he was too polite for that.

Ernesto came forward and placed the tray on the ground. "Hank," he said. But he didn't sit.

This was bad. *I wish I knew what I'd done.*

Ernesto stood quietly next to the bench, occasionally nodding his head.

Mannix knew the score now—Ernesto was having one of his inner monologues, figuring things out. Soon, he'd say something inexplicable, and Mannix would have to fill in all the missing gaps. He waited patiently for Ernesto to finish playing out whatever was going on in his head.

"I'm not like Ivan," Ernesto finally said.

"No," Mannix agreed. "You're not." He wondered how Ernesto had gotten to *that* point. Of course he wasn't like his cousin. Did Ernesto think Mannix saw him that way?

"Ernie—"

"Stop. You know my name."

Mannix closed his mouth. Was this about his nickname? "Ernie...esto, I know you're not like Ivan. Why are you telling me that?"

"He came to me that night."

Mannix raced to keep up. Was "that night" a reference to the assault at the casino? Was he talking about the American who attacked him? Was he talking about his cousin?

"Ivan? Ivan came to you?"

"Yes." Ernesto stood several feet from the bench, too far for Mannix to reach out and hold him, which was all he wanted to do. "He looked...dead."

I'm surprised he isn't.

"He said he saw me walking on the malecón. He thought I looked like I was...selling myself. Like he does." Ernesto wrapped his arms about himself, and Mannix wished those were *his* arms—comforting him, keeping Ernesto safe.

"You're not like him," Mannix said.

"I know. But he said the Americans were evil, that they all lied, and forced him to do things they said they wouldn't make him do. I think he's...he's in trouble, Hank." His voice broke, and tears shimmered in his eyes.

"Ern...Ernesto, *please* come sit down." Ernesto offered the slimmest of smiles at the stumble over his name, and Mannix scooted to the edge of the bench, trying to make himself as small as possible.

Ernesto came to the bench and sat. The koi splashed in frenzied excitement.

"But it all started...running together," Ernesto continued. "In my mind, I mean. The American who attacked me, the Americans who are abusing Ivan, the revealing clothes I have to wear..." Ernesto flashed a quick look at Mannix, then looked down. "You."

Me?

"But, Ernie!" Ernesto scowled. "Esto. Erniesto. I mean, Ernesto." Mannix took a breath to steady himself, then tried again. "I would never hurt you, Ernesto." He couldn't stop himself; he reached over and clasped Ernesto's hand, and—*thank God*—he wasn't rebuffed. "You know that. Don't you? Please tell me you know that."

"Yes. That's what I realized. I'm not like Ivan, and you're not like the American who attacked me."

It was beginning to make sense. Mannix squeezed Ernesto's hand. It was terrible Ernesto had been struggling with this for weeks.

"But, well, you *are* an American. And you're all so...foreign. There's a lot I don't understand about you. Like, what happens to the movies you and Mr. Cordero make? And what goes on around the pool late at night?"

If there was a way to explain everything to Ernesto that didn't make his life seem so sordid, Mannix would have tried. But there was such a gap between them. How could he even begin to describe his world to a young man who thought going to Catholic Mass is a form of dating?

"And I think Ivan was right about the lying. You do all seem to do that."

"No!" Mannix objected. Before he could offer further denials, Ernesto began to list examples.

"Mr. Mason lied to his boss about Hans. Matt told me you lied to the men from Allentown about not having found their underwear, and he lied to Mr. Schmidt about the trip to the farm. And Mr. Schmidt...well, I don't know... How can he dress that way and pretend to be a woman?"

"To be fair," Mannix interjected, "nobody understands Hans."

Ernesto took his hand back and turned on the bench to meet Mannix's eye. "And you lied to my aunt and uncle, and also to my father."

Mannix swallowed. It *did* look bad all laid out like that. "But that was for you, Ernie...esto."

"And you lied to me," Ernesto whispered.

"No!" Mannix exclaimed again. "I'd never lie to you."

"Mr. Schmidt told me tomorrow is your birthday."

Was it? "I never keep track of those things. And it's not a lie to forget to tell you it's my birthday."

"Hank, you told me you were twenty-five. But Mr. Schmidt said you're turning thirty."

Shit. He had said that, hadn't he? But it was back when Ernesto was just the "cute one." He hadn't even known him then. He just hadn't wanted to appear old. Still.

"Um...it's not a lie if you don't know the person...?"

"Hank." Geese and taxi horns. Mannix closed his eyes and grimaced.

"You're right. That was a lie. But truly, I'd forgotten. It's just, I thought you were younger even than you are. And I wanted you to like me." That sounded pathetic, and Mannix tried to regroup. "Besides, it was just a white lie."

"What's a white lie?" Ernesto sounded suspicious.

"It's a lie that doesn't count as a lie, because it's small and maybe makes things easier between people." But even as he explained it, Mannix realized this wasn't helping his cause.

Ernesto's frown deepened. "You mean Americans have a word for lies that don't *count* as lies?" He pressed a finger to his temple. "But they're still lies? That can't be right."

The conversation was going off track. "It's not like it sounds." Mannix ran his fingers through his hair. "Look, have you ever told Marta or your mother that something they're wearing looks pretty, even though you didn't think it suited them?"

"No."

"No? Didn't your father teach you anything?"

"What does my father—"

"Okay, bad example. Um...oh! I know. You told your aunt and uncle I was making a film about their farm."

"Yes, but that *was* a lie. And I confessed it the following Sunday before Mass. I didn't try to pretend it was some color of a lie that didn't count as a lie."

Confessed? "I'm getting confused," Mannix admitted.

Ernesto stood and threw his hands in the air. "That's my *point*. We live in different worlds."

Mannix stood also. "Wait," he said. "Enough about the lies. I'm sorry I lied about my age. It was stupid, and it didn't mean anything at the time. I would never lie to you *now*."

Ernesto sighed, and he seemed to relax—just a little. "Are there other lies, of any color, you need to clear up before we put his behind us, Hank?"

Success! Ernie was ready to get back on track. He dropped the tin of pellets to the ground and took both of Ernesto's hands in his. His mind raced, searching for any silly little half-truths he may have told Ernesto that he should confess. About his accent maybe? Or his work in the garden?

Mannix was able to see when Ernesto's interest in kissing Hank overcame his huffy concern about lies.

"You're taking too long," Ernesto said.

God, what a fool he was, searching for an inventory of lies when he should be kissing the man in front of him.

"No, nothing." Then he remembered about Arthur and the CIA and what they needed from Ernesto. But that wasn't a lie, exactly, he simply hadn't told Ernesto yet about the arrangement. And—God, he almost forgot!—he was supposed to explain all of that to Ernesto before Mason gave him the details. "Um, Arthur needs to see you."

"First it was Hans coming between us and now it's Arthur," Ernesto complained. "Maybe you should stop talking and kiss me."

He'd never seen Ernesto like this, so bold and taking charge; he liked it. And who was he to refuse Ernesto's demands for kisses? So he gave him what he'd asked for, and as the minutes wore on, Ernesto's bank of kisses must surely have been depleted. Mannix could barely breathe.

He was relieved they were back where they should be and excited about what was happening. This was it. He had his own room now.

"Oh, how I missed this," Mannix said after he'd pulled back from Ernesto's lip. "I was afraid our first time together was going to be our only time together."

"I know. Me too." Ernesto began unbuttoning Hank's shirt, then let his hand drop down to rest on Mannix's crotch. "I've been dreaming of this moment."

A soft whimper escaped Mannix's lips. "Let's get back to the house. We'll try to avoid Arthur."

Ernesto tightened his grip, and Mannix sucked in a breath. "Take off your shirt," Ernesto commanded.

And if he ever needed proof Ernesto had to stop thinking about things too much and start acting on his instincts, this was it. "Bossy," Mannix said. But he nearly tore his shirt in his haste to comply. "Now what?"

Ernesto began working on Hank's belt. He lowered himself onto the bench and maneuvered Hank in front of him. "Here in the garden?" Mannix asked, though he could already feel himself responding. "Isn't that—"

Ernesto kept working, and all thoughts of whether this was too demeaning for Ernesto dissolved.

"Oh my God," Hank moaned. "Are you sure you...?"

"It's time." Ernesto pushed Mannix's trousers and shorts down his thighs. The koi flashed their disappointment, and Ernesto was finally blinded by the glory that was Hank.

Chapter Twenty-One

ERNESTO DIDN'T KNOW what to think as he made his way back to the house in search of Mr. Mason.

He'd left Hank collapsed on the bench, an exhausted smile plastered across his face. Hank had wanted to reciprocate, but Ernesto had refused. It was more balanced now. They were equals, having each done this once for the other.

He knew he'd been inept at the task. Hank must have done it many times with far more experienced men, and Ernesto worried how he'd come across in comparison. To be fair, Ernesto had seen plenty of naked men, and Hank was definitely *not* the best choice for someone just trying to learn the art.

Still, after it was over, and they'd cleaned up as best they could and put Hank's clothes back in order, he'd said, "That was spectacular, Ernesto. *You* were spectacular."

"Is that a white lie, or a real lie?" Ernesto had asked.

"It's no lie at all," he'd responded, and Ernesto chose to believe him.

As he walked along the path, the taste of Hank in his mouth was still strong, and he couldn't decide if that was good or bad.

It hadn't been demeaning at all, even if it *had* happened in the garden. In fact, it had been exactly what he wanted, and he'd been in control the entire time. It was only now, as he made his way back to the house, that he began to worry about it, that he began to put meaning to it.

If only he didn't know about Ivan and what the Americans forced his cousin to do for money. *That* was demeaning, even if it was the very thing he'd joyfully done with Hank. If only the American at the casino hadn't attacked him.

But as he approached the house, he pushed all those thoughts from his mind. What he and Hank had done was beautiful, bringing pleasure to both of them. It wasn't about all those other things or those other people.

"Ernesto," Mason called. He was standing in the open doorway of the greenhouse, waving him over.

"I see you found Hank. Sorry about the cookies and juice trick, but he was afraid you wouldn't go to him, and he wanted to tell you himself about what the CIA is looking for before I got into the specifics."

"Uh...what? The CIA?" Ernesto was missing something.

Mason frowned. "He told me he wanted to be the one

to explain the arrangement. You did find him in the garden, didn't—" He broke off and peered more closely at Ernesto.

"Oh," Mason said. "I see. You've got, um..." He twirled a finger in the direction of Ernesto's hair. "Right there," he pointed. "Above your ear."

Ernesto slapped a hand to his head and was mortified by what he found there. How could Hank have missed that? He removed his hand only to find a sticky trail of...of...*Hank*, stretching between his fingers.

Mason bit his lip and looked away. "Perhaps you should wash up at the sink there and then join me at the table."

Ernesto did, double-checking his throat and chin and ears and his entire head before he was satisfied it was all gone. He remembered the first time he sat with Hank in this very room, when a bug had dropped out of his hair and onto the table. This was worse. Far worse.

By the time he'd finished cleaning up, Mason was already sitting at the table. Ernesto took the chair opposite.

"Obviously, Hank didn't get around to explaining why I needed to speak with you," Mason said. Ernesto blushed. "And I believe Hans has a few rules about what's acceptable behavior in the gardens."

Ernesto began to apologize, but Mason waved him off. "Oh, it's not your fault. Hank has a way of getting what he wants. He should have known better though."

Ernesto couldn't let the accusation stand, even though it would have been easier for him. "It was my fault, sir. I made Mr. Mannix do it."

Mason laughed. "Well, I'm sure you had a role to

play, young man." He leaned back in his chair. "But I'm glad to see you've...reconciled."

Silence was probably the best approach. Ernesto waited.

"So," Mason said at last. "You know my employer, the CIA, is paying for your sales office at the casino, yes?"

Ernesto nodded.

"And you know that my boss is looking into ways to help your family directly export your cigars to the United States?"

"No," Ernesto said. "I did not know that. That's... that's wonderful." It would change everything for them. He might even be able to visit America! But... "Why?" he asked.

"Exactly the right question." Mason seemed pleased. "Hans told me you had a good head on your shoulders."

Mr. Schmidt said that? It had been a day for revelations. He ran his tongue across his teeth, where he could still taste Hank.

"Are you familiar with a radical named Fidel Castro?" Mason asked.

"Of course," Ernesto replied. "Although I wouldn't necessarily call him a radical. He's a member of the Orthodox Party, running on their anticorruption platform. Or at least he was until the elections were canceled."

Mason blinked. "You're pretty well-informed."

"The torcederos are all interested in politics." And why wouldn't he be informed about what was happening in his own country?

"Torcederos?" Mason asked.

"Yes. The workers in the factory. The cigar rollers."

At Mason's blank stare, he continued. "I read to them while they work. I'm a lector." Ernesto was mildly disappointed Mr. Mason didn't already know this. He wasn't sure if he wanted to think Hank talked about him with the others, or if he was relieved to find he didn't.

"I see," said Mason. Although Ernesto thought he probably didn't. "And they like it when you read about Castro?"

"Well, not just Castro. But he's one of their favorites, probably because he's controversial, and they always end up arguing about him. Some don't like him because of his Marxist leanings, but others like that about him—especially his ideas about guaranteeing workers a share of company profits."

Mason was nodding, and he began writing notes in a pad of paper Ernesto hadn't noticed before.

"Nearly all of them like his nationalist policies though, like limiting foreign ownership of property in Cuba." It struck Ernesto, a bit late, perhaps, that he was talking to Mr. Schmidt's...partner, he supposed the right word was...and that Mr. Schmidt was a foreign owner of property in Cuba.

"I think he mostly means export industries, like sugar and tobacco, not...um, guest houses?" Ernesto hadn't meant to make that a question, but it came out that way. For some reason he wanted to make sure Mr. Mason didn't see Cuban politicians as a threat.

Mason nodded, scratching away with his pencil. "Go on."

Ernesto decided he'd said enough. He wanted to know what was expected of him. After a few moments of silence, Mason looked up from his notepad.

"What is it the CIA would like from me, Mr. Mason?"

He put down the pencil and offered Ernesto a smile. "Well, exactly this, young man." He pointed to his notes with his pencil. "You're perfectly positioned to help us out." He pushed the notepad aside and folded his hands together on the table. "You see, the government would like to know what the workers in Cuba are thinking about all the agitation for revolution coming from the radicals. Who has their support? Who doesn't? That sort of thing."

Ernesto considered that. "Why?" he asked.

Mason seemed surprised by the question. He took a moment to gather his thoughts. "The United States believes it would be bad...for Cuba, for the Cuban people, that is...if Castro and his kind came into power."

It was a careful answer, and Ernesto wondered what color a lie was if it was intended to convince someone you shared a common interest.

"And you want me to...?"

"Give us exactly this kind of information." He tapped his pencil against the pad. "And also, if you could identify which individual workers seem the most inclined to be political, that would be helpful too. Do you know them well?"

He'd grown up in the factory. Not only did he know each of the torcederos individually, but he knew the names of their wives and children too. He knew who was getting married and who had died. He knew everything about those men.

Ernesto frowned. Whenever he thought about his long history with the torcederos, he was jolted by a horrible memory. He'd done something unforgivable once—a long time ago when he was very young, but still old enough to know better—and a good worker had quit because of it. It was a shameful memory, and Ernesto always pushed it out of his head as soon it surfaced.

He locked the memory away, then realized Mr. Mason had continued talking. "So, it would be helpful if you could tell us more about these men. Do you know any of their names?"

"One or two," he answered, and there was nothing white about that lie at all.

*

AFTER HIS MEETING with Mr. Mason, Ernesto debated waiting for Hank and confronting him about why he hadn't revealed any of this earlier. He wasn't sure if it would have made a difference, if he would have refused the arrangement. He thought about the new books he'd been able to buy for the torcederos, and the better radio that sat in the family's office. And all the money he was putting aside for university.

No, it probably wouldn't have changed anything. But it still would have been nice to know ahead of time what he was getting into.

And why confront Hank about it anyway? What would he say? "I'm sorry; I should have told you sooner?" What good would that do?

He finished with the last of his morning chores— replenishing the coffee, cleaning up the remaining breakfast dishes, making sure the pool area was stocked with towels and cushions. One of the men from East Orange asked him to rub suntan oil on his back, but then one of the others made a joke of it, excusing Ernesto from the task before he had to find a polite way to refuse on his own.

At the end of his shift, he headed to Matt's room. By unspoken agreement, he continued to use a corner of the small closet as his locker, leaving his street clothes there while he worked and hanging his houseboy uniform there before he went home each day. It had seemed too...meaningful...to start keeping his clothes in Hank's new room, and Matt didn't seem to mind.

"Ernesto! Just the man I wanted to see," Matt said when Ernesto entered the room. He was sitting on his mattress, tying his shoes. He still didn't have a real bed, or even a box spring, and he'd lost the room's only chair when Mannix and Cordero had moved out.

Ernesto marveled at how the simple act of tying his shoes caused Matt's biceps and forearms to flex and bulge. He wondered if Matt would be willing to show him the trick to that someday. He stepped to the closet and began undressing. He knew Matt wouldn't look and also knew Matt was no more interested in him than he was in Matt. It was comfortable that way.

"Will you come to the university with me?" Matt asked.

Ernesto pulled on his boxers and trousers. "Now? Why doesn't Eduardo take you?"

"He doesn't want me to go. Castro is giving a rally at lunchtime today. Eduardo thinks it's dangerous." Matt finished with his shoes and climbed to his feet. "You don't think it's dangerous, do you?"

Not as dangerous as selling your body on the malecón or being a Cuban in the casino. Or falling for an American who thinks lies have colors and who forgets to tell you important things.

"Not particularly, no." And why were the Americans all so upset about Castro anyway? "And can't you get them to give you a real bed? Or at least a chair?"

"Hans says next month. I have to wait for the men from East Orange to leave, then there's a couple more coming, then Hans isn't booking the room again. Did you know he's winding things down here?"

No, Ernesto didn't know that. He shook his head. "Hank doesn't tell me anything," he complained.

"Well," Matt said, studying the floor. "Have you at least gotten over what was troubling you guys?"

Ernesto touched his still damp hair and smiled, recalling the episode in the garden. He couldn't seem to remain angry at Hank, and he wanted to see what more they could do together. "Oh yes," he replied. "We sure have."

Matt laughed. "I know that look. Makeup sex is the best, isn't it?"

Makeup sex. Another new phrase. Ernesto blushed. "I just wish I was...better at it. I wish I knew what I was doing."

"Tell you what. Be my Cuban chaperone at the Castro rally, and on the way there I'll tell you all the tricks I know. You'll have his head spinning next time."

"It's a deal," Ernesto said, and they shook on it.

*

MATT ATTRACTED ATTENTION as they made their way through the chaotic streets of Havana. There weren't many Americans in the city outside of the business and entertainment zones, and those who were there tended to be older men in suits and ties, not young, muscled men with blond hair wearing tight blue shirts and pressed trousers.

"I've never felt so *white* before," Matt said.

Ernesto thought that wasn't the right sentiment. He thought what Matt meant was that he felt different, not white. Ernesto imagined feeling white would feel like being free, untethered to the concerns or opinions of others. It was a disturbing thought, and he pushed it from his mind, then turned the conversation back to the art of sex.

By the time they reached the campus, *his* was the head that was spinning. If he could manage to remember half the techniques Matt had described he'd be lucky. Not as lucky as Hank though. He smiled in anticipation of how Hank would respond the next time they were together.

They stepped through the stone archway and into a sea of people. Hundreds had gathered to hear Castro speak.

He thought all lawyers were old, gray-haired types, but Fidel Castro was an energetic, handsome young man, with just the hint of a dark beard under his chin. He railed against the canceled elections and called out the corruption that ran through the local police offices.

Matt cheered along with the others at all the right places, but he couldn't have understood a word Castro was saying. Ernesto scanned the crowd. It was unbelievable to think that in just a few months he'd be attending classes here. Most of the students were unlikely to have experienced firsthand the corruption Castro described. Their wealthy parents probably had, but Ernesto suspected the sons and daughters of the upper classes were shielded from those realities.

He found himself nodding along with Castro at many points. Why should American companies own all the sugar production and take those profits overseas? And, of course, the elections should be rescheduled promptly. A military coup was no way to form a government.

The crowd grew in size as the rally continued. Workers from the city joined, and soon the students were in the minority. Castro urged protests and lawsuits but never once called for violence or a revolution. Nonetheless, when Castro had finally finished and stepped down from the wooden platform that had been erected for him, the crowd began chanting, *"Revolución! Revolución!"*

In the distance, over the roar of the crowd, Ernesto heard gunshots, or it might have been drums. The crowd began moving. Banners were unfurled. "Revolución!" "Jail Batista!" Ernesto and Matt were swept along, and Ernesto was sure now there was gunfire in the distance. People began screaming.

"Come on. This way," Ernesto urged, trying to pull Matt through the crowd, toward its edge. But they kept getting pushed back into the mix.

"Christ!" Matt exclaimed as a punch landed solidly against his temple. Ernesto kept him from falling and tried to pull him along. If he fell, they'd be trampled; the crowd was rushing now, ahead of the screaming and the gunfire. Whoever had punched Matt melted away. Just a protestor taking a random swipe at an American.

Eduardo had been right. This was dangerous.

Finally, Ernesto spotted an opening, and he and Matt tumbled into the relative openness of a grassy university yard. Ernesto knew where they were. His home was only fifteen minutes away. The guest house was farther, with a mob and gunfire between it and them. He glanced at Matt and the blood flowing from his brow.

There was no question of where they had to go.

He thought the bleeding had slowed by the time they entered the factory, but he hadn't paused along the way to make a thorough assessment. Several of the nearest torcederos rose from their workstations to offer help, but Ernesto waved them off. His father had already seen them and was coming onto the factory floor.

They got Matt situated in a chair by the sink, removed his bloody shirt, and began mopping his wound. The cut was on his brow, a clean, thin slice of open skin. It had bled a lot, but didn't seem to be particularly serious. He'd probably need a stitch or two though.

He translated simple introductions as his mother cleaned the blood from Matt's head and chest. Matt couldn't help how he looked, but Ernesto was embarrassed for Marta, who kept staring, then pulling her gaze away.

"It's not too bad, and the bleeding has mostly stopped, but this will need stitches," his mother confirmed.

"You can't take him to a *medico*," his father said.

"The radio is filled with news about an illegal protest. The police are looking for anyone who was involved. He'd be questioned, maybe held overnight."

Matt looked panicked. "Can you get me back to Eduardo?"

"No. It's not safe to go back to the campus," Ernesto said, as his father left the office and entered the factory. He saw him talking to the torcederos, and within a few moments he came back with Jorge, one of the older workers Ernesto knew had spent time in the military.

"Isabel, boil some water and sterilize your thinnest needle," his father said. Then he turned to Ernesto. "Tell your friend Jorge has lots of experience stitching field wounds. He'll take good care of him."

Matt blanched when he got the news. "Come on," Ernesto said. "Do you want a small, delicate scar across your eyebrow that will only increase your appeal, or a big ugly gash?" Ernesto was pleased to see that elicited a smile.

Within a half hour it was over. Jorge had done a fine job, and even Matt seemed pleased when he looked in the mirror. "I'll be bruised for a while, I think, but you were right. This scar is going to give me an air of mystery." He grinned at Ernesto. "You'll have to help me think up a good story about how I got it."

More lies. They couldn't seem to help themselves.

Marta had rinsed the blood out of Matt's shirt, and it was hanging in the kitchen to dry. Matt was wearing one of Ernesto's shirts—which pulled tightly across his chest and gaped between the buttons. His mother had made *mixtos*—and this time, when a warm drizzle of fat ran down his chin—Ernesto understood just why the sensation made him think of Hank. He colored at the memory.

They were just finishing lunch when Eduardo came through the door.

The torcederos looked up from their work. "Professor Martinez," Marta whispered when she saw who it was. Matt turned in his chair and waved at Eduardo through the glass, and Ernesto stood and went to the door, motioning for Eduardo to come into the office.

"Matt!" he exclaimed. Eduardo rushed to the table and knelt next to the American. "I *knew* that's where you went—even after I told you how dangerous it would be. What were you thinking?" He gripped Matt's chin and tilted his head for a better look. The bruise was a mottled blue and green, and the skin around the black stitches was an angry red.

He looked up at Ernesto. "They told me the two of you headed off together, so I knew right away what he must have talked you into. Thank you for looking out for him and bringing him here." He leaned in to peer into Matt's eyes. "But how did this happen?"

As Matt began to explain, Ernesto noticed the quizzical looks on his parent's faces. Although Eduardo and Matt were speaking in English, there was no mistaking the familiarity with which they were treating each other. Intimacy might even be a better word, Ernesto thought. He cleared his throat, and that seemed to bring Eduardo back to his senses.

Eduardo thanked Ernesto's parents for their help. He'd understood immediately why the wound needed to be attended to in the Ruiz's kitchen. He touched the edge of Matt's brow. "This is very fine work." Matt sucked in a breath, and the button holding the shirt closed across his chest popped and landed on the table. The two buttons above and below followed.

Eduardo swallowed, and both he and Marta looked away.

The part of Ernesto that was becoming Americanized thought the *Pumped* photographers would have loved to film that.

Marta rose and began clearing away dishes. "May I bring you something to eat, Professor?" she asked.

"No. That's very kind. But I should get Matt home. Back, that is, to his boarding house." Ernesto's parents were looking increasingly uncomfortable.

As she passed behind Ernesto, Marta leaned down and whispered, "My English is better than you think it is."

Chapter Twenty-Two

IT WAS SIX o'clock in the morning, a ridiculous hour to be awake, but since he was still in bed, cuddled against a warm and naked Ernesto, Mannix didn't mind one bit. "You should sleep over every night," he whispered as he stroked Ernesto's hair. He recognized the faint, earthy tobacco smell now and had come to associate it with Ernesto.

The room itself smelled of sex, and Ernesto wriggled more tightly into Mannix's grip.

"You know I can't," he said. "I'm needed at home."

Mannix lowered his hand and drew lazy circles around Ernesto's belly. "You work too much. Here, the casino, the factory—when do you have time to just enjoy yourself?"

"Are you not enjoying yourself right now?" Ernesto asked.

Mannix nudged his obvious enjoyment into Ernesto's backside. "Coffee doesn't start until seven. We still have an hour." His fingers on Ernesto's belly dropped lower.

"We don't have an hour." Ernesto pushed himself up and swung his legs over the side of Mannix's bed. "I need to wash, get dressed, and start prepping breakfast by six thirty. Besides, I like to be early. So does Hans."

Mannix grunted and let his hand trail across Ernesto's hip as he stood.

His new room had a sink in the corner, with a wall-mounted mirror above it, and he watched as Ernesto ran a damp cloth over his face and then under his arms. Their eyes met in the mirror, and Mannix grinned. "You missed a spot shaving."

Ernesto huffed. Mannix never tired of teasing him for his lack of body hair. He'd never shaved, and probably never would. He lifted the metal razor blade from the glass dish. "I could practice on you."

"No, I couldn't risk it," Mannix said. "My pretty face is the only thing I have going for me."

"That's not true, Hank." Ernesto turned away from the sink and began rubbing the damp cloth across his stomach, then lower still. "You also have very large *cojones.*"

Hank sat up and leaned against the headboard, clasping his hands behind his head. "I could watch you do this all day."

Ernesto rinsed the cloth in the sink and hung it on the rod to dry. He opened Mannix's closet to retrieve his uniform. It had become awkward slipping into Matt's room so early in the morning, trying not to make a sound or turn on a light. After encountering Mr. Martinez in Matt's bed one day, he decided—to everyone's relief—to transfer his clothes into Mannix's closet.

After slipping on his white briefs, he climbed back into bed. It was a total power play; he knew he drove Mannix to distraction when he was dressed only in his tight shorts. He sat cross-legged and drew a finger up Mannix's thigh. "So, I was thinking,' he said.

"Oh my God, you're killing me, Ernie."

Ernesto's caress turned into a sharp pinch.

"Ouch! *Iesto.* I meant Erniesto." He covered Ernesto's hand with his own, both to prevent further pinching and to draw him closer. "What have you been thinking about?"

"Well, we've been...dating...for a couple of months now." It was concerning how Ernesto always scrunched his nose when he said dating, like it wasn't *really* dating if it didn't include going to Mass together. Although to be fair, it *wasn't* really dating. Instead, it was lots of kissing and cuddling—and sex, of course, of a limited but highly enjoyable nature—whenever they had time alone. And that wasn't too often, given how much Ernesto worked.

Mannix was curious where this was going. "Best couple of months of my life," Mannix confirmed. He tried to tug Ernesto closer, but the last few months had taught him Ernesto was surprisingly strong when he needed to be, and he refused to be tugged.

"And I think we should go on a date." Ernesto took a deep breath and waited. Mannix could feel the tension in his hand still trapped under his.

"Like, lounging by the pool maybe?" Mannix asked. That wouldn't be too bad, assuming Golden Boy wasn't doing a photo shoot. He and Matt had reached a level of comfortable coexistence, but he couldn't have all that new Mannix stuff rubbed in his face.

"No..." Ernesto managed to wrangle his hand out from under Mannix's grip. "I was thinking more like *doing* something together, going someplace. Someplace that's not here, I mean, or the casino."

He shouldn't have been surprised. It wasn't the least bit odd. The shocking thing was to be confronted by how small his world had gotten. Back in New York he was going out and doing things all the time. Catching a movie, checking out a new club. He smiled at the memory of him and Hans and Mason and Cordero going to Coney Island one Fourth of July.

Here in Cuba, his world had contracted to a terribly tight circle. Tony had been right—they were wasting their lives.

Still, he didn't know anything about Havana. What was the point of going to a movie if you didn't speak the language? And all of the other English speakers were either in the casinos or at the beach clubs.

But he had Ernesto now. "Sure," he agreed. "Let's do that sometime."

Ernesto grinned. "Good!" He stood and began pulling on his tight houseboy trousers. "Tomorrow is my day off at the factory, and I know Mr. Schmidt would give me the morning off too. We'd have all day before we had to be at the casino."

No sense in delaying, Mannix thought. "What would

we do?"

"Leave the planning to me," Ernesto said.

"Bossy," Mannix mumbled as he watched Ernesto slowly—very slowly—button his fly.

"But you like that." Ernesto kissed him, finished dressing, and left the room.

*

THE CROCODILE WAS enormous. Mannix was no judge of such things, but he thought the reptile looked fat and almost cute, in a bony, prehistoric way, especially with one of its teeth—bigger than Mannix's thumb—poking out over the side of its lip.

The zookeeper aimed a heavy bucket filled with fish toward the animal's lagoon and sloshed its contents into the water. The man hustled out of the way as quickly as his black knee-high boots allowed him to scramble, while the crocodile abandoned all attempts at cuteness by slashing across the water and crunching through the flopping mass of its breakfast.

The water around its gaping jaw pinkened, and children screamed and squealed as they clutched the iron rail posts and pushed at each other. One young father hoisted a child onto his shoulders, and Mannix had a brief and disturbing vision of what would happen if the little boy tumbled into the enclosure.

It *was* a date, so he couldn't accuse Ernesto of lying—not exactly. But he hadn't mentioned anything about a zoo filled with children. Mannix had no idea so many children existed in the entire world, let alone in Havana itself.

And each one had sticky, cotton candy fingers and no respect for Mannix's personal space whatsoever.

At least it was June, so they were all in small family packs and not in classroom-sized gangs. That was something, anyway. Ernesto nudged him in the gut with his elbow and laughed as the crocodile climbed out of the shallow water and waddled toward the children behind the fence, bony bits of fish dangling out of its gaping jaw.

More screaming and squealing as the wiser children backed away, and the reckless ones surged forward, pressing themselves against the rails and waving their cotton candy wands at the predator.

"Not even a white lie?" Mannix asked again.

"No, Hank. I didn't lie at all."

"But you didn't tell me about all the children or the amount of death and killing there would be."

Ernesto grinned. "Those were omissions, not lies. You're the one who said those don't count."

"Well, you could have warned me about those two," Mannix complained, nodding his head farther down the enclosure's fence to where Matt and Eduardo stood transfixed by the crocodile's obvious interest in the noisy children.

"You wouldn't have agreed to come if you knew it was a double date," Ernesto said. He at least had the decency to look guilty by the manipulation.

The keeper emptied a new bucket filled with fish into the water, and the crocodile lost interest—temporarily—in eating the youth of Havana. Mannix watched as Golden Boy pinched a tuft of pink spun sugar from the cone Doctor Doolittle was holding. "That's sickeningly sweet," he told Ernesto.

A cacophonous screeching from the flamingo enclosure drew many of the children away. "Listen to that flamboyance," Ernesto exclaimed. That's what the sign on the enclosure called a group of flamingos—a flamboyance. Mannix thought it would also be a good name for a group of Casa de Ada's guests at the pool late at night.

Mannix leaned in close. "How can this be a date if I'm not allowed to kiss you? Or even touch you?" They both watched as Matt sensuously licked the sugar from his fingers, and Eduardo teetered on the edge of self-control.

"I suppose you could feed me," Ernesto offered. "Do you have anything you'd like to stuff into my mouth?"

Mannix's eyes blazed. "How long do we have to stay here?"

Eduardo suddenly appeared at Mannix's side. "Hey guys, Matt and I are going to get lunch for us. Why don't you go grab us a table in the pavilion?"

Before Mannix could enumerate any of the dozens of reasons they should *not* get a table in the pavilion, Ernesto said, "That sounds great." Then he turned to look at Mannix. "I was just telling Hank how much I'd enjoy a nice thick *butifarra.*"

Eduardo rolled his eyes. "I'll see what I can find. He's a bad influence on you, young man."

"I can guess what a butifarra is," said Mannix.

Ernesto smiled. "Yes, but you shouldn't have to guess. You need to work on your Spanish."

He'd only made half-hearted efforts at it so far. But he was embarrassed at how quickly Golden Boy seemed to be picking it up, and he vowed to redouble his efforts. "I suppose if we're going to graduate to the next level of dating—say, going to Mass together—I'll need to do better."

He'd meant it as a joke, but at Ernesto's pained expression he realized his mistake. Ernesto was a worrier; he'd known that all along, of course. But he particularly seemed to worry about his future, and his inability to visualize a path forward where they were together—romantically, as partners—caused him a great deal of grief. Maybe the double date wasn't such a bad idea. Golden Boy and Doctor Doolittle fit together seamlessly; perhaps he and Ernesto could figure out a way to follow their lead.

"Sorry," Mannix said. "I shouldn't joke about your religion."

"It's not that," Ernesto began.

"I know," Mannix assured him. "But let's not worry about the future right now. It's only our first date, after all." That coaxed a laugh from Ernesto.

They began making their way to the pavilion. "I just wish this didn't have to end," Ernesto said. His hand twitched toward Hank's but didn't touch. Mannix put his arm across Ernesto's shoulder and gave him a rough shake before letting go. It was a gesture he'd seen other men do in public—mostly younger men, but he thought it was okay.

"It *doesn't* have to end," he insisted. But in truth, he was no more capable of envisioning a future for them than Ernesto was.

*

MATT AND EDUARDO brought four large butifarras to their table, along with some fried chip things Mannix couldn't identify. They all made jokes about the butifarras as if they were twelve-year-olds and not grown men. The grilled sausages were delicious and not spicy at all, which Mannix appreciated. He avoided the things he didn't recognize and advised Matt to do the same.

"Better safe than sorry," he said, causing Matt to nearly spit out his cola.

"I've only known you for a few months," Matt said, "but I can't imagine a less Mannix thing to say." Ernesto nodded his head in agreement.

"Sure," said Mannix. "Just wait until you get food poisoning on some farm in the middle of nowhere without running water or electricity, and you start vomiting—and worse—in front of your lover's family." He took a big bite of his butiffara as the table fell silent. Three heads turned to stare at him.

Only after he swallowed did he realize what he'd said.

"Well, I...that is...I think we're...I mean...I'm very fond—"

Ernesto interrupted him by risking an under-the-table squeeze of his thigh. "I feel the same way, Hank."

"I might cry," Eduardo said.

"I might get sick," Matt said.

"Someone please change the subject," pleaded Mannix.

"Fine," said Matt. He reached into a bag at his feet and withdrew a small cardboard box. He placed it on the table and slid it across to Mannix. "Eduardo and I picked this up in the gift shop. Happy belated birthday. Your twenty-fifth, isn't it?" He winked and Mannix cringed at the reminder.

"Thanks, Golden Boy. You shouldn't have." His tone suggested he really shouldn't have.

He opened the brightly colored box to find a set of children's flashcards with pictures of zoo animals and their names. Ernesto beamed, and Eduardo said, "You need to learn some basic Spanish."

Mannix flipped through the cards. Many of them he would have guessed, even without the pictures. *El elefante. El camello. El tigre.* "Are there elephants, camels, and tigers here?" he asked. "I didn't see any."

"Not yet," Eduardo said. "Soon though. The zoo is still growing." He was busy drawing a picture on a napkin, and Mannix turned back to the cards.

"*El mono*! I never would have gotten that for monkey. Or *el oso* for a bear." He scanned more of the cards. "What are you *doing*?" The question was directed to Eduardo, who was continuing to draw on his napkins.

"I'm adding to your list," he said.

He turned the first napkin around. It was a tall stick figure, drawn with a little pot belly. "Eduardo," he said, stressing the ending syllables of his name and underlining them where he'd written it at the top of the napkin. He turned the next napkin around—a shorter stick figure with comically exaggerated biceps and a delicate little scar through his left eyebrow. "Go ahead, take a guess."

Mannix couldn't help himself. "*Chico de oro*?"

Eduardo blinked, and Matt let out a laugh. "Oh, so he has been studying."

Even Ernesto thought Hank's knowing how to say

golden boy in Spanish was funny. "Come on, Eduardo, just write Matt at the top. I want to see mine."

Eduardo finished with Matt's napkin and turned the last one around. It was a stick figure with an enormous heart bursting out of the line drawing. "Ernesto," he said, again stressing the last two syllables and underlining them. Then he took the napkin back and wrote, "*Amante*," underlining it several times and drawing another heart.

Mannix pretended not to feel the moisture pooling in his eyes.

Chapter Twenty-Three

ERNESTO WAS SITTING at the table with his family, sharing a late afternoon meal, but his thoughts were still on his date with Hank at the zoo.

Amante, Hank had called him.

His lover.

It was confusing, and overwhelming, and it felt so true.

"I wish you didn't have to go there this evening," his mother said again.

"But it's Saturday, Mama," Ernesto replied. "The casino will be busy. It's our best day of the week for sales."

"I know, mijo. But today was supposed to be election day, and there are rumors of protests planned across the city. I think it's dangerous." She ladled out more *ropa vieja* into Ernesto's bowl.

Ernesto's father chuckled. "You think crossing the street is dangerous, Isobel."

"Well, I think the casino sounds exciting," said Marta. She had finished eating and was busy putting the finishing touches on the cigar boxes Ernesto would be taking with him. She worked all the time now trying to keep up with sales. "I'd like to see it sometime."

"No," her father and mother said at the same time.

Amante. Ernesto thought Hank had meant it too. *If only there was some way to make all of this* real.

It had begun raining even as the double date at the zoo was ending, and now that the thunder shower had passed, the windows in the factory and the family's house were all open, and the ceiling fans were running on high, trying to move the thick, sticky air outside. The humidity wasn't good for the final stages of constructing a cigar.

The torcederos worked quickly, speaking quietly with one another, sharing their plans for the evening. They were nearing the end of their shift, and the factory would be closed on Sunday. The workers all fell silent when the front door opened and the *caballito* stepped in.

Two of them this time, and in the middle of the month. Ernesto thought that was a bad sign.

"Quickly, get the envelope," Ernesto's father said to him. "I'll handle this," he told the others as he wiped his hands on his napkin and stepped out onto the factory floor. The torcederos knew better than to pay attention, and they were already back at work, heads bent over their tables, seeing nothing, silently rolling their cigars.

"Señors," Raúl said, greeting the caballitos. "What a surprise. I wasn't expecting you so soon. Is everything all right?"

"It's a special day, Señor Ruiz," said the familiar one,

the one who came at the end of each month. "There are protests about the elections. We wanted to make sure you are all right."

"Everything is fine. Thank you for thinking of us."

Ernesto reappeared and slipped the envelope into his father's hand, then took a step back but remained next to him.

"I understand business has been good for your family lately?"

"Yes, we can't complain." Ernesto's father kept hold of the envelope.

"Good. Very good." The caballito nodded, then turned to indicate the man who'd entered with him. "This is my colleague. He'll be making the rounds with me from now on."

Ernesto frowned, but his father managed to avoid any reaction other than a nod of acknowledgment. "Well, thank you again for looking out for us." He extended his hand, and the caballito shook it, accepting the envelope at the same time.

"There are two of us now, Señor Ruiz."

The four men stood in silence. "Señor," Ernesto's father said. "Although business has been good, as you say, it hasn't been so very good as to…" He trailed off as the new cabalitto moved in front of one of the torcederos and reached into his workspace to pick up a handful of tobacco leaves waiting to be rolled into cigars.

He rubbed the leaves between his fingers and sniffed them. "These are nice," he said before letting the leaves fall to the floor.

Ernesto felt beads of sweat pop on his forehead. His

father only blinked.

"My colleague is new to the unit," the first caballito said. "He is a much younger man. His expenses are not so high as mine."

"I see. Excuse me a moment." Ernesto's father left the factory floor and went into his office.

"Is that your sister?" the younger caballito asked as he looked through the glass wall and to the table where Marta was busy at work, head down.

The older one elbowed him. "None of that."

Ernesto's father returned with another envelope, and also a small, undecorated cigar box. He shook the younger man's hand and transferred the envelope. "Good to see you gentlemen beefing up patrols," he said.

He held the box out to the older one. "Please accept this small token of our appreciation for all the hard work you do."

He accepted the gift. "Thank you, Señor Ruiz. That is very kind."

"When can we expect you to stop by for a visit again?" Ernesto's father asked. It seemed a brazen question, hinting too directly at the formality of the arrangement.

But the cabalitto only smiled. "We'll be making the usual rounds later this month."

Just two weeks. And twice the payment too.

*

THE WORKER'S SHIFT ended late in the afternoon, and Ernesto had to hurry to get across the city in time for his own shift at the casino, but he still needed to talk to

Francisco, one of the torcederos, before he left. He caught up with the man just as the workers were packing up and invited him into the tobacco storage room.

"Are you certain, Francisco? I don't want to get any of you into trouble."

Even though the transom windows were open, the sweet smell rising from the stacks of tobacco filled the room. Francisco leaned against the worktable, his brown fingers splayed across its surface at his sides. "Yes, we all are. We're young with no families yet. What do we have to fear from your American friends?"

Nothing. Maybe. Ernesto wasn't sure. He still didn't fully understand why Mr. Mason wanted the information about the torcederos. But he did know he couldn't lose the worker's trust; he wouldn't betray them.

The jolt of a memory—an actual betrayal, years ago—surfaced and was just as quickly buried.

So, when he understood what Mason wanted from him, he'd explained everything to the torcederos and asked for volunteers who'd be willing to share their political thoughts about Castro and his efforts to fight back against the coup.

Ernesto had collected detailed notes from Francisco and three others. No one was doing anything against the law, and none of the torcederos supported the idea of revolution—he'd made sure to stress that in his summary. The notes were simply a list of rallies, who had scheduled them, how they got the word out to the community, who were the organizers. None of it was revolutionary or even particularly radical. The message was always about ending corruption, and who could fault that?

The image of the caballito deliberately ruining the tobacco leaves burned in Ernesto's memory. He thanked Francisco, picked up his duffel bag, and told his mother he would be staying the night at the guest house.

"But tomorrow is Sunday," she complained. "You'll miss Mass."

"I need to be there," Ernesto insisted. "New guests arrive on Saturdays, so tomorrow morning will be important to give a strong first impression." He wouldn't be surprised if no new guests arrived today. Mr. Schmidt was really ratcheting back the bookings, and Ernesto wasn't sure if that was intentional or if people feared coming now after the coup.

"And besides," he added. "I can go to Mass downtown." It wasn't exactly a lie, not even a white one, because he *could* go to Mass downtown. But he knew he wouldn't, and he didn't like how American his thinking about lies was becoming.

*

"YOU KNOW HE was telling the truth, right?" Mr. Cordero asked.

They were alone in the cigar room. Hank had gone out onto the casino floor with a collection of mismatched cigars they sold for a dime each. It wasn't very much money compared to what they were getting for the gift boxes they sold, but it was still twice what the wholesaler paid them per cigar. And the tactic often drew in customers who ended up paying ten dollars or more for a box to bring back to the States.

"What do you mean?" Ernesto asked. "Telling the truth about what?"

"Hank. At the zoo this morning." When Ernesto blushed and looked at the floor, Cordero clapped him on the shoulder. "There are no secrets at Casa de Ada, Ernesto. Matt and Eduardo have been telling the *amante* story since they got back."

He wondered if that was true—that there were no secrets at Casa de Ada. They kept secrets from the outside world, after all.

"My point is," Cordero continued, "he's totally smitten with you. It would be nice to know you felt the same way." He stared at Ernesto, tightening the grasp on his shoulder, waiting for something from Ernesto. A confession of love? That was between him and Hank. "He's my friend, Ernesto. I wouldn't want to see him get hurt."

Mannix came back into the room before Ernesto could think of a reply.

"Even though I'm ridiculously handsome," Hank said, "it's hard for me to compete with those pretty cigarette girls and their short skirts."

"Sorry, Hank," Cordero said. "But those girls are the only reason I'm still willing to keep coming here to help you out." He was looking at Ernesto when he said it—staring, actually—trying to communicate something. But what?

Was Mr. Cordero *not* a homosexual? He'd thought everyone at Casa de Ada was, and the photo shoots with Hank surely pointed in that direction. But Hank had insisted he and Mr. Cordero didn't have that kind of relationship, and Ernesto believed him. And then there was

Ivan, who definitely wasn't a homosexual but who had some sort of sex with men to earn money.

He hadn't seen Ivan since the mysterious nighttime visit to his bedroom. Sometimes, he wondered if he'd dreamt it.

"We need our own pretty girl to walk the floor with a fancy tray of cigars," Hank said. Both men turned to look at Ernesto. "Say, I have an idea."

A shudder ran through Ernesto.

*

THEY ARGUED ABOUT it for half an hour but still couldn't reach an agreement.

"I'm telling you," Ernesto insisted, not for the first time, "my parents won't let her. It doesn't matter if she'd want to do it or not."

"But is she pretty?" Cordero asked, not for the first time.

"Tony, please. *Of course* she's pretty. She's like…a girl version of Ernie."

Before Ernesto could decide which objectionable part of that statement he should respond to first, Mannix moved on. "And they might come around. They weren't so keen at first on Ernie working at the guest house so much, but look how that turned out."

"Um," Cordero said, "with their only son having sex with an older American man?"

"Well, fine," said Mannix. "I suppose they wouldn't be too keen on that part. But on balance, the whole thing has been good for the Ruiz family. The money, the exposure, the new market opportunities."

Ernesto couldn't deny the truth of that.

"So maybe if we just *presented* it the right way, your parents and Marta would see it as an opportunity."

Ernesto was getting good at reading Hank, and he wondered if "presented" meant another white lie. "Maybe," he agreed. "But again, my parents wouldn't—"

"Hello?" a woman called from the doorway. "Am I interrupting?"

"No, ma'am," said Mannix. "Please come in." He waved his arm in invitation.

She stepped through the doorway, and suddenly the room was far too small. She was taller than any of the men, and Ernesto had never seen an American woman like her. She didn't seem to be wearing any makeup, and her hair was cut short in a style that only accentuated her manly appearance, as did the severe tweed skirt and blocky jacket, buttoned to the neck.

"Good," she said. "My name is Mabel Chadsworth, and I'd like to try one of the cigars that young man was offering out on the casino floor." She nodded to Mannix.

"Really? You would?" he asked. Ernesto thought Hank shouldn't have let his surprise show like that. Evidently, Mabel Chadsworth thought so too.

She narrowed her eyes, and Cordero, who always left the room when a sales presentation was being made—it was just too crowded otherwise—excused himself, squeezed past her, and slipped out the door.

Before Hank could say something stupid, Ernesto picked up the tray of cigars and approached her. "Of course, Mrs. Chadsworth," he said, holding out the tray for her to make a selection.

She added a frown to her narrowed eyes. "I'm a fifty-year-old woman dressed as I am and wearing no jewelry. Do I look like I'm married?"

"No, ma'am," Mannix and Ernesto responded simultaneously.

"Good," she said again. "Now, with that ugliness out of the way"—she turned to address Ernesto directly—"which of these cigars would you recommend for a lady?"

It was an odd question, certainly. Women didn't smoke cigars. But why not? And what if they did? Ernesto started considering what a lady might look for in a cigar, how they might smoke one. To start with, they'd probably want a cigar on the smaller size—they had smaller hands after all.

He looked at Mabel Chadsworth's thick, ringless fingers. Most women did anyway.

She cocked her head at him, waiting for an answer.

"He's thinking," Mannix whispered. "It's how he does things."

And now that he thought about it, he supposed women might smoke cigars in different contexts than men do. They wouldn't be crowded around a hazy poker table or packed into a smoke-filled board room. In fact, they most likely wouldn't be smoking in public at all. Instead, they'd gather in small groups, enjoying something secret, subversive even.

Ernesto smiled as he thought about how it must be for Hans, dressed as Ada, out dancing at the club.

Mannix leaned in closer to Mabel Chadsworth but

not too close. "The smile means he's thought of something. You see, when he—"

"Look," she interrupted. "You're very pretty, and I'm sure you mean well. But let's give the one who knows what he's doing some space to operate." Mannix's mouth gaped open. "And you're too close." She shooed him away with her fingers.

He couldn't possibly have heard any of that right, so Ernesto turned his attention back to the task. A smaller cigar, he thought, yes, but also a cleaner, shorter smoke. They wouldn't want cigars smoldering away in massive ashtrays, clouding the room unnecessarily. If women were smoking, they'd want to enjoy the experience—enjoy the *cigar*—then get on with things.

He selected a narrow, tightly rolled cigar that would have looked out of place in one of the sampler boxes. He remembered when Arturo had rolled it—he'd only had one small criollo wrapper left, and he hadn't wanted to waste it. There'd been a lot of good-natured ribbing from the other torcederos about its size, but it was high quality tobacco, and an excellent wrapper leaf, and Ernesto's father had kept it aside to enjoy himself.

Somehow, it had made its way here.

"This one, ma'am." He placed the cigar on a tray and held it to her.

She leaned in and peered at it without touching it. "Why?" she asked.

"It's distinctive," Ernesto replied. "And it's better shaped for a woman, and different enough from what the men are smoking that it wouldn't look like...like..." Ernesto waved his arm, trying to think of a way to express his thoughts in English. It wouldn't look like they were pretending to be men, but it would be clear they were doing their own thing.

"It wouldn't look like she had a big cock in her mouth," Mabel Chadsworth supplied. "And you're quite right," she added. Ernesto blushed, and behind the American woman, Mannix almost fell over. She lifted the cigar and took a deep sniff along its length. "Very nice."

Cordero passed by in the hallway, looked in, then hurried on.

She lifted the guillotine off the tray and gave an expert and enthusiastic snip to the end of the cigar. Mannix shuddered. She'd taken off more than was strictly necessary, but she seemed pleased with the result.

Ernesto lit a match and held it out to Mrs. Chadsworth. *Miss* Chadsworth, he corrected, although he thought that didn't feel right either. He was ready to seamlessly bring the flame closer and light the end of her cigar if she wasn't aware of the proper ritual.

But she was, and her eyes gleamed as she carefully rotated her cigar above the flame, allowing it to slowly warm evenly. "It's good to deal with a man who doesn't underestimate me." The way she said "man" reminded Ernesto of how Ivan had said "American" and how Mr. Mason's boss said "communist."

Ernesto lit a second match, and before long the tip of the cigar was glowing brightly and uniformly. "Very good, young man." She took a puff and let the smoke drift through her mouth before exhaling. "Oh, that is quite nice."

"Thank you, Miss Chadsworth," Ernesto said.

Mannix winced, evidently expecting a reprimand. But Mabel Chadsworth only smiled.

"Chad," she said.

Mannix's eyes bulged out of his head.

"Excuse me?" asked Ernesto.

"Chad. That's what my friends call me. *You* may call me Chad."

That would be absolutely impossible.

"This band is exquisite," she continued. "Where do you get them?

Mannix spoke up then. This was usually part of his spiel, but Ernesto thought it was probably better if he sat this one out. He tried to subtly signal his thoughts with his eyes. But Mannix wasn't looking at him. "His sister actually does them all by hand," he exclaimed. "There's a picture of her on the wall. Isn't that amazing, Chad?" He frowned. "No, Chad doesn't feel right. Chads? Chadsy, maybe? Yes, I think—"

Mabel Chadsworth turned on her heel with military precision and shot a glance at Mannix that seemed to turn him into a stone pillar. Then she turned her attention back to Ernesto.

"Please remind your pretty, but dangerously care-less, friend I still have access to the guillotine, and I enjoy using it."

Cordero had just stepped into the room but was seemingly yanked back into the hallway like a yo-yo at the end of its string.

"He may refer to me as Mabel Chadsworth. And if he *must* address me, he will use ma'am, nothing else." Behind her, Mannix swallowed and nodded.

"He understands, ma'am," Ernesto said.

This woman was amazing. Ernesto was awestruck.

"Good. And as I said, you may call me Chad."

"Yes, ma'am." At her scowl, he added, "Uh…Chad."

"Good." She took another puff from the cigar and closed her eyes in pleasure. "Now, have the pretty one bring another chair. We're going to sit, I'm going to enjoy this lovely cigar, and you're going to tell me all about your talented sister who does such extraordinary work."

Chapter Twenty-Four

"SAPPHIC CIGARS?" MASON asked, his tone incredulous.

"I know, right?" Mannix responded. They were just finishing breakfast the following morning. Ernesto had cleaned the serving dishes and was circling the room freshening everyone's coffee. The men from East Orange were grouped together at the far end of the table, their attention on Matt, who sat nearby. He was flipping through his Spanish workbook while sloppily eating cereal.

Milk would occasionally dribble down his chin, which in turn would set the men from East Orange whispering to each other.

Ernesto moved behind them with the coffeepot. One of the men stretched his arms wide while he fake yawned, and his hand came perilously close to Ernesto's backside. At Mannix's glare, he quickly withdrew. He leaned in to his companion and whispered, loud enough to be heard, "I don't know why they make him wear those pants if he's not…accessible."

Matt looked up from his workbook. "*Los hombres son cerdos,*" he said. *The men are pigs.* Ernesto smiled.

"But are you sure she was a lesbian?" Mason asked.

"Yes," insisted Mannix. "She operates a club for 'like-minded women' who sit around smoking and avoiding men. You kind of have to spit out the word *men* to get the full flavor of how she described it."

"Plus, she called Hank pretty," Ernesto said. "Then she threatened to cut off his *pinga.*" A silence fell over the table; the context provided all the translation the men needed. "She was extraordinary."

One of the men from East Orange lowered his fork to his plate, leaving the bite of sausage he had speared. "Well," he said, pushing his plate away, "Mannix *is* pretty."

"Yes," agreed one of the others. "It's just too bad he doesn't play with us anymore."

"I know," said a third. "Remember that night in the pool a few years ago? God, I could have—"

"No one remembers any nights in any pools," Mannix interrupted, loudly, and with finality.

"Not all lesbians dislike men," Hans said. "Or so I'm told anyway." He also pushed back his chair and stood, then placed a hand on Mason's shoulder. "I don't know why we're talking about lesbians anyway."

"And at the breakfast table," Mannix complained.

Cordero was picking crumbs from the muffin plate.

"We're talking about lesbians because this particular lesbian—"

"Chad," Ernesto added helpfully, to the amusement of everyone in the room.

"—wants the Ruiz family to design a line of cigars for women and wants Marta to do the artwork."

"That seems like a lot of work," said Hans. "How long will this...Chad...be staying in Havana? Is there time for all that?"

"Oh, she lives here," Ernesto said. He began collecting plates from the table. "And she's friends with Ernest Hemmingway."

"She lives *here*, in Havana?" Mason asked.

"Yes," Ernesto said. "And her club is here too. I think."

"It can't be," Hans objected. "I'd have known about it."

"It's not *right* here. It's miles away, out near where Hemmingway lives."

Cordero took a pile of dishes from Ernesto and turned to head into the kitchen. "Would Marta be interested in doing it?"

"Of course she would," Ernesto replied as he began removing the juice glasses. "But my parents would never let her."

"They might though," Mannix said. "I mean, they wouldn't need to know *everything*." Mannix stood, walked over to Matt's table, and removed his bowl.

"Hey!" Matt objected. "I'm still eating that."

Mannix ignored him. "If we told your parents it's just one commissioned job: to design a special label and box?

Why wouldn't they want her to do it?" He picked up Matt's juice glass, still half full. "And she'd be supervised the entire time. And Ernie will be there too." He glanced over for confirmation, and at Ernesto's expression he added, "Erniesto, I meant."

"I thought it was *Ernesto*," one of the East Orange men whispered.

Matt shook his head.

Mannix was warming to the strategy. "Then we can slowly build up to her working with us selling cigars. You know all the wives would love to see her paint and hear her talk about designing the boxes." He handed Matt's glass and bowl to Cordero, who'd just returned from the kitchen. "Yes, we could tell them the American women are interested in how a young Cuban woman earns a living. Oh, oh, I know…we can tell them these Americans are supporters of the arts and want to see local customs preserved and expanded!"

He looked around the room for approval. But Matt's pencil had rolled off the table after Mannix removed the plate it was resting against, and he'd stood, bent at the waist, and stretched his arms under the table to retrieve it. The men from East Orange were transfixed and paying no attention to Mannix at all.

Hans was busy looking put out that he didn't know about the—maybe lesbian—club, and Mason was staring at Mannix with a mixture of distaste and amazement, slowly shaking his head.

Only Ernesto reacted. "More white lies."

The bell dangling over the front door rang in the reception parlor.

"I'll go," said Cordero as he left the dining room.

"They're not *lies*," Mannix insisted. "They're...pieces of the truth...offered up at just the right moments to...lead people...where they need to go."

The men from East Orange nodded their agreement with that assessment. Matt put his pencil back on the table. "You're amazing," he said. Mannix offered a tentative smile in response, but he sensed a trap. "Imagine what you'll be like after thirty *more* years living in your fantasy world," Matt added.

Ernesto frowned and Mannix scowled. He hated when Ernesto was reminded that Mannix had lied to him about his age or that a future together for them was unimaginable.

Cordero came into the room with a troubled look on his face. "Uh, Hans?" That didn't sound good, and everyone turned to face him. "There are a couple of police officers here to see you. I asked them to wait in the parlor."

Hans turned to Mannix. "You didn't miss a payment, did you?"

"No. It's not expected until next week." *Was there something wrong? Was Ernie's family all right?*

"Yet here we are," said one of the caballitos, entering the dining room. "Early." The other followed close behind. Mannix recognized the first one—he was the fellow he dealt with each month. He didn't recognize the second, younger one, taking in the room with suspicious eyes.

The men from East Orange remained seated and tried to become invisible. Anger flared in Mannix; homosexuals everywhere knew a shakedown when they saw one. Hans tried to take control of the situation. "Señors, you're always welcome. Matt, would you please go see that fresh coffee is brewing in the kitchen."

That was smart, thought Mannix. Get the most volatile one out of the mix. Despite all their teasing of each other, Mannix was coming to like Golden Boy, but he had no sense of how far his idealistic view of the world was from reality. Mannix could easily see him challenging the police, which would lead to disaster.

Matt disappeared into the kitchen, and Ernesto followed him.

"Coffee?" asked Hans. "Would you like to sit? Have you had breakfast?"

"Don't worry, we won't be staying. But coffee would be nice." The younger caballito walked around the table, slowly passing by the men from East Orange, letting his finger brush across one's shoulder. Mannix thought it was meant to be intimidating but had to suppress a quirk of his lips when he considered what the caballito would think if he only knew the truth about these men.

The first officer turned to Mason. "I see the government man is back."

"Yes, señor. The United States Government is always interested in improving relations with Cuba," Mason said.

"That's good," the caballito said. "Presidente Battista would approve."

Mannix took that as an implied assertion that Battista approved of the caballito's actions on the local level as well.

"I hate to ask," the officer continued, addressing Mason directly, "but I have business to conduct with Señor

Schmidt and his house manager. Would you mind giving us some privacy?"

Mannix thought Mason looked very much like he'd mind. But there wasn't anything to do about it. The police only knew Mason as a regular guest, and a representative of the US Government, and therefore not a man who should witness the more...transactional...side of local politics. They could never be allowed to learn the truth about Mason's relationship with Hans.

"Of course," Mason replied. He placed his napkin on the table and rose from his chair. "If you'll excuse me." He nodded to Hans and walked into the hallway.

Ernesto reappeared with a coffee tray, and the caballitos began fixing their cups.

"Mr. Mannix," Hans said, "do we have the package available?" He turned to the caballitos. "My apologies. We weren't expecting to see you so soon."

"Yes, well..." The older one sipped his coffee. "Things are changing. We'll be stopping by twice a month now."

Hans didn't respond. His jaw was twitching, which was never a good sign.

"I understand business is doing very well," the senior officer said.

"Actually, no," replied Hans. "Bookings are down significantly. We're cutting back. It's the coup. Some people are afraid to come here."

"Oh, come now, Mr. Schmidt. That was months ago, and even your government has recognized our new president." He sipped his coffee. "And you'd be well advised not to use the word *coup* anymore; Batista doesn't like it. We're a legitimate, respected government."

Mannix thought of himself as an expert at stretching the truth, but considering these men were here to collect shakedown money, he thought that assertion was a few steps too far.

"And in any event, I was referring to your new cigar business doing very well."

Hans managed to hide his surprise. Ernesto had been standing silently by the coffee table, presumably waiting for a sign from Hans for what he should do next. Mannix saw him stiffen at the mention of the cigars.

"The business you neglected to tell us about," the caballito added. Mannix thought it sounded like an accusation, and it was. "We'd love to try one."

At Hans's nod, Ernesto left the room to collect the cigars. Mannix grabbed an ashtray and placed it on the breakfast table near the officers.

"Oh, I'd hardly call it a business," Hans said. "It's just a new service we're offering for our guests."

The officer glanced at the men from East Orange, still sitting quietly at the end of the table. "Enjoy a good smoke, do you?" They smiled and nodded and kept their gazes down.

Ernesto returned with a small tray holding two cigars, a guillotine, and a box of matches. Mannix noticed he'd thought to remove the Ruiz bands. Ernesto looked at Hans, who nodded to the caballitos. He offered them the cigars.

They each took one, and rather than using the guillotine to cut the cap, they both bit off the tips and spit them on the floor. Hans's jaw twitch intensified. Ernesto lifted the matches from the tray, but the younger caballito took them from him and lit his own cigar, immediately draw-ing a deep breath through it, even though the tip was barely smoldering, and unevenly at that.

Ernesto winced, and the senior officer repeated the process with his own cigar.

He inhaled deeply, and even Mannix—who wasn't much of a smoker—knew that must have been painful.

"Nice," he said, putting the cigar down directly on the table so that its smoking tip ended up dangling over the edge. "I see why you think it's worth it to rent an entire room at the casino just to sell them."

Oh. Mannix understood now. They thought Hans was selling the cigars at the casino. And they would; it made sense. He'd never discussed it with Mason, but he imagined the CIA wasn't paying the bill directly, and since Mannix appeared to run the cigar operation, the en-tire business of payments was probably being passed through the Casa de Ada account.

What a mess.

Hans looked confused. "But I'm not—"

And then the crashing realization of the risk he'd put the Ruiz family in hit home. "No," Mannix interrupted. Everyone turned to stare at him. "That is, it's the govern-ment that's paying for the room." The senior caballito raised an eyebrow. "The US Government," Mannix clari-fied.

The younger officer's cigar had gone out. It hadn't been lit properly, and Mannix watched as Ernesto strug-gled between wanting to be helpful and wanting to re-main as invisible as possible.

"And why would the United States Government pay

the casino to sell cigars?"

Good question. But how to answer it without implicating Ernie's family?

"Perhaps you should ask Mr. Mason," Mannix responded, hoping against hope that Mason would have a plausible explanation that didn't reveal Ernesto's commitment to sharing the politics of the torcederos. Who knew how the caballitos would feel about their own people sharing secrets with the US?

This is all my fault.

"Mr. Mason is here on government business," Mannix continued. "I'm sure he can't share state secrets, but he might be able to help shed light on what's happening with the cigars at the casino." It was intended as a setup for Arthur, whom Mannix assumed was eavesdropping beyond the doorway. It was the best he could do. It would be up to Arthur to come up with something, and Mannix hoped he would understand how important it was to keep Ernesto and his family out of the crosshairs.

"Did I hear my name?" Mason asked as he stepped back into the dining room.

The senior caballito lifted his cigar from the table and a column of ash dropped onto the floor. "The house manager here"—he nodded at Mannix—"believes your government is paying the casino to sell cigars there. That seems unlikely, as the payments come from this inn." Like all good investigators, he left space for someone to start talking, but no one did.

After the silence dragged on for a few moments, he took a more direct approach. "Is your government paying for that room at the casino?"

Mason made a show of eyeing the men from East Orange, as if there were things he couldn't discuss in front of civilians. He was good at his job.

"Señors," he came fully into the room and briefly touched Ernesto's shoulder as he passed. "Would you be willing to take a walk with me in the gardens?" He nodded almost imperceptibly toward the men from East Orange, and Mannix thought he might be playing the whole secrecy thing up too much. But Mason was CIA, so what did Mannix know?

The caballitos looked excited, though, so it must have worked. They nodded their agreement.

"Mr. Schmidt, might I borrow your boy to come along?" Mason asked. "It's a delicate discussion, and he might be needed to translate some of the finer points."

Mannix bristled at the word "boy." Ernesto was the smartest man in the room. But he appreciated Mason's setup to have him along; he might be able to redirect Mason if he was about to say the wrong thing.

"Certainly," Hans responded. "I'll make sure my guests afford you privacy." He glanced at the men from East Orange, who were probably preparing to bolt for their rooms and lock their doors. "When you're finished, my house manager will have your packages waiting for you."

Chapter Twenty-Five

IT WAS WARM in the garden and still damp from the thunderstorm that had rumbled through at dawn. Water dripped from leaves overhead and mosquitos buzzed in the thick air. The caballitos had left their cigars inside, where they would smolder and burn out.

Ernesto bristled at the disrespect. *All of that talent and hard work, wasted.*

Mr. Mason led the small group through the garden path, then stopped at a wide opening near the pool, which, as Mr. Schmidt had promised, remained empty.

"So, yes," he said without preamble. "The United States Government is paying the casino for space to sell cigars. This is strictly confidential, by the way, so you mustn't tell anyone." Surely, Mr. Mason knew as well as Ernesto did these men couldn't be trusted to remain silent.

"Why?"

Mason shrugged. "The usual reasons—information, intelligence, an ear to the ground, as it were." He gave Ernesto a look that was difficult to interpret. "Translate that, please."

Ernesto did his best, and he tried to hide his growing panic about what it would mean for his family to be exposed like this, to be seen as working with the United States to provide information on Cuban workers. It wouldn't matter that no one was being deceived, that the workers themselves were okay with Ernesto sharing the information. No, it would seem like a betrayal.

He had a hard time with the phrase "ear to the ground," and had to guess at its meaning himself, but the caballitos kept nodding their heads, as if what he was saying made sense.

"Why the casino?"

"Ah, well," Mason said. And Ernesto thought he was making a show of seeming embarrassed. "Things are not always done by the books here in Cuba, are they?" He swept his hand in an arc to take in the two caballitos and the inn. "Important work is done behind the scenes, out of sight, yes?" He looked to Ernesto. "Translate, please."

The conversation was becoming more awkward by the moment. Ernesto repeated Mr. Mason's comments, but he felt incredibly uncomfortable being so direct talking about the graft.

The officers squinted suspiciously, neither admitting nor denying the implications of what Mason was saying. But what could they say when everyone knew Hank was busy putting cash into envelopes back inside the house?

"And," Mason lowered his voice to a whisper,

prompting the officers to lean in, "you know about the American mob, right? The mafia?"

There was no need to translate that. The caballitos now looked as uncomfortable as Ernesto. Everyone knew of such things, but no one talked of them. "You've heard of Meyer Lansky?" Mason asked. The men sucked in their breath and leaned away. This was a step too far. Just the mention of that name in the wrong company could have dire, even fatal, consequences.

"Señor Mason," one of the men said, holding up his hand. "Be careful."

"Yes, yes, of course." Mason said. "But we're all men of the world here. We know the score. And the US Government does too. We're paying the casino to keep us informed, so we can track the mafia's operations in Cuba. We don't have a problem with Lansky right now, and neither does Batista, but we want to keep on top of things in case we need to step in."

This was far more than Ernesto wanted to know. It was dangerous information, and he wanted to unhear it.

"Translate, please."

"Do I have to?"

"Yes, Ernesto, you do."

Although his voice was trembling, he did his best, trying to remember the earlier part of Mr. Mason's statement, about being "men of the world" and "knowing the score." By the time he was finished, even the caballitos looked like they didn't want to hear more.

"Thank you, Señor Mason. You've answered all our questions. No one here has anything to worry about—"

"You know," interrupted Mason. "Maybe we could

come to some type of arrangement. We know certain police officers are cooperating secretly with the mafia, if you could find out who they are, and keep tabs on them for us—"

"No," they both said, backing away.

"Translate, please."

Ernesto couldn't possibly make that offer to the caballitos, even if he was just translating. Fortunately, he didn't have to.

"No! Don't. We understood. We've heard enough." They turned and began hurrying down the garden path.

"But your envelopes," Mason called after them.

"That's all right," the senior officer said. "Tell Señor Schmidt he can keep this one."

*

BY THE TIME he and Mr. Mason returned to the guest house, the men from East Orange had disappeared.

"The cops are gone," Mason told everyone.

"What about these?" Mannix asked. He pushed at the two envelopes sitting on the table.

Mason moved to Hans and wrapped an arm around his shoulder, pulling him close. "I've scared them off for now." Hans let out a deep, trembling breath. "I'm sorry, darling," Mason said. "I know this type of thing troubles you deeply."

"It reminds me of the first time you came sniffing around my boarding house in New York," Hans said.

"Oh, hardly," replied Mason. "I'm certain I was more intimidated by you than you were by me."

"Um, can you two finish your trip down memory lane later," asked Mannix, "so the rest of us can learn what happened? How did you scare them off?"

Ernesto admired the easy way Mr. Mason and Mr. Schmidt had with each other, the tenderness they showed. He wondered if he and Hank would ever develop that level of closeness.

"Did you manage to keep Ernie's family out of it?" Mannix asked, and Ernesto's heart swelled, despite the whole name thing. It meant a lot that his family's welfare was top of mind for Hank, and he thought, yes, if they could manage to be together long term—somehow—he and Hank could develop that type of relationship.

But not with all the public touching. Ernesto didn't like that at all. He moved to Hank, who held out an arm to him.

"No hugging," Ernesto said.

Mannix aborted his move to pull Ernesto into an embrace and instead placed a hand on his shoulder. "Don't worry," he told the room. "He's like this. He just had an entire conversation in his head about hugging. Isn't he remarkable?"

Mannix leaned close to whisper into Ernesto's ear. "You're all right, amante?"

Ernesto's heart swelled even further, and he leaned into Hank to accept the embrace after all.

"Not that all this gushy sweetness isn't fascinating," said Cordero, "But can you get to the part where you explain what happened?" He was standing by the kitchen doorway next to Matt, who gave him a thumbs-up.

"Ernesto's family isn't at risk," Mason said. "At least

not yet." He turned to Ernesto. "But, eventually, news of your success selling cigars at the casino will get back to the corrupt cops in control of your own neighborhood, and they'll want a piece of the action. We'll have to talk about how to get ahead of that."

Mannix squeezed Ernesto's shoulder, then released him. "Don't worry, amante," he whispered. "Everything will be fine."

As if wishing for something could make it true.

"But what do we do about Casa de Ada?" Mannix asked. "We do sell cigars from here too. Will the Keystone Cops feel like we lied to them about that?"

"I shouldn't think so," Hans said, indicating the empty dining room. "Business is way down. They can't expect more when we're earning so much less."

"And I think I've put them off for a while," Mason added. "I led them to believe the CIA was paying the casino to report back on mob activities. I implied the cigar room was just a front to make the payments, to have a presence in the casino."

"That's...complicated," Mannix said.

"Not for them," Mason responded. "They don't want anything to do with the mob. They know corruption runs through the highest levels of government, but they don't know who might be in whose pocket. They know enough to keep their heads down and concentrate on their own neighborhood shakedowns, leaving the mob alone."

"This is why the Cuban people want a revolution," Matt said.

Ernesto was tired of Matt thinking he knew everything about the "Cuban people." "We don't want a revolution, Matt," he said. "We just want to have elections and eliminate corruption."

Everyone turned to look at him. Ernesto rarely spoke up for himself, but now that he realized his family was at increased risk due to the cigar arrangement with the casino, he wasn't going to let others make all the decisions. He turned to Mason. "You could have warned me about all this," he said.

"Your family is just selling their cigars, Ernesto," Mason responded. "You're not involved with the mob at all. The police have no reason to think otherwise."

"But I *am* sharing information with your government, and even if it's not secret information, it still feels...dirty...somehow, now that I realize it's all part of a web of lies and deception." Matt was nodding his head. "Was it even true? What you told the caballitos about police informing on each other? Would you really pay them to turn on their own colleagues?"

Like you pay me to report on our workers.

"In my line of work, it's good to keep people guessing," Mason said. Which was no answer at all. "But if those cops aren't sure about how high up my connections go, then they might be cautious with Hans. They'll never know if their bosses might resent them putting the screws on an informant."

Ernesto realized how crazy this was—the layers of lies and deceptions. How did the Americans live this way? If only his father had known what getting close with the Americans would lead to.

"Well, that's smart," said Hans. He seemed to be recovering and allowed Mason to release him. "But they'll be coming here twice a month now—that's a lot more money we'll have to come up with. Still, they can't get blood from a stone," Hans said, sweeping his hand to indicate the empty dining room.

That was another new phrase for Ernesto, but he understood right away what it meant. He hoped Hans was right, but he had his doubts. He thought the caballitos might very well try to get blood from stones.

"And if they keep scaring our guests away," Hans complained, "the only repeat business we'll have is that awful Alan with his awful yacht."

"Oh, I don't think he'll be coming back," Mannix said.

"No," Matt said. "He will. He'll want his photos back, but they're not here."

"Photos?" Mason asked. "What—"

They were interrupted by one of the *Pumped* photographers entering the breakfast room. He yawned and took in the empty table. "Good morning," he said. "I hope there's still coffee. I saw the men from East Orange scuttling down the hallway. What did I miss?"

*

MARTA LEAPT AT the opportunity to conduct her work in the casino, and she proved to be surprisingly strong-willed in overcoming their parent's objections. Ernesto thought his father might have been overly influenced by the money they'd been making ever since he set up the cigar room there, and with her husband and both children arrayed against her, there wasn't much their mother could do.

Before long, Marta was spending as much time at the casino as Ernesto was—always chaperoned by one of the American men, of course—and she had a trunk in the corner for all her supplies. She would paint the decorative boxes and carefully apply the script to the cigar bands. And Hank had been right, the Americans loved it, especially the wives.

It took her over a month, but she completed the design project for Mabel Chadsworth, and Ernesto wasn't at all surprised to learn the boxes' images were centered around Delacroix's painting *Liberty Leading the People*, with the bare-breasted Liberty prominently portrayed on both the inside and outside of the box.

"She's extraordinary, Ernesto," Marta told him one morning at the breakfast table. "Did you know she's friends with Ernest Hemmingway?"

"Who is friends with Ernest Hemmingway?" their mother asked.

"Oh, just a woman who likes my artwork," Marta responded. Both Ernesto and Marta were getting good at only revealing to their parents what was necessary.

"This woman should not be friends with Ernest Hemmingway; he is the wrong kind of American," their mother insisted.

"What?" Marta asked. "Unlike Ernesto's Americans who help us earn lots of money?"

And I'm in love with one of them, and we have sex, and I can't bear the thought of losing our relationship, but I also can't imagine a future that permits it.

"Yes, exactly," their mother said.

Marta leaned forward, and began speaking in

English. She wasn't nearly as fluent as Ernesto, but she was improving quickly now that she interacted with Americans nearly every day. "She thinks women are too controlled, that we should be allowed to express ourselves however we choose." Their mother had moved to the kitchen sink. "I like calling her Chad. I think it's very daring."

It was certainly that. Ernesto wasn't sure if Marta understood the true nature of Chad's club.

"Well, just be careful around her. These Americans can be very confusing."

Marta simply shook her head, smiling. "Men," she murmured.

*

THE PACKARD HAD been more or less repaired, but it would never be the same. It vibrated when it went around corners and pulled slightly to the right haphazardly so it always seemed to come as a surprise to Hank when he had to tug the car back to the left.

A ghostly sour smell continued to haunt the back seat.

Nonetheless, Ernesto was happy to spend as much time as possible in the relative privacy of the car with Hank. They went on dates at least once a week now, and both men would try to make up for the fact that they'd gone about their relationship backward—starting with sex, moving on to love, then dating and trying to get to know each other.

Although maybe that was only backward in Ernesto's

world. Hank seemed to think it was the normal way of things.

It was a Sunday afternoon, one week before Ernesto was to begin his studies at university, and they were at the park next to the ancient stone fortress guarding the entrance to Havana's harbor.

The kites were Mannix's idea.

It took some level of coordination and grace to fly a kite properly, and Ernesto's kept crashing dangerously toward the sea before he'd manage to get it into the air again. Hank was much more adept and was the one who managed the added task of making sure their lines didn't cross in a tangle.

Mannix wore big black sunglasses that matched his slicked hair, and an amber silk shirt that matched Ernesto's eyes. Ernesto knew they made a handsome pair, and he paid more attention to Mannix than he did his own kite. With his arms stretched above his head, and the stiff sea breeze off the ocean, Mannix's shirt kept billowing up over his waistband, exposing his belly, and the thin line of black hair that began just below his navel.

Mannix's belly had a soft curve to it now, and Ernesto thought that made it absolutely perfect. For his part, Mannix was mortified when Ernesto caught him one day on the way back from a visit to Luigi to have his trousers let out—again.

"Don't ever turn thirty, Ernie," he'd said at the time, and Mannix had been so embarrassed that Ernesto didn't have it in him to be angry about the name.

Mannix had his kite flying in a stable figure eight pattern high above the fort, so he released one hand from the spool and trailed his fingers absently across his stomach allowing them to come to rest on the button of his trousers.

"You're doing that on purpose,' Ernesto accused him.

"Doing what?" he asked, all innocence, as his fingers dipped below his waistband.

Ernesto swallowed. "We're in public, Hank."

"We don't *need* to be," he pointed out.

Ernesto was already reeling in his kite. "Let's head back, then." He neatly coiled his kite's string around the spool, while Mannix made a hash of his and rushed to throw the kite into the Packard.

"What's your favorite *Hardy Boys* book?" Mannix called over his shoulder. It had become a game for them on their dates—asking ridiculous "getting to know you" questions like the disastrous ones they'd asked each other on their drive to the farm.

"*The Case of the Floating Underpants*," Ernesto replied. "*Cuál es to color favorito*?" he shot back. Part of the game involved Ernesto always asking his questions in Spanish. Hank was getting...better...with the language. And this was an easy one. They were both in a hurry after all.

"*Ámbar*," he replied. "*Claro*," he added. The color of Ernesto's eyes.

*

WITHOUT DISCUSSING IT, Mannix knew to head back along the malecón. Ernesto suspected Hank thought it was hopeless and they'd never find Ivan, but he couldn't just give up on his cousin. And he appreciated Hank's support.

The Packard slowed to a near crawl in dense traffic. It was a hot late-summer day, and they had the windows down, both to avoid the lingering smell from the back of the car, and to enjoy the sights and sounds of the city. The salty tang of the sea competed with diesel exhaust fumes, and the cries of the gulls nearly drowned out the calls of the cigarette and lottery ticket hawkers.

"Maybe we should get our own place," Mannix said. Ernesto turned away and looked out the window. They'd been over this before. They *could* do it, barely. Sales of cigars were strong and had picked up even more now that a few of the torcederos had learned to roll the smaller lady's cigars.

But Ernesto didn't know how it would work. What would he tell his parents and Marta? What would happen when this thing between him and Hank— But, no, he didn't want to think about that. Even though he couldn't envision a future for them, he was equally at a loss imagining an end.

"Let's see how school goes," he replied as he always did.

Mannix didn't press him. "I can't believe Golden Boy is going to be the new Ernie!" he said instead, and after a sharp pinch to the thigh, added, "...iesto."

It was difficult to imagine—Matt as the houseboy. But it was the best solution for everyone. Something had to give in his schedule once Ernesto started classes.

And the *Pumped* photographers had gone and weren't coming back. They said it was too dangerous to transport their work into the United States. The government was becoming obsessed with finding and punishing anyone dealing in "what could be mistaken for" pornography—their words. Ernesto had watched the filming, and he didn't think there was any mistaking it for anything else.

So Matt was without a job just as the houseboy position opened up. Eduardo seemed a lot more comfortable with Matt serving coffee than posing nearly naked for American magazines.

Not for the first time, Ernesto marveled at the oddities of the world he'd fallen into.

Traffic came to a stop, and after a moment, a small group of police officers pushed their way along the sidewalk next to the car. After they passed, Ernesto leaned out the window to peer ahead and saw protestors a block in front of them, waving signs about the canceled elections.

He rolled up his window and told Hank to do the same. Other drivers did too, and pedestrians either changed course or ducked into shops. It was over in minutes, and since the police didn't return in their direction, Ernesto guessed the protestors had been carted off down a side street.

"It's not like this in America, is it?"

"No, but people back home don't have the...*cojones*?" Mannix raised a questioning eyebrow, and Ernesto nodded. "The cojones to protest like this."

That didn't make sense to Ernesto. Americans prided themselves on independence. He thought about how to ask the question.

Traffic was beginning to inch along once again.

They entered the less respectable part of the malecón, and Ernesto didn't know if it was just the dark thoughts crowding his head, or if there really were more desperate-looking young Cuban men loitering about, eyeing the even larger number of greedy-looking older Americans. He was embarrassed. For them? For himself? He wasn't sure.

What did the young men see when they looked into the car? Did they assume he was one of them, riding with an American along the malecón? How much of a gap was there between him and them? Between him and Ivan?

He was still staring out the window as they crept along, being judged by the men they passed who would look in hopefully, then frown when they saw him. Disappointment? Disgust? "Hank, what are we *doing*?"

Traffic slowed to a stop again. "We're going home," Mannix replied. "But I suspect you've been having one of your deep thinks again, and maybe you mean something else?"

Ernesto was silent. Mannix followed his gaze to the corner where an American man slipped something into the palm of a Cuban teen. "This isn't us, Ernie...esto. Look at me, please." Ernesto did. "I've told you before," Mannix continued. "I love you. I don't know how that happened to me, but it did, and I do." He waited for Ernesto to say something, but he remained silent.

He wanted to say, "I love you too." And he *did* love Hank, as surprising and confusing as that was. But how could he say that here, surrounded by the destructiveness of Americans, the destructiveness of this...lifestyle? How could Hank ever fit into Ernesto's world?

"I just don't see how this"—he waved his hand between the two of them—"can work." Ernesto fell silent again. The car began rolling forward, still not moving as quickly as the woman pulling her shopping cart next to them who kept glancing quizzically at the unlikely pair inside.

"Is this the part where you say, 'But I love you, too, Honk, and we'll figure it out?'"

Ernesto was in no mood to be teased. "I *do* love you, Hank, God help me. But you're the one who gave me the job of thinking things through, and I just can't see a way for this to work. Maybe it would be best if we—"

"No! No, stop. I take it back. You are no longer responsible for thinking things through. Your job now is to relax and follow my lead. I'll figure everything out."

That wasn't the least bit comforting.

Ernesto looked out the window again, and he felt Hank's hand come to rest on his thigh. He fought against the pleasure and arousal it evoked, but it was hopeless. He long ago accepted the fact he was homosexual and even now, here in the midst of this human ugliness, the proof was irrefutable.

If only he could spend his days alone with Hank, an endless series of dates—flying kites, visiting museums, riding in the Packard. Or better yet, spending all day naked in bed, learning new things about each other.

But they couldn't do that.

"Please tell me what you're thinking," Mannix pleaded.

Ahead of them, a handful of American men had gathered at a corrugated sheet of metal that had been propped up to block access to a crumbling stone stairway leading down to the rocks of the seawall. The metal had been pulled back from one side, allowing enough space for a man to slip through. Even as he watched, Ernesto saw two Americans do just that and disappear from view.

A police officer stood nearby, his back to the group of men, scrupulously ignoring them.

Two American men came up from the steps, and Ernesto recognized something about their expressions. What was it? Satisfaction? Excitement?

No. Smugness—that was the English word for it. And he'd seen it on the faces of plenty of men at the casino when they thought they were getting away with something, like swiping a drink from a passing cocktail waitress's tray or patting the backside of a cigarette girl. Or taking three free cigar samples when they had no intention of buying any.

It was the worst of the American traits, this taking advantage of things and people because they had power, because they thought—

And then it hit him. "Stop the car."

"What? Ernie, are you—?"

"Stop the car, Hank!"

He did, and Ernesto jumped out. He pushed his way through the group of men, slipped behind the metal barrier, and leapt down the few steps to the narrow strip of dirt at the base of the seawall. It was dark in the shade, and his foot crunched on broken glass.

One of the men he'd seen descend a few moments earlier was urinating against the wall. The other loomed over a man on his knees. Ernesto pushed him aside, and he tumbled to the ground, trousers caught around his thighs. "Hey," he exclaimed as he went down.

The other hastily zipped up and moved for the stairs.

Ernesto squatted in front of the young man kneeling in the grimy sand.

It wasn't Ivan.

He looked shocked and confused, perhaps even drugged. He was filthy, and he snarled at Ernesto. "One at a time, I said." Then, when he saw Ernesto was Cuban he switched to Spanish. "What do you want?"

The man Ernesto had knocked over was getting to his feet. He was wobbly, and Ernesto briefly hoped he hadn't hit his head on one of the rocks; then he decided he hoped he had. The American seemed to be considering his options. Come back at Ernesto for a fight? Surely, he'd paid someone guarding the steps on the malecón for the privilege of coming down here.

The sound of a scuffle above decided it for the American, and he straightened himself out, then hurried away, edging farther along the seawall until he disappeared around the wall's curve. The brawl grew louder, then suddenly stopped.

Mannix appeared, his nose bleeding, and his handsome amber shirt ripped at the shoulder.

"Ernie! Amante! Are you all right?" Mannix stood over Ernesto, nervously shifting his hands as if he was unsure whether a touch would be welcomed.

"What do you want?" the Cuban repeated.

"I'm looking for someone," Ernesto said.

The Cuban spat into the dirt. "Shit. Now I won't get paid."

Hank must have understood because he pulled a few bills from his pocket and handed them to the young man. "Get yourself something to eat."

He took the money and rose stiffly to his feet. He began making his way up the steps. "That what you're looking for?" He nodded to the corner below him, where the base of the steps met the wall; then he was gone.

It looked like a pile of rags, but as Ernesto studied it, he recognized the shape of a human form underneath.

No, please God, no.

"Ernesto..." Mannix whispered.

He knelt beside the pile and peeled back a filthy sheet.

Ivan.

Was he...dead?

A soft groan proved he was not.

"Hank, he's alive." He pulled the sheet away and nearly gagged at the stench. He shook his cousin's shoulder. "Ivan. Ivan! Can you hear me?"

Ivan made no response, but he twisted his body and groaned again.

A bright red stain blossomed on his chest, just below his neck, then another, lower down his near his stomach. "Hank, he's bleeding!"

"No, that's me." Mannix pulled back.

Ernesto turned to look at him. Blood flowed from his nose, and there was a raw-looking scrape above his right eyebrow. Before he could say anything, a blare of horns from above echoed against the stones.

"I left the car blocking traffic."

Ernesto reached under Ivan and lifted him, rags and

all. "Come on. Let's get him into the car."

"Do you have him?" Mannix asked.

Ernesto nodded. His cousin was heavy, but not as heavy as he should be, and two people would make the job of maneuvering the tight steps more difficult. "Go," he told Hank.

Mannix left a trail of blood but managed to scare off the two men remaining at the top of the stairs. Pedestrians shrank back as Mannix pushed his way toward the car. The police officer was nowhere to be seen.

Hank swept the kites onto the floor then helped Ernesto wedge Ivan's body into the car.

"Where to?" Mannix asked once he was behind the wheel.

Ernesto quickly considered his options and found he had none. "We can't take him to my parents'. They'd have too many questions. Same with the hospital. We'll have to take him home with us."

Mannix grinned, revealing blood-stained teeth. "It's not the best time to say so, but I'm glad you think of home as being with me and not your parents."

"You're right. It's not the best time."

As Mannix pulled back into traffic, the blood running down his face dampened his chest and began pooling on the seat between his thighs. "That's really bad, Hank," Ernesto said. He twisted to the side to give himself enough space to pull his shirt over his head. "Here. Press this tight against your nose."

Mannix did. "Hans is going to kill me," he slurred through the fabric.

There was blood all over the Packard—on the

dashboard, smeared around the steering wheel, puddling on the driver's seat, and even splattered about the back passenger compartment from their efforts to lift Ivan into place.

Hank was right. Hans was going to kill him. Plus, they were bringing Ivan back, which surely wouldn't be welcomed. "I'm sorry, Hank."

"Oh, good. What does that make the count now?"

Chapter Twenty-Six

ALL IN ALL, Mannix thought it was probably worth it. The punch to the face, the bloody nose, the ruined shirt, the ruined car. Finding Ivan near death. It was worth everything because he was certain Ernesto had been about to break up with him at the end of their date, or at least *try* to break up with him. He'd been building up to one of his "how can this possibly work?" moments.

Mannix couldn't imagine living like that, always needing to see the future.

Of course he wouldn't have *allowed* Ernesto to break up with him. Mannix knew Ernesto didn't really want to. But the fight and the nose and the shirt and the car—and Ivan too—all meant he didn't have to think of something in the moment to talk Ernesto out of his panic.

So, yes, it was worth it.

Plus, once they arrived back home, all of the blood and swelling meant Hans didn't try to kill him. Instead,

Hans cleaned and fussed and tended. "You've *got* to stop doing this, Hank," he'd said, after bandaging his eyebrow. Did he mean the fight? The car? Ernesto? Ivan? Probably all of it.

"Yes, ma'am," Mannix had replied dutifully.

Mannix had been shocked to learn Ivan was still alive, and he was certain he wouldn't have made it much longer if Ernesto hadn't found him. They'd bathed him and dressed him in clean clothes. They could only hope food and rest might begin to restore his health.

A mattress was dragged into Matt's room for him.

When they'd pressed Ernesto as to what alerted him to Ivan's presence under the malecón, he'd only said, "I've seen Americans like that many times. I knew *someone* was in trouble." Ernesto had refused to maintain eye contact with any of them—even Hank—and had left for home shortly after being assured Ivan was resting as well as could be expected.

Mannix was uneasy about that.

"Will he be okay?" he asked Tony. "Should I go to him?"

They were in Mannix's room, and Mannix was stretched out on his bed with an ice pack on his face. Cordero had pulled the room's chair closer and propped his feet up on the mattress. "Go to him?" he asked. "How would you get there? Are you going to suddenly learn how to take the bus and then manage to find the place with an ice pack pressed against your nose?"

Mannix let out a muffled sigh. "This is too cold," he complained, lifting the ice pack a couple of inches above his swollen nose. "I guess you couldn't drive me?"

"Nope. You've ruined the car again," Cordero said. "God knows how they're going to manage to get all the blood cleaned up."

"I'm really hard on that car," Mannix said. "Maybe Mason should just get a new one."

"I'll leave you to make the suggestion to him." Cordero stretched his foot forward and poked Mannix in the side with his toes. "And besides, you can't go to Ernesto now. He needs time to think."

Mannix lifted his head and pulled the pack farther away from his face so he could turn and face Cordero. "But that's just it, Tony! He already thinks too much. It's what gets him in trouble."

Cordero mumbled something.

"What was that?" Mannix asked.

"Nothing, dear."

"Ugh." Mannix put his head back on the pillow. "I think my nose is better now." He put the ice pack on the bedside table. "Or else it's frozen, and I just can't feel anything."

Cordero brushed his toes against Mannix's side again. "Do you miss it, Hank? Your old life?"

Mannix considered the question. Tony was using his rare "serious tone," and he didn't want to make light of the question. He assumed Tony was referring to his "pre-Ernie" life, not how they'd lived in New York City.

Did he miss it—turning tricks in the garden, late-night escapades by the pool?

The casual, comfortable release he and Tony used to offer each other.

Tony's toes still rested against his side.

"No," he answered. Tony pulled his foot away. "Surprisingly, I don't. All I think about now is Ernie. Doing something with anyone else—" He glanced at Tony, then looked away. "—would feel, oh, I don't know, not like *cheating* exactly, but...pointless, maybe?"

Cordero nodded. "Spoken like a man who can have sex whenever he wants."

Mannix huffed. "Hardly whenever I want, but I understand what you mean." He sat up gingerly and swung his legs over the side of the mattress, forcing Cordero to lower his feet from the bed. "Tony, do you believe in love at first sight?"

"Yes."

"Yes? That's it? Full stop?" Mannix had expected him to scoff at the idea.

"Yes. That's all you'll get from me." He smiled at Mannix, but it had a melancholy aspect to it. "I knew that had happened to you from the first moment you told me about your awkward encounter with Ernesto in the garden."

Mannix nodded. "I still can't believe it myself sometimes. But it's true. I love him, and what's more, he loves me back! At least, when he doesn't want to break up with me. But that only happens when he gets overwhelmed by how hopeless we are."

"Nothing's ever hopeless, Hank."

Mannix leaned forward and grasped Cordero's hands. "It'll happen for you too," he said.

Cordero nodded, released Mannix's hands, and stood. "Yes, I know."

*

"CAN I HAVE more coffee, please?" Mannix asked, lifting his empty cup and wriggling it in Matt's direction.

Mannix thought there couldn't possibly be a worse houseboy, although he was glad Ernesto had given up the job. Matt let out a disgruntled huff, put down his pencil, and rose from his corner table. They all thought of it as Matt's table now. He could always be found there, studying his textbooks and Cuban newspapers.

"You've got legs, don't you?" he mumbled as he crossed the room and lifted the coffee pot off the hotplate.

"Matt," Hans cautioned. "We've talked about the attitude and demeanor necessary for a good houseboy."

Hans wore a flowing silk dressing gown in bright greens and purple. His reading glasses dangled from a beaded chain around his neck, and he would occasionally raise them to study a two-day-old copy of the *New York Times*.

"This is ridiculous," he proclaimed, shaking the paper. "Now they're saying Queen Elizabeth's coronation won't be held until sometime next year! She's been queen for months already. What could they possibly be waiting for?"

"Don't worry, dear," said Mason. He was slicing his bacon with a knife and eating it with a fork, which annoyed Mannix to no end. "I'm sure they're just trying to figure out what table to seat us at for the reception."

"Very funny," Hans replied. "First the elections here get postponed, now this..."

Matt poured the coffee into Mannix's cup. "Democracy everywhere is at risk," he muttered as he rolled his eyes.

"Exactly," confirmed Hans.

"That was a joke, Hans," Matt said. "The queen wasn't elected. Monarchies should be abolished; they're just vestiges of colonialism meant to keep the working people down."

Mason grimaced and gripped Hans's wrist. "He's just a youngster, dear."

"Speaking of working," Mannix said as he sniffed at the coffee in his mug. "I should have specified *hot* coffee when I asked for more."

"Oh, brother," Cordero said. "I'd go clean the pool for our guests, just so I could get out of here before things deteriorate, but—" He looked pointedly around the table. "—it appears we have none."

It was true. The men from East Orange were gone, and the *Pumped* photographers weren't coming back. Hans had received two unexpected cancellations for the week, and for the first time in years, Casa de Ada had no paying guests.

Mannix didn't think Hans looked concerned. He must be serious about winding down the operation.

"Well, there is a new guest arriving tomorrow," Hans said.

"It's not that fellow from Duluth, is it?" Mannix asked.

"No," said Cordero. "I looked at the guest register and didn't recognize the name—an M. Smith."

"Smith?" Mason said, struggling to get the last crumbling bit of bacon onto his fork. Mannix clenched his teeth. "Sounds like a pseudonym to me. Not that I care. I understand why some men feel the need to hide their real names."

"Especially the married ones," Mannix said. "Or the men who try to eat bacon with a fork. That would be something to hide too."

Hans folded his newspaper. "Well, as long as their money's good, I don't care what they call themselves."

*

AFTER BREAKFAST, ERNESTO and Marta arrived to check on Ivan.

Marta had been to Casa de Ada on several occasions to meet with Chad when she was designing the cigar box, but it was still unusual to have a female visitor. "Miss Ruiz," Cordero said when the two came into the dining room. He and Mason were both old-school and rose from their chairs to greet her. Mannix assumed it was part of their former FBI training.

"Thank you so much, Mr. Mannix, for helping Ernesto rescue our cousin. How is he?"

Everyone turned to Matt, who'd spent the night with him.

"Fine, I think," Matt said. "We talked a bit last night, and he was still asleep an hour ago. Can I get you two coffee?"

"Oh, say yes," Mannix said. "That way he'll make a fresh pot."

"No, thank you," Marta replied. "I'd just like to go see Ivan."

Hans pushed his chair back and stood. "I'll make more coffee. Matt, go wake Ivan and let him know his cousins are here to see him."

Matt left the room, and Mannix tried unsuccessfully to catch Ernesto's eye, to see if there was any chance of smoothing things over after they'd left everything on such an awkward note the day before.

"Are you sure I can't get you a coffee?" Cordero asked Marta. She blushed prettily and Mannix thought Cordero should tone down the chivalry thing a bit. He wouldn't want Marta getting the wrong idea.

Matt rushed back into the room. "He's gone!"

Marta gasped, and Ernesto hurried down the hallway, as if Matt might have been wrong and Ivan was hiding in the closet.

"Come on," Cordero said to Matt. "Let's check outside in case he just slipped out a few minutes ago."

Ernesto came back. "He *is* gone," he said, stating the obvious.

"We'll find him," Mason told Marta.

A few minutes later, Cordero and Matt returned. "One of the gardeners said they saw someone leave a half hour ago."

"You don't think he would have gone back to—" Mannix stopped, and everyone looked uncomfortably toward Marta.

"Ernesto explained where you found him," she said.

"No," said Matt. "He was relieved to be out of that. He told me so last night. He said by the time he'd seen what a trap it was, he was too far into it, and he thought the guy who ran that section of the malecón was drugging him."

"Where could he have gone then?" Ernesto asked. "I'm sure he wouldn't have returned to the factory or gone back to the farm."

"Um," Matt said, wringing his hands. "I think I might have an idea about that. I think he's gone to find Castro." Matt's announcement was followed by stunned silence and then a barrage of questions. How? Where? Why?

Suddenly, Golden Boy's harmless political rants looked dangerous.

"I told him about Castro and his efforts to force the government to reschedule the elections, and how Castro said he'd lead a worker's revolution to overthrow the Batista regime if the elections weren't held soon."

Marta covered a gasp with her hands, and Ernesto took her elbow.

"Now you've done it," Cordero said.

"But it's just the truth," Matt complained. He seemed nervous, glancing from face to face, pleading for someone to see his side of things. "Castro is building a worker's army, and I told Ivan he should consider joining the cause to bring justice back to Cuba."

"You encouraged Ivan to participate in *another* coup?" Mason asked incredulously.

"No! Not a coup," Matt protested. "Castro just wants to push for reform of a corrupt government."

"By overthrowing it?" Mason asked.

"Only if it's necessary," Matt said. "The best outcome would be to have Batista step down and have the people decide through elections. Revolution will only be the last resort."

Marta threw her hands up in frustration. "What gives you the right," she asked, "to come to our country and tell people they should overthrow the government?"

It was a good question, and one for which Matt had no answer.

Ernesto and Marta started speaking quickly together in Spanish. Matt must have understood at least some of it because his expression turned increasingly grim. Mannix picked up the word *Americanos* but not much else.

Marta was growing more and more agitated. Cordero was staring at the floor.

"We have to go," Ernesto said, taking his sister's arm and turning her toward the hallway. "Let us know if you hear anything."

"Ernie, wait!"

Ernesto turned. He was angry. Mannix could have kicked himself for using the nickname. It was too late to even add an "...iesto." He opened his mouth to say...something. An apology? An entreaty to stay?

"We will," Cordero said before Mannix could make things even worse. "You do the same."

After they were gone, the room fell silent.

"Asshole," Cordero said to Matt. "It's time for you to grow up."

"What were you *thinking*?" Hans demanded of Matt. "Driving that poor boy into the arms of radicals and criminals as if he didn't have enough troubles."

"But...but this country. It's horrible what Americans are doing to it. What *we're* doing to it," Matt insisted. "All of its wealth is being sucked away by American companies. Why *shouldn't* Cuban workers be the ones to benefit? It's their country."

"So, I should turn Casa de Ada over to the gardeners?" Hans asked.

"Maybe that would be better than driving the young ones into the sex trade," Matt returned.

Hans's eyes widened.

"That's enough!" snapped Mason. "Listen, Matt. I don't question your ideals or principles, but there's only two options for countries like this today—the United States or the Soviet Union. One or the other is going to come in here—and all the rest of Latin America—and start running things, either flat out or behind the scenes."

"But that's not fair—" Matt began.

"No, it isn't," Mason agreed. "But for our part, we can at least try to influence things in a positive direction, expanding human rights and growing the economy so more Cubans can find work."

"How did that work out for Ivan?" Matt asked. "Why is the US Government supporting a dictatorship that oppresses its own people?"

Mason didn't have an answer for that.

"Well," Mannix said. "I hate to admit it, but I'm with Golden Boy on this one. It does seem like this country is going to the dogs, and our government doesn't appear to be helping."

He thought about the police doubling their protection money scheme and about the American man who'd attacked Ernesto, and how American men lined up on the malecón—in broad daylight—to take advantage of desperate young Cubans. "Maybe the whole world is going to the dogs," he concluded.

No one had a response to that either.

Chapter Twenty-Seven

MARTA LINKED HER arm through Ernesto's as they made their way home.

"He won't have gone back to the malecón, at least," Ernesto said. He meant it to be reassuring, but it spotlighted the bigger question of just where Ivan might have gone instead. It was late morning, and the city was coming alive around them. Ernesto was relieved to not have people stare at him, wondering what he was doing in the American man's car.

"I know." Marta squeezed her brother's arm. "But where would he have gone? If he wanted to find Castro, I mean?"

Ernesto had been thinking about that, planning their next steps.

"Matt told me Castro holds rallies at the university all the time now. That's where we'd been the day Matt got attacked and I brought him home." Ernesto had already decided they should take the long way home through the campus. "We'll look for him now, and if we don't find him, I'll keep my eyes open next week when I'm there." Although he still wasn't sure what he'd say to Ivan even if they did find him.

"You know we're all proud of you for getting into university, don't you?"

Despite all of the events of the day before and that morning, Ernesto smiled. "Yes," he said. He was proud of himself too. It was an enormous accomplishment. And to think the third rejection had been a mistake; thank God, they'd discovered the error.

"You've become friends with Matt, haven't you?" Marta asked.

"I know it sounds odd, after what he's done, but he's a good man. He just doesn't understand us, and has all these wild ideas about the world."

"*Tal vez*," Marta replied—not an agreement, just an acknowledgment.

Ernesto colored at the memory of Matt's explicit instructions on sex. "Plus, he's helped me a lot with my English."

"These Americans have changed everything, haven't they?" she asked.

More than you could possibly know. He didn't respond. There was no need to.

"They surely are handsome though, aren't they?" Marta said. "Despite how...frustrating they can be."

Yes. That was the perfect way to describe Hank. Handsome beyond measure, but so incredibly frustrating, with his white skin and white lies and unwavering belief he always knew what was right. But how could he respond to Marta's question? He couldn't admit the Americans were handsome.

"Tal vez," he said.

Marta giggled and clutched more tightly onto his arm. "Well, *I* think they are anyway."

He remembered Marta's reaction to Matt in the office, with his gleaming chest and sparkling blue eyes.

"Be careful, Marta. The Americans are different than us. Too different. They might be able to help our family in the short term, but don't get close to them." Listen to him—giving advice to his sister he should have given to himself months ago. He hoped if Marta did let her interest be known, Matt would be polite and careful in turning her away.

It struck him then—the irony of it—that Matt and Marta could actually make a relationship work, publicly at least. No one would question Marta's choice to marry an attractive young American with a bright future ahead of him. They'd move to the United States, and she'd have American babies, even if their marriage was just a sham.

While he and Hank, who really did love each other, couldn't possibly be together—not publicly the way Matt and Marta could.

"You sound like an older brother, not a younger one," she teased.

"Well, you're only a year older than me, and I know these men." They'd reached the edge of the campus, and Ernesto guided them onto one of the paved walkways leading past open yards and gardens, heading to the classroom buildings. The buildings where he'd be studying in just days. "He's not right for you."

She laughed again. "Men," she said. "You can't see what's right in front of your noses."

Ernesto was becoming distressed about the prospect of his sister getting hurt. "No, Marta. Seriously. There are things you don't know, things I can't speak of, but trust me."

The noise of the city had fallen away. A campus bell rang in the distance. The university was different than it had been the last time Ernesto had been there. Trash had piled up in some corners, and protest banners hung everywhere. A handful of students crossed the walkway in front of them, chanting about revolution.

It was unnerving. They should be studying, preparing for their futures, not causing trouble.

"Oh, Ernesto. I know so much more than you think I do." She glanced at him as they walked. "In fact, I know about Mr. Mannix and—look!" She pointed to the group of students. "Is that...?" Ernesto looked at the protestors. He was struck by how long it must have been since Marta had seen Ivan if she could have mistaken any of those healthy young people for their cousin.

"No," she said, deflating. "It isn't Ivan."

They walked in silence for a bit as Ernesto considered just how explicit he should be in warning her about the nature of what went on at Casa de Ada. She'd be shocked, certainly, and offended, but if he could prevent her being hurt, wouldn't it be worth it? But he'd risk exposing the truth about himself too.

It was just one more example of how this entire arrangement with Hank was unworkable.

Marta shuddered next to him and took his arm again. "I just don't understand how men can do...those things to each other. It's disgusting."

Ernesto stopped, devastated. She did know! And she thought he was disgusting. A sudden wracking sob took control of him, unexpected and overwhelming. "Oh God, Marta, I...I..."

"Ernesto! What...oh! No! That's not what I meant." She moved him a few feet along the path to a bench and pulled him down beside her, then wrapped him in a hug, rubbing his shoulders while he cried. "Oh, Ernesto. It's fine. Everything is fine."

A few minutes later, when he got his breathing under control, he pulled out of her grasp. "But Marta, you don't know. I...I..."

"Shh. I *do* know. That's what I've been trying to tell you. I meant the things men did to Ivan, and the boys like him. The hurtful, abusive things—that's what's disgusting."

Was she saying...

"That's not at all like what you have with Mr. Mannix." She stroked his back. "That's beautiful and kind and...loving?"

Ernesto nodded, confirming the sentiment. The relief of someone else knowing the truth was overwhelming.

"But how did you...?"

"Oh, please. We've all worked together at the casino for a while now. Did you think I wouldn't notice how you two look at each other? How you let your fingers brush together?"

Ernesto hadn't realized they'd been that obvious.

"I think it's sweet. I might not completely *under-stand* it, but I'm happy for you, *Ernie*." She smiled at the nickname and gave his knee a shake.

"Thank you, Marta. I was so afraid you'd reject me. That maybe I'd be kicked out from home." Hank had told him that had happened to him when he was just a teen-ager.

"Reject you? I love you, Ernesto. I'm happy you've found someone in your life."

"But our parents..." Ernesto sniffed.

"Well, that is a problem," she agreed. "They'd want you to be happy, but you're right to be worried. I don't think they'd be ready for...for...this."

Ernesto groaned. "No one is ready. *I'm* not ready. How can two men love each other? How can they live their lives together? No, it's impossible. There's just no path forward for us." He slumped against the bench.

"*Tal vez*," she said and smiled again. "But maybe there is a path forward, and you just haven't found it yet."

Chapter Twenty-Eight

"IT'S PRETTY NICE around here when the place isn't cluttered with paying guests," Cordero said. Hans frowned at him from across the breakfast table.

"You're going to keep paying me though, right?" asked Matt. He made a show of stirring the eggs in the chafing dish and feeling the side of the coffee urn to ensure it was hot. No one answered him. Mannix thought everyone was still upset with him after yesterday morning's revelation that he'd driven Ivan away before Ernesto and Marta could talk to him.

He suspected it wouldn't have made a difference anyway. Ivan was a lost soul.

"The reason I ask," Matt continued, "is that Ivan took the cash out of my sock drawer before he left." He removed a small plate with crumbs on it from in front of Cordero. "Can I get you another muffin, Tony?"

"This is too painful to watch," Mannix said. "I actually liked you better when you were surly."

Cordero smiled. "Yes, please," he said to Matt. "A blueberry one this time. And I can spot you until payday." He looked at Hans. "We are going to keep him on, right? When he makes an effort, he can actually be pleasant."

Mannix made a gagging sound.

"He also took the gold chain that man from East Orange gave me."

"You know that was fake, don't you?" Cordero asked.

"What did I say about accepting gifts from guests, Matt?" Hans asked.

"Did you ever tell Eddie about that?" Mannix asked.

Matt was saved from having to respond by the jingle of the bell above the front door.

"Who could that be?" Mason asked. "The mysterious Mr. Smith already?"

"No, it can't be," replied Cordero. "The steamship doesn't arrive for hours.

"Surely it's too soon for the police again," Hans said.

"Rather than sitting around guessing," Mannix said, "why don't we send our *houseboy* to find out who it is."

"No need," said a voice from the doorway.

"Oh my God," whispered Mannix, the color draining from his face when he saw their visitor in the doorway.

"Good to see you again, too, pretty boy."

Mabel Chadsworth.

Mannix tried to recover from his shock. The woman scared the bejesus out of him, and he'd never forgotten her implied threat with the guillotine. She was dressed outrageously in trousers and a man's shirt, and she looked even more...ominous...than she did the last time he'd seen her.

Mason and Cordero both stood, but it was an awkward thing and only served to underline how unlike a lady she seemed.

Her eye landed on Matt, and she strode toward him, causing him to flinch backward involuntarily. "We haven't met," she said, holding her hand out to him. "I'm Mabel Chadsworth. You can call me ma'am."

They shook, and Matt seemed startled by the strength of her grip. "You must have replaced the authentic houseboy. Pity. I liked that one." She gave Matt a slow head-to-toe inspection, then turned to Hans. "He's a bit over the top, don't you think?"

"Mrs. Chads—" Hans began, but at Mannix's panicked head shake changed course. "Ma'am. What brings you here this morning?"

"Yes, thank you, coffee would be lovely," she answered. Matt jumped to work, and Mannix rose from his chair, then edged toward the doorway. "Don't you dare leave," she said to him. "I stopped by to personally introduce you to your new guest, to make sure there weren't any problems."

"To my—" Hans began.

"Come through, dear," she called. "The gang's in here."

A woman came into the room. A Cuban woman, bigger even than Mabel Chadsworth—which was saying something, Mannix thought—and dressed like the fieldworker she might very well have been.

"I'm afraid there's been some mistake…" Hans began.

"No. No mistake." Mabel Chadsworth said. "This is Marigold, the M. Smith I'm certain you have on your list of guests arriving today." Hans opened his mouth, probably to offer another objection. "And I'm certain her name is there because I've already popped behind the counter and taken a look."

Matt recovered quickly and brought over a cup of coffee. "I assume you take it black and strong?" he asked.

Her eyes lit up. "Oh! Aren't you a cheeky one." She reached forward and wiggled Matt's cheek in a pinch. She laughed as she did so, but Mannix thought she used enough force that she would have had to answer for it if she'd been a man. Matt's cheek blossomed red. "And such delicate coloring."

Hans put his glasses on and looked to Mason for support. "There *has* been a mistake," he insisted. "You see, Casa de Ada isn't a place for…that is, we only cater to…" Marigold came farther into the room and right up into Hans's personal space.

"*Sí?*" she asked.

"It's men only," Mason said.

"Who says?" asked Mabel Chadsworth.

Who says? Seriously?

"Look," said Mason. "Men come here to relax and be themselves. It wouldn't be a comfortable space for…" He glanced at Marigold.

Mannix wondered how he'd complete the sentence. There were so many possibilities.

"Good," Mabel Chadsworth said. "That's just what

this guest is looking for too." The Cuban nodded in agreement. Mannix wondered how much English she understood.

"I'm sorry, ma'am," Hans insisted. "Casa de Ada is men only."

They stared at each other in a stalemate. Finally, Mabel Chadsworth smiled. "I was mistaken," she said.

Mannix breathed a sigh of relief, but he couldn't quite believe she was backing down.

"Well," Hans said brightly. "No harm done. You're welcome to stay for coffee if you'd like? I can help you find alternative—"

"What I meant," Mabel Chadsworth interrupted, "is that I was mistaken in the introductions." She motioned to Marigold. "May I introduce your new guest, Michael Smith."

Marigold smiled and nodded.

Mannix did a double take and stared at the newcomer. No, despite her size and her masculine clothing, Marigold was definitely a woman. She was shaped like the primitive carvings of fertility goddesses Mannix had seen once in *National Geographic*—all breasts, thighs, and buttocks. He'd quickly closed the magazine and told Hans he needed better reading material in the sitting room. Mannix squeezed his eyes closed now to banish the image, but when he opened them, Marigold was still there.

Hans sucked in a breath. "That's—" he began. "That's not—"

"You can check if you'd like," Mabel Chadsworth challenged him. "If validating your guests' sex is something you do here, *Ada*."

Another stalemate. After a few moments of silence, Mabel Chadsworth motioned her companion to the door. "We'll just go relax in the parlor and enjoy cigars while you get the guest room prepared."

A stunned silence settled over the men after Mabel Chadsworth escorted the other woman out.

"What are we going to *do*?" Matt hissed. His left cheek still sported a cherry-colored bloom. The sweet smoke from a Ruiz cigar floated in from the parlor, reminding Mannix of Ernesto—the man he loved, yes, but also a Cuban, proud and independent.

How we've turned their lives upside down!

And not just Ernesto's life, but Marta's too. And their parents, who must be overwhelmed by all the changes their children's association with the Americans have brought. And Americans have ruined Ivan. He thought of the casinos and the young people selling themselves on the malecón. *We've ruined the whole country.*

He looked at Cordero, who offered him a soft smile and an encouraging nod, as if he could read Mannix's mind, or at least his heart.

"We should let her stay," Mannix said.

Hans cocked an eyebrow. "Explain," he commanded.

"It's what you're here for, Hans. It's what you *do*. You provide refuge. You always have." He thought of the boarding house Hans had run in New York City, and all of the desperate young men who'd found a safe haven there—himself included. "And you've said yourself this place has just become about vacations and escapism."

"True..." Hans replied, although he sounded doubtful.

"This woman and others like her need you, Hans," Mannix continued. "Haven't we just been talking about what a disservice we've done to the Cuban people? Well, now's our chance to do some good. Can you imagine what their lives must be like? Don't they deserve a space they can feel safe and be themselves?"

"Skinny-dipping late night in the pool might be awkward for the other guests," Hans pointed out.

"What other guests?" Cordero asked, waving his arm across the empty breakfast room.

Mannix shuddered at the thought of running into Mabel Chadsworth naked in the pool. But he was onto something important—transformational, even—and he pushed on. "It's something we can do that will change people's lives for the better, and maybe make up a little for what we're doing more broadly to these people and this island."

He wished Ernesto was here. He wanted to apologize to him, to explain that he saw more clearly now why Ernesto worried so much about a future with an American.

He wanted to tell him he'd work harder, and that he loved him.

"Look at you, being all enlightened," Matt said. But he stepped up to Mannix and put his hand on the man's shoulder. "He's right though. I'm with Pops. Let's provide a safe space for Cuban women."

"Me too," said Cordero.

"You know you want to, dear," Mason took Hans's hand. "You're a mother hen at heart, and the men who come here now don't need mothering."

"But what about *our* plans, Arthur? Do we really

want to take this on now, just as we're thinking about what will be next for us?"

"It's not a long-term commitment, Hans. The future will bring what it brings. And, selfishly, I'd like to feel we're doing some good, rather than me just always being the bad guy."

Hans took a deep breath. "All right." He smiled. "It *does* feel good. Thank you for making us see it, Hank." He turned to Matt. "Would you go ask Mrs....er...Miss..."

"No need," Mabel Chadsworth said, stepping into the room. "I've been eavesdropping the entire time just beyond the doorway. "Thank you, gentlemen. You're doing the right thing. You've restored my faith in mankind, so to speak."

Mannix knew they'd done the right thing, but she still scared the bejesus out of him.

"Oh, I must have carried this in from the parlor." She put the guillotine down on the table. "I won't be needing it right now."

Mannix blanched.

"You may all call me Chad."

Chapter Twenty-Nine

"IT'S NOT AT all what I expected," Ernesto told Matt. It was his second week of classes, and he and Matt were eating their lunches at an outdoor table on the campus. It was hard for them to hear each other over the shouts of a political rally happening across the large grassy yard.

"Even my business accounting class has been filled with student discussions of human rights and Batista." Ernesto took a bite of the sandwich his mother had prepared for him. On days she knew he'd be meeting with Matt, she made one for him too. "Not that the elections aren't important, but it's not what I'm paying all this tuition money for."

"I guess I shouldn't really have an opinion," Matt said.

Ernesto wiped a drip of mustard from his lips with his finger. "Okay, I appreciate the more humble you and your new awareness that it's not your job to run my country. But I've never known you not to have an opinion."

"I didn't say I don't have one; I said I *shouldn't* have one."

The fact that Matt still didn't share his opinion told Ernesto everything he needed to know. They'd talked about it before. Matt thought Ernesto should embrace the moment, be a participant in changing his country.

But Matt surprised him by sharing his opinion on an entirely different subject. "You should come back and talk to Hank."

Ernesto laid his sandwich on the table.

"He misses you and asked me to tell you he wants to go on another date." Matt wiped his hand on a napkin. "I can't believe I've become his messenger boy. Anyway, no one begrudges you a couple of weeks off from the cigar sales work, but Hank doesn't understand why you're avoiding him."

I can't keep devoting emotional energy into this when there's no future for us.

But he didn't say that. Instead, he asked about the casino. "How are the guys making out with the cigars?" He did feel guilty about leaving everything to the Americans.

"Oh, great. I've been chipping in, too, and Marta has been incredible. She's there all the time now, either making her boxes at Casa de Ada or selling in the casino. And it turns out she's really good at sales."

He didn't sense any awkwardness when Matt mentioned Marta, so he assumed that meant she'd either been very subtle in expressing an interest and accepted Matt's disinterest gracefully, or Matt had neatly deflected her with no harm done. Good.

"Sales are so good Hank said the business had its best week ever. He also said he'd give it all up if only he could talk to you." Clearly, Matt wasn't going to let this drop. Hank probably threatened him if he didn't come back with an answer.

"Do you and Eduardo ever talk about the future?"

"Sometimes. It's hard though, you know?"

Ernesto *did* know, yes.

"Eduardo wants me to stay here, but I can't. I'm not even officially enrolled this semester, and NYU isn't going to hold my space open forever. I'll need to go back in a few months if I'm going to keep my spot."

"What will Eduardo do?" Ernesto asked.

"He could come to New York, I suppose. We've talked about it, anyway. He speaks English and he's connected to academia. He could get a job." Matt looked away.

"You don't sound too excited about it."

Matt sighed. "I don't know, Ernesto. I'm actually surprised I find myself liking him so much. I've never been in a serious relationship before, and I'm afraid we might not have a future that way. I think we have *this* now."

Exactly. And "this now" might be enough for Matt, but lack of a future was tearing Ernesto apart. Especially because he *cared* so much for Hank. Because he loved him so much.

"We're not like you and Hank," Matt continued. "You guys are so in love it hurts to look at you. And you're clearly destined to be together forever."

Oh. It helped to hear that from Matt, the confirmation of what had been so heavy in his heart. Maybe he *should* talk to Hank.

"But don't worry. I'm sure even after I've gone home, Eduardo will still keep your spot for you here."

Keep my spot?

"But, once I'm accepted, I don't have to apply each year, do I?" Ernesto tried to keep the confusion from his voice. "I'm in a four-year degree program."

"Right, of course. But you're only in the program because...because..." It was never a good sign when Matt turned so suddenly white. He stood and pushed back from the table. "I need to go."

"No, Matt. What's happening?"

"He's going to kill me! I was supposed to make it better, not worse. Why doesn't he *tell* you anything!"

Ernesto stood also. "Matt...?"

"Please, Ernesto. Don't make me do this. Just talk to Hank."

"*Democrocia!*" Protesters marched past their table banging drums and waving banners.

"No!" Ernesto insisted. "I'm sick of this—" He grasped for the English word. "—*bullshit* from all of you. Tell me the truth."

Matt's face fell, and he sank back onto the bench. "Eduardo pulled strings to get you in here. Hank asked him to."

Ernesto doubled over as an invisible fist punched into his gut. He'd been so proud and foolish. He'd been lied to. *Again.*

"But don't you see?" Matt sounded desperate. "It's all

rigged! You were never going to get in. The rich and powerful keep everything to themselves. Things need to change..."

But Ernesto was already walking away—from his dreams, from his pride. From the Americans.

*

WHEN ERNESTO WALKED through the front door of the factory, Francisco put aside his work and stood from his table. "May I have a word, Ernesto?"

His mother was in the office, working on her sewing, and he didn't see his father, which probably meant he was in one of the back rooms. He'd want to talk to Francisco privately, so the two men walked outside.

The torcedero got right to the point. "I'm sorry, Ernesto, but I've talked with the others, and we're all in agreement we can no longer provide information for your American friends."

The news came as a relief, and that was surprising. Mr. Mason would be angry, or not, but Ernesto would be done with the scheme.

"Thank you for telling me, Francisco. I'm sorry I dragged you into it."

"No," he said. "Don't be. It's just that the caballitos are suddenly interested in Castro, and none of us want our names on any local lists of people to watch."

"I understand." They shook hands and Francisco went back to work. Ernesto knew he'd need to get word to Mr. Mason, and that would be best done in person.

He thought about what Matt had said at lunch before

the part where he learned he'd been lied to again. Matt believed he and Hank were meant to be together. As betrayed as Ernesto felt by not having been told the truth about his university admission, a small part of him liked the idea that going to see Mr. Mason would give him an excuse to see Hank.

Or maybe not such a small part.

*

"THERE ARE EIGHT guests there this week," Marta told him later that afternoon. They were speaking English, as they always did when they talked about the Americans, and were standing around the kitchen counter where Marta was rolling dough, helping their mother prepare the evening meal. "And they're all women! Can you believe it? Three of them are even Americans—from a place called Northampton." She tossed another handful of flour on the counter.

Their mother turned from her work at the stovetop. "Please, *mijos*, it's good to practice your English, but rude when it's just the three of us. I can't understand a word."

They switched back to Spanish and talked about inconsequential things until dinner. Ernesto was lulled by the familiarity. The shock of the afternoon, and his embarrassment from learning he hadn't legitimately been accepted at university, began to fade.

But once they were all seated at the table, his father asked, "How are your classes?"

"I don't know," Ernesto replied honestly. "It's been

two weeks, and all I see is politics and protests. The professors have let the classes become nothing more than activist meetings."

It was too soon to give up; Ernesto knew that. But it kept weighing on him—how much his family was sacrificing to send him to university. And for what?

"It'll get better when the protests die down," his mother said.

But his father had a speculative look on his face. "You know," he said. "We've been so fortunate to have great success with our brand selling at the casino. And now the clever lady cigars too. I'm sure we can develop our export business even without you getting a degree."

"Raul, no!" his mother said. "Ernesto should be a college graduate." It was about the prestige for her, Ernesto thought, not the business. "And what about Marta?" By which she meant Marta's hypothetical marriage to a hypothetical future friend Ernesto would meet at university.

But the other students only seemed interested in protests. And besides, he could sense their distance. University wasn't proving to be so much of a great equalizer as it was a litmus test for class. He knew he was different from the other students, and they knew it too. And Matt had only confirmed what he'd felt all along.

And had what Hank done really been so awful? Yes, he should have told him, but it did give Ernesto a chance he otherwise wouldn't have had, and he should be grateful.

"Don't worry about me," Marta said. "I have good prospects."

She sounded like she meant it.

"I hope you're not thinking of that white boy who sat here bleeding in our kitchen. I saw the way you looked at him."

"Mother!" Marta complained.

"I don't blame you for looking; he was quite handsome. But he's not one of us, and he's just a student. Ernesto will find someone for you."

Marta blushed furiously. But despite her discomfort, Ernesto had to agree with his mother's sentiment and for bigger reasons than either she or Marta could know.

"Of course I will," he said.

Marta glared at him.

*

AFTER DINNER, A rainstorm moved in. It drummed on the roof and freshened the air, bringing the distant scent of the sea into his bedroom, to which he and Marta had escaped to speak privately.

"Before I left the inn this afternoon, Matt came back and told us about your lunch."

"I suspected he would." Ernesto said. He wanted to ask how Hank responded but didn't.

They were both sitting cross-legged on the floor with their backs against the bed.

"Would you really quit school? It's nothing to be ashamed of—how you got in, I mean."

"I know. But seriously, there doesn't seem to be a point. I'm not learning anything. They're not *teaching* anything." He picked at the knee of his trousers. "And, yes, I'm embarrassed. I was so proud of myself. But everyone knew it was a lie. They must all feel sorry for me; or worse, maybe they're mocking me."

"No, Ernesto." Marta took his hand. "They all feel awful about how you found out. Hank still wasn't talking to Matt when I left." Marta nudged his shoulder. "But everyone agrees Hank should have told you. Even Hank! He feels awful and keeps talking about how he's failed you."

That was good to hear.

"Chad called him a spineless eunuch."

He couldn't help himself—he laughed at the image. "I can't believe all those women are there."

"It's nice." Marta looked into the distance. "They tell me stories about their lives as I work on the boxes. I never thought about what it must be like for...women like that."

"Marta, they're not trying to...recruit you, are they?"

It was her turn to laugh. "Is that what Mr. Mannix did to you?"

It was a relief Marta knew the truth, but sometimes, Ernesto wished she didn't. It wasn't something he liked to talk about. "Of course not," he said.

"Then stop treating me like a child. I know what I'm doing. I'm happy to make friends with these women, and that doesn't mean I'm a lesbian."

He was shocked to hear the word, especially from his sister. But it was the truth; Casa de Ada was a place for homosexuals. Hank was a homosexual, and Ernesto was a homosexual. He had no idea what any of that could mean for their futures.

"Not *everyone* at Casa de Ada is like that," Marta said. So, they were back to Matt. For a woman who was proving to be pretty smart, she sure had blinders on when it came to him.

When Ernesto didn't respond, Marta changed the subject. "Will you come back with me tomorrow?"

"Aren't you going to the casino tonight?"

"No. I'm not permitted to go there alone."

That meant it would just be the Americans selling the cigars. He felt bad about that. Then he remembered he had to see Mr. Mason to tell him about the end of the information-sharing arrangement with the torcederos.

"I'll come with you tomorrow." He didn't know how he felt about seeing Hank after Matt's revelation about his admission to the university, but he couldn't tolerate this continuing uncertainty about their future.

They'd need to talk.

*

ERNESTO WAS IN the middle of a disturbing dream. He was in a small elevator with Hank and Ivan, and even though he'd never been in an elevator before, he knew this one was descending far too fast. But before it could crash into the floor, he was awakened by the sound of breaking glass from downstairs.

He wasn't sure what he'd heard, but then it came again.

He swung out of bed and quickly pulled on his pants. He met his father in the hallway. "Glass," they both said, heading for the stairs. Marta was coming out of her room, and he could see his mother putting on her robe in his parent's bedroom.

His father was halfway down the stairs when he yelled, "Fire!"

Two of the windows in the factory had been broken, and small fires burned under each. They grabbed towels from the kitchen and began beating the flames. Marta ran back upstairs and returned with a blanket while his mother began filling a bucket in the sink.

Between the towels and the blanket, they were able to smother the flames quickly. Smoke filled the factory and Ernesto opened the transom windows and turned on the ceiling fans. His mother soaked the towels in the bucket, then draped them over the piles of broken glass and scorched flooring.

It hadn't been an accident.

"Why would someone do this?" his mother asked.

Ernesto thought back to his conversation with Francisco, when the man told him some of the workers were being watched because of their connections to Castro. Could this have been political?

"We should call the police," his mother said.

The caballitos.

"No," Ernesto said. His father met his eye and nodded.

"We'll wait until the morning," he said. "Ernesto and I will stay here for the rest of the night."

The two men got to work covering the broken window frames with burlap sacks. That would have to do until they could replace the glass. "You didn't tell the caballitos about the cigar sales at the casino, did you?" Ernesto asked his father.

"It's not their business." But it was clear from his

tone his father knew that had been a mistake. Acrid tendrils of the smoke burned their eyes and left a bitter taste on Ernesto's tongue.

"I think they might be making it their business," Ernesto said.

*

THEY WERE ALL bleary-eyed at breakfast. As the workers arrived, they took note of the damage but then settled themselves in to their tasks without asking any questions. It was obvious what had happened, even if the questions of "why" and "who" remained unresolved.

Ernesto had his suspicions and didn't need to wait long until they were confirmed.

The sound of motorbikes rose and then came to a stop outside. The cabalittos came in just as Marta was clearing plates from the table. Without waiting for an invitation, they strode into the family's office.

"Señors," Ernesto's father said, rising from his chair.

"It seems you had some trouble last night," the older one observed.

"Yes," his father confirmed.

The younger caballito stepped around the table and leaned against the counter by the sink, next to Marta. The older one didn't say anything. Ernesto picked up a plate and brought it to the sink, squeezing himself between his sister and the caballito.

"It seems, also," the older one continued, "you failed to mention to us that you've been selling cigars to Americans at one of the casinos."

"An honest oversight," his father said. "Please accept our apologies and a box of our finest cigars." His father offered a smile, but the caballito only shrugged.

"Was anyone hurt in the fire?" he asked.

"No, thank God."

"It could have been much worse. Rather than two small bundles of rags, it could have been actual bombs." The officer said. "It might be, next time."

They weren't even pretending it wasn't them.

"As it happens, our colleagues from across the city informed us about your venture at the casino. It was shut down last night, permanently—too disruptive to the many balances of power. All of your stock is supposed to go back to the inn the Americans own. I can't say for sure whether it will make it there."

Ernesto froze in place, and he saw Marta do the same.

All of their best cigars, all of Marta's hard work, stolen by the police.

"We'll take a few of those boxes you offered now and leave you to the cleanup."

Ernesto hurried to the back storage room and found three of the least valuable boxes he could lay his hands on, then returned and handed them to his father, who handed them to the police.

They didn't offer a thank-you; they just turned and left.

"We need to get to Casa de Ada right away," Marta said after the roar of the caballitos's motorcycles had faded.

"You're staying right here today," her mother countered, and their father nodded his agreement, sealing her fate.

"I'll go," said Ernesto, "and see if I can find out more. Hopefully, the cigars we had stored in the casino will make it there." But he doubted they would.

*

HE CONSIDERED TAKING the bus but decided to walk to give himself time to think.

That's my job, right? Thinking things through?

It was time to stop fretting about an unknown future and start planning what to do next.

A light rain had begun to fall, and as he ran his fingers through his damp hair to push it back from his forehead, he realized he hadn't had time to clean himself up. His fingers smelled of soot. At some point during the rush of events last night, he'd torn the hem on his left trousers leg, and it caught under his heel every few steps.

He made his way through the campus, eyeing the anti-Batista banners with newfound respect. Corruption wasn't just damaging, it was dangerous, and it wouldn't end on its own. Castro was right—on that front at least.

Twenty-four hours ago, before his lunch with Matt, his world had been entirely different, and the thing he was learning was that it would be entirely different again someday. Better, hopefully, but different. That's how the world worked. It changed and kept changing. All the time.

The only thing he knew for sure was that he loved Hank and Hank loved him.

If he was going to navigate a world that kept changing, he wanted Hank by his side.

But the white lies, deceptions, and omissions—those would all have to stop.

*

"ERNESTO, DEAR ONE!" Chad was the first person to greet him when he walked into Casa de Ada. He hadn't expected her to wrap him in a hug—a tight, overly enveloping hug, to be sure—but it was nice somehow. "We heard the news about your shop being shut down at the casino. Horrible."

"It's worse than that, Chad," Ernesto said. "The police set fire to our factory last night."

"Oh, no!" They were in the reception hall, and Chad came around from behind the counter and guided Ernesto toward the parlor. "They're in the sitting room," she said. "Let's go through so you only have to tell the story once."

Hans and Mason sat on the love seat doing a crossword puzzle together.

Of course men can have lives together. Why had I ever thought otherwise?

Matt was reading an actual textbook in Spanish, and Ernesto was pleased to see his university experience wasn't just limited to protests. He didn't recognize the three other women in the room. "Ernesto!" Matt exclaimed jumping up from his seat. "You've heard the news?"

"He has," Chad said. "But you haven't heard his news

yet." Her scowl communicated it wasn't good news either.

"Go get Hank," Hans told Matt.

One of the three women closed her magazine, and she and the others headed toward the kitchen. Chad took the chair by the entry hall.

Ernesto sat, and within a minute, Matt returned with Mr. Cordero.

"Hank says he'll wait for you," Matt told him. Ernesto didn't have to ask where.

He took a deep breath and told the others about the fire during the night and the visit from the caballitos that morning. No one interrupted, and when he was finished, everyone exchanged grim looks.

"I also need to talk to you, Mr. Mason, privately."

"Yes, I imagine you do," Mason replied. "But first, go find Hank."

"And whatever you have to say to him," Hans added, "please go easy. He's been insufferable without you."

Chapter Thirty

MANNIX HAD ALREADY thrown a handful of pellets into the koi pond. He'd brushed dried leaves from the bench and sat, then reconsidered and stood. He was afraid sitting would make him look too comfortable, too confident. If Ernesto was going to break up with him, he should be standing.

Then he sat again. He shouldn't send a signal he *expected* things to go wrong. Why not sit comfortably while he waited for his amante?

But what if he didn't come? Ernesto had been avoiding him ever since they lost Ivan, and after learning yesterday that Mannix had strong-armed Eddie into getting him into the university, he wouldn't be surprised if Ernesto refused to meet with him.

He stood again and smoothed the front of his shirt—the one with the brightly colored shells Ernesto liked to cry on. That sent a good message, didn't it?

Wait, no! That was a horrible message. He didn't want to suggest he was *expecting* Ernesto to cry. He quickly unbuttoned the shirt and removed it, before realizing that was even more ridiculous as he hadn't brought a spare.

And that was when Ernesto stepped around the curve of the path and stopped.

"Seriously, Hank? You're getting undressed?" Mannix froze. "A little overconfident, aren't you?" Ernesto asked.

Shit. "It's...it's the crying shirt. I thought I'd offer it to you in case...you know."

Ernesto moved closer to the bench. "That was...considerate?"

"I don't know," Mannix said. "Yes? Maybe? I wasn't thinking."

Ernesto stopped in front of Mannix. "No. That's not surprising. It's not what you do." He reached out and took the shirt.

His fingers were dirty, smudged with something black. Mannix had never seen Ernesto with dirty hands before; he was always so meticulously clean. His hair looked unwashed, and he smelled of...smoke?

Before he could ask what had happened, Ernesto said, "Why didn't you tell me about my admission to university?"

"Um...well..." He'd have to be careful here. So much was at stake. "Because it didn't matter. I mean, you got in, so—"

A flash of anger turned Ernesto's eyes into burning coals.

Mannix shivered. An unfamiliar sense of vulnerability—of exposure—overcame him. "I should put my shirt back on," he said.

"No."

No?

"Tell me the truth, Hank."

"I...I thought it might upset you...if you knew." Sweat dripped down his sides.

"So, you thought it would be best to hide something from me—something you already knew I would think was important?" Ernesto asked, still clutching the shirt.

"Oh, well...when you put it *that* way..." His mouth was suddenly dry. "Um...so...*are* you upset?"

Ernesto closed the gap between them. "Yes, Hank." He poked Mannix in the chest with his finger. "I'm upset and angry that you lied to me after all we've said about the lying."

"You know," Mannix stammered, "it's probably not a good time to bring this up, but...it wasn't actually a lie..."

"Yes, it was! Lies, omissions, deceptions. They're all the same."

Ernesto was close enough that Mannix felt his breath on his face, smelled the soot in his hair. He felt ridiculously exposed and vulnerable standing there half naked. "Can I have my shirt back now?"

"No." Ernesto took a deep breath. "The worst part, Hank, is how embarrassed I am. You knew how important it was to me to prove myself, to show I could pass the exams, to be proud of my accomplishments. To have all of that taken from me..." Ernesto shook his head. "And everyone knew but me."

"Oh! No, you have it wrong." A small spark of hope bloomed in Mannix's chest, where he could still feel the ghostly press of Ernesto's finger. "You *did* pass the exams. Eddie told me you scored higher than most of the students already enrolled."

"What? Then why...?"

"Because it's corrupt. You don't come from money, and the upper class doesn't want to let your kind in. *That's* what Eddie had to fix. You deserve to be there. You earned it."

Ernesto was quiet for a moment. Mannix could almost see the thoughts racing through his mind. "I need to sit," Ernesto said.

"Yes, sit. I cleared a space for you. So much garden debris these days." He waved a hand toward the bench, and after Ernesto sat, Mannix joined him. "Can I have my shirt back now?"

"No." Ernesto let out a breath. "Do you know what the worst part is, Hank?"

Good. A test—I can do this! "Yes. Yes, I do. I've been paying attention. The worst part is how embarrassed you are."

"No. I lied about that," Ernesto said. Mannix had absolutely no idea what to do with that admission, so he ignored it. "The worst part, Hank, is that even with all of this, with your insistence that you always know what's best—even though you clearly don't—"

"Well—"

"And your refusal to ask what *I* want, or what *I* think. Even with *all* of that, and your total inability to think about the *consequences* of your actions—"

"Hey—"

"Even with *all* of that, I still love you and can't imagine living my life without you."

Oh! Mannix's heart swelled with happiness. "That's...that's wonderful."

Ernesto grimaced. "Actually, it's scary."

"Sure," Mannix said. He was smiling so hard it hurt. "But scary in a wonderful way, right?"

Ernesto didn't respond, but Mannix didn't care. He was on top of the world. It was as if a governor had offered a last-minute reprieve, or the pope had stepped in and offered... What? What do popes do again? No, not the pope. That would be bad, given all the Catholic Mass-related dating challenges.

Ernesto wasn't breaking up with him! They were staying together.

Or were those two separate things?

"Uh...just to be clear... You're not breaking up with me, right? We're staying together?"

Ernesto leaned into Mannix's side and laid his hand on his stomach. The warmth of Ernesto's fingers soaked all the way into his soul. "Yes, Hank."

"Good. That's good." He took deep, inflating breaths—just to feel Ernesto's fingers rise and fall with his belly. He was glad he didn't have his shirt on. "Don't worry. It'll work out. I'll come up with a plan."

"No," Ernesto said, and Mannix was struck by how often he was hearing that word from Ernesto this morning. "You were right...back in the barn. It's *my* job to think things through. And instead, I've been letting you do it, flinging us into our future without a plan or any thought to the consequences."

That was a bit unfair.

"Well, Ernie, I wouldn't say—"

Ernesto slid his hand up Mannix's chest and pinched a nipple. Hard.

"Ouch! Ernie...esto, I mean." Ernesto's hand slid back down his torso, coming to rest lower this time. "This is why you won't give me my shirt back, isn't it? So you can pinch me when I say the wrong thing."

Ernesto pushed himself off Mannix and turned on the bench to face him. "It's one of the reasons, yes."

"'One of?' What's the other?"

Ernesto smiled, and Mannix decided he'd gladly suffer all the pinches of the world to have that smile aimed at him.

"The other," Ernesto said, "is that you're beautiful, and I like to look at you naked."

Oh!

"And," Ernesto continued, "I've decided I'm done taking shit from everybody... Is that the right English phrase?" Mannix nodded mutely. "And I'm going to start living the way *I* want to live. So, I'm going to make a plan for us, Hank. Not you, *me*.

"And the *first* part of that plan is that I'm going to sit here on our bench and admire you. Maybe I'll even touch you. Maybe I'll even kiss you." Ernesto dropped Mannix's shirt onto the ground. He paused and looked Mannix in the eye. "Do you have a problem with that?"

Mannix struggled to find words. "I am *so* aroused right now."

"Yes, I see. And maybe I'll get to that too."

Mannix groaned.

"But first, I'm going to tell you my plan."

"Oh God," Mannix squirmed on the bench. "Can't we do that afterward? You're killing me here, Ernie." Ernesto's hand slid up Mannix's torso. *Pinch.* Lighter this time—playful.

Mannix sucked in a breath. "Ernie..." *Pinch.* But not so much a pinch that time—more of a light brushing of a fingertip.

"Oh God, please Ernesto. I'm begging you. I can't last."

"Well," Ernesto said, "I'm in charge here, but I'm not *unreasonable.* And since you asked nicely..."

He drew his hand down Mannix's chest and past his stomach. He leaned into Mannix's side. "I love you, Hank. Don't worry; everything will be all right."

They moved on to the touching and kissing.

*

AFTERWARD, MANNIX ROTATED his shoulders to work a crick out of his neck. "The Packard is better for this sort of thing," he said.

"Yes, but it smells." Ernesto reached down to pick up his shirt, which had landed on top of Mannix's, only to find it newly splattered with several large wet stains. He lifted it gingerly and held it at arm's length—an echo of the dripping undershorts he'd removed from the pool ages ago. "Ew."

He began to put his arm through a sleeve and Mannix stopped him. "Don't you dare put that on." Mannix retrieved his own shirt from the ground and shook pieces of garden debris from it. "Wear mine," he said, handing it over. "The bright seashells suit you better than they do me. Besides, everyone here is used to seeing me half naked, whereas you'd cause a scandal if you showed up without a shirt."

Ernesto didn't object. Mannix took his amante's soiled shirt and brought it to his nose, inhaling deeply. "And I want to keep this one for a while." Ernesto shook his head, but Mannix knew he only feigned offense. Or at least he hoped so. "And speaking of things that smell, I couldn't help but notice you have a fireplace thing going on..."

As they finished pulling themselves together, Ernesto explained about the fire. Mannix knew the police were corrupt, but setting fire to the factory, risking the Ruiz family's lives—that was shocking.

Not as shocking, though, as the plan Ernesto had developed for them.

"Seriously?" Mannix asked after Ernesto had told him what they were going to do. "We're going to get our own place? Just you and me?" He'd been pushing Ernesto to agree to that for months.

"Yes. I want to and you want to, so who cares what others think?" If Mannix detected a residual fear hiding deep inside this new Ernesto, he didn't say anything. "Besides," Ernesto continued, "that way I get to admire you naked whenever I want, and we get to have sex more."

"I don't know what you did with the old Erniesto, but I like this new one a lot."

"Don't get too comfortable," Ernesto said, and his

serious tone made Mannix stop thinking about the "having sex more" comment and pay close attention. "We need to do things differently, Hank. Between us, I mean."

"Um...this is about the lying thing, isn't it?"

"Got it on the first try, Hank."

"Okay. I promise not to lie anymore. Although, really, I *don't* lie to you. It's just that—"

Ernesto put a hand over Mannix's mouth. "Stop. Listen to me. This is important." He waited for Mannix's nod before removing his hand.

Mannix took a deep breath. "Your hand smells like me, and a little bit like smoke."

"Hank!"

"Right. Sorry. Listening." He folded his hands in his lap to indicate Ernesto had his full attention.

"First, lies, white lies, deceptions, omissions—they're all the same to me, and you have to agree from now on that will be true for you too."

It made no sense. The world wasn't black and white. But the "have more sex" comment kept intruding on his thoughts. For Ernesto, he could do this.

"They're all the same, yes," he said, nodding solemnly.

How much more sex, he wondered, and what kind?

"So now is the time to come clean, Hank. I realize we might have been applying slightly different definitions of *truth*, and I'm willing to let that go, but if there is anything, and I mean *anything*, you think I would want to know, you need to tell me now."

Ernesto stared at him. *Oh, he meant right now.*

Surely, Ernesto wasn't expecting him to tell him

everything he'd ever done that he wished he hadn't, or that he was ashamed of? Everyone is entitled to their privacy. "You don't mean like the time I cheated on my math test in fifth grade by writing formulas on the bottom of my shoe?"

"No."

"Or the time in tenth grade when I told Tommy Johnson that all boys sometimes got naked together and did things to each other, and that it was perfectly normal?"

"Uh...no. But we can come back to that one later. What I mean, Hank, is anything you think I would hate learning about later. Anything that would make me angry you didn't tell me."

Oh. It was still a fairly broad net. A tiny memory—an echo of a memory, really—started softly scratching in a corner of his mind, seeking attention. But a bigger part of Mannix, the part that didn't want to screw anything up, which wanted to keep focusing on the "we can have more sex" thing, shut it down.

"Look, Ernesto, there are things in my past I don't like to talk about—things I've done I'm not proud of." Ernesto opened his mouth to say something, but Mannix kept speaking. "But, no, there's nothing you *need* to know. I won't lie to you." Ernesto cocked an eyebrow. "I won't lie to you again, I mean," Mannix said.

"Fine," Ernesto said. "Just know it's over between us if you're lying to me."

Mannix swallowed. He *mostly* liked the new Ernesto, but he was a little intimidating too.

"Second," Ernesto continued, "we need to start a formal business together, you and me."

That didn't sound like having lots more sex. "Um...what kind of business?"

"We've lost the casino outlet, but we need to keep selling cigars to Americans. That's where the money is. You're good with sales, and you're good with Americans. I'm good with cigars. We'll need to open a little shop somewhere. And it'll all be aboveboard, and we'll pay the necessary bribes, so no surprises for the caballitos."

That made sense. And they still had Mason's stateside connections. Yes, they could make that work, build a brand, set up a sales office. It would take time though. And meanwhile, he and Ernesto would have their own place, where they'd be having lots more sex.

"That sounds like a good plan," Mannix said. "I knew I put you in charge of thinking things through for a reason."

"Third—"

"Wait," Mannix interrupted. "How many of these are there?"

"Last one," Ernesto replied. "You need to take a Spanish language class. A real one, with homework and everything."

He was *not* good at classrooms. "Hmm. Just how much more sex are we going to have?"

"Hank, I can't be the only one always having to think in a foreign language. You'll be fine. And you know I'll help, and I'm sure Eduardo will help too. Even Matt would help while he's still here."

Ernesto was right. He'd been unfairly burdened with the language thing. With so many things. "Fine. I'll take a class."

Ernesto smiled, and all was right with the world. "When do we start with the lots more sex part?" Mannix asked.

"Not until after you find us a place to live. That's your next job. Find a place near the casino, where the Americans spend their time, with a small shop and maybe a room above."

He could do that. Mannix was warming to the idea. "A room above where we have lots more sex?"

Ernesto leaned over and kissed him. "Exactly. Now I have to go find Mr. Mason and tell him our deal on sharing information about the torcederos is off."

Mannix rose and considered putting Ernie's shirt on, but then he decided to simply tuck it into his waistband. It rubbed against his hip, damp and slick, but Mannix liked the reminder of their time together. "I'll go with you. I'm the one who got you into that mess."

"Yes, you are." They began making their way down the garden path back to the house. "Hey, Hank?"

"Yeah?"

"*Quién es tu Papi?*"

"You are, Ernesto. Only you." He reached out and took Ernesto's hand in his.

*

MASON WAS WAITING for them in the greenhouse.

"Coffee?" he asked when they went in. If he thought it was odd that Ernie was wearing Hank's shirt, he didn't say anything, but then he did a double take at Ernesto. "Oh, for Chrissake, Mannix." He went to the sink, dampened a cloth, and handed it to Ernesto, then indicated the spot on top of his head needing attention.

"Hank!" Ernesto exclaimed.

"I can't help it," Mannix said. "I'm like a dog marking his territory."

"Try to keep your markings outside from now on," Mason said. Once Ernesto finished cleaning up and joined them, Mason got right to business. "I expect you'll want to tell me you can no longer share information from the factory workers." It wasn't a question.

"That's right," Ernesto said.

"Not surprising, and perfectly understandable," Mason said. "For what it's worth, I don't think our arrangement had anything to do with the fire last night at your factory. I think that was all about your local police feeling left out when they learned about the business with the casino."

"I agree," said Ernesto. "That's why Hank and I are going to do it differently this time."

Mason cocked an eyebrow. "This time?" He looked at Mannix for an explanation.

Mannix smiled. "I'm not in charge anymore; you'll have to ask Ernie."

Mason turned his gaze to Ernesto. "Smart move, young man, wresting control from that one." He nodded his head at Mannix. "What are your plans?"

"Hank and I are starting a business. We'll be manufacturing cigars for export. Hank's American, so he'll be in charge of sales and marketing. I'm handling production and operations." Mannix was pleased to see the look of respect on Mason's face as he listened to his amante.

"I thought they weren't teaching you anything at university," Mason said.

"I read the textbooks," Ernesto replied.

"Good for you." A thoughtful look came over Mason's face. "Where are you setting up shop?"

"Hank will be looking for something, preferably with a room above."

Mannix blushed at the thought of "lots more sex."

Mason stood and poured more coffee for everyone. "Well, in that case, there's something you should know that might impact your plans." He put the coffeepot back on the hot plate and rejoined the others at the table. "I'm being transferred to Miami."

What? Hans hadn't said anything.

"I've just learned about it. It seems we—the US Government, I mean—miscalculated badly here. We didn't realize how much support Castro had, or how close the country was to revolution." He turned to Ernesto. "I'm sorry if this is difficult for you to hear."

Ernesto shook his head. "It's not. I knew the torcederos liked him, but it didn't hit home until last night how corrupt the police were."

"Exactly," Mason said. "That was our assessment too; the government now believes Castro has a good chance of overthrowing Batista unless the corruption ends. And we don't think it's going to end on its own. So, my bosses decided they couldn't get caught flat-footed again. They're opening a centralized office in Miami to track communist agitators throughout Latin America. And I'll be heading it up."

Mannix knew this was big news, but he was still

trying to figure out what it would mean for him and Ernesto. "But what's going to happen here?" he asked. "At Casa de Ada? I'm assuming Hans is going with you."

"Of course he is," Mason said. And Mannix was embarrassed he'd asked. That's how it is when you love someone; you stick together. Always.

He'd never leave Ernesto in a million years.

"Right. Sorry. It's a lot to take in," Mannix said. "What's going to happen to the guest house?"

"Interestingly, even before the news that we'd be leaving, Mabel Chadsworth had been asking about a partnership. It seems she's quite well-known...well, within very specific circles anyway. She wants to create a safe space for women from both Cuba and the States to relax and be themselves."

"Just like what Mr. Schmidt did," Ernesto said.

"What he *tried* to do," Mannix corrected. "It worked back in New York. Here it's been more about men coming to party."

"Yes," Mason agreed. "I don't think Hans knew how much that was frustrating him until he saw how far he'd come from his original vision for Casa de Ada."

"And Tony and I were blind to it too," said Mannix, "until my amante came along and saved me." He reached over and squeezed Ernesto's hand.

"But, now that you two are looking for a base for your new business, perhaps this would be a good start? Most of your stock was returned here overnight by the police. I think they're still a little bit afraid of me. For now, at least."

Mannix could see Ernesto thinking it over, and he

didn't want his amante making any promises until they had a chance to talk about it. "I don't know," he said. "Could Ernie and I really work around Mabel Chadsworth all day long? She has that guillotine, you know."

"Of course we could," Ernesto said with what sounded an awful lot like finality.

This whole "Ernie is in charge now" thing is going to take a lot of getting used to.

Mannix tried again. "But how could we sell cigars to Americans with that Amazon Marigold lumbering about the place?"

"Oh, come on, Hank. We'll think of something. Maybe we'll set up separate spaces for Chad's guests in a different part of the building from where we sell cigars. And we wouldn't want to interfere with her efforts to create a safe space for women, would we?" Ernesto asked.

"Well, actually—"

But Ernesto interrupted him. "I think we should try." And what could Mannix say to that?

Mason tried unsuccessfully to hide a smile. "It's not my place to say so, but I think between the two of you, the right one is in charge now."

Mannix did too, but it still stung. "What about Tony?" he asked.

"I don't know. This is all brand new, but I plan on offering him a position in Miami. He has the FBI background I could use."

Mannix frowned. As much as he and Tony had talked about change recently, he hadn't thought about what his life would be like without his friend around. He'd miss him. "But he could stay here, right? Work with us on the cigars?"

"It would be up to him, of course. If he thought that would be the best fit for him..." Mason sounded as if he thought it highly unlikely Tony would choose cigars over cloak and dagger stuff in Miami. He was probably right.

"Hank?" Ernesto asked.

Mannix hated the look of concern on Ernesto's face. Why was he so hesitant? He had everything he needed right here.

"You're the boss," he told Ernesto. He placed his hand on Ernesto's knee. "And there's so much more room here for...well, for all sorts of things."

He let his finger slide up Ernesto's thigh and smiled at his amante's blush.

Chapter Thirty-One

THEY COULD BARELY hear each other over the drumming.

Ernesto and Matt were sharing a bench in a campus courtyard, eating a lunch of sandwiches and pickles Ernesto's mother had made that morning. A group of protestors was circling the university grounds, shouting their anti-Batista slogans, banging on drums or pots and pans. There were banners supporting Castro, and shouts of *Viva la Revolutión*, which made Ernesto uncomfortable.

Reform? Yes. But revolution?

The cacophony echoed against the brick walls of the courtyard's buildings, and Matt leaned in closer. "I'm going to miss your mother's lunches," he said.

Me too, once I'm no longer living at home.

Matt swallowed a bite of his sandwich and licked mustard off his lip. "I need to tell you something," he said. Ernesto didn't like the sound of that at all.

"Eduardo and I saw Ivan here yesterday evening. He was with a group of militants that sometimes gathers at night on campus. They don't protest. They're very secretive. I think they just plot."

"Did you talk to him? How did he look?" Ernesto was relieved Ivan was still alive and hadn't gone back to the malecón, but he hated to think he'd gotten involved with subversives.

"We tried to. But the group broke up as soon as they saw us approaching." Matt put his sandwich down and placed his hand on Ernesto's arm. "He looked...better, Ernesto. I think he's eating, at least, and probably has a place to sleep."

The protestors had circled back around, and their noise made conversation impossible for a minute. One of them aimed a rude gesture at Matt as she passed. "I'm sorry," Matt said once the group had moved on—as if he was the one who needed to apologize for what was happening to Ernesto's country.

"I hate it here," Ernesto replied, leaning in to be heard. "I've decided I'm dropping out. There's no point to this."

"I won't try to talk you out of it." Matt finished his lunch and neatly folded the waxed-paper wrapper. "I was wrong. These people aren't looking to just end corruption or have peaceful elections; they're looking to overthrow the government, and I think they'd use violence to have their way."

He thought about the fire at his family's factory. "Everyone is using violence now. It's not black and white."

"I liked it better when it was," Matt said.

And maybe, when you go back to your own world, it will be again, at least for you.

Ernesto stood. "I'm going to find Eduardo, tell him I'm dropping out. Maybe if things get better, he can help me get back in."

"Maybe, but I don't think you'll need to. What you and Pops have set up at the guest house is really impressive."

In the weeks since Ernesto and Hank had talked to Mason about setting up their business at Casa de Ada, things had moved quickly. The greenhouse had been turned into the cigar room, and already three of the torcederos, as well as Marta, were working out of the space. It was an ideal setting because the humidity and temperature could be managed through opening and closing the many windows.

And it had its own entrance, so Americans could be escorted through the garden and directly into the cigar room without bumping into the "Amazon"—as Mannix referred to Marigold. He'd need to talk to Hank—again— about being more respectful.

"Maybe you're right," he replied to Matt. Things are really going well for us.

"You know," Matt said. "I could drop out too. From NYU, I mean. I could stay here in Cuba, work for you guys?"

Selfishly, Ernesto was looking forward to Matt going home. He liked Matt and enjoyed his friendship, but the sooner Marta could stop thinking he was a possible match for her the better. "That would be up to Chad, I guess.

She's the one who books guests now, and they're all...women."

"You can say lesbians, Ernesto. It's who they are."

"Well, either way, I guess Chad would still need help. Not so much a *houseboy*, maybe—"

"Oh, I almost forgot," Matt said. "Speaking of guests, you won't believe who's listed in the register as arriving tomorrow."

Ernesto didn't know enough about the various Americans who came and went through Casa de Ada, men or women, to hazard a guess. Nor did he particularly care. "Who?" he asked anyway, just to be polite.

"Alan!"

The fellow who wants photos back. The ones Ivan stole.

"I don't think he's going to show up," Matt said. "He knows no one wants him here. But if he *does* show up, I want to see the look on his face when he realizes it's all lesbians now."

*

ALTHOUGH ERNESTO SPENT most of his nights with Hank at Casa de Ada, once or twice a week, he'd work late at the factory processing a new delivery from the farm, and on those nights, he'd sleep in his old room, and his mother would make a big meal as if it was a celebration of some sort to have Ernesto home.

"I like working in the greenhouse," Marta told him. "It has good light. It's easier to do the fine painting work." They were in the storage room behind the factory floor, separating bundles of wrapper leaves and selecting the ones they'd decide to send over to the cigar room at Casa de Ada. The Americans enjoyed learning about the production process, and Marta wanted to make sure she had a sufficiently varied selection of leaves to show them.

"Sales are almost back to where they were before we lost the casino," Ernesto told her. "But the payments to the caballitos are expensive."

"It's better than having our house burned down," Marta responded. "And Francisco is nice. I've never worked with the torcederos before. He keeps asking me to teach him English words."

Yes, thought Ernesto. Francisco *is* nice, and he'd be a much better match for Marta than Matt. He was one of the three torcederos who'd set up shop in Casa de Ada's cigar room, demonstrating their craft to the Americans.

Hank said the authentic experience is what interested the tourists, and they were even talking with Chad about offering specific tour packages for travelers interested in learning about cigars. They could stay at Casa de Ada, watch the cigars being made, maybe even visit the farm. Hank said there could be good money in that.

Ernesto and Marta began wrapping their selected *manos* into burlap bundles.

"I think you should tell Mamma and Pappa about Hank," she said. "Not *everything*, of course, but... enough? So they know he's...special in some way."

He made a noncommittal noise and began wrapping another bundle.

Maybe he should. He'd decided he was going to run his own life, after all. Why not be more honest with his parents?

"Why do you think I should?" he asked.

"So it'll be easier for me when my turn comes," she said.

"What are you trying to tell me, Marta? You're moving in with Marigold now?"

"Very funny. No. I mean, if they suspect you're a...homosexual...*and* know you're happy, then maybe they'll be less upset if I do something...unconventional."

Hmm. Marta's American man would be less shocking than Ernesto's American man. She was right about that, and it was probably a good strategy. But it didn't change the fact she'd never be happy with Matt. He didn't think Matt would lead her on, but he was going to be very angry if he found out he had.

"You're right about Francisco," Ernesto said. "He is very nice. Handsome too."

Marta slapped his arm. "Stop. Are you trying to marry me off to a factory worker?"

"Torcederos aren't just factory workers, Marta. You know that. They're artists and professionals. They're very respectable, and Francisco is a good man."

She sighed. "I know. I just want more now. I've learned so much working with the Americans. My eyes have been opened to a whole new way of life."

Ernesto couldn't disagree with that. He felt the same way.

"Promise me you'll support me, Ernesto, when the time comes." She seemed nervous, like *when the time comes* might be sooner rather than later. Had he missed something entirely with Matt? He hoped not.

"I can't promise you that, Marta." He wouldn't let her ruin her life by marrying a man who couldn't love her. If it came to it, he'd tell her the full truth about Matt, but only if he had to. That wasn't his secret to share. "But I promise you I'll always look out for your best interests."

"Ernesto, how can you say that when you don't even know who—"

She was interrupted by their father stepping into the room. "Come to the table, mijos. Your mother has dinner ready."

*

DINNER WAS AN unusually strained affair. Marta seemed increasingly nervous throughout the meal, and Ernesto was distracted by how to tell his parents he'd officially dropped out of university that afternoon.

Or how to tell them about Hank.

He wasn't used to keeping secrets, and his own insistence to Hank that omissions and deceptions were the same as lies was weighing heavily on him.

"It seems our children are filled with distractions today," his mother said.

"Eat your dinners," their father said. "Your mother worked hard to make this meal."

Marta kept glancing at the wall clock. At times she opened her mouth to say something but then appeared to reconsider. Finally, near the end of the meal, she said, "Father, there's something you need to know. There's someone...that is...I want... Please, when he—"

They were interrupted by a knock on the door.

"Ernesto, see who is at the door," their father said.

As Ernesto began making his way toward the factory floor, Marta stood suddenly. "Father, please. Just hear him out. He's a good man." Before Ernesto's mind could come fully up to speed on what was happening, he opened the door.

Tony Cordero stood there, an unopened bottle of whiskey in hand. He wore a suit and tie and his free hand tugged at his collar as if it was choking him. "Um, surprise?" he said softly enough that only Ernesto could hear him.

"But...but you...you're..." Ernesto trailed off, dumbstruck.

"Look, much as I'd like to stand here in the doorway and chat, I'm actually here to see your father." He shifted the whiskey bottle between his hands and, when Ernesto still hadn't said anything, added, "May I come in?"

Ernesto took a deep breath and moved out of the way. His father stepped out of the family's office and onto the factory floor. "Who is it, Ernesto?" he asked. Marta stood in the office doorway, their mother with a hand on her shoulder keeping her in place.

After Marta's frantic last-minute efforts to pre-stage the meeting, it must be clear to his parents what was happening.

He recalled his inability to introduce himself to Hank, and then to Hans, a million years ago, and smiled. He recovered himself and waved Mr. Cordero into the room. "Father, may I present Mr. Tony Cordero, an...associate...of my..."

Amante

"Business partner, Hank Mannix, whom you've met. Mr. Cordero has been extremely helpful with selling the cigars, both at the casino and also now in my shop." And I've seen him nearly naked, wrestling with my lover in transparent bathing trunks. He shook the thought out of his head.

"Tony, may I introduce my father, Señor Raul Ruiz."

All of this he'd delivered in Spanish, and he wondered what Mr. Cordero's next step would be, now that the introductions had been made, and the fact that neither man spoke the other's language sat between them.

"*Mucho gusto en conocerle*, Señor Ruiz," Cordero said. It wasn't exactly right, but at least he'd made the effort.

The men shook.

"Thank you, Ernesto," Mr. Cordero said. "I hate to ask this for such a private thing, but would you please be my translator while I convince your father to allow me to marry your sister?"

"But...but aren't you...?" Ernesto didn't know how to finish his question, given the circumstances.

"Ernesto?" his father prompted.

"Please, Ernesto," Cordero pleaded. "I love her, and I swear I'll be good for her. Can't that be enough for you for now?"

He supposed it could. It would have to be. Enough for now was all any of them really had.

He turned to his father. "Mr. Cordero would like to speak with you privately in a matter concerning Marta, as I'm sure you've surmised. But unfortunately for me, he has asked me to be his translator. Will you permit that?"

"You know this American," his father said. "Should I let him approach me about this?"

Ernesto thought of all the hints Marta had dropped and how blind he'd been. He also considered Hank's assurance that he and Mr. Cordero didn't have a...romantic...relationship, that it was just business, pictures for a magazine, nothing more. Perhaps Mr. Cordero wasn't like the rest of the men at Casa de Ada.

And Mr. Cordero was a good friend to Hank, which said something. Plus, he'd helped tremendously with the cigar business. Although when Ernesto considered how much time that allowed him to spend alone with Marta, he thought perhaps the American hadn't been entirely altruistic.

But still, Marta loved him.

And he'd even managed to find a suit and tie somewhere, which made him look very handsome and professional—not at all like someone who loafed around the guest house posing nearly naked with Ernesto's amante.

He'd have to have a heart-to-heart with Marta before it became irreversible, but he couldn't stand in the way of this. When he thought about it, he found he didn't even want to.

"Yes, Father. Mr. Cordero is a good man. He's kind, and smart, and has strong prospects. And Marta seems fond of him."

Ernesto recognized the speculative gleam that appeared in his father's eye. Raul Ruiz wasn't a man to turn away from an unexpected opportunity. And Cordero was an American, as would be Marta's children.

His father smiled and waved an arm toward the back

room. "After you, Señor Cordero."

*

AFTER IT WAS all over—the toasts to good health, the explanations about his new job with the government in Miami, the repeated assurances that, yes, Mr. Cordero was a Catholic, the proposal itself, with Cordero on one knee offering a delicate gold ring with a pink-hued stone, Marta's joyful acceptance—after all of that, and after Mr. Cordero had left, and their parents had finally gone off to bed, Ernesto poured himself and his sister another small glass of whiskey, then sat across from her at the kitchen table.

She was happy, and Ernesto wasn't going to ruin it for her. Still, he had to make sure she knew.

"He's a good man, Marta."

"Yes," she replied. "We both have our American men now."

Ernesto cringed. He still wasn't comfortable talking openly about his love for Hank, and certainly not about their romantic relationship. But it was about to get worse. This was no moment for discretion; he needed to be clear.

He cleared his throat and took a sip of whiskey. "Marta, you know about the photographers that used to come to Casa de Ada to take pictures of Hank and Mr. Cordero."

"He's about to be your brother-in-law," she said. "You need to call him Tony now."

"Right. Tony, then. But you know the nature of the pictures they took, don't you? And the movies too?"

"Ernesto, please. Don't. Tony has told me everything. He's even showed me the magazines. If women can make money by appearing scantily clad in photos for a magazine, why can't men?"

Ernesto took another drink. "Of course. But the photos, they're...sexual...or meant to seem so anyway. You did see that, right? The two of them together, almost naked?"

Marta swirled the whiskey around in her glass. "Now you're just embarrassing me. Yes, I know all that. And I know they are made for a homosexual audience, and I *think* I can understand that—they're both very attractive men."

He cringed again, listening to his sister talk about men. Men like him.

"And the movies, Ernesto! I haven't seen them, but Tony told me there are tiny little theaters in New York City where men gather to watch them. Can you imagine such a thing?"

He could, and he sincerely hoped she couldn't—not in too much detail anyway.

But it was enough. She knew the truth, and Ernesto didn't feel like he needed to explain further.

But Marta wasn't quite through. "He even told me—" She lowered her voice and leaned closer, as if they weren't alone in the family kitchen. "—about the other pictures."

Other pictures?

She leaned back. "You can imagine that was...concerning. But he was *honest*; that's what's important. It was a difficult time, and they did things they weren't proud of but had to do to survive."

They?

"It's not so different than what some of the women at Casa de Ada have talked about. The things Marigold has gone through..." She finished most of her drink in one swallow. "But none of that matters. I'm getting married, Ernesto! And moving to Miami!"

"I know, and I'm happy for you, Marta. I just want to make sure Mr. Cord—uh, Tony—loves you and can make you happy...that way."

"Oh *that*." She waved her hand, dismissing Ernesto's concern. "He's considerate and kind and careful, and *very* attentive." She smiled at a private memory. "Why the first time we actually made—"

Ernesto had had enough. "No! No more, please. You're my *sister*."

"That's right, and you love me." She lifted her glass and held it toward Ernesto. "To the Ruiz children, and the American men they love."

It was good toast to end the night.

*

IT WAS LATE by the time Ernesto made his way up to his bedroom. He wasn't accustomed to drinking whiskey, so he was confused at first when he opened his door and felt the damp air. The briny smell of low tide filled the small space.

Ivan was sitting on Ernesto's bed.

"Ivan!" Ernesto fumbled for the lamp on his bedside table. "Are you all right?"

"Leave it off," Ivan said. "I can't be seen."

Ernesto put his hands on his cousin's shoulders, then sat next to him, twisting him to study his face in the dim glow of the lights outside. He seemed alert, and his eyes sparked with excitement. He was shirtless, but at least he wore shoes, and his pants were relatively clean. It was hard to see, but Ernesto thought he looked better than the last time he'd seen him when he'd been close to death under the malecón wall. "I wanted to thank you for saving my life that time," Ivan said.

"Oh, Ivan, of course—"

"And to say goodbye," Ivan added.

"What do you mean? Where are you going? Where have you been living? Marta will—"

"The revolution starts tonight. Castro is leading a group of us to attack the army." Ivan sounded...not drugged, exactly...more like he was in a trance. The spark Ernesto had noticed in his cousin's eyes began to seem more like delirium.

"Ivan, stay here tonight. We don't need to tell anyone. You can sleep in my bed and in the morning—"

"Here. Take these." Ivan reached beside him and slid the white envelope toward Ernesto.

Alan's photos. The ones Ivan stole.

"I know you wanted them back, and I wasn't able to sell them. No one wants to buy stolen pictures that are illegal to have anyway. Maybe you'll have better luck."

Ernesto pushed the envelope aside. "They don't matter, Ivan. Please stay here. Can I get you something to eat? Marta will want to see you. She has news about—"

"You should look at them, primo." He glanced down

at the envelope.

"No. I don't want to see them. It doesn't matter. You need—"

"I think you should look at them." Ivan stood from the bed and looked around the room slowly as if he was seeing it for the first time—or the last. He spotted Hank's shirt—the one with the shells—draped across the top of the desk chair. Ivan lifted it from the chair and held it out like an accusation. "You even dress like them now." He spat on the floor.

It was a shocking thing to do. "Ivan, no. It's not even mine." Panic threatened to overwhelm him. "Put it down."

Ivan spat on the floor again, and Ernesto felt it like a blow to the face. His cousin refused to relinquish the shirt, winding it around his fist instead like a boxing glove.

This couldn't be happening. "Hank—Mr. Mannix and I—we have plans. You could—"

"The Americans lie, Ernesto. All of them. All the time." He hoisted himself up onto the window sill. "It'll all be over soon. I'll come find you after its done."

Tears welled in Ernesto's eyes, making it even more difficult to see his cousin. He reached his hand out, but Ivan was already pulling himself through the window. "But where are you going?" Ivan didn't answer. Instead, he turned one last time to look at his cousin, then disappeared into the shadows.

Ernesto picked up the damp envelope and placed it on his bedside table. First thing in the morning he'd return it to Casa de Ada and tell Hank and the others what

Ivan had said about the revolution. Maybe someone would have an idea about how to stop him.

Chapter Thirty-Two

"I KNOW SHE said 'yes,' but how did the rest of it go last night?" Mannix asked his best friend, who was getting married and abandoning him for a life in Miami.

It was early in the morning, and Mannix and Cordero sat at the table in the greenhouse, where they could speak freely without bothering—or being bothered by—the women in the parlor. Matt and Hans were busy in the kitchen preparing breakfast.

"I think your boyfriend was the one who had the hardest time with it," Cordero replied. "Between having to translate for me while I told his father how much I loved his sister, and his extremely evident discomfort about me—I mean, he's seen us filming, after all—well, I was impressed he managed to hold it together."

"Does Marta know? About the films, I mean?" Mannix asked.

"Of course she does. I told her everything. I've

watched the two of them together. There was no way Ernesto was going to let her marry me unless she knew the truth."

Mannix put his coffee down and widened his eyes. "Everything?" he asked.

"Not in detail, but yes." Cordero grinned. "Don't look so shocked. She's a modern woman. I showed her a couple of the *Pumped* magazine spreads and told her about the films."

Mannix shook his head. Ernesto knew about the magazines and the movies, but that was different. But Cordero had said *everything*. "You didn't tell her about—" He waved his hand between the two of them. "What we used to do sometimes."

"No, Hank." Cordero looked out the window into the garden. "As I've said all along, if two friends lend each other a helping hand occasionally, it's nobody's business but theirs. It's not like we had commitments to others as we do now." Mannix was glad to hear that.

Cordero leaned in closer. "But I did tell her about the other photos. The bad ones."

Mannix's stomach fell. "What? Tony! Jesus, how could you?"

"Calm down. I wasn't explicit. But I did tell her you and I did things for that rich New Yorker so we could afford a roof over our heads and food on the table for a few months. I told her it was demeaning and probably illegal and that the asshole should probably be in prison for pressuring us into it."

Demeaning. Like forcing Ernesto into having sex in the garden. Oh God.

"Hank, it's okay. I told her enough that she could probably piece together the details, but I'm sure she doesn't want to. She knows it was in the past, and she's learned a thing or two from Marigold and the others about having to do unpleasant things to get through a tough spot."

This couldn't be happening. It would be disastrous if Ernesto found out about that from Marta. He'd have to tell him, and soon. God, and after he'd sworn he wasn't keeping any secrets. It *wasn't* a lie, not really, no matter how broadly Ernesto defined the term. It was just a shameful moment from his past he'd like to forget forever.

Mason chose that moment to rush into the greenhouse. "Emergency in the reception hall, gents." Mannix and Cordero stood and followed Mason into the house.

It was crowded in the reception hall.

A very red-faced Matt was pointing an accusing finger at—oh, God—Alan. He *had* come back, the bastard. A young, muscled fellow who looked just like Matt stood uncertainly behind him. Hans drummed his fingers on the desk with one hand and clutched at a floral-patterned, lime-green scarf draped around his shoulders with the other. Chad, dressed inexplicably in what looked like a Boy Scout uniform, towered disapprovingly over Alan. Marigold filled the rest of the open space.

When Mason reentered the room, he put a hand on Matt's shoulder, presumably to keep him from launching himself at Alan.

When Mannix and Cordero piled in behind Mason, causing everyone to pack even more tightly into the room,

Alan said, "Oh, good, the porn stars are here." Mason glanced over, and Mannix could see he was suddenly re-assessing whether Matt needed constraining more than Mannix did; then he simply backed away, evidently deciding he'd let the chips fall where they may.

"He stole my photos," Alan said, pointing at Matt

He must have made the accusation earlier because Matt began to respond with, "I *told* you I didn't—"

But Mannix interrupted. "Hello there, you poor boy," he said to the hapless young man at Alan's side as he stepped forward and offered his hand. "You must be the new Matt."

"Um…" said the poor boy in question.

"He's not—" began Alan, before taking a closer look at Matt. "Why is he dressed like a whore?" he asked.

"Don't be ridiculous," Cordero responded. "He's dressed like a houseboy. Matt's the new Ernie."

"Who's Ernie?" Alan asked.

"He used to be the cute one," Hans said, "But then he became the new Mannix, and—"

"No," Cordero interrupted. "It was Matt who became the new Mannix, before he became the new Ernie."

The new Matt looked increasingly bewildered as he tried to inch away from the crowd in the room. Alan reached out a hand and gripped his elbow, holding him in place. "Stop," Alan said and turned his attention back to the old Matt. "I need that envelope right now."

Mannix knew the envelope had pornographic pictures in it. They'd all conducted a thorough search for it. It wasn't something Hans could risk someone stumbling upon inadvertently. And what an idiot Alan was to travel around with them—risking arrest and exposure at any moment.

The front door pushed open, squeezing Chad even closer to Alan, just as Matt said "I don't have your damn pictures!" Ernesto shouldered his way into the room holding an envelope in front of him.

Was that...?" But how could Ernie have ended up with Alan's stash of porn?

He looked awful, as if he hadn't gotten any sleep. "Ernie..." he began, stepping toward his amante.

"Those are mine!" bellowed Alan as he lunged toward Ernesto and made a grab for the envelope. Ernesto flinched back, and although Alan had managed to grab the edge of the envelope, neither man was able to hold onto it as Ernesto pulled away, and the envelope dropped to the ground, scattering its contents across the floor.

Marigold stepped forward and pushed herself in front of Alan. She pressed a thick palm against his chest. And then, the woman who had previously given every indication of being a field-worker, said, in perfect English, "Do not touch that boy. If you lay one hand on him, I will rip your balls off and feed them to you." Marigold leaned right into Alan's face. "Do you understand me?"

Alan gulped and nodded, and the new Matt scrunched his eyes closed and seemed to shrink in upon himself, as if he could somehow make everything go away by not looking.

"Ernie..." Mannix began. But Ernesto had turned a ghostly white and was staring, openmouthed, at the photos that had spilled from the envelope. Mannix followed his gaze.

His own face leered up at him, and Tony's too, as he and his best friend engaged in a variety of highly explicit and illegal sex acts on the reception room floor.

Time slowed down. And in the frantic part of Mannix's brain that was watching the disaster unfold in slow motion, he thought maybe he could slow time even further, slow it so much that it started moving backward, and the pictures would slide back into the envelope.

But instead, into the stunned silence of the room, Ernesto looked up, tears in his eyes, and whispered, "You lied to me."

Mannix watched his world fall apart, as everyone else stared in mute horror at his shame displayed across the floor. Chad, bless her heart, was the first to recover. She hip checked Alan out of the way—"You miserable little prick"—and bent to retrieve the photographs.

I want to die. I can't live with the hate and disgust in Ernie's face.

The front door was flung open again but only made it a few inches before it collided with Alan, who was in the midst of regaining his balance after Chad's shove. Alan collapsed onto the floor, and it may or may not have been intentional when Chad's scouting boot came down hard on his fingers.

"Oh...what..." said Eduardo as he peeked his head around the door frame, then leveraged himself through the small gap and stepped over Alan. "Oh no, you're back," he said, looking at the man lying prone on the floor, grimacing in pain.

Alan rolled onto his side and stared up at Eduardo. "Who the hell are you?" he demanded.

"Seriously?" Eduardo asked. "Still? The man with the big boat and the little..." but he trailed off when he noticed the tone of the room, and the looks on everyone's faces. "What's happened? What's wrong?"

A few incoherent mumbles dissolved into silence.

My life just ended; that's what happened.

"Well, it doesn't matter. We have an emergency," Eduardo said. He craned his neck around to look between Chad and Marigold. "Oh! Matt, thank God. I was afraid you'd gone with him. Ivan is headed into an ambush!"

*

EVERYONE STARTED TALKING at once, which, Mannix supposed, was better than everyone quietly staring at pictures of him having sex with Tony.

Hans was making a visible effort to pull himself together. "Let's all go into the parlor where at least there's room to breathe, and Eduardo can tell us what's going on." They all began to shuffle out of the reception the hall. Chad slipped the envelope of photos into Mannix's hand as she passed and gave his arm a soft pat.

Mannix cursed every moment he'd ever thought something mean about her.

Tony whispered into his ear as he passed. "Thank God I was on top." Then he punched Mannix in the shoulder.

Ernesto refused to make eye contact, and he made sure to get around Mannix and into the parlor while others were blocking the space between them.

Once everyone was in the next room—everyone

except Alan, who could still be heard groaning on the reception hall floor—all eyes turned to Eduardo. But Eduardo had just noticed the newcomer, and his face lit up in appreciation. "Hello! Who are you?"

"I'm the new Matt, evidently," the young man said.

"Oh, I'm so sorry."

"Don't worry. I don't think it will last for long."

The old Matt came over and put a claiming arm around Eduardo's waist. It would have been sweet if Mannix's life hadn't just been destroyed, and if Ernesto didn't look like he'd just been brutally betrayed.

"Eduardo!" Ernesto demanded. "We need to focus on Ivan. He came to me last night and told me the revolution is starting. He gave me the...you know..."

No one looked at Mannix.

Eduardo pulled his attention away from the new Matt. "Yes, that's what I came to tell you. The police have been tipped off, and they warned us to be prepared for unrest at the university. Ivan has joined up with Castro's army. They're going to start the revolution by attacking the Moncada Barracks. It's a suicide mission."

Poor Ivan. To have survived everything he's been through, and now this.

Ernesto looked devastated. "Can we stop them in time?" Ernesto asked. "Or can we at least stop Ivan?"

"Where are they now?" Chad asked. "When did they leave?"

"They left before light this morning," he responded. "But they're in two old buses, and there's at least a hundred of them. We might be able to catch them."

"No," Hans said. "The Packard can barely make it

around the block these days."

The Packard. Mannix didn't need something else to feel bad about. He thought the group had moved on pretty quickly from "the end of his life as he knew it" to stopping the revolution and making sure Ivan didn't die, but maybe he was being too self-centered.

He glanced at Ernesto, who still refused to make eye contact, and who was looking even more anguished than he had been—a hundred years ago—when everyone's attention was on him and Tony having sex on the reception hall floor.

Marigold cleared her throat—a deep, rumbling noise reminiscent of the caballito's motorcycle engines—and pushed her way to the center of the room. "I have a truck."

Of course she did. And based on other people's expressions, he wasn't the only one who'd already forgotten the shock of learning Marigold spoke English. There was simply too much going on.

"Let's go," said Ernesto, and for the one who was supposed to think things through, Mannix thought it was a terribly impulsive thing to say. But people were already moving, and Eduardo was speaking with Marigold as they headed toward the door, presumably providing specifics regarding the where and when of the revolution.

Everyone moved through the reception hall, variously stepping over or around Alan, and gathered out front as Marigold headed off to get her truck.

"Will it rain, do you think?" Hans asked as he untied his scarf then reset it to cover his head and shoulders.

"I'll get your umbrella, dear, and a rain jacket," Mason said.

How long was this trip going to take? And why is no one else asking any of the planning questions? Come on, Ernie, do your job.

Ernesto stood as far away from Mannix as he could. Tony moved up to him, and Ernesto didn't turn *him* away. Mannix wished he was close enough to hear what they were saying, but he knew better than to approach.

After a few moments, Mason returned with the rain-gear, and Marigold returned with her truck. It was somewhat bigger than the run-of-the-mill pickup truck Mannix had been envisioning, and it had wooden panels running along the sides of the bed that would, presumably, keep people and goods from bouncing out.

He looked at the unnecessarily large crowd milling about and concluded no matter what happened, he was joining Ernesto on this reckless dash to save Ivan, even if Ernesto didn't want him along. "You need to sit up front with me and Chad," Marigold told Eduardo. That made sense, since he was the one who knew where they were going, but it would be a tight squeeze in the cab.

The open truck bed was strewn with the remains of sugar cane stalks and leaves, and there were piles of none-too-clean blankets scattered about. "She uses it to transport the field-workers between her farms," Chad explained.

No turning back now. Mannix leapt into the open bed just ahead of Ernesto. He reached down to help pull his *amante* up, but Ernesto stepped aside and let Matt clamber in first, then he helped Hans, and then Mason. By the time Mannix had managed to settle Hans more or less comfortably in a corner, Ernesto had already climbed in and hunkered down far from Mannix.

Cordero was next, then everyone looked at the new Matt, who seemed confused and uncertain. He glanced back at the house just as an angry Alan hobbled out of the door. "I can't stay here with him," he said.

The old Matt reached down a hand. "Come on, then."

The new Matt climbed on board and squeezed in next to Mannix. The truck rumbled to life and began bouncing down the drive.

Let's hope these barracks are close by.

*

MANNIX LEARNED *A lot* during the next six hours.

He learned that the new Matt—who'd seemed so shy and uncertain—was anything but. "I liked your pictures," he said to Mannix as they jostled against one another in the back of the truck. "Can I see them again?" Thank God Ernesto hadn't been close enough to hear. Mannix found an excuse to switch places with Mason and settled next to Hans.

He learned that the old Matt didn't only suffer motion sickness at sea. The swaying, bouncing motion of the truck set him off as well, and Mannix spent quite a bit of time holding Matt's waistband, as he vomited over the side.

He learned that even Mason could lose his cool eventually, after enough spittle from Matt flew back onto the passengers huddled in the truck bed. "For God's sake, Matt, use the other side of the truck!"

He learned that exhaust fumes from a poorly tuned

diesel engine smelled bitter and cloying and magically pooled in the bed of the truck and stayed there, in seeming defiance of the fact the truck was—very slowly—moving.

He learned that the Moncada Barracks must be in Africa somewhere.

And he learned that, even with everything else, he'd rather be stuck in the back of that truck with Ernesto than be anywhere else in the world.

Marigold pulled off the road and into a dusty lot next to a...what? There must be a word for these roadside venues that seemed to be a combination of workshop, junkyard, food stand, and retailer, selling hats, lottery tickets and unidentifiable food-like things from a deep fryer.

Starvation and dehydration never looked so good.

"Don't eat anything," he advised the other Americans as the men piled out of the back of the truck. The Cubans and Chad stepped around a few live chickens and disappeared into the depths of the...whatever it was.

"I guess I could live here," the old Matt said, surveying the bleak landscape. "I mean, I don't *have* to get back in the truck."

"Die here, more likely," Mason added helpfully. "I'm afraid there's no way but forward."

Hans unwrapped his scarf and flapped it in the wind, which would remove the pieces of straw and sugar cane, but wouldn't do anything for the droplets of vomit. "Is this real?" he asked. "Did all of that just happen?" No one answered him.

Tony approached Mannix and placed an arm around his shoulder. "It's looking grim," he said.

"Oh, I don't know," Mannix replied. "A refreshing country drive…"

"I appreciate your fake optimism, but I was referring to Ernesto. He's beyond simply being angry."

The photographs in his pocket weighed a hundred pounds. For a moment, Mannix entertained the notion of slipping into the—whatever it was—and leaving the photographs there, on a tabletop or tucked into some mysterious piece of machinery. But he couldn't do that to the Cuban people.

"Of course he is. I betrayed him."

"You should have told him."

"Gee, thanks. I hadn't figured that out on my own yet. Anything else I might have missed? Should I have asked how far the barracks were, maybe?"

The new Matt wandered over. "I keep thinking about those pictures," he said. Mannix cringed, and Cordero put a hand on the new Matt's shoulder and pulled him close.

"Can I tell you a secret?" he whispered.

The new Matt smiled and leaned in.

"If you mention those photographs again," Cordero said directly into his ear, "I will break your kneecaps and leave you to find your own way back to Alan."

After the young man slunk away, Mannix said, "You're a good man, Tony."

"So are you, Hank. We'll get through this. I promise."

*

EDUARDO REDEEMED EVERYTHING he'd ever done wrong by appearing with a wooden tray piled high with bottles of cola. They were warm, but they were sealed, and that was the important thing. Everyone gathered around. "Small sips," he said to Matt. "I'm sorry I let you come. I wasn't thinking about the distance."

"It's all right; I wouldn't miss it. I want to see what happens."

With the revolution? With Ivan? With him and Ernie? Whichever it was, Mannix felt the same way.

"How much farther?" Mannix asked Eduardo, who began studying the ground intently.

"Well, it's still some distance away."

"Eddie. How much farther?"

"The good news is the people inside said two buses came by here very early this morning. And we're probably making better time than they are."

"Eddie...?"

Eduardo popped the cap on his bottle and took a deep swallow. "We're not even halfway."

Oh, why not? His life was over, he was sore and bruised from all the bumping, and he was flecked with Matt's vomit. Why not make an eternity out of it?

Ernesto appeared, carrying loaves of bread, blocks of cheese, and some bananas. Bread couldn't kill you, could it? Mannix counted it as an enormous victory when Ernesto tore off a chuck of bread and handed it to him along with a banana. "Don't eat the cheese," he said before turning away.

At least he was talking to him.

The men began piling back into the truck, and Mannix pushed the new Matt aside just as he was lowering himself next to Ernesto. "Sorry," he said. "I've reserved this seat." Then he plopped down next to Ernesto, who rolled his eyes, but—another victory—didn't move away.

The truck crunched over stones and back onto the roadway. Matt closed his eyes and took delicate sips of soda as the diesel fumes began swirling about the truck bed. Mannix turned to Ernesto. "We're really bad at road trips."

Ernesto's lips *might* have twitched. "Hank, please. It would be so much easier if you just acknowledged it's over between us and we got through the rest of this ordeal pretending we don't know each other."

Mannix nudged Ernesto with his knee. "It would be easier, but it's not true. It's *not* over between us. And since it's not true, we shouldn't pretend it is. That would be like lying, and we *definitely* shouldn't lie to each other."

Ernesto flopped his head back against the wooden board. "That's...that's..."

"That's Hank," Cordero supplied. He was squeezed up against Ernesto's other side, and occasionally pushed in even tighter when the new Matt got too close on his other side. "You know not to try to reason with him when he thinks he knows what he's talking about."

"But he's *wrong*," Ernesto told Cordero. "I was quite clear if he lied to me again, it would be over between us."

"Suit yourself," Cordero said and closed his eyes, pretending to settle in for nap.

Mannix struggled not to say it, but in the end, he lost the battle. "It wasn't a lie," he whispered.

The truck hit a pothole and bounced violently. "What!" demanded Ernesto.

"He said it wasn't a lie," Cordero replied.

"I wasn't talking to you," Ernesto snapped.

"But, Ernie…" Mannix began.

"And I'm not talking to you either." Ernesto crossed his arms and withdrew into himself. Months ago, before any of this had started, he *might*—once or twice—have entertained a fantasy about being squeezed between the white twins. Never again.

They'd only driven a few miles before the truck came a halt. Mannix stood and looked over the roof of the cab. Workers were setting up a detour, and one of them was approaching the truck.

Marigold leaned out the window and called to the man. They spoke for a few minutes before he walked away. A moment later, Eduardo climbed out of the cab. "We have to take a detour. They're putting in a new culvert. But they've just started."

"So, Ivan probably passed through hours ago, and will now be even farther ahead of us?" Ernesto asked.

"I'm afraid so," Eduardo said. "Marigold wants to know what she should do."

Everyone looked at Ernesto. No one wanted to be in this truck one second longer than necessary, Mannix thought. But what a horrible burden to put on Ernesto. It was his cousin, after all, and he knew Ernesto well enough to know he'd be torn between his duty to Ivan and his reluctance to make everyone suffer further on his behalf.

That wasn't right.

"We're going to go find Ivan," Mannix said. Cordero

nodded his agreement. "Ernie and I can find other transport if we need to. No need for everyone to continue along." He hoped they would all ignore the fact they hadn't passed anything like a bus station or a hotel in hours. Thankfully, no one objected, and Hans even said, "Oh, the things we do for love," which Mannix thought must clearly be a point in his favor.

"Onward it is, then," Eduardo said with a tap on the roof of the cab.

*

THE DETOUR TURNED out to be on a poorly marked road that branched and meandered through farms and brushland. They soon began to lose the light, and Marigold pulled the truck onto a drive leading to a farm with a scattering of barns and outbuildings.

"Déjà vu," Mannix said to Ernesto.

Chapter Thirty-Three

THE SUGAR MILL, where Ernesto and the other men had been directed to bed down for the night, was open on all sides, and much of the interior space was dominated by a steam-powered press. The press was used to extract juice from sugar cane, and thankfully it wasn't operating this time of year, so the building was quiet and dusty.

The air smelled sweetly of alcohol, reminiscent of the last time Ernesto had slept in a barn—when he'd first learned Hank was a vulnerable man filled with self-doubts just like Ernesto. "I'm washed up," Hank had said then.

Chad and Marigold had been invited to sleep in the house.

Ernesto was surprised to learn Marigold was the daughter of landowners who operated several sugarcane farms. He shouldn't have been surprised, and he chided himself for judging that book by its cover. They were much the same, the two of them, children of middle-class parents, looking to make a life for themselves and improve their family's circumstances.

He hoped when all of this was over, one way or another, they might become friends.

A bright moon softly illuminated the interior of the mill. Ernesto had brought his blankets to a far corner. It was too warm to use them as anything other than a means of softening the hard dirt floor.

He wondered where Ivan was. Had the attack happened? Had the revolution started? Was he alive?

A figure approached him, and he prepared himself to tell Hank in no uncertain terms to leave him alone.

But it was Hans. He surprised Ernesto by lowering himself on top of the blankets and snuggling in, wrapping him into a hug from behind. "How are you, dear one?" Hans asked. He smelled good, in a light floral way, and Ernesto couldn't imagine how he'd managed that after the day they'd had.

"Awful," he responded.

"I did warn you," Hans said softly.

Ernesto rolled over and created a small distance between the two of them. "You did no such thing. And you probably knew about the two of them," he said. He tried to keep the resentment from his voice, but he didn't think he succeeded.

"No. I meant I warned you that you could hurt him."

Hurt him? *Was Hans saying this was Ernesto's fault?*

"That's not fair," Ernesto insisted. "He *lied* to me. And he knew that was the one thing I couldn't accept from him. *I'm* the one who got hurt."

"Of course you did! God knows, we all saw that coming, what with Hank's history and...recklessness. But you did hurt him, Ernesto. Even though you didn't mean to."

"I don't see how I could have. I'm not the one who cheated and lied." He didn't like how he sounded, and there was no need to snap at Hans. "But it doesn't matter. It's over."

"It does matter," Hans insisted. He pulled himself into a cross-legged position on the blankets, and Ernesto did the same. "And you hurt him because he made himself vulnerable to you. He's never done that with anyone before. And when you saw all his flaws, you rejected him."

He wasn't going to let Hans make him feel bad for having principles and standards. "Cheating and lying aren't *flaws*, Hans."

"Cheating," Hans scoffed. "Think Ernesto. Where did those pictures come from?"

Alan had brought them. And to think he'd done so just to blackmail Hank. What a snake. These Americans were—oh. Alan had brought them with him before Ernesto and Hank had even met. So maybe, *maybe*, cheating was going too far. But still, he'd lied, and after everything they'd talked about.

Hans nodded as he watched Ernesto think it through. "Exactly," he said. "And you're really so certain he lied?"

"Yes, absolutely." On this, Ernesto was clear. "He told me he and Hank had never...done that."

"What did he say exactly, Ernesto?"

He thought back. They'd been in the car, driving

along the malecón. He'd said…what exactly? Ernesto had mentioned the rumors about Hank and Tony that Ivan had shared with him, and Hank had said…

"'We're not like that.' That's what Hank said—about Tony and him." And by *that*, he'd meant not like and Hank and Ernesto were.

"Well, they're *not* like that," Hans confirmed.

"But the *pictures—*" Ernesto insisted.

"Were from before he knew you." Hans finished for him.

Ernesto couldn't get the graphic images out of his mind. "But still…"

"Yes," Hans said. "But still." He stood and steadied himself with a hand on Ernesto's shoulder. "I'm not making any judgments. But you *have* hurt him, and now you have the opportunity to utterly destroy him." He bent down and kissed Ernesto on the forehead. "He's a good man, Ernesto. Be careful what you choose to do."

*

HE COULDN'T SLEEP. He tossed and turned, thinking about Ivan, thinking about Hank, thinking about Tony and Marta. Had she truly known about the photos and been all right with them? She said Tony implied he'd had to do things he didn't want to do, and that seemed to be enough for her.

He hoped she'd never see them. They were difficult images to unsee.

"I can hear you thinking from all the way across the barn," Hank said as he dropped down next to Ernesto.

Earlier, he'd been resigned to forcing Hank away if he showed up. Now he wasn't sure what he thought or what he wanted.

"It's not a barn; it's a mill."

"Well, whatever it is, I'm not throwing up in it, and you haven't kicked me in the *cajones* yet, so there's two good things."

The man was infuriating. He sat up to face Hank. "You promised not to lie to me, Hank."

"I know, and I shouldn't have made that promise."

That wasn't the defense he was expecting. "What!"

"Hear me out. I shouldn't have agreed to your silly definitions of lies. They don't make any sense! I wouldn't have lied to you if you hadn't made lying so impossible to avoid by defining it so broad—"

"Do *not* put this on me," Ernesto interrupted. "Don't you think I would have wanted to know you had sex with Tony?" He tried to keep his voice down. "Don't you think I had the right to know?"

"Ha," Mannix responded. "For the smart one who's supposed to think things through, you can be pretty dense sometimes."

"If this is your way of apologizing—"

"It is *not*!" Mannix shot back. "I'm not apologizing. You asked two very different questions. Yes, I think you would have wanted to know that Tony and I had sex. You want to know *everything*. You obsess over details, trying to figure out what everything *means*. You...you...*dwell* on things, until everything looks dark, then you end up wanting to break up with me."

Did he dwell on things? He didn't think so. Sure, he

always reasoned things through and tried to see all the different angles. And it was natural for part of that to include understanding what could go wrong, how things could—

"See! You're doing it now." Hank made it sound like an accusation.

When Ernesto didn't respond, Mannix continued. "And as to your second question, no, I *don't* think you had a right to know about what Tony and I did years before I met you. It was a horrible time I'd like to forget. Some asshole in New York paid us a lot of money to let him take those pictures. It was just our bad luck he turned out to be part of the same asshole circle Alan is a part of."

Marta *did* say Tony told her they'd been desperate.

"And it was demeaning and embarrassing and shameful, and I wish I'd never done it. Tony and I could barely look at each other for days afterward." Mannix sniffed and wiped at his eyes and then lowered his voice. "Tony wasn't even that good at it."

From across the mill, there was a muffled objection, followed by a soft *thunk* and then "Ouch."

"My point is," Mannix continued, "you don't have a *right* to know that about me. I'm not obligated to put every horrible thing that ever happened to me out there for your inspection—for your *judgment*."

Ernesto hadn't thought about it like that. Still, it was something Hank had chosen to do—sort of, under a lot of pressure he now saw. "I wasn't judg—"

"Yes. That is exactly what you were doing. Calling the worst decision I'd ever made, and tried to keep private, a *lie* because you think you have a right to know my darkest, most shameful secrets."

Was that what he'd done? Hank was clearly in pain. Ernesto hated thinking he may have caused that.

"And the thing is, Ernesto, I think I may have chosen to tell you those things about myself someday. To keep opening up to you, making myself more vulnerable. It felt...liberating, what we were building together. But I guess now we'll never know."

He stood, and, unlike Hans, he did not kiss Ernesto on the brow. "They were right though, Hans and Tony. We really are capable of hurting each other."

Then he walked away.

*

ERNESTO TOSSED AND turned all night, thinking, dwelling, *obsessing*—just as Hank said he would. He wanted to figure it all out, to carefully weigh everything Hank had said against what Ernesto knew to be the truth. But he couldn't think clearly; his mind kept drifting back to Ivan.

In the morning, he still hadn't reached any conclusions about what everything meant. It seemed important to learn Hank had been nearly forced into having sex with Tony, but how important? Did that excuse Hank's not telling him about it? Sure, he could understand why Hank would like to have forgotten about the whole thing, but he must have known how horrible it would be for Ernesto to find out the way he did.

Well, no. No one could have foreseen the photographs scattered about on the reception hall floor.

Then he kicked himself for doing the very thing Hank had accused him of—turning things over and over in his mind, studying them every which way, and never letting anything settle.

He pushed it all from his mind and headed for the truck. He'd think about it after they found Ivan.

He didn't deliberately avoid Hank as they all climbed into the truck bed, but he was relieved nonetheless to find himself sitting between the old and new Matts. "Oh good, we're going to do this again," Hans said as he settled himself into a corner. Marigold had borrowed a flowered bedsheet from their hosts, and Mason helped Hans wrap it securely around his shoulders.

"How are you feeling, Matt?" Mason asked. Everyone wanted to know the answer to that question—wanted to know if they needed to brace themselves for more vomit spittle—and Ernesto smiled when the new Matt began to answer. Either his name really was Matt, or he'd decided to adopt it for his visit to Cuba. Someone should probably ask him.

"Not you," Mason said.

"Fine, I think," the old Matt said. "I'm just sipping my soda this morning."

Everyone nodded. Surely, if they all believed that would be enough, it would be.

Within an hour they were off the detour and back on the main road, where they were able to pick up speed. Matt began to look a bit green but managed to keep it together for the next two hours, at which point the truck came to a stop. Mason stood and looked over the cab to the road ahead.

"We're almost there," he said. "That's the church they told Marigold we should look for. The barracks are just a mile down that road." Everyone looked at Ernesto. This was what they had come for—to stop Ivan from joining a suicidal attack against a fortified army barracks. There was no activity on the road ahead of them. Perhaps they'd gotten there in time?

The truck started up again and swayed wide into the turn, causing Matt to leap up and lean over the side. Mannix stood and held onto him, and everyone waited to see if he would vomit or recover as the truck continued its lumbering way down the road.

He did vomit, but his retching didn't cover the sound of gunfire and explosions they began to hear in the distance.

We're too late.

Marigold stopped the truck. Everyone listened to the sounds of battle until a small group of young people came running down the road from the direction of the barracks. Two of them were bleeding. "Help!" one called. "Can you get us out of here?"

Mason was still standing, braced against the cab, and Ernesto joined him, knowing that Mason wouldn't have understood the request. "No," Ernesto responded. "We're heading to the barracks. We need to find someone. Do you know an Ivan Ruiz?"

"Don't go any closer," another one said. "It's a massacre. If your friend hasn't run off, he's dead for sure."

Matt vomited again, and the young people—*revolution-aries*?—continued down the road in search of a savior.

Mannix was helping Matt steady himself, and maybe it was because he was the only one facing that side of the truck, away from the fleeing fighters, that he spotted something. He settled Matt onto the floor and banged on the roof of the cab. "There!" he shouted, pointing at—nothing Ernesto could see—far into the distance, across a fallow sugar cane field.

"I saw someone fall on the far edge of the field."

"Was it Ivan?" Hans asked.

"Maybe," Mannix replied, "I don't know. It could have been. I thought I saw Ernie's crying shirt—the one I wear with the shells on it. But Ernie has that shirt."

"Ivan took it!" he shouted to Hank. "Two nights ago when he—"

But Ernesto didn't even get a chance to finish the thought before Mannix leapt over the side of the truck, landing ungracefully with a grunt, and took off at a run across the field. Ernesto jumped out and took off after Mannix.

It hurts *to run through a field of dead sugarcane stalks.* But he was rapidly gaining on Mannix, and a small, betraying part of his mind thought that later—if everything ended well—he'd enjoy teasing Hank about being faster.

By the time they reached the person lying in the field, they were both winded, and Mannix was panting heavily.

Ivan. His chest rose and fell, but he appeared to have passed out, and there was a lot of blood. "Help me lift him so I can get him back to the truck," Mannix said.

"Is it safe to move him?" Ernesto asked.

Mannix was already stooping to secure a hold on Ivan. He squinted up at Ernesto. "Do you see a pay phone in this field to call for an ambulance? Should we leave him for the army to find?" Ernesto blinked, caught off guard by a sudden realization.

Sometimes it wasn't useful to be the guy who thought through all the risks. Sometimes, you just needed to act.

Mannix hoisted Ivan up onto his shoulders, and Ernesto saw blood flowing down his cousin's arm and onto Hank's shirt, the one he was wearing—not the one with the shells that Ivan had on, although that was blood soaked too. The jagged cane stalks tore at their trousers and poked at their shins.

Marigold and Mason moved forward to take Ivan, and they laid him on the tailgate. After a quick inspection, Marigold said, "I think he's been shot, but it looks like it grazed his arm, and the bullet isn't lodged inside." Thank God for that, and thank God for Hank, for seeing Ivan fall across the field and for acting so quickly.

"We need to get out of here," Mason said. The sound of fighting had stopped, but there were still distant screams. "Reinforcements will be coming soon. We can't be questioned by the police."

Everyone jumped into action. Mannix and Ernesto sat next to each other, backs against the truck's wooden sideboards, Ivan on the floor between them, his head resting between their thighs on one of the blankets. Matt did his best to clean the wound with water Eduardo had bought at the same stop where he'd gotten sodas for the

Americans.

Marigold had been right. It was a serious wound, but the bullet had passed through the edge of his bicep, and wasn't lodged inside. "Give me your shirt," Matt told Mannix. "It's ruined anyway, but I can use the clean part to bind his arm until…" He trailed off then. What *would* they do with Ivan?

"Again, with the men insisting I go shirtless," Mannix mumbled.

They settled in for the long ride. At one point, Ivan was jostled awake. He looked up at Mannix, pain, confusion, and panic turned to recognition. "Maricón," he spat.

"Now, now, Grubby," Mannix replied. "There'll be no name calling here."

"He saved your life," Ernesto said to his cousin. "Again." Ivan closed his eyes.

Mannix reached over Ivan and touched Ernesto's shoulder. "Are you all right?" he asked.

Ernesto had been thinking about that very question all night. Dwelling, obsessing, weighing. But all of that had dropped away when Hank ran into the field, and something important had locked in place in his heart.

He loved Hank. He'd known that already, but he kept letting his principles and…and…*purity* get in the way. His insistence that Hank conform to the very highest standards. But that's not how love worked, was it?

When Ernesto didn't answer, Mannix let out a soft sigh. "Okay. I know that look. You're thinking. I'll wait."

I can't keep turning away from Hank—not when he's the best thing in my life. Not when he has my cousin's blood on his hands, and on his chest. Ernesto did his very best not to focus on the rise and fall of Hank's belly as his breathing returned to normal.

Not when we love each other so much.

But he'd hurt Hank. Badly. He saw that now. When Hank's deepest shame was exposed, and he was completely vulnerable, Ernesto had rejected him. *Judged* him, yes, and found him unworthy. But how could he convince Hank he understood now that he'd been wrong and that he deserved a second chance?

"We need fish," Ernesto said.

Mannix squinted, a puzzled look on his face. "Um, well, I wasn't expecting that. But, okay, though fish might be hard to find here in the middle of nowhere, and we probably shouldn't detour, what with your cousin—"

"No," Ernesto interrupted, "our fish, in our pond." He reached across Ivan and took Hank's hand. "It seems these conversations always go better when we're there with our fish keeping us company, getting us back on track."

Mannix broke into a tentative smile at the mention of getting back on track.

Ernesto knew what he had to do. "I want to tell you something," he said.

Everyone in the crowded truck bed pretended not to be listening. Mannix didn't say anything but squeezed Ernesto's hand.

Ernesto took a deep breath and began. "When I was thirteen, my father tried to teach me all the aspects of our business. I was good at some of it. Matching wrapper leaf colors, knowing when the manos needed to be turned, managing the fans and windows to keep the humidity at the right levels."

Between them, Ivan blinked, then settled.

"But I was horrible at rolling cigars. They would fall apart or come out oddly shaped, or I would tear the wrapper leaves. I just couldn't manage it."

The truck bumped along, and the diesel fumes pooled in the bed. No one spoke a word.

"There was a young torcedero then. His name was Ramon. He was very talented and always tried to prove himself to my father. He wanted to be recognized, maybe earn more money. One day, I stole several of his cigars and told my father I'd made them."

Ernesto stopped as shame flamed in his face. He hadn't let himself think about what he'd done in years. But he owed it to Hank to get through this.

"My father was so pleased with me and praised my work. I was foolish enough to be proud of his approval. It was all I wanted—to have him tell me what a good job I'd done." A tear slipped down his cheek. "Later that day, I heard him tell Ramon he did fine work but needed to be more productive. He needed to be able to make more cigars in an afternoon."

Ernesto thought about the conversations he'd had with Matt about workers' rights and privilege and power.

"Of course Ramon never said anything. How could he risk claiming the owner's son stole from him? He left shortly afterward. I never told my father the truth, although I think he eventually came to suspect they hadn't been my cigars."

Ernesto didn't make eye contact with anyone. It was his most shameful moment, and it still haunted him.

But it was his gift to Hank. And just as Hank's shame had been displayed for everyone to see, now Ernesto's was too. It equalized them, put things back into balance.

After the silence dragged on uncomfortably for a few moments, Hank asked, "Ernie, is this your way of...of...apologizing to me?"

Ernesto nodded. He decided not to look at Hank or the others. Instead, he looked down at Ivan, who blinked up at him once, then closed his eyes again. He could feel the small pool of blood from Ivan's arm that had formed at his thigh.

"You know," Mannix said. "None of this would have happened if you'd just told me the truth from the beginning."

Ernesto swallowed against the lump in his throat. "I know."

"This is all your fault," Mannix continued.

"I *know*. Please...I'm so sorry." He was crying now, and he looked up to see if he could ever to hope to find forgiveness in Hank's face.

But Mannix was grinning from ear to ear. "Got you," he said. And although it seemed impossible, his grin grew even wider. "We're starting the count over. Go."

Ernesto smiled through his tears as relief washed through him. Hank had been right. The vulnerability *did* feel good. "One," he said softly.

"I'm collecting that right now," Hank said, as he leaned over Ivan—squishing him tighter against Ernesto's leg—and brought his lips to Ernesto's.

It wasn't a chaste kiss, and the Matts whooped their

approval. Hans politely applauded as if he were at a fashion runway show. Mason raised an imaginary glass, and Cordero said, "Get a room." Beneath them, Ivan groaned.

Mannix pulled back. "Let's not do that to each other again."

"Never, Hank. Never again."

*

A FEW MONTHS later, long after Hans and Mason had left for Miami, Hank and Ernesto were sitting at the kitchen table writing a letter to Hans.

"Tell him we finally had our Catholic Mass date," Mannix said.

"It wasn't a date, Hank. It was my sister's wedding."

"Maybe, but you invited me. I think it counts as a date." They hadn't sat together at the wedding, but Mannix had caught Ernesto's eyes on him several times. And if his parents were puzzled as to why their son invited his business partner to his sister's wedding, they didn't show it. The fact that Marta had invited Chad and Marigold stole some of the attention, and that helped.

Even though Ernesto knew Hank couldn't understand most of it, he seemed moved by the ambiance of the small candlelit *iglesia*. The reception was a true feast, and he and Hank danced with Marta and all of his cousins. They brought home a mountain of churros they were still snacking on nearly a week later.

"Tell him about her dress," Hank said. "He'll want to know all about the dress."

Ernesto paused his scribbling and hovered his pen

over the paper. "Uh…it was white?"

"And frilly," Mannix added. "Tell him that."

"Oh, for God's sake," interrupted Chad. She and Marigold were at the counter working a loaf of dough. She wiped her hands on a damp towel and came to the table, took Ernesto's pen, and began to write words like *tulle, crinoline, bodice,* and *bustle.*

Marta had been beautiful, and Hank told him it was the first time he'd understood what the word radiant applied to a bride could mean. "And Cordero!" Hank had said. "Holy smokes. He looked like a fellow who'd reached into a box of caramel corn and found a pot of gold instead of a toy." Ernesto thought that was exactly what he'd done.

So had he and Mannix.

Ernesto tapped the pen against his teeth, while considering if they needed to write anything else. Hans's last letter was open on the table. Hans always had questions—how are Matt and Eduardo getting along? Did the bougainvillea by the greenhouse recover? Is Hank remembering to feed the koi?—and Ernesto wanted to make sure he answered each one.

"Should I tell him about the name, do you think?" Ernesto asked.

"Maybe not just yet," Mannix responded, and Marigold chuckled.

The Casa de Ada sign over the guest entry had been replaced with *Sapho's*—Chad's idea, of course. The cigar tourists from America didn't read anything into it, but the ladies in the smoking lounge loved it.

"Oh," Ernesto said. "He wants to know—now that the

revolution is over—if Ivan has given up on the idea and gotten a real job?"

Was the revolution over? It seemed to be. Castro was in prison, his supporters who attacked the barracks were either dead or in prison themselves. A lucky few, like Ivan, had drifted away discreetly and gone back to their lives. In Ivan's case, that meant back to the farm and, Ernesto hoped, to the civilizing influence of Elena and her churros.

"Tell him Ivan's fine, business is booming, and we're looking forward to visiting all four of them in Miami soon," Mannix said with growing impatience. Ernesto did, and closed the letter with a request that Hans let them know as soon as he had even a suspicion Marta might be pregnant.

"Come on, amante," Hank said. "It's getting late. I want to take you to bed and have you do filthy things to me."

Marigold cleared her throat.

Mannix leaned close to Ernesto. "How do I keep forgetting she speaks English?"

"She can hear too," Marigold said without turning to look at them.

Ernesto laughed. It was just an act the two of them put on together, but they never seemed to tire of it— Mannix pretending Marigold couldn't understand him and Marigold pretending Mannix was just an obnoxious clown. At least, Ernesto *thought* she was pretending. Chad picked up her guillotine and clicked it a few times. That was all a pretense now too. Maybe.

But it *was* getting late. "Did you remember to feed

the cat?" Hank asked. They didn't have a cat; the question was part of a different and much more pleasurable game Mannix liked to play.

"No," replied Ernesto. "I didn't. I'm very, very sorry."

"Again, with the apologies," Mannix said, rising from his chair and taking Ernesto's hand in his. "Come with me, young man. I shall have to collect what is due." Ernesto went willingly enough. When they passed into the hallway, Mannix whispered. "*Te Amo*, Ernesto."

"I love you too, Hank."

Epilogue

DECEMBER 31, 1958

THE LAST OF the koi pellets disappeared into a flashing swirl of gold and orange, and Ernesto snuggled into Hank's side. Hank handed him the envelope. "Open it," he said. It had become a tradition for them, waiting to read letters from Marta or Hans until the day was over, and they could sit on the bench and share the news.

This letter was from his sister, and Ernesto felt the envelope to determine if there was a photograph in it. There usually was. No matter how he braced himself, it always came with a jolt when a picture slid out of an envelope.

How close I'd come to letting those photos ruin us!

He held the picture in front of them. A small boy of about five, with a serious look on his face, stood on a beach and stared distantly across the sea toward the horizon.

"Aw," said Mannix. "He has your scowl."

Ernesto laughed and turned the photo over.

Ernesto Ruiz Antonio Cordero his sister had written. She'd captioned the scene: "Ernie waiting for his uncles, December 1958."

"Ouch," Mannix said. "That's pointed."

"Well, they've been gone nearly six years, and we've only been over twice."

"We've been *busy*," Mannix complained. He let his fingers climb up Ernesto's thigh.

Ernesto slapped it away. "I don't think that kind of *busy* counts as an excuse."

He began to read the letter as Mannix studied the picture. "Oh, listen to this, Hank. 'You better come visit soon, or we won't have a guestroom to put you in.' She's pregnant!"

"That's wonderful," Mannix said. "I wonder how Tony survives it all?" Ernesto smiled. He knew Hank wasn't serious. When they last visited, Hank and three-year old Ernie were inseparable. "Is this picture from their new place?" Mannix asked. "It's pretty."

"Yes, she says they look out on Biscayne Bay." Ernesto studied the photo. "That sounds nice, doesn't it?"

"Yes. Does she mention how Tony and Mason are getting on with hunting communists?"

Ernesto continued reading. "Here it is. She says she's included a separate message from Tony for you." Ernesto picked up a folded square sheet that had dropped out of the envelope with the photo. "This must be it." He handed it to Mannix.

"Oh, listen. Hans is managing a boarding house again, taking in Cubans fleeing ahead of Castro's advance." He looked at Mannix. "It can't be that serious already, can it? We'd have heard if there was an actual threat, wouldn't we?"

"Well, Castro's been back from Mexico for two years now. And this time he seems to be making some progress." Mannix opened the little piece of paper. "I can absolutely see Hans doing that for the Cubans; maybe Matt would want to go back to the States and help him."

"Ha," said Ernesto. Matt and Mannix had settled into a not-quite-friends relationship that was moderated by Eduardo's steady presence. The four of them got together now and then and always shared dinner on New Year's Eve when they'd be joined by Chad and Marigold and would offer toasts to their friends in Miami before Matt would start into politics and Eduardo would have to take him home.

Ernesto had already set the dinner table; they'd be arriving soon.

"They probably can't believe we're still together either," Mannix offered. He began reading Tony's note. It was short and to the point.

"Nonsense," said Ernesto. "Everyone knew we were meant to be together from the start." Mannix had a troubled look on his face. "What does Tony have to say?"

Mannix refolded the paper and placed it in his breast pocket. "Nothing. Everything's fine."

Ernesto sighed. "Hank. Is this one of those situations where I would want to know the truth, and you would think you know better and were protecting me by not telling me, and I would get very angry when I found out?"

Mannix shrugged in a noncommittal way.

"And then we wouldn't have sex until I'd forgiven you," Ernesto added.

"Yikes," Mannix said. "You sure know how to play hardball. Here." He handed him Tony's note.

Get your asses out of there now, he'd written. *There's no time left.*

He'd underlined the word *now* three times.

Ernesto looked troubled. "What do you think we should do?" he asked.

"Well," said Mannix. "Maybe it *would* be a good time to visit Biscayne Bay. An extended family trip, perhaps, just until things blow over?"

Ernesto cocked his head as if he'd heard something. Then Mannix heard it too. Screams and breaking glass, coming from the area near the casinos. They both jumped when they heard gunfire.

It was six years late, but the revolution had finally arrived.

About John Patrick

John Patrick is an author and a Lambda Literary Award finalist who lives in the Berkshire Hills of Massachusetts, where he is supported in his writing by his husband and their terrier, who is convinced he could do battle with the bears that come through the woods on occasion (the terrier, that is, not the husband).

John is an introvert and can often be found doing introverted things like reading or writing, cooking, and thinking deep, contemplative thoughts (his husband might call this napping). He loves to spend time in nature—"forest bathing" is the Japanese term for it—feeling connected with the universe. But he also loathes heat and humidity, bugs of any sort, and unsteady footing in the form of rocks, mud, tree roots, snow, or ice. So his love of nature is tempered; he's complicated that way.

John and his husband enjoy traveling and have visited over a dozen countries, meeting new people, exploring new cultures, and—most importantly—discovering new foods.

Email
john@johnpatrickauthor.com

Facebook
www.facebook.com/JohnPatrickAuthor

Twitter
@jpatrickauthor

Website
www.johnpatrickauthor.com

Instagram
@johnpatrickauthor

Other NineStar books by this author

Paradise Series
Franklin in Paradise
Undercover in Paradise

Tides of Change Series
Dublin Bay
Turtle Bay

Connect with NineStar Press

www.ninestarpress.com

www.facebook.com/ninestarpress

www.facebook.com/groups/NineStarNiche

www.twitter.com/ninestarpress

www.instagram.com/ninestarpress

www.ingramcontent.com/pod-product-compliance
Lightning Source LLC
Chambersburg PA
CBHW060300100726
47907CB00002B/218